**ROSSLYN THE BEAUTIFUL,
ROSSLYN THE PASSIONATE—
WHAT MAN COULD CLAIM HER
FOR HIS OWN?**

Surely not Jarvis, fourth Lord Burton, the handsome but insensitive man who married her, brought her to Burton Hall, and shattered her dreams of marital happiness.

Who, then? Would it be Tom Stanley, whose lustful powers were the talk of the county and whose wandering eye now rested provocatively on Rosslyn? Or Camille, the fierce revolutionary with the power to take what he wanted and to destroy what he could not have? Or Armand St. Clare, who was so strong, so noble, so irresistible—and so loyal to his wife?

Rosslyn wondered if she would ever know the answer. For wherever she went—hate-filled Burton Hall or Revolution-torn Paris—dangerous adventure awaited her, even as she longed to taste a woman's fullest joys.

LOVE'S DEFIANT PRISONER

Patricia Phillips

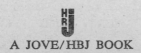

A JOVE/HBJ BOOK

First Jove/HBJ edition published January 1978

Library of Congress Catalog Card Number: 77-80697

Printed in the United States of America

Jove/HBJ books are published by Jove Publications, Inc. (Harcourt Brace Jovanovich) 757 Third Avenue, New York, N.Y. 10017

CHAPTER ONE

Buffeted by the rising wind, and exhilarated by the fury of the elements, Rosslyn watched the summer storm gather over the Channel. Heavy clouds formed a curtain over the choppy water. Rain-scented gusts tangled her mane of black curls, whipping bright color into her usually pale cheeks and bringing crackling life to her expression which too often of late had appeared as an oval mask of perfection. Riding over the deserted headland Rosslyn was free to be herself, glad to shed the narrow confines of her social position as Lady Burton. Suddenly the wind billowed the skirt of her amber redingote like a sail, the flapping sound startling her high-strung mare who whickered in nervous excitement.

"It's all right, Alice," she said as she bent low, patting the animal's sleek neck. Then she was forced to clutch her tall crowned felt hat and anchor it tighter beneath her chin before it went bowling over the cliffs to the tossing ferment below.

On a clear day the French coast was visible from here. The violence raging through France was nearing some terrible climax now in this year 1792 as the Revolution accelerated to spawn a reign of terror. Though Rosslyn did not wish to share in the danger of her French counterparts, she would have welcomed a little excitement in contrast to the depressing sameness of her life.

She reluctantly turned her mare's head towards home. Yellow tinged light colored the downs an unnatural green. Raindrops stung her cheeks as she galloped over the rolling hillocks until Burton Hall became visible in the hollow below, its classic columns pristine white against the dark sky.

She would have preferred to ride out the storm on the downs, racing through the tingling wetness instead of returning to oversee the last minute details of the party they were holding to celebrate the marriage of her husband's cousin Letty.

When Rosslyn came to Burton Hall on her wedding day the sun had sparkled diamond flashes from the masonry walls, the portico was smothered in yellow roses and she had found the house as beautiful as a palace surrounded by its acres of landscaped parkland. With her handsome young husband beside her, in the romantic dreams of youth she had pictured them living happily ever after on this spacious estate.

Her mouth turned down bitterly to recall her own girlish naivety on that day, swathed as she was in virginal white, a wreath of orange blossoms crowning her silk gauze veil.

Flicking impatiently at a buzzing circle of horseflies, Rosslyn dismounted.

These past seven years spent with Jarvis, his drinking, his gambling, his wenching, and his disagreeable nature had shattered those myths. Used to amorous interludes with servant girls whose jobs depended on his favor, Jarvis was unprepared to woo his bride. That she expected it aroused his indignation. Terrible disappointment in the act of love moved Rosslyn to tears during those early months, and her emotion sent Jarvis off to the nearest ale house. And so the pattern was established . . .

"There be company indoors, my lady."

Interrupted in her intimate thoughts, Rosslyn blinked owlishly at the open-faced groom unsaddling her mare.

"Company," she repeated blankly.

"Aye, m'lady, and the master be gone riding. Don't reckon the storm's brought him back though. Bain't never one to mind the weather, his lordship bain't."

The admiration in the young groom's voice was not lost to Rosslyn, who knew he would not have believed her had she made him aware of Jarvis's less admirable traits. The servants thought of Jarvis as a real man's man. And he was determined their young son should be raised in the same athletic manner, despite both her own

6

and Doctor Watkins's pleas for caution because of the six-year-old's weak heart.

Noticing that there were three empty stalls, Rosslyn snapped: "Did the master take Will out in the rain?"

"Oh, aye, young master went too. Told 'im the sky looked threatening. I done just like you says, m'lady, being mindful of young Master Will's delicate condition like, I done that," the groom said defensively, seeing the anger flash in her eyes, turning the violet to navy.

Forcing down her flaring temper Rosslyn managed a weak smile. "It's all right, Heath, I'm not blaming you. Perhaps they'll be back soon."

The groom nodded in relief. "It's Lady Redding who be up at the house, m'lady. Come to stay the night by the looks on it."

As she crossed the cobbled yard to the rear entrance, Rosslyn found she was in an increasingly foul humor. Jarvis's disregard for the doctor's suggestions about their son, coupled with the discovery that his sister was here for an afternoon of chatting and meddling, only increased her bad temper. Her sister-in-law was an incurable gossip. In fact, it was thanks to dear Stella that she had had the first crushing revelation of her husband's infidelity. Rose was the girl's name, the daughter of the village blacksmith. Their honeymoon was barely over when Stella confided the details which she had from her maid, Rose's cousin. Jarvis rewarded the girl with a striped calico gown for being so obliging. For a long time Rosslyn could not bear striped dresses; now she wore them often as proof that she was immune to the pain. There followed so many stories of seductions that she ordered Stella to reveal no more. Those first tears of disillusion washed the stars from her eyes, leaving her vomiting with self-pity through the early months of pregnancy. Love and tenderness were not required for that natural function, she thought bitterly as she slammed the blue-painted door against the masonry.

Her full red mouth, which had once been softly sensual, assumed its usual set line as she marched indoors, thumping her riding crop against her gloved hand as she went.

"God, what a thundercloud you look!" Stella greeted

7

cheerfully, her fleshy body overflowing the narrow seat of a blue satin chair beside the drawing room hearth. "Thought you'd need some help with Letty's party."

"Thanks, but everything's arranged. Sorry if I'm not too charming, the weather affects my disposition. Will you excuse me while I change?"

"Of course. By the way, I took the liberty of ordering the fire lit. Devilish cold for summer, isn't it? Oh, and I sent for tea and cakes. I'm starving. I knew this shocking weather would drive you indoors. A pity about the rain, it'll ruin Letty's big day. Where's Jarvis?"

"Still on the downs I suppose."

"Oh, I thought you went together."

"We never ride together. Your brother's an inconsiderate clod taking Will out in the rain when he knows how easily he takes cold," Rosslyn exploded, knowing Stella could do little to regulate Jarvis's actions, yet needing to voice her resentment to someone. Even Stella would do.

"Oh, but I agree, darling, totally inconsiderate. Aren't all men? My Jackie certainly is. That man—sometimes I could wring his neck. But then, my dear, where would we be without them at certain important times?" Stella finished with a throaty chuckle, leaving little doubt that she referred to the bedroom.

After some deliberation, Rosslyn changed from her riding habit into a new flocked dimity afternoon dress, lavender and white with a wide green sash.

"So becoming, Madame," her French maid said as she attempted to straighten Rosslyn's wind-tossed hair, tugging ineffectually until Rosslyn motioned her aside.

"Here, I'll brush it. You choose some jewelry to match the dress." Though the dark-haired girl was obliging, Jeanette was far from efficient. Her lack of skill convinced Rosslyn that she had little experience at the job, a fact echoed in the girl's proud carriage and genteel manner suggesting that she was more at home being waited on than performing the service herself.

"Here, Madame, purple amethysts to match the color of your gown."

Rosslyn accepted the delicate gold necklace, trying its

gem-studded length against her creamy skin before nodding her approval.

"Perfect. You may not be able to brush hair, but you've certainly got good taste. Tell me, what on earth did you do before Clarence rescued you from the Folkstone packet?"

"Do, Madame?" Jeanette asked stiffly.

"For a living, girl. Don't think for a moment I believe that twaddle about you being a lady's maid. Why, if I wasn't keeping you on as a favor to my brother, I'd have sent you packing when he brought you here last autumn."

"Oh, Madame!"

Hearing the tearful catch in the girl's voice Rosslyn glanced towards the shadowy face above hers in the mirror.

"There now, don't take it to heart. I didn't mean I don't like you." Tears were sliding down Jeanette's pale cheeks and Rosslyn exclaimed beneath her breath at the girl's sensitivity. "Come on, don't cry. Here, help me tie this sash."

Sniffling back her grief, Jeanette struggled to anchor the leaf green satin sash beneath her mistress's full breasts in the new fashion, while Rosslyn tied a matching ribbon around her dark curls. When her arms were down the sash became uncomfortable; with a sigh of aggravation Rosslyn tugged the thin fabric in place over her bosom, wishing the dressmaker had allowed more room in the scant bodice. The Frenchwoman who had sewn this frothy creation was a relative of Jeanette's, purportedly dressmaker to the French Queen before the Revolution, but as so many emigrant seamstresses made the same extravagant claim, she took the latter with a pinch of salt.

Seeing her mistress's usually sulky face curve into a smile of approval, Jeanette asked, "Madame likes the dress?"

"Very much. The work's exquisite. Only tell your relative to give me more room in the bodice next time. I declare, I'll suffocate before the day's out."

"Yes, Madame."

"What are you doing with that?"

9

Jeanette glanced up guiltily, a miniature clasped in her fingers. "Just admiring it, Madame," she faltered.

Rosslyn held out her hand for the necklace, surprised to behold her own face staring back. It was the miniature Papa commissioned on her fifteenth birthday. How fragile she looked beside her twenty-one-year-old brother.

"Well, what do you think of me in those days?"

"You were just as lovely," Jeanette whispered generously, smiling at the young painted faces nestled in the palm of her mistress's white hand.

"That was two years before I married Jarvis. You'd have liked me better then—not as bitchy as I am now," Rosslyn added with a grin, recalling her frequent outbursts of temper directed at the girl. "No reason for it then, I suppose. Papa doted on me, said I was the image of my mother. She was French. That's why I speak the language. Even Clarence was nicer then. In those days we both had dreams. When all your dreams are dead it's never the same. Now my brother's become a wastrel who barely manages the family business between horse races. And me . . . I'm an overdressed doll as my husband so aptly puts it. When we married he called me a spoiled brat; since then he's tried his damnedest to unspoil me."

"Yes, Madame," Jeanette agreed, returning the jewelry to its case, uncomfortable sharing her mistress's rare confidences.

Hand on her chin Rosslyn scowled at her own reflection in the beveled glass. "I act the brainless, pretty plaything because that's the only female Jarvis understands. Apart from dressing me like a queen, he ignores me. There's Sunday nights of course . . ." she paused, finding she had revealed more than was intended. That part of it was none of the girl's business. Jeanette probably knew Jarvis had other women; servants gossiped constantly, how else would Stella collect her gems about who was sleeping with whom. The girl probably knew too that Sunday was the night of duty reserved for "the little woman" as he laughingly referred to her amongst his cronies. What Jeanette could not know was the joylessness of those occasions, the speed with which the act

10

was completed to allow more time for a final game of cards and another drink. And to think she had once offered Jarvis her heart and the passion locked within her shapely body. Like the insensitive clod he was, he had trampled those delicate emotions, extinguishing the warmth, the flowering love, leaving cold emptiness in its place . . .

"Will you need your wrap, Madame? It's chilly since the rain."

Rosslyn sighed. She had almost forgotten the storm and Will's presence on those windswept downs. Oh, Jarvis would hear about that! It was one way she could reach him, the one way to command his attention. Sometimes the arguments were almost pleasant, for they gave vent to emotion too often buried beneath the composed facade known as Rosslyn, Lady Burton.

"Do you know how long they've been out?"

"Almost an hour, Madame. I heard Nana go to her room while I was pressing your gown."

"Lord, an hour in this. He'll be wheezing half the night." Seeing a peculiar expression flit across the girl's face, she snapped: "I suppose you think I'm overprotective too?"

"Oh, no, Madame," Jeanette protested.

"That's what my husband says. But Will is delicate. The doctor tells me he needs special handling. I'm right to protect him from Jarvis, aren't I?"

Jeanette laid a sympathetic hand on her mistress's arm.

"You are right to love him as you do. Men don't always see things a woman's way. My own papa was harsh on my brother, insisting he ride in all weathers, forcing him to fencing lessons when he raged with fever . . ." Jeanette's voice trailed away as she saw her mistress's eyes brighten attentively as she listened to secrets unconsciously revealed.

"Fencing? The brother of a lady's maid?"

"We met with reduced circumstances later in life."

"There's no need to keep up the pretense. I'm aware you're a Royalist sympathizer; up to now I've not divulged your secret. I couldn't care less if you're cousin to Marie Antoinette herself. Here, give me that thing, I

11

suppose I'll need it." Rosslyn took the gossamer wool shawl the girl clutched in trembling hands. "If you're ashamed of being in 'reduced circumstances' you needn't be. Though we kept it from him, my father was almost bankrupt when he died. All he left me was a cottage near Dover—Jarvis won't let me go near the place, calls it a hovel. He really hates it because Father left it to me. There's quite a lot of jealousy to Jarvis's nature."

"It's not pride which seals my tongue, Madame. My brother recently escaped from Paris. His life's in danger because he took part in the plot for their Majesties' escape last summer. There are others still in prison for whom I have so little hope—oh, dear Madame, you've been most kind to take me in, most patient with my shortcomings, but of you I ask a little more patience. Someday I can reveal. Not now."

The earnestness of Jeanette's words was a surprise. Rosslyn noted the stricken expression on the French girl's face and gave her a comforting pat. Then clutching the lacy green shawl about her shoulders, she hastened downstairs to the brightness of the warm drawing room.

When Stella saw Rosslyn's new gown she clucked in appreciation and boldly came forward to finger the fine material. She had always envied Rosslyn her high-breasted, small-waisted figure, for at twenty-eight her own body, in keeping with the Burton family trait, was becoming fat. "What a delight you are, my dear," she cooed, assessing the cost of the gown. "You look sixteen again. I'm madly jealous."

"Hardly that, but I thank you for saying it. Madame Mercale sews so exquisitely in the latest modes. She was dressmaker to the French Queen, you know."

"Oh, really," Stella gasped quite impressed. "You'll have to introduce her to me. Though I doubt if my Jackie'll consider spending half the fortune on clothes that Jarvis does. You're an expensive hobby to him, darling."

Rosslyn smiled with feigned sweetness at Stella's comments, accepting a china cup of steaming tea which Stella, who had automatically assumed the role of hostess, poured for her. One had to say Stella made herself completely at home when she visited.

Settled at last, Stella launched into her scandalous revelations. Speaking rapidly, her voice grew husky from the exertion while her blue eyes bulged with eagerness as she recounted all the delicious tales she had gathered since their last meeting.

While Stella talked, Rosslyn turned so she had a clear view of the winding path through the parkland along which her husband and son should soon return from their ride. It had stopped raining now, though the beeches were drenched. As the hour lengthened into two, Rosslyn mentally rehearsed what she would say to Jarvis, in reprimand for his thoughtless behavior. She hoped Will had taken shelter or he would be soaked to the skin.

"For heaven's sake, Rosslyn, haven't you heard a word I've said?"

Rosslyn swung her attention back to Stella who was viewing her with ill-concealed annoyance, her protruding pale blue eyes bulging in disbelief that so important a dialogue could have passed without acknowledgment.

"You're wearing yellow silk at Letty's wedding."

"Yes, but there was so much more . . . well, I won't bore you again with a repetition."

"Sorry. I was listening, it's just that I started watching for Jarvis. Poor Will's been out so long, I know he'll be soaked."

"Soaked! Since when did a thorough drowning hurt a lad of six?" Stella exploded, wagging her finger. "I declare, you worry about that child as if he were made of spun sugar candy. My boys survive worse than summer storms."

Forcing a smile, Rosslyn refrained from pointing out that in keeping with the usual male progeny of their family, Stella's boys were as healthy and cumbersome as oxen. Will, on the other hand, favored her, dark and slender with the unfortunate addition of an inherited heart ailment from his French grandmother.

"When you only have one you worry more, especially when everytime I turn around he's ill again."

"Only one. Well, whose fault's that? From what I recall of Jarvis's escapades it can't be from want of trying."

Deciding to change the subject before Stella succumbed to the temptation to delve into the past, Rosslyn said: "It's hard to believe Letty's going to be Mrs. Tom Stanley this time tomorrow."

"Isn't it. Who'd have thought a spirited man like Tom Stanley would marry such a milksop as Letty."

"Oh, Stella—Letty's quiet, but I'd hardly call her that," Rosslyn defended. Though the rest of the Burtons were somewhat scornful of their soon-to-be-rich cousin, Rosslyn, not sure if from genuine affection or in defiance of the collective family decision, rather liked the pale blonde girl.

"Quiet! That's putting it mildly. When that handsome brute pins her down on the marriage bed what do you suppose she'll do? For my money she'll expire with an attack of the vapors. Though I hate to admit it, that's a night I envy her, the twittering fool. No doubt she'll not appreciate her good fortune. I'm burning with curiosity about something I heard the other day. Can you even guess what it was?"

Dutifully Rosslyn shook her head, knowing Stella was just bursting to reveal the facts. "No, but I'm sure it's something very juicy."

Stella chuckled. "How well you know me, poppet." Leaning her fair head close to Rosslyn's she whispered: "Jack tells me last spring our handsome Mr. Stanley took on six whores in less than an hour. Can you believe that staying power? And also," now her voice dropped to a barely audible whisper, "they do say his anatomy rivals that raw-boned brute he rides. All the women are talking about him."

Six women! Jarvis could even be jealous of that record. Yet perhaps six purchased bodies were far easier serviced than one wife who expected some tenderness and consideration . . .

"Well, my dear, what do you think of that?" Stella prompted.

"I think they were all probably very drunk."

"Drunk or not, you must agree, it's an intriguing story. Oh, how can I find out if it's true? I'm just burning with curiosity. Too bad I'm not ravishing enough to find out the obvious way—I know, I'll ask Letty if the naughty rumors be true."

"About the six women?"

"Oh, no, silly. About his overdevelopment."

Stella's peal of laughter was interrupted by Agnes the downstairs maid who brought a silver platter of cucumber sandwiches and a plate of iced cakes.

Barely managing to harness her tongue till the maid was out of earshot, Stella leaned closer. "Will you hazard a small wager on the outcome, my love?"

"No, thanks. Jarvis gambles enough for both of us."

Rosslyn went to the windows for a closer view of two dots moving towards the espaliered apple tunnel on the west lawn.

It was them, she was sure of it.

Recalling the prodigious feat of Tom Stanley at one of their wine-besotted gatherings at the casino, Rosslyn wondered when Jarvis would insist on taking Will to the more seamy entertainments he enjoyed with his drunken friends. After all, Will was the heir, the *only* heir, as Jarvis constantly reminded her. The Burton heir must fit comfortably within the scandalous pattern of behavior established by the gentry of Burton Hill. How often Jarvis compared their six-year-old boy to Veasey, Stella's oldest son, who, still in his early teens, was fast becoming an apprentice rake under Jarvis's able tutelage. An arrogant lout, Veasey was the perfect reproduction of a Burton male, so alike to Jarvis, he seemed more his son than did Will . . .

"As I was saying," Stella pointedly cleared her throat to secure Rosslyn's complete attention, "this perfectly marvelous Frenchman who arrived in London last month is rather a mystery. A lucky gambler—my dear, he was absolutely penniless when he came off the packet. Now he has a suit made by the best London tailor. And rooms in Marylebone. I ask you, is that luck or not?" Stella momentarily paused to stuff a cucumber sandwich between her thick lips.

"A gambler! I might know it'd be something like that to stir you up—or a man who could take on twelve women in thirty minutes," Rosslyn suggested with a grin. Gambling and sexual prowess were Stella's yard-sticks in the measurement of a man's potential.

Stella grinned back. "He says he's Armand St. Clare, but Jackie thinks he's a marquis or a comte newly come from France. When he arrived he had nothing but the clothes on his back, and none too clean at that. The story is he'd escaped from prison. Do you know there's a secret society right here on our south coast that helps them escape? Backed by a mysterious millionaire. It's so exciting! They literally drag them from the guillotine! Of course, St. Clare neither agrees nor disagrees which is infuriating. I expect he's afraid of spies. Jack tells me they're all over London."

"How exciting," Rosslyn agreed, turning her attention to the riders who were on the walkway leading to the stables. Her heart began an uneasy pounding as she observed Will's fatigue, head drooping, barely able to sit upright in the saddle.

"You'll see St. Clare tomorrow at the ball. Tom Stanley's invited him. Your Clarence knows him too, but he absolutely refuses to discuss Armand St. Clare with me, the beast."

Good for him, Rosslyn felt like saying, but she did not: Stella made a better friend than enemy. "He sounds very intriguing."

"Oh, he is. There's not a woman there who won't be mad for him when the night's over," Stella assured her. "By the way, Rosslyn, dear, what do you know of the little French maid Clarence found for you?"

"Little beyond her name and inefficiency," Rosslyn said guardedly, refusing to add grist to Stella's gossip mill. "Why? What else should I know?"

Stella grinned wickedly at the innocent question. "Well, of course you've guessed she's an escaped Royalist. Oh innocent, don't you know? Your Clarence has far more than a friendly interest in her, pretty little thing that she is. Where do you think she goes given half the chance?"

Rosslyn stared at Stella's plump face, deceptively angelic with its bubbly halo of curls. "Not to see Clarence?"

"Exactly."

A fluttering wave of nausea halted the next words from her mouth. Though what Stella said was probably true, she despised her for the revelation, for the gloating smile of satisfaction splitting her face in a Cheshire-cat grin. To think Jeanette had betrayed her trust in that manner. More than likely her interest over that portrait, at which she had gazed with such rapt attention this morning, was centered on Clarence's likeness and not her own. Though her brother had not always been faithful to his wife, the news of his latest deception was made more disturbing because it was with her own maid. What if Adela too had heard the gossip?

As if reading her thoughts, Stella shook her head.

"Don't worry, darling Adela hasn't heard a word. Of course, if you think I should tell . . ."

"No. You could be mistaken," Rosslyn blurted, hearing heavy steps ringing along the marble-tiled corridor. Jarvis must have received news of their visitor from the groom and was coming straight from the stables.

"I've also heard your little Jeanette is quite attached to our mysterious Frenchman. With the usual alleycat morals of those Frenchwomen, it's likely she's warming both their beds—Jarvis, sweet."

Brother and sister embraced.

"Where's Will?" Rosslyn demanded, barely allowing them time to exchange greetings before she began chastising her husband.

"Coming to join us, me dear. Why, how pretty you look. Is that a new gown?" Jarvis asked, his slightly bulbous blue eyes rolling in lascivious delight as he surveyed the skimpy bodice. "By Jove, that must have set me back a pretty penny with those flouncy folderols round the hem. Hand embroidered too."

Rosslyn nodded in agreement, surveying her husband's neatly brushed hair as he stooped towards her for a perfunctory peck on the cheek. In the naive, girlish time of her initiation she had found Jarvis madly attractive. Tall, broad-shouldered, with a deep, well-developed chest, he had seemed so manly and protective. His high florid complexion surmounted by nut-brown hair lightened by sun streaks had portrayed her ideal of an English gentleman.

17

Half-turning to watch him, she assessed Jarvis candidly where he stood puddling moisture on the oriental carpet from his redingote and then making twin rivers from his sodden footsteps as he crossed to the hearth. At first he had been somewhat attentive until he discovered she demanded something of him, something he was either unable or unwilling to give. All thoughts of tender delight in their lovemaking disappeared behind the closed bedroom door, for he was a hasty, bungling lover. He was still physically attractive, though his wavy hair was not as thick and his waistline not as slim as it once had been. The milkmaids and the nubile servant girls were not as plentiful either these days, or so she heard tell. Approaching thirty, Jarvis had already squandered the best years of his virility. Now for solace he turned more to dice and cards and the ever-present decanter of port. Yet this change brought no new tenderness to their relationship; it was far too late for that. Always a creature of habit, over the years Jarvis had come to regard her merely as a potential mother for his heirs, their one sickly boy not being enough to cement the inheritance. And it was to this end he came to her bed. The fact that she was a beautiful woman made his husbandly duty far more pleasant. No, it was too late to ask for tenderness, too late for any expectation of awakened passion.

"Mama, we're back," the boy called from the doorway. His clothes were dripping. Beneath his eyes, bright with fever, purplish circles spread downwards over thin cheeks to reveal his fatigue, making the dark eyes seem gigantic in his small face.

"Oh, Will, how wet you are! Let me ring for Nana to change your clothes," Rosslyn gasped as the boy hugged her, the cold, rain-wet contact chilling through the thin skirts of her gown.

"Stuff and nonsense! Nana! My God, the boy needs a man to shape him. We're hiring a tutor for our Will next week. Already have a fellow in mind, as a matter of fact. A splendid horseman, good swordsman—best of all, he's a damned fine gambler. He'll make a man of him, you can be sure of that. Only drawback is the fellow's a Froggy. Damned unlucky that, but it can't be helped."

"I forbid it. The doctor told you we couldn't put Will through a rigorous schedule. Can't you see how ill he is today, yet you took him on one of your infernal rides, not caring what anyone says, always having your own way. I've told you before," Rosslyn shrilled, her face hot with anger. She viciously tugged the embroidered bellpull to summon Nana in defiance of her husband's wishes. Throughout the exchange Stella had listened avidly, absorbing the latest to tell at next week's tea parties, disappointed when Rosslyn became aware of her interest and bit back her words. "We'll discuss it later in private," she hissed, her jaw tense.

"Nothing to discuss," Jarvis said, turning a smug smile on her as he unbuttoned his caped gray coat.

As he held it out to the blaze a billowing cloud of steam arose. "The matter's settled. A tutor for Will starting next week. That'll bring the boy out. Time to untie the apron strings, Ross, time to let him learn how to be a man."

"Oh, Jarvis, do tell. Could I dare hope this man, this gambler, is the same Frenchman Jackie told me about last week?"

Jarvis smiled indulgently at his sister, tweaking her fluffy curls. "Now how do I know what Jack told you, Stella? You'll have to give me more clues than that."

"Armand St. Clare—oh, is it him?"

He smiled, infuriating her by his silence. Thrusting his leather boots towards the brass firedogs, he stretched, sighing with pleasure at the warmth. "Could be right, me dear, some fancified Froggy name. A Saint something."

"Oh, Rosslyn," Stella gasped, her eyes round with delight. "How fortunate you are. Why, I declare, I'll be a daily visitor to see how young Will manages his studies," she vowed breathlessly.

The sparkle in Stella's eyes foretold more than she had revealed to Rosslyn about the mysterious Frenchman's life story; if her guess was correct, the man must also possess a reputation for amorous conquest, for only expertise in that subject was capable of sparking that special gleam of excited anticipation in her sister-in-law's eyes.

"Well, laddie, what'll you think of having a French tutor to give you your lessons?" Jarvis asked, pulling his small son against his chair where he tickled him good-naturedly.

"If it please you, Papa, I shall like it very well."

"That's my boy! A real man we're going to make of you someday, despite your Mama."

And Rosslyn could not fail to notice that look of triumph her husband flashed over the dark curly head leaning so trustingly against his shoulder.

By evening Will's fever had soared to frightening proportions. Rosslyn stayed at his bedside until his nurse persuaded her to go to her own room to sleep. High fevers were not uncommon amongst children, she assured herself, as she hurried through the chill corridors of Burton Hall. Will often ran fevers at night and was cured the next day. And, as Stella pointed out, a dousing never hurt a boy of six; sore throats, earaches, headaches, those were symptoms of common childhood maladies, nothing more.

"Well, coming to bed at last? It's about time! Thought I'd fall asleep before you got here."

Rosslyn backed from the open door as her husband's hearty voice boomed forth to greet her. This was not the night! Of all the times over the years she had wished he would deviate from his pattern of obligation to have him do so now, when Will tossed in a feverish sleep upstairs.

"It's not Sunday," she protested illogically.

"Not Sunday, eh," Jarvis repeated, a smile of amusement lifting his mouth. "Are we so well regulated in our lives we allot a specific day for a husband to make love to his wife?" Blundering tipsily to his feet, the smile faded as Jarvis viciously knotted the silk cord of his blue dressing gown about his waist. "Close the door."

Rosslyn obeyed, finding the fledgling nervous headache she had contracted in Will's bedroom pounding now to full maturity. How insensitive Jarvis was! Instead of comforting her over their son's illness, instead of trying to soothe her fears, he merely demanded her wifely obligation. No response on her part was required; that way he assumed no guilt for his own lustful haste.

"Will's very ill," she snapped accusingly, suddenly wanting to punish him. "Thanks to your idiotic thoughtlessness his fever's dangerously high."

"He'll recover. Children always do." Jarvis dismissed the matter impatiently, other more pressing things on his mind. He reached for her hands. "Come to me. It's torture to see you looking so ravishing and not be allowed to touch you."

A flicker of his long buried charm coming forth, Jarvis drew her to the circle of his arms. A whiff of port-laden breath blew in her face, making Rosslyn turn aside so that she received his wet kiss on her cheek. Fumbling in his pleasure, Jarvis grunted at the hindrance of the fastening of her dress.

"Will you see my new gown for Letty's wedding?" she ventured, seeing a rose silk flounce protruding from the wardrobe door.

"Eh?" Jarvis murmured, completely occupied by the ample contents of her tight bodice which he had managed to unhook.

"My gown for the wedding. Considering how many hundreds of guineas it cost you, it's your right to see me in it first," she said, adeptly slipping from his grasp. "Now, stay there while I put it on."

Miserably Jarvis obeyed, indulging her, thinking perhaps it would improve his chances for pleasure when he entered the blue and white sprigged softness of her vast bed.

Taking her time, Rosslyn changed her gown in the corner behind a China silk screen, pleased Jarvis did not attempt to raid her privacy. This was an idiotic thing to do when her head pounded like a drum, yet it was merely a delaying action. She did not care whether he recognized it as such or not. Perhaps if she took long enough about dressing Jarvis would succumb to the vast quantity of port he had imbibed after dinner.

Rosslyn finally swept from behind the screen, gliding over the blue carpet to stand before him, a delightful picture in her rose silk gown. The full puffed sleeves capped her shoulders, seeming minuscle against the broad expanse of gleaming arms and swelling bosom. She swept the rose-edged train over her arm as she pirouetted about the room, warily conscious of the eye-popping effect she was having on her husband.

What a terrible mistake this had been. Far from deterring him from his intent, it had merely increased his ardor.

"You may be cold as a January night inside, my dear, but on the surface you make any man's blood boil. And you're all mine. We've had our differences, but I'm still proud of you, Rosslyn. Proud that you want to look pretty for me. Proud when other men undress you with their eyes, the devils. And I alone know what they can only guess about."

He seized her wrist, pulling her to his lap, burying his mouth in the hollow between her breasts. His robe opened slightly until she felt the heat of his furry chest against her bare arms, the contact sending a shiver through her body. Her reaction was taken for immediate desire by Jarvis, whose pleasure was reflected in the clamoring rise of his masculinity.

"Ah, Sunday or not, my dearest, we'll make a brother for our Will tonight, you mark my words," he gasped, bearing her rapidly to the bed.

And once again, those stirrings of pleasure at his touch, the sparks of warmth, were extinguished by the chilling reminder of her duty as a mere receptacle for the sacred Burton heir.

Later Rosslyn lay staring at the ceiling, hearing the rustle of tree branches below the windows. She felt hollow, empty, used. Long ago he had gone to sleep, rolling abruptly to his side, the task accomplished. No caresses, no kiss, nothing more than the act itself was required to produce another boy.

Though he had been snoring gently a moment before, Jarvis creaked to a sitting position beside her, toyed with her dark hair spread over the pillow before he heaved his large frame out of the soft mattress, cursing beneath his breath as his feet touched icy tiles.

"God! What a climate! When this idiotic revolution's over I think we'll take one of those tours on the

Continent, my dear. This Froggy fellow has my interest up when he talks of foreign parts. Might be interesting for you, new clothes and such. I know you'd like that, if nothing else."

Rosslyn turned away not wanting to watch him put on his robe, the act which finalized the duties until next week.

"That would be nice, Jarvis. Perhaps we can go someday when the wars are done and the revolutions over," she agreed placidly.

"Yes, we'll plan on it then, when these fool Frenchmen come to their senses and stop offending His Majesty with their confounded threats. I tell you, if this Froggy chap wasn't such a damned likeable fellow, and down on his luck into the bargain, I'd never give him houseroom. You'll have to meet him, Ross. We won't regard him as a servant, ye know, more like a poor relation, especially since the rumor is he's titled. Actually it's quite a feather in our caps, having a titled tutor for the boy."

Jarvis, feeling generous in his assuasion, patted her soft form under the mounded covers. Absently Rosslyn squeezed his arm, her mind straying to the possible problems to be encountered over Will and his French tutor. "If the man's of the nobility, as you suggest, he may be receptive to Will's special needs. I'll discuss it with him."

"By all means. I can't wait to face him across the tables. Now that's where he really shines. Stanley says our little Froggy's bold as brass over his game, sure of hisself and damned lucky. They say he's the same with the ladies too." Jarvis chuckled. "Did you see the way Stella almost went into heat when I mentioned his name? It's a pity you're not more like her, Ross, a real pity."

She bore his hidden accusations of frigidity in silence. Once she would have shouted and wept, she would have told him where the blame lay. But that was once. And it was an argument of which she had tired. Let him think what he wished.

Sensing his wife's disinterest, Jarvis returned to his original subject. "We'll have a game to beat all games here tomorrow night. It'll make Stanley feel right at home. Though I'll have to watch my step, not drink too much. Need a cool head to pit yourself against those fellows. Don't want to end up losing my shirt, ye know."

Chuckling, Jarvis plopped on the edge of the bed evoking a symphony of groans from the protesting bed-frame.

"Promise not to gamble the night away. After all, it is Letty's wedding night. The groom . . ."

"Be damned to Letty. I'll do what I want," he growled, swinging his large frame about with surprising agility. "A man like Tom Stanley would find it a fitting tribute on his wedding day. Why do you think I offered them the use of the Hall? Not out of the kindness of my heart, I assure you, especially not to a common casino owner."

"Why did you offer it to them?"

"So I can have him in *my* debt for a change." Jarvis chuckled, his good humor returning as he prodded her sharply in the buttocks to emphasize the point. "I want him to see what I've done to this place these past few years. Lord, he'll be green with envy. We'll be the talk of all London once his friends get back. It's too bad that stupid Letty has anything to do with it all, she's the only fly in the ointment. Besides, if Lady Luck ever runs me foul, it'll be wise to have Stanley in my debt. I could need his assistance."

"Your gambling's like a sickness," Rosslyn spat. "Someday we'll all be wandering the countryside with-out a roof over our heads. Don't think I don't know how much has been frittered away since our marriage. How many debts there are."

"You worry too much. Stanley would never see us starve," Jarvis dismissed, lumbering to his feet. "Be-sides, before I'd give up this place we might go through a few interesting alternatives. I'm thinking of one right now which would be especially appealing, considering your peculiarly frosty nature," he sneered.

He turned to look at her, his lip curled in contempt. She was the picture of desirable womanhood sprawled indolently on the bed, only it was a cruel mockery be-cause her perfect body was as cold as ice.

"The only alternative I can see is for you to give up gambling entirely. As far as I'm concerned it'll be the only way we can be sure of Burton Hall staying in the family."

"If you don't guard your tongue I might wager a small lease on the Hall with all its amenities, including a bedmate. Tom Stanley's always coveted this estate, covets you too, more fool him. It'd serve you right, always criticizing me, never content with anything I do. Stanley may even awaken a few sparks in your chilly soul, because I've damned sure not been able to."

"How dare you stand there and blithely suggest such a thing to your own wife? It's almost as if I was a prize filly . . ."

Jarvis spluttered at her description in high delight, his heavy eyelids rising in surprise at her unexpected burst of indignation. "A little black-maned riding filly; yes, Tom would appreciate that, you know how much he admires good flesh."

"Don't you dare link my name with his again."

"I'll do any damned thing I please and there's nothing you can do or say about it," he growled, his mouth set pugnaciously as he grabbed for her, but Rosslyn twisted from his grasp. "You don't fancy being part of his stud stable, eh! Well, let me tell you, Stanley would soon bend you into shape, something I should've done long ago, but I've been too kindhearted with you, you spoiled bitch. A good thrashing's what you need. Someday you'll make me angry enough to do it."

Long after he had left her room, his ugly threat ringing in her ears, Rosslyn still trembled with anger. Tonight she had come closer than ever to loathing her husband. His suggestion of bartering her to make good his gambling debts may have been merely something with which to taunt her, or in his drunken state Jarvis may have hit close to his true wishes.

His audacity in associating her name in such a repulsive plan with that of Tom Stanley made matters worse; though the man owned property in London, he was more famous for Stanley Casino, a fashionable West End gambling spot. At one time such a common person would never have been considered worthy of Letty, granddaughter of an earl, but these days eligible nobility was scarce around Burton Hill. The fact that Stanley's family originated from a band of itinerant actors mattered not a whit to the New Society where money was fast becoming king. And Tom Stanley was very wealthy. Letty's children would be heirs to a fortune accumulated from the very aristocracy her husband aspired to, given in payment for bad gambling debts.

If Rosslyn had been in a more humorous mood, she may even have found the situation comical.

CHAPTER TWO

Despite early morning clouds, by ten o'clock, Letty's wedding day had turned sunny, promising a perfect Kentish summer day of lazy, grass-sweetened warmth. The village church of St. Martin's was awash in a sea of white roses, their heady fragrance filling the Norman stone structure with perfume. Pink-and-white-satin lover's knots adorned the end of each pew, borne aloft by plaster cupids holding sprays of maidenhair fern and moss roses. Vast urns full of white flowers formed a bank behind the altar where the nervous minister appeared to be in a hothouse almost eclipsed by the elaborate floral arrangements.

Rosslyn smiled in satisfaction at the minister's obvious nervousness as he fumbled with the prayerbook while waiting for the ceremony to begin. She had lost her respect for Parson Smedley when she had asked his advice about Jarvis's handling of Will, needing a disinterested third party to talk some sense through that port-befuddled brain. Intimidated, however, by his wealthy parishioner, Smedley had advised her to say nothing and abide by the wisdom of her husband's judgment, for after all, a son needed the firm hand of his father. Stupid nonsense! No wonder the man hadn't courage enough to marry; though several local girls had their sights set on the eligible parson, he had never made up his mind about the chosen lady.

The church was packed with Tom Stanley's well-dressed acquaintances who had driven down from London. Some would return to the capital after the ceremony; others would stay as Jarvis's house guests, privileged to join the non-stop gambling Rosslyn knew would be the highlight of the gentlemen's celebration.

Unconsciously tightening her mouth, she thrust the unpleasant reminder away, concentrating instead on her son who sat beside her, curiously observing the wedding preliminaries. Will was so much better this morning, though it was not without reservations she had allowed him to attend the ceremony.

How handsome he looked, she thought. Tears of motherly pride moistened her eyes. His suit was pink satin frothed with cream lace at neck and wrists, specially tailored for the occasion in the same shade as her own Lyons silk gown. She squeezed Will's hand, swallowing a lump in her throat as they exchanged smiles of affection. He winked outrageously at her until Rosslyn was forced to smother an exclamation of surprise while she wondered which servant had taught him the trick. Then she decided bitterly it was more likely a mere observance of his father's habitual salutation to a pretty woman.

A commotion in the doorway heralded the arrival of the wedding party. All eyes swiveled towards the sunlit opening as the first attendants came forward, sweeping towards the altar in cream muslin gowns trimmed with pink and white satin ruffles with pink sashes around their waists and deep fichus of cream Alençon lace to add decorum to the low necklines. The bridesmaids carried bouquets of sweet peas and white moss roses set in a circlet of ribbons and lace, while on their heads they wore straw picture hats tied with pink ribbons.

When at last the bride entered, to be given away by Jarvis, for she was an orphan, Rosslyn had to admit Letty looked almost attractive today in white lace, a billowing veil dwarfing her thin features. The groom's twin nephews carried her voluminous train of tulle, caught at intervals with bunches of roses, miniatures of the huge bouquet that she clasped before her.

Tom Stanley was splendidly dressed in a wine cutaway coat faced wtih cream, his britches of the facing fabric, and the outfit completed by a cream satin waistcoat embroidered with pink moss roses. Craning forward for a better view of his face, Rosslyn decided Stella's outrageous stories about him were probably true, for he spared little attention to his trembling bride, preferring instead the six virginal bridesmaids who smiled shyly at his boldness. Typical behavior from one of Jarvis's friends who always found the grass greener in forbidden pastures. How stupid of her to be surprised.

When the ceremony was over the brightly dressed guests congregated outside the gray stone church, tranquil in the warm August sunshine. Even the headstones in the churchyard, half-covered with lichen, were less forbidding today as everything seemed bathed in an ambience of nuptial happiness.

Rosslyn had to admit this enchanting aura was due partly to the admiring glances she was receiving from the London gentlemen and the spiteful glares from the ladies who had accompanied them. This morning Jeanette had dressed her hair in elaborate curls which cascaded from beneath the upturned brim of a chip straw picture hat, clasped with a confection of rose silk flowers and ruched satin ribbons. One especially handsome gentleman ogled her, even took out his eyeglass to have a closer look at her charms. When they passed on the gravel walk he contrived to brush her arm, the encounter requiring an apology, thus enabling him to gaze unabashedly into her deep violet eyes. His admiring smile made her heart beat faster and Rosslyn wondered what it would be like to kiss this attractive man, to feel his arms around her crushing her possessively against his body, to experience the promised emotion reflected openly in his handsome face. Blinking in surprise at her own thoughts, she stepped back with a smile. The gentleman nodded to her in farewell and rejoined his friends beside their canary yellow phaeton, where a matched pair of chestnuts pawed the road, impatient to be off.

On the return journey clattering through the rolling parkland to Burton Hall amongst the laughing members of the wedding party, Rosslyn reviewed the discovery she had made this morning. Why, even now, when she pictured the admiration in that handsome face, her heart thumped erratically. She must put it down to sheer sentimentality over Letty's wedding; after all, it was seven years since she had been a bride. Yet she did not envy the girl her wedding night, as Stella seemed to do. Though attractive and his appeal somewhat heightened by Stella's scandalous gossip, Rosslyn assumed Stanley was cast in the same mold as Jarvis. After the haste of the first couple of days his ardor would drive him to easier, more familiar conquests. Being a bride was easy compared to being a wife. A bride was cherished, if only briefly; a wife, never.

For a wistful moment Rosslyn wondered if life would have been different had she married that handsome blonde gentleman who had caused her to experience a flurry of excitement. But the bitter experience of seven married years gave her a ready answer: There would be no difference in the long run, silly fool. Men like that were all alike. He would treat her exactly the way Jarvis did.

Forcing her sunniest smile, Rosslyn sat erect against the black padded seat. Why should she feel sad? She was more beautiful than the bride, her new dress was the envy of many women at the wedding; besides this, she had Will for company. Somehow today, even that was not consolation enough for what she vaguely felt she was missing. All this depth of feeling she kept locked within her heart was a magnificent gift she had saved for someone who did not exist. A passionate, caring man who gave her comfort when she was lonely, who was receptive to her moods. Everything she had thought Jarvis would be and was not.

Wistfully she watched Letty's simpering devotion to her husband as they alighted before the hall, and Rosslyn felt pangs of jealousy for Letty's innocence, for her hopes for the future—a road which, for Rosslyn, was already grown bitter, paved with dead hopes and dreams.

Burton Hall was crowded wtih toast-proposing well-wishers, champagne flowing by the bucketful though it was not yet noon. The tall-ceilinged rooms with their swagged moldings seemed to burst into bloom as laughter and voices echoed through their vastness. Into this false world Rosslyn immersed herself, brushing away those disturbing emotions which robbed her of her peace of mind. So much so, that it was difficult for Stella to draw her aside to reveal the very latest gossip.

Trapped as she was beside the French windows, Rosslyn made a futile attempt at escape to the terrace, but Stella held her fast.

"Before you go, my dear, I must tell you the most shocking thing. Our bridegroom wagered your Jarvis's gambling debts against . . ."

"Jarvis's gambling record is not my favorite subject," Rosslyn said icily, wishing, just for once, Stella could forget her absorbing weakness for gossip.

Ruffled by her attitude, her sister-in-law released her arm. "Well then, my dear, don't say I didn't try to warn you. If fate's against Jarvis you may just find out for yourself on his next birthday and what a shock that'll be. For myself, mind you, the idea would be intriguing; but you, dearest, will hate it like poison."

Leaving her with the unexplained riddle, Stella hurried away, knowing Rosslyn seethed inwardly with curiosity about the disaster she had sketchily revealed, knowing also she would have to be begged to enlighten her sister-in-law any further after that brush-off.

What idea could possibly be so unpleasant? Rosslyn wondered as Stella flounced away. A lavish party had been discussed for Jarvis's thirtieth birthday, but nothing definite had been set. Why worry about it? He had celebrated his twenty-ninth birthday less than a month ago. Surely little importance could be attached to his drunken boasts about casting the biggest wager of his life at his next party. Was that suggestion of last night more than an idle threat? But she would not ask him if it were true; she preferred not to give him the satisfaction of thinking his threats disturbed her.

Rosslyn glanced towards Tom Stanley who stood beside the marble fireplace, his arm resting on the ornate laurel leaf ornamentation as he surveyed the gathering with a smug smile on his wide mouth. It was as if he was lord of the manor, beaming like a simpleton because at last he had bought himself into the aristocracy, a position which he had been desperate to acquire all of his thirty-two years. It was a pity Jarvis and his gambling relatives had been so ready to supply Letty as sacrificial virgin to aid Tom Stanley's delusions of grandeur.

At precisely one o'clock a delicious luncheon of roast game, cured hams, creamed potatoes and minted garden peas was served, the meal ending with silver platters of exotic fresh fruit and delicate black-currant ices topped by whipped cream and glacé cherries. After the festive luncheon Rosslyn felt pleasantly appeased. Her good humor was abruptly shattered when she went into the hallway to find Will at the foot of the stairs, his face flushed, his brow moist with perspiration.

"Oh, sweetheart, what is it? Are you ill?"

"Things look so funny, Mama. My eyes are going fuzzy," he whispered, leaning against her, his hand tight against his chest. She took away the small clenched fist, alarmed to feel the shuddering, wracking breath in his lungs.

Concern over her child's illness dispelled the happiness over her new dress; even her anger over Jarvis's foolish, drunken schemes was forgotten. There was only Will and the fear in her heart as he slumped unconscious against her rose silk skirts.

Calling for help, Rosslyn swept him from the carpet in her arms and crouched there until a passing gentleman seeing her predicament assisted with the child, laying him full length on the shallow bottom stair. A knot of concerned guests formed around them; it was through this group Jarvis finally pushed his way.

"What is it?" he demanded, full lips thrust pugnaciously forward, irritated by the commotion.

"Will's collapsed! Send for Dr. Watkins. He's so hot. Getting wet yesterday must have caused more than a chill. How often have I told you . . . " she began, hissing in an angry undertone until she remembered others were listening.

Jarvis's florid face paled, then recovering his old bombast he turned aside with a crooked grin. "Nothing to worry about, the lad suffers from these periodic attacks. Get him up to bed, my love, no cause for alarm. Come, everyone, let's to the gaming room. I'll wager today's stakes are higher than most of you care to indulge in."

Aghast, Rosslyn watched him lumber away, soon to be joined by a laughing, animated group of gentlemen who swept him along in their midst. Across the hall he went and up the opposite stair, giving no further thought to the ill child in her arms. Tears came to Rosslyn's eyes, but they were not of sorrow, only an expression of blazing anger.

"Damn you! Damn all of you," she ground out, gritting her teeth until she thought they would snap under the pressure. Struggling to support the boy, she shakily got to her feet. Fortunately Will was light, his bones birdlike in their fragility so that he was no great burden to carry.

"Give him to me, Rosslyn, I'll carry him for you."

Tom Stanley's deep voice sounded at her elbow. In surprise Rosslyn relinquished her burden to the broadshouldered casino owner who had materialized from the seemingly empty hallway. She had supposed him to be in Jarvis's group of gentlemen gamblers as had been the handsome man whom her heart had fluttered over this morning. To think she had wasted even a moment's admiration for such an insensitive clod, when here was Tom Stanley, whom she had never held in high regard, coming to her rescue.

"Did you send for the doctor?"

"Not yet, I'd thought Jarvis would . . . " her voice cracked, until she could no longer trust herself to speak for all the hate and resentment that might come bubbling forth.

"Some men have little time for small children's ailments," he said smoothly. "Which way?"

At her direction they soon reached Will's bedroom where he deposited the boy on his bed. At their arrival Will's nurse came from the dressing room, her round face paling in shock at the sight of her young charge appearing so lifeless.

"Oh, my lady," she gasped, "what ails Master Will?"

Rosslyn shook her head. "I don't know, Nana. Probably too much excitement. Anyway, I'm sending for the doctor just in case it's more serious."

"Very well, my lady. I'll undress him and put him to bed. Poor little love," Nana crooned, stroking back Will's damp hair with a tender caress.

Silently Tom Stanley accompanied Rosslyn downstairs, offering to dispatch a servant himself to save her the inconvenience. Tight lipped, she accepted his proposal, waiting until he had gone to allow herself the luxury of tears as she leaned against the cold pillar at the foot of the stairs for comfort.

"Rosslyn, oh, what is it, dear?" Her brother's wife slid her arm about Rosslyn's heaving shoulders in concern, wondering at her grief.

Blinking back tears, Rosslyn gripped Adela's hand. "I'm glad it's you. Will seems so ill. And Jarvis, who cares not at all about his son's health, has gone to . . ." unable to finish her sentence, Rosslyn turned away trying to gain her composure.

Adela's small heart-shaped face was lined with worry as she understood her friend's distress. When Rosslyn regained herself enough for speech, she said: "Jarvis has gone where? You've got such a dreadful habit of not finishing your stories, Rosslyn, you've always driven me wild by it. Now where has he gone?"

Remembering Stella's gossip about Clarence and the French maid and feeling sorrow for Adela when she too heard the rumors, Rosslyn swallowed her anger.

"Gambling comes first as usual. Tom Stanley had to send for the doctor," she explained while a picture of Jeanette lying in Clarence's arms flashed through her mind. That deceiving little baggage with her genteel ways! To Adela, who virtually worshipped indolent Clarence, the discovery would be a crushing blow. It was enough for her to endure Clarence's passion for horses, his mania for racing around the countryside in his light phaeton, taking corners like a madman, without being confronted by his unfaithfulness as well. The inevitable drinking and gambling which beset the gentry of Burton Hill was commonplace. Rosslyn had always believed Clarence's loving attentions toward Adela made up for all the rest.

Gripping her friend's freckled arm, mindful of Adela's recent miscarriage, Rosslyn rested her dark head momentarily against Adela's auburn one with its frothy, ribbon-tied cascade of curls.

"You mustn't worry about Will. Children suffer from tremendous fevers and are right as rain in a couple of days. Jarvis thinks I overreact to Will's ailments—perhaps he's right."

Adela smiled in sympathy, squeezing her friend's arm.

"I never cease to marvel at your bravery. If I didn't know you I'd think you were cold as ice, because you must be the most composed person ever. How glad I am that you show your real self to me. Somehow that makes our friendship all the sweeter."

Touched by Adela's sincere words, Rosslyn made a great effort to squash the niggling feeling of disloyalty for not revealing what was being whispered behind her back by the others. At the first opportunity she would tackle Jeanette about the story. She might not be able to prevent her brother's amorous adventures, but a maid's behavior, even that of an aristocratic one, was a different story. She linked arms with Adela and led the way up the broad staircase to Will's room.

When Dr. Watkins arrived Rosslyn hovered anxiously beside her son's bed while the doctor gravely went through the usual examination. Will was alert now, his eyes unnaturally bright, the familiar wheezing in his chest audible above his speech.

Leaving his young patient with an admonition to be good, Dr. Watkins motioned for Rosslyn to accompany him into the corridor. Exchanging worried glances with Adela and Nana, who fluffed Will's pillows and coaxed him to sip lemonade, Rosslyn went with the doctor.

"Now, Lady Burton, there's no need for me to repeat what we've already discussed about Will. I must say though, his heart seems to have been overtaxed. I can't advise too strongly against prolonged activity. As you can see, his asthma has recurred, the old throat trouble along with it, direct results of distress and exposure. The boy needs plenty of rest and nourishing food, and above all, an atmosphere of loving security." Seeing the worried frown on Rosslyn's face, the old man smiled and patted her cheek. "Come now, Lady Burton, not to worry. He'll sleep soundly with the medicine I gave him. Weakness is normal for a child with Will's heart defect. Just has to take things easy, that's all, has to get through that stubborn little head he'll never be a cart-horse like those young cousins of his. Sooner he realizes that, the better it'll be."

"It's not Will, but my husband, who fails to accept that fact, Dr. Watkins. Have you time to speak to him?"

"Of course, there's always time to soothe a concerned father. Where is he?"

Rosslyn's face flushed at having to admit Jarvis's whereabouts, for it seemed to give the lie to his concern. "He's in the gaming room at the moment, but I'll have him fetched."

"No, don't bother, my lady," the doctor hastily decided, "some other time perhaps."

He made his escape, knowing it was more than his practice was worth to approach Lord Burton over the card table for something as effeminate as illness. The pretty little woman would have to wheedle him around which was to follow, racking her brain for her own knowledge of the Burton men, that should not be a difficult task.

When her mistress stalked through the doorway, with a look of determination hardening her features, Jeanette cleared her throat in nervous anticipation of the tirade which was to follow, wracking her brain for her own part in her lady's displeasure.

Her nerves tautened by Will's illness and her anger sharpened by Jarvis's humiliating indifference to it, Rosslyn came directly to the point, sparing little thought for the maid's feelings.

"Jeanette, I've heard some distressing rumors lately concerning your conduct with my brother."

"Me, Madame!"

"Yes, you—Look, girl, I'm in no mood for evasions. Is this just another of Stella's malicious stories, or is there something to it? I warn you, don't lie to me . . ."

"I've no intention of lying to you, Madame," Jeanette announced stiffly.

Though the maid's attitude annoyed her, Rosslyn found a flicker of admiration for her composure. "Tell me then, are you and Clarence having an affair? Oh, what a blind, stupid fool I've been, why else would a man like Clarence be interested in a penniless French miss with little to recommend her but a pretty face . . ."

"Madame," Jeanette interrupted, drawing herself up to her full height which only brought her level with Rosslyn's mouth. "I assure you, Madame, nothing of an immoral nature has occurred between your brother and myself."

Taken back by the icy assurance revealed in the words, Rosslyn made an effort to master her anger at the girl's insolence in speaking thus to her mistress; she forced herself to remember that unusual circumstances surrounded this maid's life.

"Very well then, Jeanette, if I have made a mistake I'm sorry," she managed, studying the girl's white face, convinced she was speaking the truth.

"Certainly, Madame, I accept your apology."

Biting back an acid comment at the haughtiness of those words, Rosslyn spun on her heel. "I think you should be aware of the nature of the things being whispered in certain circles."

"Thank you for your thoughtfulness. Need I remind you we are powerless to prevent the malicious tongues of idle women . . ."

"That will be quite enough!"

Blushing, Jeanette bobbed a curtsy. "Yes, Madame. Will you look over the menu cook has submitted for the buffet?"

Rosslyn approved the selection, instructed Jeanette what garments to lay out for her evening appearance, then left for the ballroom to oversee the floral arrangements. She was still seething in anger at the icy composure with which the maid received her accusations. What had begun as a lovely day was fast becoming another of those trials she so often had to endure. What with Will's collapse, followed by Jarvis's inconsiderate behavior, now the maid with her aristocratic ways, it was enough to bring about one of those terrific headaches from which she suffered when tension brought her nerves to a breaking point.

Rosslyn did not see Jarvis again until evening when it was time to dress for the ball. Letty had shyly thanked them for allowing her the use of their beautiful mansion, exclaiming in genuine delight over the silk damask draperies, the gilded chairs, even the inlaid marquetry cabinets in the library. Though Letty's admiration was flattering, nagging worry about Will took the edge off Rosslyn's pleasure in her compliments. Letty gushingly suggested that when she and Tom refurbished Burton Chase, the small home her father had left her overlooking the Channel five miles to the west, Rosslyn should advise her on the furnishings. Then, with a disarming smile which surprised them both, Letty asked Jarvis if he would personally oversee the landscaping of their ten-acre park because he had done such a splendid job with his own property.

When she tripped away, still laughing and fluttering, Jarvis's gaze followed her, admiration awakening for his pale cousin who had exhibited such excellent taste in asking for his assistance.

"Come on, me dear, time to pretty yourself up. You can leave everything else to the servants, that's what they're for, ye know. Our guests are anxious to see the famous beauty they've heard so much about."

Rosslyn smiled at the unexpected compliment, taking his kiss on the mouth, though he had aimed for her cheek.

"Surely it's too early to change."

"Not at all. The afternoon's game's been over an hour. We must circulate before they start the night game. This weekend's turning out so well, can't think why I've waited so long to have a party like this."

Jarvis ambled away, his new suit of strawberry pink brocade a bright splash of color against the gloomy, slate blue walls.

Rosslyn sought the sanctuary of her darkened room where she lay listening to the muted sounds of party preparations from the lower floor. Thankful that she was no longer needed downstairs, she luxuriated in the downy comfort of her bed, regretting the need to exchange her solitude for the noisy throng of guests who would soon await her presence.

Letty's shy praise had been a surprise, as had Tom Stanley's considerate assistance over Will's indisposition this afternoon. Perhaps in the future they could become as good friends to her as Adela and Clarence, who lived less than ten miles from Burton Hall. Having friends close at hand improved her life with Jarvis whose daily timeclock revolved around the hours of the next card games. Had she been forced into seclusion with him for the rest of her life, Rosslyn was sure she would be driven insane.

Burton Hall resounded with noise as the guests congregated in the glittering ballroom, brilliantly lit by hundreds of candles which turned the vast mirrored room bright as day and twice as hot.

Rosslyn paused to watch the scene over the bannister, surveying the colorful throng below as a steady stream of guests moved through the ballroom entrance. The huge double doors had been flung back; the ladies headed for either the terrace or the powder room; the gentlemen gravitated towards the gaming rooms where baize-topped tables had been set up for the evening event. Both brilliantly clothed groups met briefly in the ballroom where the lulling music of a minuet was nearly drowned by their chatter. On a dais at the far end of the room the white-wigged musicians doggedly labored at their instruments despite the noise, playing even louder in a desperate effort to be heard. Buffet tables extended the length of the room where an army of servants doled out spiced wine punch in crystal goblets, or assisted guests with heaping plates of delicacies ranging from roast pheasant to pâté. Everything appeared to be running like clockwork, thanks to her meticulous planning and the servants' efficient execution of their duties.

Though the colorful scene excited her, Rosslyn hesitated to become part of it, almost as if to enter the picture would be to destroy the grandeur it presented when viewed from this vantage point.

A movement below alerted her to a gentleman standing in the shadow of the Chinese lacquered cabinet directly opposite. As his pale eyes met hers Rosslyn read his bold appraisal, for he made no effort to hide his outrageous thoughts. Flushing, she jerked upright, suddenly conscious of the gaping bodice of her blue-striped ballgown as she leaned over the balustrade, the low-cut neckline revealing even more than the dressmaker had intended.

Noticing her swift action, the expression of effrontery flickering coldly over her face, the man chuckled as he stepped into the light, giving her a mock salute before he strode away.

Blood warmed the broad expanse of her bare chest and shoulders as Rosslyn glared after him, the sound of his amusement still echoing in her ears. His boldness was an insult, yet there had also been something compelling about those eyes which had fastened on hers for what seemed an eternity, startlingly pale in his dark-complexioned face. Something so compelling, in fact, that now, as she relived the boldness of that stare, her arms prickled with goosebumps as something not quite buried from the days of her girlhood romanticism was revived.

Swishing about, her frilled skirts dragging over the stairs, she made a determined descent. Whoever he was, the stranger's naked appraisal of her body had been insultingly out of place. How dare he, this Mr. Impertinence in the severe dove gray coat and charcoal-striped britches, the gray suede boots turned down with vivid citron to match his cravat . . .

Clasping her hand to her flushed cheek, Rosslyn paused on the fifth stair; if the stranger had been so uncouth, why did she remember the details of his dress so accurately? Or clearly picture the lean darkness of his face with its high-bridged, aristocratic nose and sensual, well-shaped mouth, the firm chin where a cleft deeply marked the flesh, the dark brows drawing a straight line above those startling gray eyes which promised something forbidden and exciting . . .

"There you are at last, my dear, thought you'd had an attack of the vapors. Come, we're waiting for you. I had to greet everyone alone."

Jarvis waited at the foot of the stairs and Rosslyn hastily thrust the disturbing picture of the stranger's face from her mind. Seeing her hesitation, he seized her cold fingers, hastening her impatiently to the lighted ballroom.

When he entered the hot room, splendid in his brilliantly colored suit, a snow white cravat tight about his thick neck, Jarvis beamed in pleasure to behold the sumptuous party he was hosting, basking in the gasps of delight he had received from the London guests who marveled at his ingenuity over designing the formal layout for the gardens. This was the culmination of his dreams: the woman on his arm, with her perfect features and desirable body brilliantly attired in a diamond-sparkled necklace to compliment her French ballgown, his crowning delight.

The envy in men's eyes more than made up for what it cost him to present her thus arrayed, exquisite as a painted masterpiece. No need to reveal the distaste with which they sometimes viewed each other in private. On the surface they made a splendid couple, and as appearances were what really mattered in life, he was able to bask in this myth he had created of his own perfect taste in both estate and women. The nagging worry in the back of his mind about the health of his pale, shadowy heir asleep upstairs must not be allowed to destroy his well-earned pleasure over tonight's ball, and resolutely Jarvis thrust the picture from his mind.

Accepting a welter of compliments on her appearance, Rosslyn smiled, assured that as soon as they returned home those ladies would beg and plead with their husbands to let them have a dress by that new French dressmaker Rosslyn Burton had used. The idea was pleasing. To be a leader in her circle was a position she strove to maintain, one of the few absorbing pleasures of her life. That detached, serene woman they knew might have been one of the marble statues surrounding the lily pond, as she smiled at them all, remotely in her flawless appearance. And as cold and unyielding, she was sure the gentlemen added; for beyond mild flirtations which went no further than discreet hand holding, Rosslyn had stayed immune to the advances she received from Jarvis's gambling cronies, much to the collective disappointment of those gay young blades who were forced to adore her from a safe distance.

Knowing her nature well enough, Jarvis viewed other men's admiration of his wife in the benign manner of a doting parent, confidently assured of her fidelity.

Too assured perhaps, for when Rosslyn again encountered the bold, searching gaze of that insolent stranger when they met by chance beside the punch bowl, she felt her heart flutter sickeningly. His scrutiny flustered her so much she was forced to lower her lashes to hide her own confusion at his stare. His interest turned her inwardly giddy as a schoolgirl, bringing blood throbbing in congested heat in reply to the unspoken question she read in his eyes.

A few moments later Stella battled her way through the throng, looking like a Jersey cow in yellow-brown satin, her blonde curls tortured into hornlike protrusions wrapped with purple silk pansies. At the sight of Rosslyn, she grabbed her arm.

"Do come with me. He's here at last. Oh, you really must meet him."

"Who is here?"

"That marvelous Frenchman I was telling you about. The handsome one. You know, the mysterious comte the women are raving over. I swear, he's the handsomest man I've ever seen. You'll just adore him."

"Yes, do introduce me, I'd love to see him. I'm sure the gentleman couldn't be half as delicious as you'd have me believe, Stella dearest."

"Just wait and see."

Swept through the ballroom by her sister-in-law, Rosslyn perceived a gathering at the far end of the room where a group of ladies laughed and chattered to someone hidden in their midst, his presence betrayed by a glimpse of a dark masculine haircut amongst the beribboned, flower-decked topknots. This must be the French charmer. Rosslyn's mouth curled scornfully as she listened to the other women's foolish laughter. No wonder the man thought himself so handsomely desirable with all this unwarranted attention lavished on him.

"After listening to all that flirtatious nonsense, the Frenchman will think our ladies came out of a convent. I declare, one would think there were no English gentlemen present at all," Rosslyn said, amused to see Stella's growing annoyance over her attitude.

"Wait till you've met him to pass judgment. You can't deny these foreigners have a certain something."

"Merely an unwarranted reputation, my dear, nothing more," Rosslyn drawled.

"Out of the way, everyone. Do let poor Rosslyn meet our charming Mr. St. Clare. I know she'll love him as we all do," Stella gushed with sugar sweetness, maneuvering her silk encased bulk with tripping coyness as she dragged Rosslyn after her. "Do meet your hostess, Mr. St. Clare—Rosslyn, Lady Burton."

"I am your servant, Madame."

The man who confronted her when the adoring ladies parted like waves to allow her to enter the hallowed circle, bowed politely. When he straightened up, a set smile on his mouth, Rosslyn was shocked to behold the insolent gentleman in the dove gray coat.

Unprepared for his appearance, Rosslyn found she was at a momentary loss for words. So this impudent stranger was the mystery Frenchman about whom Stella raved, this man, who had virtually undressed her with his eyes. Forcing cold reserve to her face, she politely held out her hand to him.

"At last, Monsieur," she drawled with a bored air. "I declare, your reputation has assumed such gigantic proportions in the retelling, I'm almost afraid to touch your hand. Tell me, is everything they say about you true?"

He brushed her fingers with his mouth; still with that same impersonal smile he shrugged. "Unless you acquaint me with what is said about my exploits, Madame, I'm afraid I cannot answer that question."

A titter spread around the simpering group at his retort, causing Rosslyn to fume inwardly, annoyed that her words had been turned so neatly aside. "I'm afraid by the nature of some of these rumors, such a discussion between us would prove unseemly," she said with sugar sweetness.

"In that case, Madame, I will vouch for the authenticity of the stories."

Stella led the others in laughter, nudging Rosslyn in high delight at his words.

The smile froze on Rosslyn's face, until she felt like a plaster image. He stared back at her with that same smile as he awaited her next retort in this game at which he was fast proving her master.

"Why, Monsieur, are you wearing boots? The customs of your country must be very different from ours. Well-bred gentlemen do not dance in riding boots in England," she observed spitefully.

"Nor do they in France. But there are so many delightful ladies present tonight, I'd be spoiled for choice. Those with whom I did not dance would feel affronted; therefore, Madame, if I dance with no one, all the ladies will remain my friend. Your servant, Madame Burton."

With a curt nod he walked away, several of the adoring females clinging to his arms, giggling up at him as he strode to the punch table for a refill. Rosslyn seethed inwardly at his answer, aware she had received several triumphant glances when her spiteful words were vanquished. This was so humiliating she wanted to hit him. The shock of his public insolence had sent pains shooting through her temples.

"If you'll excuse me, Stella, I have a headache."

"Don't you dare leave the ball."

"I'm coming back. I'll get my maid to mix a potion for this frightful headache, then I'll pop into Will's room to see how he fares."

"Mind that's all you do, now," Stella cautioned, giving her an affectionate peck on the cheek. "Letty would be crushed to think you'd left her wedding ball so early."

A cool breeze wafting through the deep windows of the upper stories of the house soothed Rosslyn's throbbing head. Her own dark bedroom seemed a welcoming haven from the noise and hot brilliance of the ballroom. The excitement downstairs was the cause of this excruciating headache, that, and the insolence of that French emigré. To think he had shown no remorse for ogling her openly; even when he discovered she was his hostess, there had been no word of apology on his fine chiseled lips. How dare he treat her as if she was merely a buxom servant girl!

44

Clenching her fists in anger, Rosslyn thumped the soft down pillow as she imagined it was his face, fighting tears of humiliation which burned like fire between her closed lids. Somehow she had expected more from him after the frank revelation of his sensual thoughts. More consideration, more flattering attentions—yet it was she who had gone to battle, determined to put him in his place. All these years of fighting with Jarvis seemed to have ruined her dealings with men once she became personally involved. And she was involved, though she tried to ignore the force of attraction drawing her to the stranger. Damn Jarvis for spoiling what had promised to bring such pleasure! Damn her own bitchiness—oh damn the Frenchman too for making a fool of her before those jealous twittering cows in their provincial fashions, voraciously gobbling up her ideas to transpose on their bovine bodies in so ridiculous a fashion, she wanted to laugh out at the bulging bosoms and sagging bellies protruding in their uncorseted dresses. Well, let them ape her, it was flattering to be the fashion leader of the local gentry. They were fifty miles from London; if only she could go to court where she could really shine. Then it would not matter if Jarvis ignored her, just as long as he bought pretty clothes and jewels to deck her in sumptuous style. And he would, the very thought of his wife being at court would loosen his already lax purse strings even further. She would have to urge Jarvis to accept all invitations into London Society next season. They could even buy a house in the city. Bloomsbury was a delightful district, fashionable though still rural in aspect, and the Duke of Bedford owned an impressive mansion there. Better yet, there were fields at hand where they could indulge their passion for riding. The change of scene might be good for Will as well. They would be able to go to the park in the carriage and she could take him to watch the horse-guards' parades.

The exciting idea had cheered her so much, the throbbing headache had almost disappeared. Still, she would ask Jeanette to prepare one of Dr. Watkins's headache powders, just in case. Those white powders usually worked like magic to alleviate the pain for hours, albeit making her rather intoxicated, yet tonight those sometimes alarming aftereffects would only serve her purpose. She needed some of her usual enthusiasm to endure the rest of this ball; worry over Will's health had robbed her of some of her pleasure, now that insolent foreigner had completed the process. True, he had humiliated her before the neighbors, yet that should not bring about this gloom which was out of all proportion to the crime. He was at best an impoverished aristocrat; at worse, a flagrant imposter.

Rousing herself to action Rosslyn took one of Dr. Watkins's white powders from the flower-inlaid cabinet where she kept her medicines.

Impatiently waiting for Jeanette to appear after she had rung the bell several times, Rosslyn went in search of the girl. Foreigners could not be trusted—those words began one of Jarvis's favorite homilies on why His Majesty should have no dealings with other nations. After the insolence of that man downstairs and Jeanette's unreliability, she was beginning to feel perhaps he was right about something at last.

A movement in the alcove which was situated directly over the portico attracted her attention. Moonlight flooded the corridor making it light as day so Rosslyn had not bothered to bring a candle; now, in the curtained area, she could identify the woman who stood there. It was Jeanette. And by her impatient actions as she repeatedly glanced downstairs, clasping and unclasping her hands in anticipation, she was plainly waiting for someone. Was the strumpet awaiting a rendezvous with Clarence? Had she lied to her then?

Her mouth set in anger at the discovery, Rosslyn stepped into the shadow of a pair of Grecian vases overflowing with ornamental grasses, determined to confront them with her scandalous knowledge whenever her brother appeared. For Adela's sake she definitely would not stand for it under her roof; whatever they chose to do elsewhere, at Burton Hall their behavior must be beyond reproach.

A few minutes later heavy masculine footsteps echoed on the stair. Jeanette strained forward to identify the person, her face assuming a tremulous smile as the dark figure bounded the last two steps and seized her in his arms.

Instead of marching forward to denounce them as Rosslyn had intended, she shrank deeper into the shadow, sickened by what she had witnessed. The French girl was whispering to the man, uttering soft cries of pleasure in his embrace, yet the lover Jeanette had awaited was not Rosslyn's brother Clarence: The man in her arms was that insolent Frenchman, St. Clare.

Though Rosslyn spoke fluent French, she would not demean herself by translating their exchange, closing her ears to Jeanette's breathless endearments as she clung to him lovingly amid tears of joy.

Silently, afraid to betray her presence, Rosslyn crept the length of the corridor to the other stair, fighting anger and disappointment as she went towards Will's door. Her reaction was puzzling, for it mattered not a whit to her that those two embraced back there in the darkness. A maid and an insolent upstart deserved each other. By this discovery she was at least assured of one thing, French gentlemen were exactly like their English counterparts, breaking their necks to tip some servant girl on her back. Yet she had to acknowledge, though she professed indifference, there was more than a twinge of jealousy that Jeanette of all people should have the privilege of owning that arousing man if only briefly. Privilege—good God, the wine had turned her brain.

Forcing his image to the background Rosslyn assumed her usual, somewhat cynical smile as she turned the doorknob to her son's room and with a swish of ruffled skirts disappeared inside the gloom.

CHAPTER THREE

During the next couple of days Will made a remarkable recovery until he pleaded with his mother to be allowed to go outdoors. He grew more fretful by the hour as Nana insisted he keep to his bed, stoically ignoring his pleas to let him sit on the terrace in the sunshine.

On Wednesday Dr. Watkins pronounced him able to go outdoors. Rosslyn planned a picnic on the downs, choosing all Will's favorite foods to please him and tempt his flagging appetite. When she held the boy she must use her utmost restraint to keep from crushing him breathless out of relief at his recovery. As it was, Will struggled in her embrace, somewhat embarrassed by his mother's overwhelming demonstration of affection. Rosslyn released him, blinking back tears of joy as he skipped outdoors, laughing and chattering like any normal boy.

Jarvis was not invited to join them on their picnic, not that he would have come, for he had ridden into the village with his nephew Veasey to look at some animals a horse trader was offering at the marketplace. Veasey had told his uncle what good horses they were, and though the mounts were undoubtedly stolen, Jarvis decided to view them with an eye to replacing Will's small gelding with a better horse. Uneasily Rosslyn wondered if Jarvis would have enough sense to buy an animal appropriate for a six-year-old. More likely he would choose a towering brute suitable only for an experienced horseman, and unreasonably expect the boy to master it.

The sun beat down warmly on her face and Rosslyn lay, eyes closed, enjoying the peaceful serenade of wheeling gulls and buzzing insects. Will hummed as he crawled through the grass hunting for ants and grass-hoppers for his insect collection.

Tomorrow the tutor would come for his interview and Rosslyn was determined to outline what she expected of him. Visions of how she would put him in his place brought a smile to her lips. She would show him how she felt about taking a penniless Frenchman into her household, especially after their encounter at the ball where he had publicly humiliated her. Yet despite her resolve to keep him in his place, Rosslyn could not help dwelling on his handsome face with those heavy-lidded pale eyes which had appraised her so boldly. And though she told herself his manner toward her was outrageous, shivers of excitement prickled along her spine when she relived the promise in his eyes. Other men ogled her; in fact, there were any number of fast-riding, hard-drinking younger sons who would have come eagerly to her call. They would have relished the conquest, and then next week bandied the story from ale house to ale house. Though sometimes in the past the idea of a lover had intrigued her, the cold assessment of the aftermath of the encounter had always tempered the desire. Besides, up till now no man had sparked her interest sufficiently for that! She smiled at the revealing honesty of her thoughts, which for her was a rare indulgence. "Up till now"—that phrase, while intriguing, could also prove dangerous.

The interview was set for ten o'clock. Rosslyn dressed with utmost care, choosing a lavender muslin gown with a deep-pleated fichu at the neck, the ends caught with a cameo brooch which had belonged to her mother. It was unseemly to appear in a low-necked gown before her son's future tutor; besides, she wouldn't give that impudent Frenchman the satisfaction of ogling her breasts again this morning.

When she had faced him in the ballroom Rosslyn noticed he was not much taller than she in her three-inch heels, so she searched through her wardrobe for a pair of suitably decorous day shoes with tall heels. Mouse gray velvet with a violet rosette seemed appropriate.

Flicking her curls artfully over her brow, she dismissed Jeanette, who was clumsily abstracted this morning. On the whole Rosslyn had found the maid failed to please her in any way since she had discovered her affair with that man. Picturing them together in a close locked embrace made her seethe with anger, until at times she could barely restrain herself from confronting the simpering little ninny with her knowledge. The force of that anger was bewildering. It was not that she cared a jot for St. Clare; it was more jealousy over the fact that Jeanette should be fortunate to have the complete attention of a man who aroused her ire.

As Rosslyn approached the study, still simmering over Jeanette's romance, she realized the probable reason for the maid's added clumsiness this morning. Her lover would be here in the house, and today would be just a forerunner of months of blissful reunion for the pair. That man with his brazen assurance must be laughing up his elegant sleeve at Jarvis's foolish cooperation in hiring him as tutor. This way he could be sure of continuing those tender moments he had shared with Jeanette in the corridor, financing his outrageous amour at their expense.

With unaccustomed vigor she wrenched open the study door and strode aggressively inside the room.

"Oh, there you are, Mama, we've been waiting almost half an hour for you," Will piped, coming to stand at her side while he cast a furtive glance at the stranger who stood in the bright flood of sunlight through the deep windows.

Her gaze was drawn like a magnet to St. Clare who again wore his gray coat and striped britches, but today his boots were modest black as was his cravat, completing the picture of subservient decorum. Yet even the drabness of his clothes seemed lit by an inner vitality which was quite remarkable. That, coupled with the compelling attraction she felt towards him, forced her to gird herself for battle, determined the men should not have the best of her over the situation. Jarvis was seated behind his desk, lordly and commanding as usual, toying with his initialed letter opener while he waited. He nodded towards his wife in greeting, ruffling absently through a sheaf of papers before him on the polished oak desk.

"Do forgive me if I've kept you gentlemen waiting," Rosslyn said. Though she had taken care over her dressing, she had not intended to be that long. It was amazing how the time had flown.

"Your servant, Madame Burton," Armand St. Clare said, stepping towards her and making a stiff, half bow over her hand.

When their eyes met Rosslyn deliberately looked away, venturing only a small, frosty smile in answer to his greeting. When Jarvis indicated a chair beside the desk for her use, she glided regally towards it, the model of a lady of quality. Will came to her side and she took his hot sticky hand in her own, smiling at him with reassurance. Then she nodded for the interview to begin.

"Well, me dear, we haven't much left to discuss," Jarvis drawled, stretching in his chair. "Only a formality, really, having you here."

"What! I understood the interview was for ten. I can't be more than a few minutes late. How could you start without me when you know how much I wanted to talk to this man about Will's schedule?" Rosslyn exploded, taken off guard enough to allow her genuine emotion to shine through for once.

"That's when I asked *you* to come here, yes. Monsieur St. Clare and I have already discussed most matters of importance."

"You agreed I should interview him too."

"Yes, of course. Well, we have a few minutes left. Carry on, my dear, if it'll make you happy," Jarvis allowed indulgently.

Her husband's condescension had so unnerved her, the cold aloof personality Rosslyn had intended to display was hard won as she found it difficult to swallow the anger which bubbled to the surface when she realized she had been tricked. Clearing her throat she began evenly: "Monsieur St. Clare, I trust you do speak English?"

"Fluently, Madame."

"Good, although I was prepared to converse with you in your own language."

"That's very thoughtful of you, Madame, but not necessary."

"I'm sure my husband has warned you about our son's delicate health."

"Yes, I have been made aware of his needs."

Jarvis snorted. "You see, St. Clare, how my wife worries about the lad. He'll grow out of it, be hardy as a weed in a couple of years given the proper grounding. Hardy as a weed."

"Despite what my husband believes, Dr. Watkins tells me Will may never grow to be a robust child. His heart's weak and he suffers from asthmatic attacks when he becomes upset. He also has headaches, earaches, a persistent throat problem . . ."

"Gad, my dear, don't bore us with this. Run along, lad, no need for you to have to listen to Mama's tiresome speeches, is there?" Jarvis boomed at Will, winking at him in a conspiratorial manner. "Go romp with the new pups. Splendid animals those, St. Clare, you'll have to have a look at them, give me your opinion."

Biting back words of angry retort, Rosslyn watched the small figure depart. "Please don't take my words lightly, Monsieur, it's vital that he not become chilled. This alarming athletic program my husband wishes the boy to embark upon can only be dangerous to his health. He can exercise if rest periods are allowed at least every half hour."

"I assure you I'll be mindful of the boy's needs."

The quiet acceptance of her words was something Rosslyn had not expected, his manner taking away much of her aggression, for she had expected him to disagree with her ideas.

"Are you to live inside the house, Monsieur?"

"By George, do you expect me to house the chap in the barn? Of course he's going to live in the house. But that's all taken care of, my love, no need to worry your pretty head about it," Jarvis dismissed, creaking to his feet with a bellow of laughter.

"I worry about it only because of the moral welfare of our maids," Rosslyn snapped, looking pointedly at the Frenchman so that he should understand she knew which maid in particular concerned her.

"You have my assurance, Madame, I shall make no attempt to seduce them."

Fuming at the man's impertinence, Rosslyn could have struck Jarvis when he chortled in glee.

"Well, my good fellow, from what I've seen, the little fillies may come scratching on your door instead."

"Will you please be serious," Rosslyn said icily, her voice sobering even Jarvis's humor. "This interview should at least be conducted with dignity, not like some cheap theatrical farce. I must be concerned with the moral welfare of my female staff as no one else spares a thought for them. It's hard enough to maintain decorum in a staff of this size without introducing single men into the household, especially one with different standards of behavior, and strange habits from another country. We have no idea . . ."

"Madame, allow me to set your mind at rest. Your women servants will be safe from me. Though apparently I do not meet with your special standards of morality, I assure you I am used to a reasonably genteel way of life. You need not go on to remind me to eat with cutlery instead of fingers at table, nor to take off my boots when I sleep, nor warn me about relieving myself in the gardens . . ."

"How dare you speak so to me!" Rosslyn sprang to her feet, her face hot with anger. At least in her tottering heels she was at eye level with him, she thought with passing satisfaction, yet the amusement she saw sparkling there only added to her anger.

"Oh, dammit all, Ross, give the fellow credit, you have to admit he has you bested," Jarvis gasped, recovering from a burst of laughter at the new tutor's words. If the man wasn't an aristocrat he would have him flogged for his insolence, but to see his wife as ruffled as this was worth enduring the fellow's cheek.

In stony silence Rosslyn viewed the two men, seething inwardly, using her utmost control to keep from slinging something at her husband's red grinning face, or slapping the somber-faced employee who had the audacity to mock her.

"I can see there will be no satisfaction gained from any of my requests, therefore, I shall take my leave."

Mustering her utmost dignity, head held high, she tottered precariously from the study, Jarvis's infuriating chuckle accompanying her departure.

For the next few days every time she thought of that farcical interview, Rosslyn became freshly annoyed. It was typical of Jarvis to have dismissed her questions as nonsense. Determined to have her revenge on them, she watched Will like a hawk for the first sign of fatigue, her intention being to summon Dr. Watkins to have him explain to Jarvis why the tutor must be dismissed. For her husband to win this argument would give him a tremendous advantage. And she could never allow that.

To her aggravation, nothing went awry. Not that she wanted Will to suffer; she needed only a minor failing to pounce on the new routine condemning it as dangerous. Begrudgingly, however, she had to admit Will seemed to be blooming under the Frenchman's guidance, his whole personality brightening as the days passed.

For two weeks Rosslyn kept her distance, allowing the men to schedule her son's days, immersing herself in the banality of Stella's whist drives and social teas, even choosing her daily ride at a time when Will and his tutor were safely in the schoolroom so that she would not be forced to encounter the man and be reminded of her humiliation.

Stella's cross-examination about their exciting employee became so insistent Rosslyn could have slapped her for her inquisitive tongue, which pried into all manner of intimate feelings. Not content with Rosslyn's sketchy information about Armand St. Clare, Stella had the audacity to ride over to Burton Hall at least three times a week, often accompanying Will and his tutor on their afternoon rides.

Watching their return from her vantage point on the south terrace, Rosslyn was determined to speak to Stella about the unseemliness of her behavior. What was the matter with the woman? Wasn't it enough to have Jeanette simpering around the house like a lunatic, without Stella acting like a bitch in heat? Look at her openly ogling him as she deliberately brushed against his arm, then giggling like a schoolgirl when he apologized, fluttering her sparse eyelashes, her toad's eyes even more prominent as she watched him!

"Stella, have you no home of your own?" Rosslyn snapped when at last, the stable activity over, Stella sauntered towards the garden chairs where Rosslyn pretended to read a novel.

"Don't you want me to be interested in my nephew's welfare?"

"Yes, I would certainly prefer that to your unseemly interest in his tutor," Rosslyn remarked acidly.

Stella grinned. "Am I that obvious?"

"I half expect you to attack him."

"If I thought it would be advantageous, I might consider that," Stella said, squashing her large body into a delicate wrought-iron garden chair. Unbuttoning her bottle green serge habit, she wiped streams of perspiration from her neck. "Deuced hot today, isn't it? Or maybe it was the company which made me sweat."

"Oh, Stella, really," Rosslyn admonished, but could not help laughing at her sister-in-law's complete honesty.

"Yes, really, my cool-as-a-cucumber girl. Haven't you ever had one surge of passion in your entire life, my dear?"

"I never discuss matters of that nature," Rosslyn dismissed primly, quick to look away from Stella's probing gaze. Was that fluttering heart, the hot confusion she experienced during St. Clare's appraisal, the forerunner of passion? Rosslyn turned back to Stella to ask: "What do you think of Will's progress so far?"

"Excellent. You certainly did right in choosing Mr. St. Clare. Why, the boy absolutely adores him."

"Does he really?" Rosslyn echoed in surprise, looking back towards the parkland where a tall figure and a small one walked slowly beneath the trees. "Where are they going?"

"To find an anthill I think. Your boy certainly has a liking for those creepy-crawly things. You have to hand it to the tutor, he takes it all in stride."

"The study of insects is not considered creepy"

"By me it is. What have you got to eat, anyway?"

"Nothing out here, but I can ring for something if you like."

"Oh, Lord, don't bother. How you ever keep up your strength, I'll never know. I'll be off home, the boys are having a picnic later anyway. Can Will come?"

"I'd rather he didn't, the ride was tiring enough."

"All right, whatever you think. God, if you ever dismiss that man, send him to my place. These rides over here are wearing me out."

Rosslyn smiled at Stella's outrageous statement as she watched her sister-in-law lever herself from the chair with effort. "You know, you could give up your pursuit. A tutor is rather beneath your station, is it not?"

"But you forget, I'm not interested in a tutor, my dear. My interest is in a mysterious French comte who must be the most fascinating man in Kent. I'll have to say, the man is keeping his place, never a word or a glance out of the way. It's absolutely infuriating. Why, I could probably offer myself to him and he would give me that inscrutable stare and apologize for misinterpreting my words. Damn him!"

"Please don't embarrass me by testing him."

"Well, if I do, I certainly shan't tell you about it. Good-bye, dearest. Will I see you tomorrow? We're having a little game after lunch. Letty's finally coming to visit me, tearing herself away from her new husband for a whole afternoon—oh, I despise her for her good fortune."

"I'll probably be there, but with Will's uncertain health, I never know from one day to the next if I'll be able to go visiting."

"I just dare him to be ill. We're having some of those French crepes with whipped cream, um, delicious. That little Charlotte is certainly worth her weight in gold. All in all, this revolution hasn't been bad for us British, having such good cooks and dressmakers just begging for work. And men like Armand St. Clare." Stella winked meaningfully. Then, with a wave, she stumped over the grass to the stables.

After Stella's departure Rosslyn went back to her book, but her interest in Lady Stanhope's tragedies had waned. The shadowy figure of Armand St. Clare flitted through her mind as she pictured him dismounting in the bright sunlight, his tight-fitting clothing reminding her of the muscular beauty of his body. Wide shouldered, he had the wiry, slender frame of an athlete. Indulging her fancy a moment, she shuddered to imagine their bodies pressed close, having the intoxicating sensation of knowing that he would soon make love to her. His face had been in shadow when he spoke to Stella so she could not see his expression. For a moment Rosslyn substituted herself for the portly figure in bottle green serge, wondering if he would appear so indifferent then. After that revealing exchange at the ball she doubted it. However, the idea was exciting.

Banging the book closed, Rosslyn decided to go indoors, wondering at the foolish nature of her thoughts. It was no accomplishment to have a man desire you, heavens knows, even Jarvis did that. It was that special tenderness which accompanied it she craved. To assume Armand St. Clare offered such a rare commodity was little more than romantic dreaming, despite the promise she read in his pale eyes.

"Mama, wait."

Shielding her eyes from the sun, Rosslyn saw Will racing over the lawn towards her. She turned from the French window to watch his progress with pleasure, noting how vigorous he seemed this afternoon.

"See what I've found," he cried, breathless as he eagerly thrust a snuffbox in her hands.

Opening the silver lid with care, half-expecting the box to be full of crawling things, she smiled bravely as she tried to overcome her natural aversion to insects in order to please her son. Inside the box a huge black beetle scrabbled over the silver base.

"Isn't he grand? His name's Freddy. Monsieur helped me catch him by lending me his snuffbox. This kind of beetle is very rare, Mama."

"Yes, he's lovely, sweetheart. Now here, you keep him. Mama wouldn't want to drop Freddy." Thankfully she relinquished the box into Will's grubby hands, and looked up to see the amused smile of his tutor who stood beside the shrubbery at a discreet distance awaiting his charge.

"It is a pleasant afternoon, Madame."

"Yes, early September is usually nice."

"Would you care to see Will's riding? He has improved."

"No thank you. I was just going indoors."

"Oh, Mama, at least come see the horse Papa bought me. He's a monster."

"What, is it here already? I wasn't told."

"Yes, but I don't ride him. Monsieur says he's far too big."

Rosslyn looked towards the man for confirmation, further alarmed when he gravely nodded his head in agreement.

"Well, in that case, I'd better come see just in case Papa decides to overrule Monsieur's decision someday."

The trio walked stiffly towards the stables, Rosslyn feeling ill at ease with the Frenchman after her intimate thoughts of him just moments ago. Only Will prattled on as if nothing was changed.

The acrid stench of the stables met them in a hot wave as they entered the yard. Inside the building the summer afternoon heat accentuated the animal smell until Rosslyn wrinkled her nose in distaste.

"Here he is. Isn't he a big one, Mama?"

Rosslyn gasped at the mammoth raw-boned hunter plunging about in his stall. The horse was over sixteen hands and his flashing, rolling eyes and dilated nostrils bespoke his temper.

"Good heavens! Whatever was Papa thinking about to choose such a fierce animal for you?" she gasped, taken back by the horse's evil glance.

"As Will told you, Madame, I shall not allow him to ride the horse until he is ready."

"I hope that will be about ten years from now."

"It will be never if I have my way."

In surprise she turned to the tutor, seeing the smile of understanding on his face. Will had gone to fondle his small gelding, leaving the new horse thrashing about in his stall as he attempted to break his restraint.

"Thank you, Monsieur," she said humbly, wary in

case the boy was listening. "My husband has poor judgment where Will is concerned, therefore I must leave these decisions up to you. Jarvis doesn't listen to me."

"That horse is a challenge even for me, though I've ridden him twice already. He knows who's master," the Frenchman assured, fixing the animal with a stare as he reached for the long, sinewy neck. The chestnut suffered his touch, gentling after a few minutes. "Will you ride with us someday? The boy is anxious to show you how much he's improved."

Rosslyn hesitated, fighting her first impulse to refuse, convincing herself that agreement was for Will's pleasure, not a sign of capitulation.

"Perhaps tomorrow if the weather is nice." At least that would make a good excuse not to attend Stella's card party.

"I shall look forward to it, Madame. Would you like me to ride the animal to show you how he can be handled?"

"If you wish."

Rosslyn watched him carefully sidestep the plunging beast to unhook his halter and lead him from the stall. In alarm she grabbed Will's arm in case the animal broke loose, wary of those rolling eyes. The groom saddled the chestnut after much effort and Monsieur St. Clare mounted the leaping, thrashing horse who was fiercely rejecting the idea of bearing a rider. Bending close to his ear and whispering to soothe the animal, they moved to the paddock where Rosslyn leaned against the fence to watch. The horse was a fine animal though by the way he fought the bit, plunging repeatedly to rid himself of his burden, he had obviously at least once been cruelly handled.

Will perched on the fence to cheer as his tutor brought the animal under control. "We're going to call the horse Attila, Mama, because he's such a barbarian."

Squinting against the sun Rosslyn watched the man taking the horse into a canter, sitting in perfect control in the saddle, thighs tensed, hands relaxed. Jarvis was right, he did appear to be a superb horseman. Perhaps this was not such a bad idea after all, having him as tutor for a few months.

59

"If Will would like to go indoors to rest, I'll take the brute for a gallop on the downs to run some of the vinegar out of him."

Rosslyn looked up at the dark face above her as he leaned towards the fence, a smile on his mouth which made her grow uneasy. Why should she feel this way when he looked at her? she puzzled. Today at least the man was being respectful to her. Never once had she caught his eyes straying below her lace-flounced neckband. And he did seem to have a genuine affection for Will and a sympathy for his needs. Why then, was she so uneasy in his presence?

"Yes, by all means, Monsieur St. Clare," she agreed calmly, deliberately turning on her heel to indicate their conversation was at an end. "Come, Will, the sun's too hot for you."

Rosslyn watched the man ride out of the yard, admiring the easy grace with which he sat in the saddle, the arrogance to the set of his chin. Now that she had observed him at length, she was convinced Stella's suggestion that he was a French aristocrat was true. No tutor rode like that, or carried his body as well, or dressed as well, she added, reviewing the way his coat fitted smoothly over the broad expanse of his shoulders, his britches molded tight as a glove to display the perfection of his lower body. She forced her gaze from him, thinking it somehow unseemly to stare at his buttocks and thighs lovingly encased in brown doeskin, revealing each muscle and sinew strained taut against the animal's side.

"Do you still wish Papa to dismiss Monsieur?" Will asked.

"What do you want him to do?"

"I want him to stay, of course. I like him a lot."

"What of the fencing lessons, are they too strenuous?"

"No, Mama. Monsieur is not like Papa, he makes me rest before I'm tired. Sometimes he's very funny and makes me laugh. He says we'll do all kinds of different things outdoors if I'm diligent with my lessons. He even showed me how to manage the dogs; now I'm not afraid

60

when they jump on me, or even if they knock me down. Isn't that nice, Mama?"

"Yes, very nice, Will."

Rosslyn squinted against the bright sunlight as she watched the paragon of virtue disappear over the crest of the hill. The Frenchman's presence angered her; or was it more that his presence disturbed her?

The sun beat down from a cloudless blue sky, the day holding a balminess that spoke of September. Rosslyn breathed deep, enjoying the warm, sea-scented breeze wafting against her face, listening to the comforting thud of the turf beneath the horse's hooves and she felt at peace. She moved rhythmically with her mare until she became part of the animal. That she was a born horsewoman was one of her few virtues Jarvis acknowledged, though they almost never rode together now, for her husband's presence robbed her of enjoyment. Alone, lulled to tranquility by the sound of the sea, she could indulge herself in daydreams.

"Do you not think his riding has improved?"

The voice at her elbow was distracting. Rosslyn nodded, pulling ahead, yet he kept easy pace beside her, quickening his own mount accordingly. Not wishing to seem rude, in view of his much appreciated concern for her son, Rosslyn did not tell Armand St. Clare that she found his presence annoying.

"Can I go down to the beach, Mama? I've brought my pail."

"I think the cliff path's too steep for you."

"Monsieur showed me an easier way down. Can I, Mama?"

"I'm sure he'll be safe if you don't mind his clothes getting sandy."

Finally Rosslyn gave in to their combined pressure and Will shrieked with joy as he scrambled from his mount. The tutor assisted Rosslyn to dismount and she held herself coldly aloof from any contact with his body. When he took the horses' reins she nodded curtly to him, striding away over the rough, gorse-dotted headland, allowing him to tie the animals to a stunted, sun-bleached tree stump beside the chalky path. A puddle

61

of blue flowers caught her attention and crouching, Rosslyn plucked a handful of delicate stems, dropping the flowers in the hollow of her skirts. Voices blew to her on the wind, distracting her. No one else was here, yet the giggling, lisping character of one voice suggested that of a woman.

Rosslyn stood, shading her eyes from the sun as she looked towards the sound. Behind her she was aware of the tutor's steps crunching over the springy turf, but he remained at a distance, allowing her some privacy. Two figures became visible in a hollow thirty feet towards the inland curve. As she stared at the hunched forms surprise tainted her feeling of pleasure as she realized what they were doing. A girl and boy were rolling in the weed-rank grass, arms entwined about each other, first the girl's gray skirts and white apron were visible, then the boy's dun-colored britches. They came to rest eventually after much giggling, the boy on top, but now the skirts were pulled up and sturdy white legs protruded indecently from the jumble of fabric.

Rosslyn paled to see the girl's flaming red hair, recognizing her as Molly, the new scullery maid who had reported sick this morning. Sick indeed! Indignation brought the blood back in a fury until her face burned and her ears sang with it. Rosslyn took a determined step towards the couple, then hastily retreated, for now they had begun to move rhythmically and instead of speech they made other, more urgent noises.

Turning quickly away, disturbed by the animal grunts of pleasure carrying in the wind, Rosslyn set her mouth tight against the sounds which encroached on her privacy. She walked briskly through the gorse-strewn grass to the chalk path of the headland, gleaming stark white in the sunshine.

"Madame, do not be so disapproving—they are in love."

Color heightened her cheekbones at Armand St. Clare's words, but she did not stop, walking instead towards the tethered horses. From the beach came Will's cries of glee, faint against the battering surf as he made dams and fortresses from the tawny sand, only to find his defenses flattened before the onslaught of the incoming tide.

"Don't go. The boy's enjoying himself and he won't understand. It's quiet here. You won't be able to hear them. I assure you, Madame, such is their passion they have not the least intention of offending you, or of even being discovered. The servant girl and her groom believe themselves to be quite alone."

Rosslyn hesitated, her hand on the mare's reins. It was quiet here except for the distant roll of the surf mingling with Will's laughter, the sounds echoed by the screeching sea birds on the cliffs. The warm sun fell on her cheeks casting an elongated shadow of her body over the grass. She needed this peace, to be far away from the indignity of eavesdropping on Molly's amours, yet still this man invaded her privacy, this Frenchman who had the effrontery to counsel her about her reactions. She was forgetting however, that he was no penniless French tutor; he had betrayed himself by his boldness this morning if by no other action. A tutor knew his place: A nobleman felt himself to be her equal.

The horses whickered in pleasure, nuzzling each other and Rosslyn turned to her son's tutor with a forced smile. "It would seem as if everyone is in love today, Monsieur."

"Such a beautiful day is meant for lovers." He smiled at her as he spread his dark cloak on the grass. "Please, this is the best I can offer," he said, indicating the cover was meant for her.

Rosslyn spread her blue skirts daintily about her ankles. The unaccustomed warmth of the sun had made her perspire and a slow irritating trickle slid between her breasts. Modestly unfastening the first three buttons of her habit to allow a breeze to cool her neck, Rosslyn looked at the far horizon, noting the faint blurr of green on the French coast, so far away her eyes had to strain to distinguish shape and movement. That was where he belonged, this man who presumed so much, across that glittering water, so narrow a stretch, yet separating them by worlds of difference.

"Do you suppose Molly and her man are happy?"

she blurted unexpectedly, surprising herself by the blunt question.

"Yes, passion is an exhilarating experience, by far the best part of love."

"You discuss the subject like an expert, monsieur," she reproved, imperceptibly drawing herself away from him, growing more aloof at the impudence of his intimate tone.

"Perhaps on passion, I am; love is another matter," he explained, flashing her that quizzical smile from which she always looked away.

"Well, I'm no expert in either," Rosslyn admitted, surprised once more by her frankness. He made it easy to say hidden things, this hired tutor; talking to him was somehow so impersonal, Rosslyn found she was on the verge of saying far more than she intended, of confiding in him what she had hidden from the world for the past seven years. Instead she said: "I've often wondered what being in love was like, if it was the heavenly feeling I've read about in novels. There men and women die for love. Papa used to scold me for filling my head with such romantic nonsense. Do you really think people ever die for love, Monsieur?"

"Yes, I'm sure some have."

"Don't you find our discussion rather amusing? Love is a subject about which I almost never think these days. You see, I've quite grown out of such foolish notions."

His face was grave as he leaned towards her, his pale eyes meeting hers. "Love is not a foolish notion, Madame. Men and women of our class rarely experience the emotion, least of all with our spouses. Sometimes I think the chambermaids and valets are more fortunate, they have no blood lines to propagate, no titles to cement. They may pick and choose as fancy dictates. We must . . . " he paused, realizing he had betrayed himself.

His unguarded confidence revealed to Rosslyn what she had speculated upon since she first met this man. Plain Armand St. Clare he was not, some title preceded that name, just now he had admitted as much.

"You envy your valet?"

"No, Madame, I envy only the freedom of his soul."

"Do you believe love lasts forever then?"

"That I don't know. Perhaps it is more like this flower," he said, plucking a golden blossom from the grass at their feet. "Love is like a flower in season, it buds, it bursts forth golden till it's full grown; then it fades, withering, until one day it is dead."

She watched him crush the flower between lean, olive-skinned fingers before dropping it to the ground. Now he laughed at her, amused by the seriousness of her face.

"I'm not always so philosophical," he explained. "It's just that everything I thought life was made for has gone; yet I am still alive. I've discovered an entire world I didn't know existed. Land, money, titles, heirs—once my life hinged on them. Now I live only for today."

"Who are you really?"

He sighed, squinting across the shimmering water towards the distant coastline. "A fugitive from my homeland. Have you any idea what it's like to be an exile, to crave the scent and the sight of the place where you were born, yet to know once you set foot on that soil again you are condemned. I learned today there have been terrible massacres at prisons throughout Paris. Thank God I'm free, yet there are other members of my family who are not so fortunate."

"So you did escape from prison?"

"Yes, though I hope you will keep my secret. It is one thing for gossiping tongues to speculate on one's identity, another for that identity to be confirmed."

"I'll reveal your confidences to no one. Only tell me, for my own satisfaction, who you are? You are no tutor. There's not one jot of subservience to your character. Sometimes you make me feel almost as if you should be master of the hall."

"Forgive me, Madame, I had not meant . . ."

"You need not apologize, at least knowing you are not just plain Armand St. Clare, tutor, salves my conscience somewhat. I declare, it has shocked me to the core to think I would confide such secrets to a mere tutor."

"Does the thought I may have a title make them any less secret?"

"No," Rosslyn admitted thoughtfully, "it makes me feel more comfortable about revealing them when I think we are equals."

He laughed, the expression on his face as he looked at her making Rosslyn prickle ice cold down her spine. It was as if for once both their defenses were down, as if in this meeting of eyes they revealed their inner selves. The confrontation was alarming. Hastily she scrambled to her feet, inwardly panicking to be away from him.

"You still have not told me who you are or where you are from, Monsieur. You leave me at a disadvantage."

"Thanks to the ruling of '90 forbidding the use of the preposition 'de', I'm plain Armand St. Clare. That edict also forbids me the use of my title. To be correct, Madame, you should address me as Monsieur le Comte."

His revelation was surprising. Rosslyn blinked up at him, standing so close, shielding her from the glaring sun, his face darkly shadowed. His nearness frightened and exhilarated her at the same time, bringing blood pounding hot through her limbs, creating the insane desire to reach for him. She wanted to press her breasts against him, to see the reaction in those gray eyes—

"Why are you working for us?" she whispered.

"Beyond what I've won at the gaming tables I'm penniless. My chateau outside Paris was destroyed by the mob. Except for the purchase of two outfits of clothes, every penny I've won has gone to France to support my family who are still in prison. When your husband pays me the amount agreed on at the next quarter, I'll go back. There's much unfinished business left for me."

"Oh, but you said your life would be in danger if you went back. I don't . . . " Rosslyn gasped at her wayward tongue, spilling more secrets of her heart, secrets as yet unacknowledged even to herself.

"I find your concern very touching."

Imperceptibly he had drawn closer still until all Rosslyn could see was her own minute reflection in the glitter of his pale eyes. She was aware of the fierce longing to touch those firm lips with her own, to taste the heat of his mouth, to smell his skin. The warmth of his breath fanned her brow as she found herself drawn nearer to him, attracted as if by a magnet, falling . . .

"Mama, look, Mama! See what I've found!"

Gulping painfully, for her breath seemed trapped in her throat, Rosslyn spun about to face Will. The boy raced over the grass, holding out a struggling creature for her inspection.

"What is it, sweetheart? Oh, a crab, yes, you can keep him if you want."

"Thank you, Mama. See, Monsieur, how he wriggles. Shall I put him in water?"

Rosslyn stood aside while they studied the crab, which at the tutor's suggestion was dropped in Will's small, water-filled pail. How timely was the boy's intervention, she thought, a few moments more and heaven alone knew what foolishness she would have become involved in. Plainly Armand St. Clare's eyes told her a harmless flirtation was not the game he played. Rosslyn surprised herself even further by contemplating the alternative which at the moment seemed the most natural conclusion in the world. For those few insane moments she had desperately wanted him. The question uppermost in her mind: How satisfying a lover would he be?

On the return journey she did not speak to the Frenchman, riding ahead of the boy and his tutor, who, to her annoyance did not seem to notice the change, for he was too engrossed in discussing the habits of crabs, a subject about which Armand St. Clare seemed extremely knowledgable. Brooding over their recent conversation and the treachery of her own emotions, she decided there must be few subjects about which the dispossessed comte was ignorant, least of all the subject of women, for he had played her correctly throughout the morning. Angered at her own gullibility for making his advances so easy, Rosslyn quickened her pace, kicking the mare's flanks until she began a careening gallop, sending turf flying as she thudded over the grass and leaving the two plodding figures far behind until they were no more than specks against the sunlit sky.

CHAPTER FOUR

"Will that be all, Madame?" Jeanette asked nervously, wary of her mistress's flaring temper. She had been like a fiend these past weeks, screaming in anger one minute, then bursting into gales of repentant tears the next.

Rosslyn thrust aside the tray of weak tea and water biscuits, indicating that she was finished. "Be sure to press my pink dimity for tomorrow—oh, and get the green silk hat refurbished with that garland of roses for the weekend."

"Anything else, Madame?"

"No—oh, go on, get out, I suppose you've got far more important things to do than wait on me."

Seething, Rosslyn watched the French girl scurrying about to collect the garments, timid as a mouse lately. After all, she could not blame her, even she must admit her mood had been that of a virago. Jeanette gave her no actual cause for the storms, unless her affair with St. Clare was reason enough. No, it was more her duplicity after worming her way in to share confidences, all the better to carry on behind her back unchastised, the hussy.

Jeanette left, dropping a hasty curtsy before she shut the door. Rosslyn followed her, pulling the door slightly open to allow her a view of the corridor. At this hour the Frenchman met the little strumpet at the head of the stairs. True, she had caught them in no more than a friendly embrace, but she was convinced that although their meetings were innocent in appearance, during this time they were arranging another, more private meeting place. She ought to go out there and shock them with her knowledge, but such display over their private lives was beneath her, especially after the last time she confronted the maid about Clarence. Rosslyn was not anxious to endure another bout of that icy control and certainly not in front of that man to boot. It would be too humiliating. The truth would be out eventually; until then she would bide her time.

Tonight Armand St. Clare was without his coat, clad only in brown doeskin britches and lawn shirt, the thin white fabric molded to his body by the brisk autumn wind which had risen at nightfall and whipped relentlessly through the deep windows. Stella was right about one thing, Rosslyn begrudgingly acknowledged as she closed the door: He was an attractive man. Even though she did not view him in the fashion in which Stella pictured a man, she nevertheless found herself stirred by his beauty. It was merely aesthetic appreciation, she convinced herself primly as she went to the windows. Nothing more. As if he were a statue of a perfectly proportioned male.

Alone in the twilight Rosslyn felt the blood coursing to her face as she reviewed the disturbing dreams she had experienced lately in which Armand St. Clare played a prominent part. The content of her subconscious was so rewarding to her, that in the soft wakefulness of morning she wept to find the dreams untrue. Sheer love for her had radiated from his face, his eyes grown limpid with emotion, and the delight with which she had reciprocated made her blush. His mouth had been hot on hers, stirring her blood with a strange sensation that she could not control. He had touched her breasts, until finally they lay on the scrubby, salt-bleached grass of the headland where their lovemaking far surpassed that of Molly and her groom.

Choking emotion at the memory made her clear her throat. Rosslyn leaned miserably against the window-pane, staring at the wind-tossed gardens: The moon was rising, buoyed like a silver vessel on the clouds, bathing everything in radiance. Only the cypress walk stood out like tall black sentinels guarding the splashing fountain where a nymph poured water in a never ending stream from her marble pitcher. The night was lovely, a beauty meant to be shared by lovers; yet there was no one who was even aware of her sadness. Jarvis was at his London club, but even had he been home, there would have been no comfort forthcoming from his presence. Oh, Lord, why was she suddenly so lonely, so restless, so discontent? Tears of self-pity slid from her eyes, plopping to her bare arms as Rosslyn gave herself up to grief, finding the emotion calming to her ragged nerves.

The anticipated gaiety of the coming Christmas season eclipsed that emptiness, until Rosslyn had to smother laughter when she pictured the pining melancholy creature she had become. Determined to leave that sadness far behind, she thrust herself feverishly into the preparations for the upcoming events.

A cold bleak wind screamed about the house as she carefully wrote out the gilt-edged invitations to the Christmas Ball in her neat rounded hand. Sitting beside the hearth, toasting her feet on the brass surround, she was at peace. A warm dish of buttered muffins at her elbow with a plate of pink-iced sponges for dessert added to the cosy feeling of well-being. Hopefully the weather would be far warmer on the great day, for she intended to wear a fine silk gown of purest white decorated with bands of lace and knots of scarlet ribbons around the narrow skirt. In her hair she would have a lace cascade attached to a satin ribbon, her curls caught up in red satin bows. A pearl-encrusted reticule with ivory clasps would be perfect with the dress, and to her delight she had found just the thing at a delightful shop on Bond Street during her visit to Letty's London home last week.

Smiling, Rosslyn leaned against the wing of her chair as she relived the excitement of that week-long visit.

Letty's new home was decorated in the latest mode, with yards of swagged satin draperies in a glorious shade of heliotrope. Tom Stanley had been flatteringly attentive, in fact, everyone had been most charming to her. The men had ogled her outrageously and she had loved every minute of it. Reigning as the current beauty of Tom Stanley's lavish parties had quite restored her confidence. It was unthinkable that this same person had stared through a crack in the door at a mere tutor, or had gazed at the moon with schoolgirlish hunger, weeping for a dream world which did not exist. Ridiculous and really rather pathetic.

"Mama, may I see you for a moment?"

Will interrupted her thoughts and with a charming smile Rosslyn beckoned him inside the room. "Of course, sweetheart, you don't need to ask permission to see me. What is it you want?"

"Did you purchase my gifts like I asked you?" Will cried eagerly, racing to the blazing hearth to warm his hands.

"I have them in my bureau. Surely you didn't think your Mama would forget, did you?"

Rosslyn brought a box to the fireside and together they knelt on the scarlet needlepoint hearth rug to examine its contents. There was a large box of cigars for Papa, hastily cast aside in favor of a secret gift which Will had requested Letty to purchase for Mama, his instructions contained in a note sealed with wax. Indulgently Rosslyn smiled at her son as he caressed the small box mysteriously wrapped in silver-striped paper and tied with silver lace banding.

"Aunt Letty bought just what you asked. And do you know, she wouldn't tell me a thing about it."

"That's good. I wanted this to be a real secret. Oh, here it is. I thought maybe you'd forgotten."

Rosslyn's humor clouded somewhat as the boy held up a pair of fine leather gloves, his special request for his tutor.

"Monsieur will like these. His old gloves are becoming threadbare. Did you get them from his tailor?"

"Yes, and they were terribly expensive."

"That's all right. I don't mind spending a lot of money on Monsieur. Thank you, Mama. Shall I take these to my room? I probably ought to wrap these linen handkerchiefs for Nana, and I think I'll give one of the hair ribbons to Jeanette, if that's agreeable to you, Mama?"

"Whatever you wish," Rosslyn agreed coldly.

"Monsieur says she has had such an unhappy life lately so I wanted to cheer her up with a gift. I think she's very pretty and Monsieur agrees with me. He thinks scarlet ribbons will suit her best."

"Not scarlet, Will."

"Why not?"

"Mama will be wearing scarlet ribbons at Christmastime, therefore, you should give my maid another color," Rosslyn explained stiffly, burning to think St. Clare had dared discuss his mistress with a child. She would have to speak to him about it.

"Very well." Will sighed, fingering the other ribbons. "I suppose yellow will suit her as well. Thank you for being so thoughtful, Mama. I'll pay you when I get my next allowance."

"There's no hurry, darling. Mama was glad to be of help."

After the boy departed, struggling with the box of presents, Rosslyn fumed over their discussion. To think that man had the effrontery to discuss his private life with the boy, heaven knows to what lengths they had gone. She would really have to speak to him about it, though since that revealing experience on the headland she had managed to keep her distance, reviewing Will's schedule from the safety of the drawing room. Fortunately the tutor did not take meals with them, so apart from an occasional confrontation in the schoolroom, she had not needed to see him at all. She had even refused to discuss him with Stella, who, finding her devotion not returned by the object of her affections, had reduced her unwelcome visits to once a week.

Bursting with good cheer and generously primed with wine, Jarvis had insisted on having Will's tutor as a guest at the Christmas Ball. Rosslyn was forced to agree, though it was with ill grace. Certainly she was grateful to him for his kindness to her son; Will had blossomed as she had never expected him to do these past months, having only two bouts of illness in the entire time. And, after she had told the man not to discuss his women with the boy, he had assured her it would not happen again. The truth of the matter was her own attraction to him created such crackling tension and unease between them, each encounter had become a battlefield. And it was all wrong. This was not what she really wanted. What she wanted made her face hot with the mere thought. If her life depended on it, she was freshly determined with each pang of interest, he would never know she spared him more than a passing thought.

A charming smile permanently fixed on her face, Rosslyn wafted about the brilliantly lit ballroom, laughing gaily at the gentlemen's jokes, entering into discussions about children and clothing with the ladies, fulfilling her role as perfect hostess. This type of gathering was a pleasure for she enjoyed displaying her home and its contents to the envious neighbors. It was well worth the effort of organizing, the hours spent choosing just the right food and drink.

The women still crowded around Armand St. Clare, though some of his mystique had rubbed off as he was no longer a romantic newcomer, his attraction dimmed somewhat by his becoming the Burtons' tutor.

Rosslyn nodded politely to him as she stepped out on the terrace for a moment, finding the ballroom unbearably hot. The day had been very mild for December, the evening turned damply muggy, more like early autumn than winter. The cool night breeze fanned her bare arms, a pleasant refresher after the furnacelike atmosphere generated by the blazing hearth and sputtering candles she had just left.

What a lovely picture the ball presented, she thought, watching the colorful moving throng through the French windows as the guests bounced past in a spirited dance. Being outside looking in added an extra charm, turning the scene as remote as a painting. What sumptuous colors there were set against a backdrop of leaping orange flames and monstrous ribbon-tied garlands of glossy evergreens looped about the walls. The mantel was festooned with holly boughs jingling with silver bells, while fragrant bayberry candles blazed in the elaborate wall sconces, the picture reflected many times over in the deep mirrors which lined the ballroom walls over twelve feet high. This wall of glass had the effect of opening the room to endless size until it seemed a veritable palace of color and light.

Marveling at the sight, like a little girl peering at a grown-ups' magnificent party, Rosslyn pressed her nose to the glass. Christmas was really the loveliest holiday of the year, she decided with a sigh of pleasure. The other women had worn velvet and satin making her stand out in her tissue-thin silk. To her surprise she stood out more than was intended, for, when silhouetted against the light, the gown revealed far more than she felt proper, but with her usual nonchalance, Rosslyn carried the discovery well as she pretended the near transparency of the fabric had been her intention. Thank heavens she had worn a satin petticoat, at least now the skirt only suggested the shape of her legs as it clung seductively; the bodice molded like a second skin, hugged the ample curves of her breasts leaving her dark nipples blatantly prominent through the fabric. Jarvis had been enchanted by the unexpected development, taking vicarious pleasure from the desire flickering in the men's eyes. Rosslyn too found their appreciation flattering as long as she was able to keep them at arm's length.

A movement at the end of the terrace attracted her attention. At once Rosslyn saw who the man was and she stepped hastily towards the windows, not anxious to confront Armand St. Clare out here in the darkness.

"Don't leave. Please, stay a moment longer, it's so pleasant outdoors tonight."

At the softness of his voice, Rosslyn hesitated, knowing she should not heed his request. Too late now, her hesitation had given him time to reach her side.

"Yes, the evening is unseasonably warm."

"Your party's an overwhelming success, Madame. And your appearance also."

Hearing the smile in his voice, yet unable to see his face, put her at a disadvantage. Rosslyn frostily acknowledged his compliment as she twisted the stubborn window catch. To her annoyance she found someone had fastened the window from the inside, trapping her on the terrace.

"Is the window latched? Come, there's an alternate means of entry," he suggested politely, ushering her forward.

Knowing she could bang on the glass for attention, Rosslyn hesitated, aware of the pounding of her heart. She could attract someone's attention to open the window, or she could walk with him to the drawing-room entrance. Out here in the clammy darkness it seemed safe, almost like the world of her dreams where they became two different people.

"Thank you, Monsieur, it's kind of you to offer to escort me," she said.

They stepped away from the broad expanse of lighted windows, past the huge bow-fronted glass panes at the other end of the ballroom, around the corner into total darkness. Rosslyn was aware he had stopped and she paused, her hand on the icy balustrade.

"Why have you avoided me lately?" he asked bluntly.

"Avoided you?"

"Yes, after our discussion on the cliffs I thought we would become friends. Did you betray too much of your inner nature? Is that why you avoided me?"

"I've no idea what you are talking about," she muttered, unable to think clearly, only wishing to see the escape of the open drawing-room window.

"Yes you do. What of that talk of love? Did it mean nothing?"

"It meant no more than you caught me at a vulnerable moment," she said icily.

"It's good to be able to tell someone things we sometimes hide from the world."

His voice had grown husky and she found they were moving again, the heat of his hand lightly guiding beneath her elbow. Down the shallow terrace steps she walked like a sleepwalker, over the lawns to the vine arbor. Rousing herself at last, Rosslyn gasped: "Where are you taking me?"

"I was under the impression we walked together, Madame."

"I must go indoors."

"Why?"

"I do not wish to discuss anything of a personal nature with you, Monsieur, not tonight, nor ever again."

"Are you afraid I will learn the truth about you? Or

75

is it more that you are afraid you will learn the truth about yourself?"

"I haven't the faintest idea what you are talking about."

His hand slipped into hers, engulfing her with heat.

"You told me you knew nothing of love. I thought it sounded like a regret," he ventured, drawing her closer, though she tried to stay stiffly apart.

"I hate to disappoint you, Monsieur, but I'm no gullible young virgin. I've been a married woman for seven years. I doubt there's much left for you to teach me, though I thank you for your concern."

He heard the sarcasm in her voice and smiled in the darkness, stepping towards the arbor. Moonlight washed the vines with softness, brightening the last white flowers of the season with silver, turning the air fragrant with dew-wet grass and cloying perfume from the flowers. Lazily he drew her inside the shadows, plucking a flower which he pressed into her hands, curving her fingers around the damp softness.

Rosslyn trembled at his unexpected nearness, bewildered by her reaction to him. In the half light she could not distinguish his expression, but instinct told her what her eyes could not see. She was intensely aware of the dark shadow of his face so close to her own, of the faint, unaccustomed smell of the pomade which clung to his clothing.

"So you are a married woman of seven years' standing, of seven years' experience who cannot, or who will not, be taught anything."

Regaining some of her composure, she backed away.

"You forget yourself."

"Do I? I think not."

"I'm warning you, if you come any closer I'll scream."

"Will you?"

"Yes," she hissed in anger, backed against the wooden pillar of the arbor, suddenly afraid of him, but her fear was a wild, heart-racing emotion.

"How charmingly you lie."

His mocking words spoken so smoothly made her

throat constrict. He reached for her, his hands firm on her upper arm, his fingers burning through the flimsy fabric of her cap sleeves.

"How dare you say that to me? How dare you lay your hands on me?"

"Because you have not screamed, Madame."

Astounded at his impudence, Rosslyn stared into the glitter of his eyes, aware that she could even smell his skin; feel the heat he gave off, something she had never noticed about a man before. Then his lids closed as he kissed her. Emotion surged through her limbs with shocking fury: panicking, Rosslyn struggled ineffectually against the hot constriction of his mouth. When at last he moved away, she did not escape, longing to go, yet desperate to discover what it was about this man which intoxicated her so. Before tonight she had been in complete control of her emotion, now her limbs trembled and she felt a wild urge to reach for him, to draw him against her body, to press herself intimately to him.

"Shall I forget myself even further?"

Immobile she waited for his next move as if she watched another on a stage, as if this was not happening to her at all, yet it was she who experienced the gnawing, physical ache in her limbs, that strange sensation of being overcome. She shuddered as the heat of his hands slid over her breasts, burning her flesh through the thin fabric. At the intimacy of his action she felt twisting, burning contractions deep between her thighs, until the pain of the sensation made her gasp. Gently he unfastened her bodice, his fingers deft on the tiny pearl-domed buttons. Gasping at his bold actions, Rosslyn was powerless to prevent them, blood flushing hot to her face as he stripped back the thin fabric to expose her breasts; still gentle, he cupped their weight in his hands, his thumbs slowly tracing the prominence of her nipples which erected pointedly beneath his touch.

"I always knew you would be beautiful, but not quite as lovely as this," he whispered ardently.

Thrilling to his touch, more excited than she had ever been before except in those forbidden dreams, Rosslyn wondered what it would be like to live that ecstasy in reality. What would it be like to lie with him, to uncover the seat of his passion, her intimate curiosity a delicious warmly leaden sensation. He aroused such desire in her, with an emotion more intense than she had known possible. In shock she raised her eyes to his, vulnerable in her discovery.

"Do you still want me to stop?" he whispered, smiling lazily at her, stroking her flesh gently with the back of his hand.

"No," she gasped, "please, don't stop." Her voice was low, throbbing with the emotion he aroused.

Standing was becoming increasingly difficult so that she fell towards him. His arms went around her back, the buttons of his coat pressing a flower design on her breasts. Now Rosslyn became startlingly aware of the renewed pressure of his thighs against hers, the contact revealing the surging, clamoring rise of his desire.

"Let me love you," he whispered hoarsely against her ear. "Come, I know you want me. No more lies, *cherie*, no more modesty. I need you so . . . oh, God, I need you."

Shuddering at his words, pressing towards him, passion allowed her no room for modesty as she molded herself against the thrust of his body.

"There's a bench over here," he breathed, "come."

Rosslyn nodded, reluctant to end the exquisite pleasure of their embrace, words of aquiescence on the tip of her tongue, when an angry voice cut through their insanity with chilling tones.

"Rosslyn, dammit, where are you? We have guests. If you aren't indoors in five minutes, by God, I'll flog you myself."

With an oath Armand swung her deeper into the shadows, anxious not to betray their presence by the flimsy whiteness of her gown. Beneath his breath he cursed again.

Gasping, Rosslyn clutched her open bodice together, pushing him aside in shock and guilt as she tried to fasten the buttons with trembling fingers.

"Let me help you."

She suffered him to fasten her bodice, steeling herself against the heated delight of the pressure of his hands against her flesh. When he stooped to kiss her breast through the fabric of her gown, she shut her eyes, squeezing back tears of frustrated desire, then she turned and ran over the lawns towards the lighted windows.

It took her several minutes to gain enough composure to rejoin the guests. Hastening through the drawing room, she patted her hair in place, glancing at her reflection in a shrouded gilt mirror before she stepped into the light. As a guilty afterthought she clasped her hands over her bodice assuring herself all the buttons were in their correct loops.

"Well, by God, there you are. About time," Jarvis thundered, seizing her arm and swinging her around. Too much brandy had turned his good humor to belligerence. "Where've you been?"

"It's too hot in here. I stepped on the terrace for a breath of air and some fool latched the window. How could you humiliate me by parading about the lawns bellowing like a prize bull?" she demanded in anger, not entirely feigned. Despising him, she glared hostilely at his red sweating face, resentful that it should be he who had interrupted such exquisite delight, who had stolen a moment which may never come again. Now she was back inside the lighted room, Rosslyn saw the sheer insanity of her actions, though she was not without regret for her incompleted passion.

"Well, it's damned rude going off and leaving the guests like that. If I didn't know you better I'd think you were fumbling some dandy out there in the bushes."

"How dare you suggest such a thing," she hissed, reddening to find him coming so close to the truth.

"Suggest any damned thing I want, any damned thing," he repeated, his voice slurring, then pulling her arm, he dragged her towards their waiting guests.

During the night Rosslyn woke trembling as she relived Armand's embrance in her dreams. Armand, that is how she would think of him in future. He had held and kissed her, he had said he needed her: recalling the vehemence of that statement made her grow hot and aching with passion. He loved her, that is what he had meant. And clutching her pillow in ecstasy, Rosslyn

79

slithered deeper into her bed to luxuriate in her stirring memories.

During the following week Rosslyn accompanied Will on his morning rides enjoying the crisp woodland air scented with decaying leaves, admiring the damp winter-black trees etched starkly against a pale sunlit sky. Infuriatingly Armand acted towards her as if nothing had happened between them, until she caught him looking at her, his eyes darkening with the memory of their embrace; then she smiled with shy pleasure at their shared delight, feeling young and vulnerable. Understanding her thoughts, Armand winked impudently at her behind the boy's back, creating a new and wonderful feeling of intimacy between them.

On Friday they rode as far as the village where Will wanted to purchase a hunting knife. Though not in favor of the acquisition, Rosslyn allowed it, assured Armand would safely direct its use.

"You know, Mama, Monsieur really knows what boys want. That's a lot better than some tutors," Will confided, as they surveyed trays of knives in the dingy shop.

Armand carried a display of pocket knives to the doorway to view them in the weak winter sunlight and Rosslyn turned to admire him, shuddering deliciously as her eye traveled the length of his body. He had ordered a new outfit of clothes for the winter season which became him as admirably as his other suits had done. The bottle green coat of fine velour wool fitted snugly across his broad back, tapering to a perfect fit at his small waist. As was his habit, the buff riding britches fit close as a second skin, displaying to advantage his strong, taut thighs and buttocks, before the fine fabric disappeared into the tops of his tall, mirror-bright black boots.

"I suppose that's because of his own boys, don't you, Mama?"

Guiltily turning her attention back to her son, Rosslyn flushed. While probing her memory of that night in the arbor she had found her mind straying to the most intimate aspects of Armand St. Clare's body, her bold speculation surprising her with a delicious, forbidden shudder as her vivid imagination rushed forth to supply a ready answer.

"What was that, Will? Mama was dreaming."

"I said Monsieur knows about me because of his own boys. Being with them has taught him how to get along with me. He misses them dreadfully."

Blood pounded slowly to her face, thundering in a deafening tattoo at her son's words. "Own boys," Rosslyn croaked.

"Did you know Monsieur had two sons of his own? There's Charles, who's my age, and Louis who's two years older."

Rosslyn swallowed, suddenly feeling faint. "I had no idea," she mumbled. "Did he tell you this?"

"Oh, yes, we often speak of them. They're in prison in France with their mother. I'm certainly glad my mother isn't in prison, aren't you?" Cheerily he smiled at her, then turning his attention back to the knives he said, "This pearl-handled one's for me. Don't you think it's splendid, Mama?"

The small dingy shop reeled about dizzily for a moment before righting itself while Rosslyn clutched her riding crop in a frantic grasp, feeling terribly nauseated. A wife! Oh, God, when he had spoken about his family, she had never thought of a wife. It was to her he wanted to return; his wife and sons were the reason for taking this job so beneath his station, for sending all his money to France. While he dallied secretly with her in the darkness, all the time his thoughts were of his wife!

During the ensuing transaction over the pearl-handled knife, Rosslyn watched everything through a haze of frustrated tears. When Armand spoke to her outside the shop, she deliberately turned her back on him, disdaining his offer of assistance as she hoisted herself in the saddle, not waiting for them to mount before she headed up the cobbled street, her face burning with humiliation. What a gullible fool she had been! He had known exactly what he was doing, the cad, using her like that, taking advantage of her vulnerability.

Well, thanks to Jarvis, he had been thwarted in his plans, the ultimate conquest snatched from him until she took near fiendish pleasure in contemplating his painful frustration, hoping to God it was even greater than her own had been. She would never put herself in his reach again. Will had inadvertently armed her with the truth.

For the next couple of weeks she ignored Armand St. Clare, being icily polite when forced to speak and haughtily disdaining when not. Af first he accepted her mood; then realizing she was not going to come around of her own accord, he cornered her outside the schoolroom when Will went upstairs to be examined by his doctor.

"What's wrong with you these days?" he demanded, catching her arm to detain her. "You are barely civil to me."

"Take your hands off me. How dare you?"

He grinned then, releasing her so that she haughtily swung away. "Have you forgotten I've dared far more than this, Madame."

Rosslyn stared at him, fighting the last remnants of attraction he still held for her, deliberately picturing him in Jeanette's arms, or the arms of that unknown French comtesse across the Channel. "You deceived me."

"How is that?"

"I was such a fool to be taken in. To allow you to . . . oh, how I despise you."

"Is it guilt which brings forth this condemnation?"

"No it's not. You did not think I'd find out you had a wife, did you?" she flashed triumphantly, awaiting his reaction of shock, disappointed when it did not come.

"It was no secret."

"Then why did you not tell me?"

"Because you never asked me, Madame."

Aghast she watched him bow mockingly to her before striding away. Oh, how she hated him for his nonchalance, for his triumphant departure when inside she was so pitifully alone and hurt.

Seething with pent-up emotion she glanced about the

corridor, her eyes lighting on a hideous oriental vase on a bookcase. Seizing the monstrosity, she vented her fury on it, rejoicing to see blue and purple fragments scattered noisily at her feet.

CHAPTER FIVE

Throughout the spring, Jarvis grew more discontent with the Frenchman's handling of his son, jealousy mounting as he recognized the growing dependency between the boy and his tutor. Now it was never, "Papa this, Papa that," it was always "Monsieur says."

Brooding, he watched the two crossing the lawns, envious of the man at whom his son smiled in affection. There was one way to end that part of it anyway. These rides could be stopped; the lad had shaped up surprisingly well in the saddle. There was no earthly reason why he couldn't try out the new chestnut, nothing beyond that Froggy fellow's stubbornness. A bit like a woman, these foreigners, he thought, curling his lips in scorn. The fellow was nearly as concerned as Rosslyn about the boy's health. A lot of unnecessary pap this rest business, unnecessary and unmanly.

"From now on, Will's going to take his rides with me, my good fellow. I know you'll understand," Jarvis announced as he met them on the terrace steps. "And I certainly have to congratulate you on handling things so well. A fine horseman the lad's proving to be, fine horseman."

"You will no longer require my services?" Armand asked in surprise, his hand tightening on Will's frail shoulder.

"Well, not on the rides, but the lad still needs some work on his fencing, then of course the studies will continue."

"Did Madame suggest the change?"

"Lady Burton? Not at all, my idea entirely. Come on, Will, show Papa how well you can manage your horse."

"The new chestnut, Papa?" Will asked softly, fear flickering on his pale face.

"Of course the new chestnut, not that little baby's gelding, ye know."

"Will has not been allowed to ride the animal, my lord. I felt the horse was too vicious for a small boy."

Jarvis glared at the tutor who had the effrontery to stand his ground before him and overrule his decision. "By God, I expect him to ride the animal, that's what it was bought for. Good horseflesh that, worthy of the Burton heir. Why, Veasey, who's no more than a slip of a boy, can manage him. Rode him up here from the village, now, what do ye say to that?"

"Master Veasey is fourteen years old and big for his age. Will is only seven."

"Don't need you to point that out, St. Clare. Come on, Will, what ye waiting for, lad?"

Armand stepped forward. "Though I do not wish to disagree with you, sir, I feel Will is far too small to handle such a vicious and willful beast. I cannot urge more strongly that you wait a few years. Will can show you how he takes the jumps on his own horse. He has mastered them all . . ."

"Stuff and nonsense. And if you value your position you won't disagree with me very often, St. Clare, not often at all."

Bulbous eyes staring, lip thrust belligerently forward, Jarvis straddled his legs, a formidable adversary, daring the other man to say one more word of disagreement. Then without further ado, he grasped Will's arm and propelled him towards the stable. Glancing over his shoulder he saw the tutor coming after them. "No need to come, St. Clare. Mark some exercise books or something, we're off to the downs."

When Rosslyn walked around the stable building it was to find Armand waiting for her at the gate. At his unexpected appearance, she backed away, not wishing to be caught in a situation where she must speak to him. When she heard the horses leave a few moments before she had naturally assumed he had gone with them.

"Madame, forgive me for bothering you with this, but His Lordship has taken Will out on the chestnut.

Shall I go after them? He told me to stay here, but I could ride at a distance to see how things are going, close enough to intervene if necessary. That is if you permit."

She stared at him, dumbfounded by both his attitude and his news. "God, the fool!" she gasped. "Stay here, I'll go. Damn him anyway." Muttering under her breath, she ran to the mare's stall.

Armand watched her depart, admiring her courage, knowing how futile a thing it was to pit her strength against that bombastic husband with his twisted ideas of manliness.

Rosslyn thundered over the downs, driving the mare to her limits, wondering which direction they had taken. Jarvis was stupid enough to ride the boy through the village to boast of his manly prowess at handling the big brute. The wind was sharp for March and she felt it singing past her ears, numbing her cheeks with icy fingers. With this storm blowing in, the weather was not even suitable for Will to be outside, let alone risking his neck on that savage brute.

Reining in, she surveyed the empty miles of rolling grassland all the way to the coast without seeing a sign of riders. Damn him, he had gone to the village after all.

Changing direction she pelted along the road, anger churning within her, anger and resentment, and a certain thanks that at least Armand had the decency to tell her about the situation. She must thank him for that consideration when next she saw him. Despising him for being married was a fool thing to do; after all, she had Jarvis, yet somehow she did not think of her own marriage as any hindrance to falling in love.

Coming past Brow Farm she spotted them; Will clinging desperately to the animal's mane as an extra handhold, the reins wound about his arm, his eyes wild with fright as they careened over open country. Cursing beneath her breath, using oaths which would have done justice to the toughest huntsman, she cut them off over the pasture.

"What in God's name are you thinking about? Are you mad?" she screamed at Jarvis, too angry to take

86

pleasure from his pop-eyed amazement at her intrusion.

"What do you mean, mad? We're going for a ride."

"Can't you see he's terrified?"

"Well, he shouldn't be, told him so myself. I've got no use for squeamish cowards and I told him that too. Crying like a girl—I'll not stand for it. Not have it at all, do you hear?"

Rosslyn pulled alongside the boy, reaching out to him; when she would have taken him from the saddle, Jarvis whacked her arms sharply with his riding crop.

"Don't you ever do that to me again," she spat, her eyes dark with rage.

"Leave the lad alone. He's doing fine without your interference. No wonder he's a milksop with you and that foolish Froggy to coddle him. No more coddling. I'm done with it. We're riding this animal to hounds on Saturday. Made my mind up, so don't try to change it. Will had better get used to the idea. Now, back to your needlework like any other respectable woman and leave us alone."

"I'll see you in hell first," she muttered, pulling her mare back to safety as Jarvis spurred his horse, giving the chestnut a rap on the flanks until he bucked forward into a loping gait.

When Saturday dawned, however, Rosslyn found her threats were empty. There was absolutely nothing she could do to prevent Will being taken to the hunt. Jarvis threatened to have her locked in her room, relenting only when he realized he would have to explain her absence to their neighbors. During the season Rosslyn had ridden avidly with the hunt and he had been proud of her capabilities, taking the tallest jump on that spirited mare of hers, representing the name of Burton in grand fashion. This final hunt was more of an exhibition than anything, a social get-together after the season, so it was vitally important she attend or there would be embarrassing talk.

In the brisk morning chill the riders waited before the Hall, breath steaming in the nippy air as the stirrup cups were passed, the mulled drink warming the company to their toes. For this special event, and to show there were no hard feelings between them after their disagreement over Will's mount, Jarvis asked Armand to accompany them.

With two concerned people to keep an eye on him Will gained confidence. Since Armand had been handling the chestnut, the horse seemed more docile. So Will finally began to sit straighter in the saddle and relax his death grip on the reins. Nevertheless, Rosslyn viewed the morning event with trepidation, unable to squash a nagging fear at the back of her mind that all would not go well, her apprehension robbing her of her usual enthusiasm for the chase.

They went through Burton Wood as the sun came up. It glinted golden on the farm ponds, tinging the hedgerows with light. Armand rode at Will's side, Jarvis slightly ahead, until annoyed by the arrangement, he insisted Will ride with him, forcing Armand to drop back beside Rosslyn. She did not speak, determined to ignore him to discourage further attentions, for she was freshly annoyed after she had heard him whispering with Jeanette outside her door last night.

At the crossroads Stella hailed them with exuberance. She was galloping at the head of her small party, taking fences and hedgerows in her stride as she cut across the browned pastureland to join the hunt. Her husband Jack, swathed in a caped coat of scarlet serge, panted and gasped in his efforts to keep up with his boisterous wife. Behind them streamed their assorted progeny led by Veasey, cocksure on his black hunter, head held high as he surveyed the open countryside.

Rosslyn viewed this first encounter with distaste when Jack clapped Will on the shoulder to compliment him on his bravery for tackling such a big horse, oblivious to the violent arguments which had raged for weeks over the ugly beast. She glowered next at Veasey when he rode close to Will, jostling him, laughing scornfully to see fear start in those big dark eyes as the chestnut grew restless. Rosslyn maneuvered her mare between them, her interference rewarded by a glowering glance from Veasey before he rode ahead to scent out easier sport.

By the time they reached Brow Farm, the entire hunt

88

had assembled, streaming across the winter-browned land like a colorful banner spread over the fields, the master of the pack and the whippers-in leading the parade, bright splashes of color in their scarlet coats and white britches. All was progressing well as they rode through the village where the cottagers came out to wave, cheering the party on its way. It was not until they reached the open land beyond Burton Hill that Rosslyn's unease returned.

Horses stumbled over the wide hedges, spraddling in ungainly heaps in the icy water of the brackish ditches edging the country lanes. Will closed his eyes in terror at the jumps, hanging on, allowing Attila his way, and to do him justice, the big horse did seem surprisingly competent.

Noting his son's remarkable progress, Jarvis beamed wider and wider, mentally applauding himself for his own good sense in overruling the advice of those two nervous old maids about the lad's welfare. Will made a splendid horseman, almost as good as Veasey had been at his age.

It was at the dangerous jump of Badger's Hollow that Rosslyn's premonition of doom came to fruition. She had just begun to relax, even venturing a forgiving smile at Armand who cantered beside her, impressed by the sheer skill of his riding as he obtained the utmost from the young, untried hunter Jarvis had begrudgingly loaned him. He was so handsome, she acknowledged wistfully, whether he cuddled in dark corners with Jeanette or not. In fact, if she was not careful, he could still bring her blood pressure to pounding heat. If she was totally honest with herself, something she indulged in sparingly, Rosslyn had to admit her body flagrantly disregarded his marital status, his infidelity with Jeanette, in fact everything but the rushing surge of nerve-tingling sensation he produced in her.

The sun was warmer now and the air smelled fresh, that old exhilaration at the chase was gradually working to dispel her apprehension until Rosslyn was almost enjoying the hunt.

"Whoa! Whoa!—oh, my God. Oh, I say," Jack

Redding cried, the rasp dying to croak as a cry and a thud echoed through the crisp morning air.

Rosslyn stood in the stirrups and she screamed in shock at what lay before her. During the last half mile she had become separated from Will who rode between his father and his Uncle Jack as they neared Badger's Hollow with its treacherous jump of hedge, fence, and broad stagnant ditch. Now only the huge chestnut pawed and tossed on this side of the fence, having refused the massive barrier at the last moment. Will was nowhere to be seen.

"Stay here," Armand yelled to her as he spurred forward, clearing the jump with inches to spare. Shouting, Jarvis followed, with Jack Redding close behind him.

Sickening dread clutched Rosslyn's heart. Feeling suddenly unable to manage the treacherous jump, she raced down the lane to a break in the hedge where she forced a reluctant Alice through the bramble-infested hawthorn. The rest of the hunt thundered past, finding no cause for suspension of their pleasure; riders became unhorsed quite frequently, there was no calamity to it.

Her heart sounded loud and hollow, thumping audibly while she impatiently kept aside to allow the riders to pass, watching them stream excitedly across the rolling fields as the hounds bayed over a scent. At last she was free to go to the three men who crouched over a small, still form, now carefully cradled against his father's massive bulk. Armand had reached him first, lifting the child from the ditch, silently relinquishing his burden when Jarvis thundered over the hedge, his face flushed with concern.

"Let me have him. Oh, is he all right?" Rosslyn cried in anguish, fighting a feeling of nausea which rose bitterly in her throat at the sight.

"Knocked a bit of the stuffing out of him, me dear, that's all," Jarvis chuckled, holding the limp child protectively against his chest.

"By George, the lad's out like a light," Jack echoed, his florid complexion paling as he leaned over Will's face. "No bruises though."

"The water must have broken his fall. I could see no bruises either."

Rosslyn turned beseechingly to Armand, waiting for him to say more, questions in her eyes, but he only shrugged and turned aside.

"There's a cottage over there. Let's see if we can get help. Someone can summon Dr. Watkins," she suggested breathlessly.

"No need to drag that old sawbones out of bed, me dear." Jarvis chuckled, bearing the frail boy effortlessly in his arms. "Lead on."

Because Jarvis did not refuse to go to the cottage, because behind the bombast there seemed to be creeping a gray frown of worry, Rosslyn's terror increased. Will was so still. He should have come around by now, yet he lay like a rag doll, bouncing limply in his father's arms.

An old woman in a soiled mobcap opened the door before they knocked, for she had watched the slow procession wend its way up the incline. "Took a tumble did 'e?" Eyes twinkling, she ushered them inside the smokey, low-ceilinged room. And though Rosslyn would not have chosen these surroundings for her injured son, she had little choice, for this was the only dwelling at Badger's Hollow.

Kneeling on the beaten earth floor, with trembling hands she unfastened Will's serge coat as he lay on a blanket-covered pallet beside the smoldering hearth. The old woman brought a cup of well water and Rosslyn tried to pry the cup between his lips which seemed unnaturally blue.

"Here, let me help you."

Armand knelt beside her, raising the boy's head and he undid the small cravat and tightly buttoned neckband of Will's shirt. Jack and Jarvis stood laughing in the doorway, blocking most of the light as they discussed the merits of the pack and the odds on the likelihood of flushing anything out so late in the year, until Rosslyn could have screamed for them to be quiet. They acted as if nothing was wrong.

At their arrival the old woman's grubby nephew had been dispatched for Dr. Watkins who lived less than a mile from Badger's Hollow.

In worried silence Rosslyn waited for the doctor.

Finding Will's shirt wet she unfastened the sodden material, whispering endearments to him as she worked. Once his eyelids flickered and his mouth twitched in the beginnings of a smile as he recognized her voice and she wept with joy and love at his reaction.

Armand covered the child with his coat. Rosslyn leaned against the fieldstone hearth, watching him tenderly sweep Will's curly hair from his eyes, watching him slip his hand casually inside the covering coat, pausing to finger the neck, then jerk forward in sudden alarm as he pressed his ear to Will's chest.

"Oh, God, what is it?" she cried, dropping to her knees.

"I can't feel his pulse."

Frantically he ripped aside the dark coat and pressed his ear to Will's bony chest. Then, to Rosslyn's anger, he pounded his fist hard into Will's body, thumping his chest, before crouching again to listen.

"Stop it! Oh you're hurting him, you fool!" But he thrust her aside, thumping the inert form even harder.

The men stopped talking at the door, staring in shocked surprise at the scene beside the hearth. "Now look here, St. Clare . . . " Jarvis began, stepping towards the pallet, puffing in angry resentment at the tutor's actions.

"He's dead."

"What! Don't be such an ass! He can't be dead, you said yourself there weren't any bruises," Jarvis exploded, his face turning from flaming red to sickly pale green.

"Listen for yourself."

One by one they listened to the cold chest. In amazement the men stepped back, leaving only Rosslyn frantically cradling her child, murmuring, begging, pleading for him to speak, to open his eyes. She was still crouched when a few minutes later Dr. Watkins, who had been on his morning walk, stooped to enter the farmer's cottage, taking in the scene at a glance. The country lad had already gabbled the gist of the story, he could fill in the rest.

Sagging at the knees, Rosslyn allowed her husband to lead her outdoors while the doctor examined their son.

The freshness of the March morning warmly awakened by the newly risen sun seemed torture to bear, while down the hill that murderous horse cropped peacefully at the hedge, his presence a hateful reminder of the cause of her agony.

In a nightmare she heard the doctor's pronouncement, followed a moment later by Jarvis's angry denial. Her husband even managed a few tears of genuine grief as they carried the little body out of the smokey cottage, down the hill to the waiting horses.

Numb as she was with shock, her husband's grief failed to move Rosslyn. "Too late," she muttered to herself, "your concern for him's too late, you murderer." Unseeing she scrambled into her saddle, the motions out of touch and habit rather than consciousness; then she spurred her mare flat out towards the woods, tears of agonizing grief drenching her face, her mouth one gaping cry of anguish. After a few miles Rosslyn gradually became aware of a rider following at a distance. When she glanced back she recognized Armand, but she took no comfort from his obvious concern for her welfare. Will was dead. Her whole life had stopped at Badger's Hollow on this crisp morning in March.

Will was buried on the twenty-first day of March in the year 1793 in the small private cemetery of Burton Hall, where the freshly chiseled headstone read:

William Jarvis George Burton, beloved only son of Jarvis, fourth Lord Burton, taken to his Heavenly Father in the seventh year of his life. "He shall give His angels charge over thee to keep thee in all ways."

Rosslyn stood in the shadow of the dank trees in a cold drizzling rain, her voluminous black veil hiding her face from view. Arrayed as she was in somber black, shrouded and veiled, leaden grief weighting down her limbs, she felt the embodiment of the angel of death. Gray mistiness curled smokily amongst the upper branches of the tall oaks like thin wraiths of the past. A mournful bird call broke the stillness, echoing the forlorn cry of an injured child. And she turned against a blackened tree trunk, clutching the slimy cold for support as her knees buckled.

"Come, Madame, it is time to go."

His voice came through her pain, low, heavy with grief, for he too had loved Will in his way. Clearing her vision, Rosslyn stared up at Armand's face through the dark wisps of her veil, seeing unshed grief for her son glistening in his eyes, seeing the lines of pain around that set mouth. She allowed him to take her hand, to lead her like a sleepwalker past the mourners to the funeral carriage where tall plumes waved majestically on the bobbing heads of the six black horses.

"Dearest Rosslyn, don't hesitate to come by if you're lonely," Stella whispered, as Rosslyn was handed inside the coach.

Nodding, not able to trust herself with speech, Rosslyn gripped her sister-in-law's gloved hand reassuringly. Letty was here and Adela too, wrapped about in voluminous cloaks, their small black hats emerging from smothering yards of veiling making them appear like giant carrion crows waiting in the graveyard to pounce on little Will who would soon begin to mold beneath the clean marble headstone.

It was so unjust his dying now at the dawn of spring, when things should be reborn, when the land was bursting with hope and life . . .

"Thank you, everyone. We'll see you later at the Hall," Jarvis rumbled, taking his wife's head against his shoulder, sharing the bleakness of her pain. He felt no guilt at the boy's death, for hadn't Dr. Watkins said it was due to his heart stopping, not an injury from the fall. Fright is what killed him, and after all, whose fault was it the lad was always frightened?

Distastefully he put the weeping woman aside, allowing her to slide against the padded carriage in misery. Then he rapped on the glass for the driver to begin the return journey.

Back at the Hall during the days following Will's funeral, Jarvis began to pick up the threads of his life. The French tutor, no longer needed, was paid off, thanked, and promptly dismissed. All in all it was a relief to be rid of the fellow, even though he had proved a deuced fine gambler, Jarvis thought, as he watched him ride slowly down the sweeping driveway beneath the trees. A sight too good, he thought, tightening his mouth in regret at the loss of his favorite diamond stick-pin. The man had won it from him two weeks ago, and the saddle and horse he rode today were both winnings from another unlucky game. Yes, it was good to be rid of him.

From her window upstairs, Rosslyn watched the lone rider enter the tunnel of greening trees and she wondered where he would go now. Part of her went with him, that hot primitive self whose existence she often failed to acknowledge. He had not come to bid her goodbye—she had not really expected it. Yet Rosslyn knew deep inside she had hoped their parting gave him enough grief to seek her out. Well, he was gone now, the pleasure, the uncertainty of their relationship, riding with him. All she had left for comfort was Jarvis. And at the realization, she threw herself across her bed in an uncontrollable fit of weeping.

Rain misted the trees, turning the lake water leaden, blending with sky and ground to draw a gray curtain over the park, shrouding like death. At the comparison ready tears welled in her throat and Rosslyn leaned against the nearest tree trunk for support, allowing grief to take possession of her senses. Dear God, it had been a month since Will had died, every day since his death she had shed torrents of tears, more tears than she had imagined the human body could produce, yet still they came as if she were powerless to prevent the flow. She was no longer sure she cried for Will, now it was more for Rosslyn as tears and pain twisted together in her heart, tearing it to shreds with destructive thoughts.

She hated Jarvis for what he had done to her child, hated him enough sometimes to kill him. But what could she, a woman alone, do against his strength? Somewhere out there in the mist did her child wait for her to join him? A movement in the trees brought her head up, but she saw no one. If Will waited for her it would be over by the water, for he had enjoyed sailing his paper boats on the lake.

Stumbling, blinded by tears, Rosslyn moved towards the water as a sleepwalker. Her cloak had turned black with rain, but she did not notice. How deep was the lake. It was comforting somehow in its infinite grayness. Crouching, she trailed her hands in the shallows, listening for Will's voice, yet even as she listened she could not really believe his shadowy presence was here. He waited in that place where the dead must stay, their memory treasured by those left behind. In death alone would she meet her child again.

The water beckoned seductively until she leaned further and further. When at last she tipped forward, lightly breaking the surface, it was as if another fell into the iciness, as if another was slowly sinking to those vast gray depths . . .

Hands grabbed her, wrenching her from the comforting blackness and Rosslyn fought her rescuer, protesting at the cruel injustice of it.

"Leave me. Oh, God, let me go," she gasped through bursting lungs, for unconsciously she had held her breath with the instinct for survival, fighting the enveloping water.

"Stop it, you little fool."

A stinging slap on her cheek made her gasp with pain and shock. Half-carried, half-dragged, Rosslyn suddenly found herself gasping and sobbing on the plank floor of the summerhouse while a dark shape loomed over her. Blinking rapidly to clear her vision, she unwillingly recognized the face which swam into focus above her.

"Monsieur le Comte! Oh, God, what miserable fortune brought you by?"

"Do you want me to slap you again?"

"By all means, if it gives you pleasure."

"I saved your life."

"Did it ever occur to you perhaps I did not want it saved?"

"It did, but as you are temporarily insane, I overruled your decision."

Struggling to sit, Rosslyn disdained his assistance. Dragging herself against the white-painted wall, she wiped a stream of water from her face. Glaring hostilely at her rescuer she noticed he too was soaked, his clothing plastered to his body in a most revealing way. In embarrassment she found her own garments clung in the same manner, the thin blue merino dress molded against her like a second skin. In self-defense she drew the sodden cloak about her chest, finding the thick material cold.

"Must you stare at me," she snapped, "I find your gaze insulting."

"Do you? I did not find yours insulting," he countered, straightening up. For a moment he watched the increasing fury of the storm through the white latticework before turning back to her to ask:

"Can I trust you not to heave yourself back in the lake if I leave you alone?"

"No."

"Very well then, I shall stay."

"Do as you please. I am leaving."

"Stay where you are."

In shock Rosslyn stared up at him. "How dare you command me? This is my estate. Besides, you no longer have any right to be here, my husband dismissed you weeks ago. Why are you still here?"

"There was some business to attend to before I left for France."

His words took her by surprise and Rosslyn had already gasped in dismay at his news before she was aware of her reaction, then she could have bitten it back for he laughed at her.

"I'm sorry to upset you so, Madame. By now I've saved enough money for a passage to France and a little over for living expenses. When I've sold my mount, that money also will be useful in bribing jailors. This time I'm determined to bring my family back with me."

"And if you are caught?" she whispered.

"You already know the answer to that question."

"When do you leave?"

"Tomorrow on the early tide."

"Then we'll not see each other again?"

He shrugged, half-turning away. "Who knows."

Rosslyn was silent; all her pain over Will's death, all the anger, strangely deflated by hs unexpected news.

Perhaps this time tomorrow he would be under arrest. Though it was not of her choosing, he had gallantly saved her life.

"Thank you for rescuing me. I didn't mean to be such an ungrateful fool. It's just that since Will's death nothing about my life has seemed worthwhile, as if I was an empty shell just drifting aimlessly through the days."

"It's a pity to throw away your life when there are so many who'd give anything to live. I, for one, would like the assurance I shall see the sun come up next week." He turned towards her and smiled fondly, touched by her bleak expression. "We always seem to be antagonists. Shall we declare a truce at this our last meeting? Somehow I once thought things between us would be different after . . ."

She flushed at the unspoken conclusion to his speech, knowing full well he meant the Christmas Ball when she had nearly succumbed to him. What delight it had been, however stolen, however regretted in the chill sanity of day, to feel his strong arms around her, to have his mouth against hers . . .

"Ah, you do remember then," he whispered, crouching before her, hand extended as he saw her wistful smile.

"Good-bye, Armand, God speed. Please let me know how you fare when you return," she whispered, refusing to say "if." Tears choked absurdly in her throat and his face swam through a haze of moisture. He gripped her fingers, the warmth tingling a burst of blood through her chilled limbs. Alarmed by the unexpected reaction, Rosslyn scrabbled to free her hand, blinking back that treacherous display of grief. In the gloomy, rain-darkened light she saw that blood-quickening expression on his face, saw, and recognized, and was glad.

"Good-bye, Rosslyn *cherie*, you'll live in my memory forever."

"I thought men only said that about their conquests," she whispered, trying to be humorous, trying to make light of the emotion that was licking heat through her icy limbs. "Do they also say it about the ones who got away?"

"Ah, but you have not got away yet," he whispered huskily.

Leaning forward he lightly kissed her brow. When he would have pulled back she caught the lapel of his coat, desperately gripping the wet material. There was one thing left for her in life; fate had granted her this temporary relief from nothingness. Insanity took possession of her then, for she drew him towards her, searching those eyes, startlingly pale in his dark face, seeing the speckled surface, the thick fringe of black lashes as she tried to read his thoughts. And failed.

"I want . . . " she paused, unable to find the right words, knowing he knew what it was she wanted, she knew also that he wanted her to voice that need to satisfy some twisted part of his character.

"Say it," he urged. "You don't know how much I've longed to hear you say that to me," he whispered, wrapping her about with the warmth of his arms, driving the chill from her body with his pulsating length of vital muscle and bone.

"First kiss me properly, on the mouth."

He did as he was bid, shuddering at the response he kindled from her lips. "Remember, you are far too mature for romance, Madame."

"Oh, damn you, don't mock me now."

"On the contrary, I intend to do something far more pleasant to you."

His throaty laughter echoed in her ears, competing with the thundering blood which pounded there. The storm must have ended for rays of feeble light cast a latticed design across his face when he went to secure the summerhouse door. Without shame she noted his state of arousal, too difficult to conceal in the wet, clinging garments.

When he crouched beside her she sought the embodiment of that passion, timid at first, then growing bolder, thrilling when he shuddered at the searching warmth of her hand.

"Does my touch give you so much pleasure?" she asked in wonder, her mouth smothered against his neck as he crushed her to him.

"Your touch is ecstasy, all the more delightful because it's yours," he whispered hoarsely. Then preventing further speech, he clamped his mouth hotly to hers, taking her breath until she trembled in his arms.

He lay beside her and forced himself to be patient, to touch, to kiss, until she wept with delight at the manipulation of his hands.

"Oh, Armand, how much I love you," she whispered, all defenses gone, speaking from the secret depths of her heart. "Finish what you started that night. All this time I've wanted you to love me."

"I only thought to hear you say that in my dreams—if I'm dreaming, please God don't let me wake."

"No one has ever really made love to me."

With a tender smile he cradled her softly against his body. "Poor little girl," he whispered, but his words weren't mocking. "After today you'll never be able to say that again."

"I want to know how it feels with you, just this once."

She smiled as he caught his breath, freshly inflamed by her request. In his arms Rosslyn felt secure. She was a virgin in all but the technical sense of the word; this time the act would be without pain, bringing instead that abandon her aching body promised. His mouth and his hands, the electrifying discovery of the intimate part of his body dispelled the last vestiges of chill, bringing about a fierce emotion which frightened her in the enormity of its possession.

"What is it, *cherie*?"

"I don't know. This feeling makes me afraid of what's going to happen when I give in to it."

He kissed her tenderly, moved by her confession. "You mustn't be afraid, trust me. Your body's so lovely, here . . . and here."

Rosslyn trembled at the gentle touch, at the inquiry of his fingers into the secret places of her body until the loosening, flooding warmth seemed more natural now. She wanted to return the pleasure, to make him shudder as he had done before in the delight of her hands on his bare flesh.

When at last he positioned her, she panicked, struggling beneath the confining weight of his body, beating ineffectually against the muscled expanse of his back.

100

Armand ignored her feeble protests; when he entered her, he drew back, tormenting her until her fury was redirected, until in frustration Rosslyn seized his hips and drove him deep inside her. And she wept, but this time for the pain of fulfillment.

Awakening as if from a deep slumber, Rosslyn gradually returned to reality, confused until she became aware of a trilling bird in the trees overhead. In wonder she stroked Armand's back where he had half-rolled from her.

"I've never felt like that before."

"I'm happy you shared it with me," he whispered, a lazy smile lifting his mouth.

Propping herself on her elbow, Rosslyn gazed at him, finding his eyes not as pale now, his face softer. Gone was that grimness she had observed a few moments before as passion tensed his features.

"You are so lovely," she whispered generously, stroking his face, shuddering anew at the touch of his flesh. "Now you are all mine. Tell me it is so."

When he looked away from her adoring gaze, pain stabbed wounding and deep.

"You know I can promise you nothing."

"But you can't leave me now, not after . . . "

"Our passion was mutual. I made no vows with it."

"But I let . . . " at his mocking grin she stopped, looking away from his eyes in embarrassment. He was right. It was she who had asked, who had encouraged, no blame for it was his. Tears prickled her eyes, slipping down her small nose until he brushed them away gently with his fingers.

"*Cherie,* don't cry, please. Don't spoil what we shared. Don't be ashamed of wanting me. God knows, I've wanted you since the first time I laid eyes on you. It was very good between us, can't you let it stop at that? I may not live long enough to fulfil any vows I make, so I won't try to deceive you with lies. And I have a wife in France."

Her heart turned leaden. In the wake of her evaporating bliss Rosslyn had become freshly aware of her wet clothing and the chill which it struck through her limbs, while the contour of his body, still not totally returned to normal, mocked her beneath the clinging sheath of his sodden britches.

"Oh, how could you use me so?" she hissed, fighting tears, ashamed now for revealing the depth of her own feelings for him.

"I thought the use was mutual, Madame," he reminded, his face hardening.

Rosslyn scrambled to her feet, backing away as he stood to face her. "Don't you dare tell anyone about this," she threatened, his amused smile only inflaming her anger. "Oh, how I wish I'd never met you . . . you . . . tutor."

Amusement flickered on his face as he made a swift, half-mocking bow. "Your servant, Madame. I'm sorry you feel your bargain was ill repaid. When you think this over in the months to come, I'm sure you'll realize what excellent measure you had for your money."

Spluttering in anger at his impudence, knowing full well what he implied by his smooth oiled statement, Rosslyn swung at him, but Armand dodged adeptly through the doorway, leaping the three steps to the sodden grass.

"*Au revoir, cherie.* And I was not lying when I said I would always remember you."

"Damn you . . . I hope I never set eyes on you again, you conceited . . . " Cradling her bruised flesh in its clammy wrappings she huddled moaning out of shame and loss and anger.

For a long time she stayed in that position sobbing in despair until finally she dozed. When she awoke the sun had shifted to the west and puzzled, she stretched her cramped limbs, wondering how long she had been asleep. A strange, heavy-limbed relaxation had washed over her during that most satisfying sleep, something she had not known for a very long time.

Scrambling to her feet Rosslyn pushed open the summerhouse door, recalling in a daze the stolen passion she had shared with Armand St. Clare on the dusty floor, or had it only been a dream? After that deep drugged sleep she was no longer sure, the only thing she was sure of now was a renewed determination to live. All the anger and the passion that man had caused, whether real or imagined, had kindled some faltering sparks of life in her numbed soul.

Tossing her head back, her sodden hair slapping icily against her shoulders, Rosslyn breathed deep the sweet fragrance of rain-drenched grass, filling her lungs with the new life of it. Then picking up her wet skirts, she ran along the path to Burton Hall.

CHAPTER SIX

"Come here, my little princess, won't you honor us with your presence?" Jarvis guffawed, reaching for Rosslyn who swished away coldly from his grasp.

"You're drunk!"

"Damned right, drunk and happy. Would do you a sight of good to get drunk once in a while, remove some of those long icicles from your soul."

The other gentlemen guffawed loudly at his thick-tongued humor and Rosslyn felt her face flushing with indignation. "I'm going to my room," she announced, drawing herself up stiffly to maximum height from where she surveyed them with a cold stare of disgust.

"All right, me dear, deuced if we want to keep you up. Do you need some kind gentleman to show you the way?"

"Jarvis," she hissed threateningly, "watch your tongue."

His foolish smile faded at her words. "Could give you the same advice, you nagging hussy," he growled, his mouth jutting belligerently.

"Come on, Burton, let's get back to the game. I haven't been waiting a year to listen to your domestic squabbles," Tom Stanley drawled, winking impudently at Rosslyn. "For this famed birthday event all you've offered so far is a damned fine meal and buckets of port. Now, let's get down to the meat of the matter."

At this, the others went into gales of drunken laughter and Jarvis grinned, staggering to his feet, anxious to comply with his guest's wishes. "All in good time, gentlemen. All in good time. Well, me dear, goodnight. Sleep well."

Another round of laughter greeted his remark and

growing impatient with their drunken absurdity, Rosslyn stalked from the room, glad to leave the leering, wine-besotted creatures to their gambling.

Jarvis's thirtieth birthday was to have been a lavish party, one to which she had looked forward with mild interest. Today, to her amazement, only gentlemen had arrived, each bearing a lame excuse about their wives' ailments. It was so strange as she had spoken to Letty only last week and she had not mentioned feeling ill; yet Tom Stanley told her his wife had journeyed to take the early season baths at the spa.

This discovery of Letty's surprise visit to the spa left Rosslyn vaguely uneasy, even Tom Stanley's attitude towards her tonight of bantering flirtatiousness, to which Jarvis took no exception, added to that unease. So much so, that she decided to take all precautions and lock her door. It would be safe to assume Jarvis and his birthday guests would keep their game going well into the early hours of the morning; yet it might be wise to lock the door in case a wandering gambler decided to storm her room, brave after the consumption of all that liquor. Jarvis had a key, but after such an absorbing game as this special birthday celebration promised to be, it was not likely he would have any interest in exercising his husbandly rights and for that small favor Rosslyn was immensely grateful.

The upper stories of the house afforded an unobstructed view of the coastline from where she watched the orange sun sink to a fiery rim on the horizon. With a shiver of emotion she spared a thought for Armand St. Clare who at this moment might be in a French prison, or worse—then that other side of her nature raced forward to pluck out the tender thoughts. He was no gentleman to use her so callously, to leave without so much as a promise of fidelity. At first she had waited for him to contact her, but when the weeks slipped by without a letter she knew he had no intention of writing. Then her wounded pride directed her emotion towards anger instead of love, until she would have burned any letter he had written without opening it, so rejected had she felt.

Restless, she swished the blue brocade draperies

closed, dimming the fading twilight. From the stables came the rumble of carriage wheels indicating at least one of the gamers was departing, ruined no doubt by an unlucky throw of the dice. Traitorously her mind strayed back to Armand, to the tenderness of his smile and the way his gaze held hers, revealing the thoughts of passion uppermost in his mind. Even the few endearments he had whispered to her that rainy day in the summerhouse had often been dwelled upon with delight. The fierce emotion he unharnessed within her was a confusion of love and hate, though at this moment, when she thought of him so intimately, the memory kindled a response of mingled need and rejection.

She thumped her pillow, angry to have those thoughts invade her mind, to be lying here recalling the feel of his body, the sight, the smell of him, was more than she could endure in the sadness of the long summer twilight. Instead she would think about the new gowns she was having made for the coming season. There was one especially beautiful dress of ecru silk organza, the full skirt dotted with clusters of carmine roses and forget-me-nots. A beautiful silk straw bonnet piled high with a confection of ribbons and silk flowers completed the costume. That was what she would wear to church when they visited the Duke of Bedford's estate later in the year. And for the upcoming hunt season she would have the red guardsman's coat for which she had been fitted yesterday, complete with tall black hat and silver buckle. Lord, she must have something to occupy her time now that Will was gone. Since his death Jarvis had grown worse about his pursuit of wine and card games, growing unluckier too, although he insisted that was a streak which couldn't last. He was even worse about comparing that odious Veasey to his ideal of a son, going as far as to accuse her of not providing him with another heir to spite him, as if she had any control over the matter. Men were the most unreasonable fools! For a time she had hoped she was pregnant following that rain-washed interlude in the summerhouse, but later, when the blood came and she knew she was not, she was glad. It would have been too much of an indignity to be forced to carry that foreign scoundrel's child.

Several hours later, after a fitful sleep, Rosslyn was sharply awakened by the grating of a key in the lock. The sound brought her wide awake, her eyes straining in the dark room. The gaming had obviously not been stimulating enough this evening, or Jarvis's desire for an heir was increasing.

Rosslyn rolled to her side and pretended to be asleep; this ruse sometimes worked, though it was hard to keep from smiling when he peered close at her face by candlelight in the futile hope she would wake. Occasionally the results were disappointing when Jarvis was in his demanding mood, but Rosslyn was usually prepared to accept what fortune sent her way in the matter.

It seemed an eternity while she practiced even breathing, mentally preparing herself for the onslaught of flickering light accompanied by Jarvis's winey breath as he peered close to her face. Instead there was only the soft swoosh of clothing being dropped beside the bed, followed by a groaning sound as the bed dipped when a heavy weight slipped inside the light bedcover. Rosslyn held her breath, wondering in surprise at Jarvis's new method of operation, having to admit the change left her somewhat intrigued.

From the staircase below a man's laughter echoed upstairs; the unpleasant sound made her shiver, the reaction bringing a chuckle from the inert body beside her. Knowing she was doomed now, Rosslyn felt the sudden heat of a large hand on her buttocks, moving upwards along her spine, yet the warm pressure slid seductively and was far more pleasant than she remembered.

Half-turning over, she allowed herself to relax. The down pillow was soft beneath her face. Jarvis was using a new pomade on his hair too, the fragrance reminding her of spices, not unlike bay rum. The caressing hand traveled upward to her breasts, until she found blood pulsating hotly through her stomach at the exploring touch.

"Jarvis," she murmured in astonishment, totally unused to this preliminary caressing.

He did not speak, merely took her hand, moving it to the heat of his hairy chest, sweeping it slowly downwards. Then, as her fingers were clasped gently around throbbing, searing flesh, Rosslyn snatched back her hand with a cry of alarm, this final gesture convincing her as no other had.

"You're not Jarvis! Who in God's name are you and what are you doing in my bed?"

"That's a hell of a reaction. You disappoint me."

Rosslyn froze as she recognized the drawling voice of Tom Stanley. "Get out of my room," she gasped, trying to fight herself free of his grasp. At her angry words his fingers bit harder into her shoulder, until she winced at the bruising pressure on her flesh.

"When I tell you I've no intention of doing anything of the sort, will you thrill me and scream? I think I'd like that."

"Take your insolence and your barnyard attributes out of my room before I ring for the servants and have you thrown out."

"Don't threaten me with that. We both know you'd die rather than let them think I'm up here with you naked in bed."

She shuddered as he drawled out the sentence, her flesh crawling as he followed his statement with a sweeping caress. He was right and what made it worse he knew it.

"Jarvis would have you whipped if he even suspected you were here," she hissed, struggling to release herself from his hands.

"Come now, who do you think gave me the little silver key to this haven of enchantment?" he mocked.

At his words Rosslyn tensed, remembering he had indeed let himself in her room with a key; Jarvis's key.

"What did you do, rifle his pockets when he passed out?" she asked with contempt.

"Wouldn't you be surprised to—no, for this little revelation I want to see your face. Shall we have candles, dearest? Promise you won't charge naked through the halls when I release you, think of the servants' talk."

Huddled beneath the covers, pulled up now to her chin to hid her body, Rosslyn glowered in the darkness, blinking at a circle of light flickering on the ceiling. As Tom Stanley came towards the bed she closed her eyes, knowing he was unclothed and, unlike Stella, not wishing to be privy to the secrets of his body.

"You are a disappointment—closed eyes. For shame! I'd heard I was a point of speculation in certain circles and here you are missing a golden opportunity to enlighten them."

"What is it you want?"

"That should be obvious, but first I must present you with the legal claim to what I seek. In exchange for wiping his slate clean of a tremendous debt, Jarvis has given me this. Here, read it."

Rosslyn found a crackling paper thrust in her hands. She began to read the parchment by the candlelight held aloft, gasping as she became aware of the contents of the document:

"I, Jarvis, fourth Lord Burton, do hereby grant the use of the property known as Burton Hall, all furnishings and amenities thereof, including my champion hunters, carriages and contents of larder and cellar, to Thomas Stanley for a period of two weeks beginning on the night of my thirtieth birthday, July . . ."

Rosslyn allowed the parchment to flutter to the bedcovers, stricken by nauseating shock. Jarvis had done what he threatened; no doubt the document went on to state the terms of the wager where she may even be mentioned by name.

"Shall I read you the part about 'my black-maned riding filly, Rosslyn'?"

"Don't you dare," she hissed.

Respecting her emotion he remained silent for a few moments until, tiring of the inactivity, he reached out to put the candle on the nightstand. She turned away when he moved. Tom Stanley caught a handful of her hair and yanked Rosslyn's head towards him.

"Now, my black-maned riding filly, kiss me of your own accord."

"I'll see you damned first."

"Tut-tut, what language Jarvis has taught you, hardly becoming to a lady. Come now, behave yourself, or I'll have to spank you."

"Those papers were drawn up by that half-soused scoundrel Millington, I suppose, damn him. He's another of your gambling cronies up to his neck in debt. Well, take your claim if you can, but you'll have no help at it from me."

In the candleglow his eyes narrowed to slits, his hair appeared dark in the shadows, his coarse face turned ugly. "Then I'd best waste no more of my valuable time."

He grabbed her and Rosslyn squirmed away, crying out afresh as he seized two fistfuls of her hair, shaking her, pulling her face against his, laughing cruelly at the tears of pain spilling from her eyes.

"Now, kiss me, damn you."

When he pressed his mouth to hers she bit his lips; it was only a minor wound, but he went white with anger, slapping her across the face until her ears rang. Nursing her bursting head she cowered in the bed, sobbing out of anger and pain.

"Look at me, and so help me, if you close your eyes again, I'll knock you senseless."

Rosslyn looked at his towering nakedness and a primitive part of her was stirred by the sight. He was so brutal, so disgusting, but the treacherous flame that damnable Frenchman had kindled within her was awakened.

"Now, little filly, I'm going to ride you until you beg for mercy."

The imprisoning weight as he fell on her took her breath. During the brutal claiming Rosslyn fought in vain against the entrance of his body. Once, twice, he rallied; when she began to sob, her tears did not halt him until he was assured her resistance was vanquished; only then did he stop.

"We'll begin again in the morning. I'd like to see you in the daylight, this lighting leaves much to be desired," he promised, when at last he got up from the bed, leaning over to kiss her, knowing Rosslyn was too weary to repel him. "You must be the most expensive whore in history—you know, for the past two years I've dreamed of having this house and everything in it mine for the taking. Soon I'll own it for good because your husband's a drunken, unlucky fool. Will you look forward to that day, Rosslyn, dearest?"

"With the same joy as my own funeral," she gasped.

Throwing back his head in a throaty chuckle at her retort, he sauntered from the room.

So this was the cause of that meaningless, absurd laughter downstairs. How many others knew the odds of Jarvis's birthday wager? No doubt Stella had revealed the shocking odds to all who would listen. The carriage she heard earlier must have been Jarvis relinquishing ownership to the winning hand, probably at this moment he was skulking in his club, drowning the memory with fresh decanters of port. Now he was out from under a morass of debt. When he sobered up in the morning would he still feel the sacrifice was worthwhile?

In the morning light, Tom Stanley appeared huge and frightening standing beside her bed. He bore a tray of tea and rolls, their fresh-backed fragrance stirring her hunger.

"Here, sweetheart, let's eat."

Though she did not wish to eat with him, Rosslyn decided that being passive was probably the best course. Later, when she was dressed, she would go to the stables to saddle Alice and ride as far from Burton Hall and its hateful indignities as she could manage.

"By the way, if you're thinking of escape, don't," he threatened as if he read her mind, shocking her so much that she gasped. "Oh, then I'm right, you were thinking of it. Come now, Rosslyn, I'm not that bad. I'm damned good, as a matter of fact, even though I say so myself. We're going to ride over the downs later just to show everyone we've no hard feelings."

"You're insane if you think I'd ride with you in public after . . . this."

"Don't disappoint me, or you'll be very sorry. I wouldn't want to think I'd been cheated. Your drunken husband owed me thousands; as a matter of fact, you should be flattered to think how much money I deemed you worth."

When he was finished eating he put the tray aside and lounged on the bed, wearing one of Jarvis's brocade dressing gowns.

"I bet poor Letty doesn't know about your wager."

He smiled at her naive statement. "My dear Rosslyn, after Stella's tongue stops wagging everyone will know."

She gasped, her face flushing dark red in humiliation. "I'll never be able to hold my head up again," she mumbled, shrinking deeper into the pillows in shame.

"It's not that bad."

"That's your opinion. What do you think Letty will say about your infidelity?"

He grimaced. "How pompous that word sounds. I much prefer 'change of pace.' Anyway, I'm sure she's fervently praying her thanks that I'm otherwise engaged for two blessed weeks. She may even be adding a few extra prayers for poor, poor Rosslyn who must suffer so excruciatingly. By the way, I know you weren't nearly as cold towards me as you wanted me to think. I could tell from the start."

"You're wrong. I loathe you."

In answer he snatched the plate from her lap and seized her viciously in his arms, crushing her face to his, banging their teeth in the savagery of his kiss. Deftly he ripped open the pink flowered wrapper she wore and with a sigh of satisfaction, pinning down her arms so that he would have an unobstructed view, he gazed in admiration at her body.

"We're a damned good couple, the two of us. I may be the best made man you've ever set eyes on, but I'll be damned if you're not the best made woman."

And though she despised him, though she was afraid of him, Tom Stanley's undisguised admiration for the beauty of her body was pleasing. This reaction shocked Rosslyn, also the fact that when he brushed his hand over her breasts she was stirred by his touch. He pulled her upright in the bed, molding his body to hers and the feeling did not leave, until she found that that quick explosion of bodily comfort she had discovered in the summerhouse could be generated by more than one man.

By the second day, Rosslyn was no longer distraction enough. Tom Stanley explored the cellars and the stables, riding Jarvis's champion hunters one by one until he found one that pleased him. She even joined him on an evening ride, though she hated the idea; to her surprise he only ventured on the downs, hastening back to the Hall by twilight for he had promised himself a night ride in Jarvis's new red phaeton. When Rosslyn declined his invitation to accompany him he swore at her in anger, striking her viciously across the face before storming from the room.

She could hear him racing downstairs, his boots thundering on the wide treads. His former good humor had been tainted this afternoon by copious amounts of Jarvis's aged brandy, until Rosslyn found she was more afraid of him than usual; the drunken Tom Stanley being even more vicious than the sober one.

Having some time at last to herself, Rosslyn used it to bathe, rubbing her skin with oils to eradicate the smell of him, not ringing for Jeanette to assist her as she did not want the girl's inquisitive eyes to see the bruises and teeth marks, all battle wounds of the bedroom. Several times during the past hours Rosslyn had contemplated killing Tom Stanley; yet what good would that do, other than bring the magistrates after her. Jarvis, her kind and thoughtful husband, had arranged things legally and so well, his wife but a chattel of his vast estate without legal voice to protect her body.

The phaeton rattled in about midnight. Shuddering, Rosslyn knew what that meant; she must be prepared for another assault. Urging Jeanette to leave after readying her for bed, Rosslyn plumped her pillows and tried to compose herself before he arrived.

A commotion on the stairs attracted her attention, then Rosslyn heard the French girl's shrill screams of terror. Like a flash she was out of bed and wrenching open the door to find Jeanette cringing at the stairhead, Tom Stanley leaning over her as he ripped her bodice, laughing cruelly at her fright.

"Variety is the spice of life, or haven't you heard that expression in your country, sweetheart?"

"Monsieur, please have mercy, I am a good girl . . ."

A resounding slap ended her pleas and he dragged her upright against the bannister. "Come on, you'll not be sorry," he urged breathlessly, reaching down to unfasten his clothing.

"Take your hands off that girl."

Half-turning in surprise, he stared at her, uncomprehending for a moment, made foolish by an excess of brandy. "Rosslyn, that you? Jealous, my love? Don't fret, I'll attend to you when I'm done with this one. I didn't get my stalwart reputation for nothing, you know."

"You despicable animal," she spat, taking a couple of steps towards him. "Leave her alone. Is no one safe? There's an aged cook in the kitchen, must I guard her also?"

Throwing back his head he bellowed at her humor before returning to Jeanette, who, unnoticed, had reached for a candlestick from the oak table on the landing. Baffled, he watched the missile descend. As the metal base neared his brow, he harmlessly deflected the candlestick, thrusting Jeanette aside. With a wild cry of fright the maid tumbled downstairs, bouncing and thumping as she went down the first flight before stopping at the bend.

"Now, my jealous little black-maned filly, first I'm going for some more brandy, then I'll be back to deal with you. I don't like interfering women, you might be sorry you didn't let me dissipate my vigor first on the French bitch."

Heart thudding with terror, Rosslyn raced down the stairs to rescue Jeanette. The maid was still, but she was not dead, for she cradled her swelling ankle in her hand.

"Is it broken?" Rosslyn asked, crouching beside the frightened girl.

"Oh, Madame, it hurts so. That man is a beast."

"Never mind him, let's get you to bed."

Struggling, she supported the slim girl, surprised to find, for all her curvacious body, Jeanette was light as a child. Rosslyn staggered downstairs with the injured maid to the couch at the foot of the stairs where she knelt to massage the ankle, keeping her ear open for the sound of Stanley's return.

"Oh, don't leave me, Madame, please don't leave me," Jeanette pleaded as Rosslyn stood.

"I'm just going for cold compresses for your ankle. It'll only take a minute."

114

"Don't make me stay here with that man."

"Where else can you go?"

"Take me to your brother's house. He's always been so kind to me."

"To Clarence! You're out of your mind. Adela's a very good friend of mine. I won't insult her by taking you there, whether you deny there's anything immoral going on or not," Rosslyn snapped, drawing back, the old doubt beginning again.

"You have my word. Besides, Adela's away from home visiting her parents. Please, take me to The Hollies. I must talk to him. It's vital. Oh, I'm in so much pain."

Crouching in the draughty hallway as the minutes ticked away her margin of escape, Rosslyn wondered what to do. The girl had become hysterical, lapsing into French. Barely able to comprehend the words, she knew she would do no good with her until she agreed to take her to The Hollies. A disjointed story was emerging between the sobs, all about Armand St. Clare and someone named Marie, who was perhaps another of Jeanette's relatives. At her mention of Armand, Rosslyn could barely contain her anger. What if she revealed to the forward hussy what had taken place between herself and Jeanette's splendid French lover that day beside the lake? That would put an end to her rambling about him; on the other hand it could mean only that she had put a valuable weapon in the hands of a servant.

Struggling to support Jeanette, Rosslyn went through the garden room into the moonless night. The breeze was chill against her bare arms for she had not taken time to fetch a wrap. The scarlet phaeton was still hitched after Tom Stanley's reckless ride, so it was only a matter of talking to the horses to quiet them, then hoisting Jeanette into the padded seat, where she moaned in renewed pain as her ankle banged against the footboard. Clicking impatiently to the team Rosslyn could hardly wait to be out of the yard before Tom Stanley discovered their flight and came thundering after her on Jarvis's hunter.

The thought of Tom Stanley brought a flush to Rosslyn's face when she recalled his vicious attack. The man was odious, yet with fresh disgust she recalled the sparks of arousal she had known, sometimes being unable to quell the treacherous flame. Who had she to thank for that reaction? This whimpering slut's lover, that's who. Before Armand St. Clare arrived at Burton Hall she had been serenely detached from all earthy communication between men and women. Now, thanks to him, she knew what the craving was like, the animal part of it where there was no pretense at romantic love to excuse the feeling. Even Tom Stanley could arouse her in that primitive way. And she hated him for it.

"We'll be there in a minute, can't you stop that noise," she snapped at Jeanette who huddled against her for comfort.

Racing the phaeton over the last stretch of road, Rosslyn delighted in the reckless speed as fully as any man, as if she was possessed by another being. This was a fierce, untamed spirit boiling with all the primitive passions of love and hate, who rejoiced in the wind whipping against her face as it tossed her hair in a tangling banner, in the brute strength of the straining horses, exhilarated as much as she by the wild ride. The moon had risen now and the rolling countryside was bathed in white light. She might have been Queen Boadicea driving her war chariot over the downs, racing to meet the enemy and to kill, yes, tonight she had enough passion within her to kill.

Thankful Adela was visiting her parents at Bath, Rosslyn charged through the stable entrance, skidding the animals to a stop. Like a man she yelled for the grooms, who appeared bleary-eyed and startled at this amazon with flying black hair all bathed in ghostly light who had suddenly appeared in their midst.

"Get your master, you fools, don't stand there gaping," she commanded.

When Clarence did appear he assessed the situation in a moment, exclaiming in distress and anger when he beheld Jeanette's pain.

"What in God's name happened to her?"

"She didn't fancy Tom Stanley's gentle services. When she tried to defend herself, he pushed her downstairs. I don't think anything's broken, sprained maybe, that's all. I couldn't make much sense of her story except she must be brought here. Something about the tide . . ." Rosslyn hesitated, wondering in view of Clarence's tender ministrations to the girl whether she ought to mention that cad of a Frenchman. Despite Jeanette's firm protestations to the contrary, her brother's face betrayed his deep concern. Perhaps Clarence was in all innocence over the deplorable state of pretty Jeanette's morals. Then, as she recalled her own recent experiences, she flushed, knowing she had no room to condemn.

"Armand—oh, God, what damnable luck!" Clarence groaned, bearing the girl inside the house.

He knew. The discovery took Rosslyn by surprise. "You know about her and Armand St. Clare?"

"Yes, he's her brother. Didn't you know?"

Rosslyn's gasp was loud in the deserted corridor. Her brother! To think she had despised him partially for his amour with the maid when after all there had been no more than family affection there. "I . . . I had no idea," she mumbled.

When Jeanette was settled upstairs with one of the serving women to pack her ankle and ease her pain, Clarence took Rosslyn's hand and led her to the study. Locking the door to assure privacy, he turned to her, his face grave with worry. "Will you help me?"

"If you mean in keeping this affair from Adela, you have my word. That girl lied to me, saying there was nothing going on. I'd have to be blind to believe that now after watching your face. It's not because I approve, Clarence, it's merely because I have such high regard for Adela's feelings . . ."

"Not about that," he dismissed impatiently. "You must do as you see fit about that situation. I truly love Jeanette, which is an emotion I doubt you'll be able to understand, as spoiled as you've always been. There's little room in your heart for the type of genuine affection we share. She did not lie to you about our love— I've never laid hands on her. I respect her. At least now that you know she's not merely a serving girl, perhaps you'll be more able to accept it for the truth. You're just

117

as prudish and hypocritical as Adela, but I value your family loyalty."

Eyes rounded in shock at Clarence's cutting words, Rosslyn stared, speechless to think her own brother could be so unkindly blunt in his condemnation. It was disillusioning to understand his true feelings after all these years.

Disregarding her stunned reaction he continued: "The help I ask is in something more important than deceiving Adela. Many lives hinge on what I'm going to ask you to do for me."

"Lives?"

"Yes. Mine, possibly yours too, assuredly that of Armand St. Clare, his wife and sons. This may come as another shock to you, Rosslyn, but the numerous races and house parties to which I'm purportedly addicted are merely a cover. For the past year I've been actively involved with several other gentlemen in rescuing condemned emigrés from France."

"What!"

"At first I did it for the excitement, for believe it or not, I'm bored to death with the futility of our lives. Now I cross the Channel out of genuine commitment to those poor souls. I was drawn into this by my regard for Jeanette St. Clare who confessed her true identity the day I rescued her from a rabble of drunken seamen on the quay. I helped her brother escape, and though I was greatly against his return to France, I understood why he must make an effort to save his family. It's for him and more especially for little Jeanette that I've agreed to a plan to rescue his wife from the Temple prison. His sons are also imprisoned there, but their rescue may be far easier. Marie St. Clare was a confidante of Marie Antoinette, therefore she's far more valuable to the tribunal than some. Her resuce will cost Armand considerably more than the usual amount."

Rosslyn, finding her legs too tired to support her, stumbled to a leather chair beside the hearth. All the surging life which had sped her on to The Hollies seemed to have evaporated at Clarence's startling news, leaving her a quivering mass.

118

"What do you want me to do? What can I possibly do?"

"Jeanette was supposed to accompany me to France on the evening tide. Dressed as Marie's maid, she was to change places with Marie, once inside the prison. From that point we have an elaborate chain of bribes set up from the jailors to Armand's cousin Bernard Desjardins, who's a member of the Assembly—albeit a traitorous one—yet he enjoys a rich living style which takes a considerable amount of money to support. Armand tells me there were valuable heirlooms buried on the grounds of the ruined chateau before the mob destroyed it, only he's privy to their whereabouts. He intends to sell what he can, then bring the rest to sell in England so that he can pay Bernard whatever sum he asks in return for safe conduct passes for the family and passage aboard a ship for the Americas. Now, as Jeanette's no use to me with a sprained ankle, the whole plan will fall through unless I have a replacement. You speak fluent French, I thought you could take her place."

"Me! You're out of your mind. If you think I'd risk my life to save that man . . . to even think about it . . ."

"I see you prefer Tom Stanley's company. Well, Sister, come, we should be just in time. About this hour of the night he comes up for second wind. Poor Letty, no wonder she chose to visit the spa."

In alarm Rosslyn watched her brother stride towards the door; he clicked the lock and a picture of Tom Stanley's lustful, mocking face whirled before her. The thought of another week of assaults, of cruelty—"Wait. Oh, wait."

"Changed your mind?"

"Yes, close the door. I can't go back to him."

Clarence obeyed, coming to kneel before her where he took her hands in his large square ones, remarking on the iciness of his sister's fingers. "Sorry I had to make it this way, but I'm desperate, love," he said at last. "You understand that, don't you?"

Rosslyn nodded. "If I do this for you, will I have to see him? I mean . . ."

"Armand? Casually, nothing more. I don't intend to

119

authenticate the story that far, rest assured. Besides, it's not been his habit to make connubial visits. Have you forgotten he's a wanted man? Poor Rosslyn, if only I could have challenged Stanley's right, but I could not risk it. Someday maybe you'll understand and forgive me. When Jarvis signed that paper he had a fifty-fifty chance of winning, you must realize that. I gambled too—and lost. Did he . . ." Clarence colored at his thoughts, glancing away. "Was it too bad?"

Rosslyn laughed bitterly. "From whose viewpoint?"

"I'm so sorry," Clarence whispered, embracing her, holding her chill face in the warmth of his neck. "You were a necessary sacrifice so that others . . . please try to understand."

Rosslyn managed a few tears, though the reaction cost her some effort. Amazed at her lack of emotion she was comforted by her brother's affection, though she had no idea what he meant by sacrificing her for others. It was as if her emotions were spent after that moonlight ride, as if Tom Stanley and his brutality were inhabitants of another world. She suffered still, but not because she dreaded tomorrow. Clarence had offered her an escape, one which gave her a chance to do something selfless for once. How more selfless could a woman become than to risk her life to save the wife of the man she . . . Rosslyn stopped, shocked to review the next word in her mind. It had been loves. Is that what she genuinely felt for that man who had taken advantage of her, who had ruined her for the coming years by souring her detached pleasure at this life she was forced to live? Leaves pattered against the windows, her chair creaked, all sounds of peace, while tonight the Paris streets ran with blood as ragged mobs howled for victims. There Armand waited for help which might not come, waited to save the lives of his sons and a woman named Marie.

"I'll come with you. Nothing seems very important to me anymore. Perhaps the last week of my life will be spent doing some good for someone," she said nobly, blinking back the emotion which at last her selfless words had awakened.

"Don't talk such ridiculous twaddle, for God's sake,

Rosslyn," her brother exploded, taking her by surprise. "For once can't you be Rosslyn Burton instead of acting like some stupid condemned heroine? I must be able to count on you. This is not an amateur theatrical, the blood is always real."

Clarence's angry words sobered her, making her feel ashamed of her stupid sentimentality. "Sorry," she apologized, giggling at the humor of his words. "Despite that unkind assessment of my character you made a little while ago, you should know I won't let you down."

At her comment he grinned sheepishly. "Sorry about my candid observations, but it's true you know."

"No, Clarence, not all of it."

The plans for their departure were so quickly made, Rosslyn was sure she must be dreaming. Clarence ordered the phaeton returned to Burton Hall in the morning along with a letter which Rosslyn took great delight in writing, in which she stated she was going into seclusion to recover from the tremendous assault to her nerves brought about by Jarvis's despicable gambling arrangement. If he would forgive her sudden departure, then she would forgive him his insensitive, immoral wager. So ashamed would he be when he sobered up, Clarence assured her, Jarvis would not dare attempt to trace her whereabouts.

It was rather exciting as she stepped into the balmy summer night to embark on the short ride to the coast. Dressed in a ragged, though clean at her insistence, homespun gown with sagging skirts and a waist in the appropriate place, Rosslyn laughed to think what her friends would think if they could see her now with her black hair tumbling untidily about her shoulders, clumsy leather shoes on her feet, looking every inch the scullery maid. Though Clarence had omitted it from the costume, she insisted on a dingy white apron of the type usually worn by the lower classes to add a further touch of authenticity to the role.

Though she told herself repeatedly this was no charade, she could not prevent the great flutter of excitement she always felt when entering into the spirit of amateur theatricals, much to her brother's despair. The danger of their mission did not register even when they rode towards the coast in the breaking summer dawn, fragrant with sweet meadow grass, the deep country silence disturbed by a trilling bird in the woods.

To her surprise they embarked on a ramshackle boat from a nameless cove tucked away in the straits of Dover; though with a smile at her own stupidity, Rosslyn realized they could not march pompously to the Folkstone packet for such a mission. It was chill on the water and one of the rough men who manned their small boat threw her a length of sacking for a cloak. The sun was struggling through morning mist when at last they met their France-bound vessel, transferring to her in mid-Channel, the precarious operation turning Rosslyn white with shock as the water lapped at her feet, swaying their fishing boat like a leaf on a pond.

It was only when they scrambled on board the merchant ship, the slippery deck rolling like a top, and Clarence greeted the Captain in French, that the enormity of their situation began to penetrate the frivolous layers of her consciousness. A bearded sailor reached hungrily for her, stroking her cheek with an exclamation of pleasure, his advances curtly repelled by Clarence who swore at him, fluent as any Marseilles tar. Rosslyn was forced to reply to the man in French, shakily at first, then gaining courage when she saw Clarence's eyes widen in alarm at her hesitancy. Only then did she finally understand the enormity of what she had so lightly undertaken. The shock and the rocking vessel were too much for her; with a cry of distress she raced to the rail and vomited into the choppy green water.

CHAPTER SEVEN

Armand St. Clare stepped quickly into the darkened doorway, pulling his battered black hat lower on his brow as the body of men tramped past.

"Good evening, citizen."

"And to you, citizens."

Warily he sidled back into the street, watching the group swinging jauntily down the Rue St. Antoine to the weekly meeting of the Revolutionary Committee, proudly sporting red caps of liberty and thumping their pikes along the cobblestones like walking sticks. He had recognized their big burly leader with his cross eyes and harelip as Robert, the cartman from the brewery at the corner of the street. Hopefully Robert had not recognized him. For the past week he had successfully dodged the patrols, becoming wilier than he had believed possible, trying to stay alive at least until tonight when he would meet with his cousin Bernard, who was the only link with his imprisoned wife and sons.

Pausing to wipe sweat from his brow, Armand leaned against the peeling shutters of a darkened house, holding his breath against the unspeakable odor wafting from the alley beside the house. A choking fog composed of refuse and excrement mingled with the nose-prickling odor of many urinations hotly awakened by the July heat. The clean air of the English South Downs seemed an eternity away.

Just then a young woman with curly black hair ran from a house across the street and something about her reminded him strikingly of Rosslyn. Perhaps it was the small waist, or the overflowing bodice; maybe it was just the hair, but whatever it had been the memory tugged painfully deep inside the soiled cambric of his shirt. With a shrug of annoyance for his idiotic thoughts, he began to walk again, wishing for the hundredth time Bernard's rendezvous had been in a more pleasant faubourg of Paris.

How easy it would have been to have stayed in England, not to have made this final crossing at all. Even after his dismissal from Burton Hall, his post as tutor gone, there would have been other chances to make a reasonable living. That panting relative of Jarvis Burton for one, he could have managed an assignment there had he been clever. True, more than riding lessons would have been required, but the other was an occupational hazard he could have endured.

Down the street, around the corner. Fortunately it was getting dark now, the brazen sun sinking, an orange globe over the Seine. Perhaps Bernard would invite him to sup with him; the idea was certainly appealing, for beyond a crust of bread and a rotten orange, he had not eaten all day.

The wine shop appeared to be closed, but when he tapped on the rear window as he had been instructed, a frowsy head poked inquiringly over the sill.

"Yes, citizen?"

"Have you the shipment of Spanish sherry?"

"The new stuff from Jerez?"

"Yes, fresh in last week."

"A minute, citizen, I'll see."

Armand waited in the close fetid darkness, sweating profusely in the high-walled yard where the temperature must have been at least twenty degrees hotter than in the street. Having completed his dialogue as instructed, he had not anticipated a wait. Perhaps things had not gone well and Bernard was not expecting him.

"Citizen."

"Yes, I'm still here."

"The master says you may come in and wait."

"Thank you, citizen, a thousand times."

The door creaked loudly as Armand was admitted to a room which reeked of wine casks and the dark pungence of ales and brandy, definitely a welcome change from the ordure of humanity fouling the gutters outside.

"This way, citizen."

They came into a brightly lit room where the sudden burst of light made Armand blink painfully. Two men sat at a table playing cards, a plate of bread and cheese beside them, tawny wine coloring their glasses with a jeweled glow. At his appearance one of the men disappeared through a back door to leave him alone with his cousin Bernard.

"Thank you, citizen. Will you bring another glass."

The shuffling servant departed and Bernard waved towards a chair. "Don't stand on ceremony, Monsieur le Comte," he said with sarcasm.

Armand thankfully sank into the cushioned chair, eyeing Bernard's pallid face with a wary gaze. Lines creased his cousin's formerly smooth brow, seaming the fine skin about his dull black eyes. He looked older but far more prosperous than the last time they had met.

"So, belonging to the Assembly seems to be suiting you. How sleek and fat you've become."

Bernard patted his developing paunch, cradled by a green brocade waistcoat and laced in by a huge gold watchchain. "It has its compensations. And you, my dear Armand, have you been sleeping with goats?"

"Goats would have been preferable to some of the inhabitants of doorways I've been forced to share."

"I suppose you want fresh clothes?"

"The offer is definitely appealing."

"Have you money?"

"Some. There's more to come when I can find transportation to Saint Clare. But what of my sons, tell me, are they well?"

"Yes, as well as can be expected."

"And Marie?"

Bernard shrugged, stroking the beginnings of a silken mustache on his short upper lip. "Stubborn, arrogant; she would do herself a favor to forget that her birthline stretches back to the fifteenth century."

Armand managed a smile. Yes, that was Marie all right. Aloud, he said: "How soon can you have my papers? And when can we get the safe conduct passes?"

Bernard shrugged, crumbling fragments of white bread to powder between his long thin fingers, the sight making Armand's mouth water. Narrow eyed, they surveyed each other, each regarding the other with a certain contempt, entering into a bargain merely out of business considerations.

"Are you hungry?"

"Ravenous."

Armand seized the plate of food Bernard thrust disdainfully over the table, hardly able to believe how good the bread tasted after so long a fast. The servant brought a fresh decanter of wine and another glass before Bernard waved him away.

"Something's wrong at the other end, for I've not heard from the Englishman yet. He agreed to my clever plan of substituting our charming little Jeanette for Marie."

"Are you sure it's safe?" Armand asked, worried lines drawing his dark brows together. There was something about Bernard's bland, girl-smooth face he did not trust.

"Nothing's safe, not even our conversation. If you mean, am I sure it will work, yes—perhaps. But it will be expensive."

"I'm prepared for that."

"Good, then we have a bargain, Cousin. Shall we drink to it?" Bernard raised his glass, his eyes dark as sloe berries in his pale face as he held the wine glass high. "To the success of all our plans."

"How many days must we wait?"

"I'm prepared to wait no more than a week. If we have heard nothing before then, we'll abandon the idea. They've been transferred from Temple."

Armand's eyes widened in alarm at the unexpected news.

"Why?"

"None of my doing, I can assure you. Anyway, Conciergerie is easier to crack, the staircases are crowded every day with sightseers. Temple's like a fort with that ditch and those unscaleable towers. We're much better off."

"Isn't Conciergerie the beginning of the end?"

Bernard shrugged. Standing up, he crossed to the corner of the room where he took a bundle from a table.

"Sometimes it is, that all depends on who you are, and whom you know," he added with a knowing grin. "Here's some clothing, not what you're used to, but I'm sure it will be pleasanter smelling than what you're wearing at the moment. The unpowdered style of your hair's becoming. I wouldn't have recognized you like that."

Deftly Armand caught the bundle, burying his face in the clean-smelling cloth. Filth and the lack of washing facilities was the part of being a fugitive he most deplored. "Your clothing seems to be of the first order. What say they to such extravagance from a citizen of the new republic?" he asked. With an experienced eye he had assessed the probable cost of the lime green suit his cousin wore, a splendid cut, the fabric luxuriously soft. His boots were of glove leather turned down with crimson. His striped silk cravat was held by a jeweled stickpin fashioned like a miniature guillotine from gold, an emerald taking the place of the victim's head. Such macabre taste seemed appropriate to Bernard Desjardins's strange sense of humor.

"It is not for anyone to question me, too many are in my debt already with favors unrepaid. Now, you'd best go. I'll meet you here in a week with the first papers. Give me all the cash you have, no jewelry, I can't exchange that today."

"And eating, how shall I do that with no money?"

"Steal it, beg it, anything—better yet, find a woman with lodgings near the prison."

"I don't know a woman," Armand protested.

"With your looks, Cousin, that should not be an insurmountable barrier," Bernard said with a grin. "Find one, charm her, bed her, but above all lodge in the neighborhood."

"Prostitute myself! By God, what do you think I am? I have my pride . . . "

"And little else at the moment, Monsieur le Comte," Bernard sneered. "Prostitute is a strong word, besides, it will not be bad at all. Think of it . . . some sturdy laundress or flower seller, scented with honest, garlic-tainted sweat, some lovely nymph begotten in a piss-stained alley and birthed on a lousy straw pallet," Ber-

127

nard suggested, as he poured himself more wine. Then his smile faded as he brought his fist down on the table. "If you would save your family, or at worst your own neck, then you'll do it and be glad. Besides, when she gets her legs around your back you'll never notice. You can even pick a pretty one, but pick one, Cousin, before the week's out or I'll wash my hands of you. This is a dangerous assignment, I want some insurance nothing will go wrong. Meet me at Jacques' Wine Shop on the corner. I'll bring you an identity card for that section, also an affidavit swearing you've been a continuous resident in France since May '92 sworn by eight honest citizens: You must bring the jewels to buy other papers."

"But what if I can't get them?"

"Then your fate's in your own hands, Cousin," Bernard said, glancing at his elaborate gold watch. "You can ask for no better odds than that, now, can you?"

Armand said nothing as he reluctantly turned over the linen bag of coins which he had worn inside his clothing while he awaited this moment; he clearly understood nothing had been settled. The fate of his wife and sons and his own life, hinged on the whims of Bernard Desjardins who was not known for his integrity.

Counting the money, Bernard thrust the bag inside his pocket. "Putting this with what you've already paid may buy the necessary papers, it may buy a few cooperative blind eyes, but little else, my dear Armand."

"I had thought to take the jewels to England, there would be more chance of payment there, don't you think?"

"Perhaps, but you have no time in which to bargain hunt, Cousin. My patience is short. Bring them to me at my apartments. I have ways of liquidating such things."

"Only when the affidavits for safe conduct are in my possession."

"Impossible."

"Then you shall not have the jewels."

Bernard smiled, the expression without humor, and he took out a snuffbox and delicately took a pinch of the white powder, sneezing convulsively a moment later.

"Ah, my dear cousin, if such is the case, then you shall not have your family."

Anger bubbled to the surface and Armand was forced to exert his utmost control to keep from grabbing that old-maid's neck and wringing it. He must go along with Bernard's plans; he had no other choice. "What assurance have I of security once I relinquish the jewels?"

"None, besides my integrity, dear Armand. To think you doubt me causes great anguish."

Clutching the bundle of clothing, crushing tight, acting out in symbol what he could not afford to do in reality, Armand bore Bernard's sarcastic smile. "Very well, one week from tonight at Jacques' Wine Shop. If all is set, I'll attempt to get the rest of the money within a couple of days."

"There's not that much haste. Once we know the plan's in operation, you have several weeks; I'll see to that. Better to establish your identity in the neighborhood first. I have much at stake in this scheme, after all, Marie's valuable to the tribunal. I shall be leaving for the country at the end of the month. My villa puts me closer to Saint Clare. Perhaps we can come to some arrangement for transportation."

"Thank you. Is there somewhere I can wash and put these on?"

Bernard waved his hand towards the doorway. "Through there. I'll send for some bath water."

Armand cautiously entered the room where an old-fashioned bath took up most of the space beside a small unmade bed. The meeting tonight had left him uneasy. Bernard was treacherous: how simple it would be to double-cross him once the jewels were handed over, to order his arrest and not release Marie and the boys.

A few minutes later an old woman tramped through the doorway with a steaming copper kettle of water. She dumped the water in the bathtub and without speaking tramped back for more. Stripping off his odorous clothing Armand examined some shaving supplies on a shelf beneath a broken piece of mirror in the corner. A clean basin stood on the shelf and he dipped some of the bathwater into it preparing to shave.

"Eh, what a fine guest you are," a woman's gruff voice remarked in admiration.

Glancing over his shoulder, Armand found a much younger woman this time bringing the water kettles. He winked at her and turned back to stropping the razor, surprised a moment later to feel her hands stroking his back.

"Come, I'll shave you if you wish."

"Thank you, citizeness, I'd prefer to do that myself."

"Eh bien, shaving is not my best thing, after all. I'll scrub your back."

Admiration for his lithe body was reflected in her eyes as she produced a bar of soap and a soft-bristled brush. Though Armand found the situation unexpected, he decided there were some compensations to Bernard's schemes after all. The young woman was in her twenties, not unpleasant to look at, and she smelled clean. Beyond that there was that sparkling eagerness in her eyes as she set about her task to recommend her; the expression promised far more than the proffered back rub.

"This is an unexpected pleasure," he sighed, leaning back, luxuriating in the hot bath as she soaped him vigorously, her strong hands kneading his weary back muscles with expertise.

"Ah, and for me too, citizen. The old one who let you in—he's my husband," she explained with a meaningful laugh, leaning lower so that her dress gaped to present him with a clear view of ripe brown flesh. "All in all, this is my lucky day."

Rain beat unceasingly against the roof of the cafe as Armand huddled in a corner of the room, trying to make his cheap wine last long enough to shelter till the rain let up. He had kept back in his boot a few coins from the money paid to Bernard, trying to eke out a meager existence until the week was up. There were two days still to go and he had no more money, his last coin going for this vinegar-sour slop flatteringly called wine and a chunk of coarse black bread. The doorway of St. Marguerite would already be crowded in this weather, so there was little point in hurrying through the rain to

130

stake out his few feet of flagged bedspace. Better to wait here until the customers were thrown out at closing time.

The first night he had spent in comfort at the rear of the wineshop, entertained right royally by the eager young wife of its owner, thrust out regretfully at dawn with a bundle of bread and cheese to tide him over. Twice since he had stopped by for meals, but the relationship was a dead-end one. He needed something far more permanent with a woman who had no grandfatherly husband who slipped inside her room twice nightly to make a bed check. He had had to hide in the murky recesses beneath the wooden bed, holding his breath so as not to choke on the dusty atmosphere and betray his presence.

A girl beside the door kept watching him, smiling when he caught her eye, undisguised admiration and interest shining forth. Perhaps she would be the answer. He had seen her in here the evening before, alone, though not for lack of possible companionship, for several drovers had already been loudly rebuffed by her this evening.

Armand smiled at her invitingly, feeling that unspoken message crackle through the air as she walked towards him. Hopefully she was not a whore, for she'd give him short shrift when she found out he was broke. She did not look like a whore, more like a plump, rosy-cheeked country girl, her brawny arms chapped from hard work. In all possibility she was a laundress. Bernard's sarcastic suggestions flicked through his mind and he smiled again, hardly expecting to be living out those suggestions in reality.

The girl in the blue-striped gown and gray calico apron was beside him now, her dark eyes sparkling, her rosy cheeks flushed pinker as she gazed at him, obviously not disappointed now that she saw him at close quarters.

"I've noticed you before," she said as she squeezed in place beside him.

"And I have noticed you."

The girl smiled at him. "What's your trade, citizen?"

"I'm an artist."

131

"Ahh!" She struck an attitude, hands on hips, breasts thrust forward and she fluttered her eyelashes coquettishly. "Paint me."

"Not a painter—a poet," Armand corrected hastily.

"A poet." She curled her lip. "What do you write about, Monsieur Poet?" she asked, drawing up a stool. She leaned forward on her elbows to gaze rapturously at him.

"About love."

"Read me one of your poems."

"I haven't written any lately."

She threw up her hands in exasperation and left, but a few minutes later she returned with two steaming bowls of soup. "Here, poor, starving, Monsieur Poet, eat."

Armand did not argue with her and when the soup was gone she grinned impishly at him. "You are an artist who doesn't paint, a poet who doesn't write—no wonder you are hungry."

"There's been no inspiration lately," he exclaimed lamely.

"When did she leave, your inspiration?"

"Three weeks ago," he lied, "since then I haven't written a word."

"Poor Monsieur Poet." She sighed, her dark eyes sad. "I know what it's like. I had a man who left me— he was no good, that rat. I'll kill him if I ever set eyes on him again," she vowed, eyes flashing in anger. "He left me for a red-haired Marseilles trollop, the fool."

"You can sympathize with me then." Armand sighed, entering into the spirit of the performance. "My inspiration took all my money and now I've no place to live."

The girl clucked in understanding, taking his hand in her own square roughened palm. "Threw you out, did they? Ah, life is bad sometimes." She guzzled a tankard of cheap wine and wiped her mouth on the back of her hand. "Well, I have lodgings and no man, you have no lodgings and no woman—*eh bien,* we shall both be happy. You must come home with me," the girl suggested generously, winking at him.

Armand stared in surprise, for he had not realized it would be this easy. "Do you mean that?"

132

"Yes, Monsieur Poet, unless you prefer boys. I knew a poet once who was like that . . ."

"No, Mademoiselle," he interrupted hastily, "it sounds an admirable arrangement from both our viewpoints."

"It's far too wet to sleep out tonight. My room's dry and there's a good bed," she paused and leaning close to him she whispered: "I've admired you since the first time I saw you. Your body is very fine. Will you make love to me, Monsieur Poet?"

Armand stared into her dark eyes to see desire flickering there, tinging the brown with gold; perhaps it was only the cheap wine.

"I will make love to you as often as you wish, Mademoiselle," he promised huskily, clasping her hands in his.

"*Bon Dieu,* what a stallion you must be." She laughed throatily, rising to unsteady feet as she spoke. "Come, Monsieur Poet, I'm very impatient."

Rain blew in gusts against the window, rattling the casement, and the girl in his arms shivered at the lonely sound. She burrowed beneath the covers with a laugh, stretching out her hand in a demanding caress. His flesh responded and Armand heard her sigh of pleasure close against his ear. Her thick dark hair smelled of cheap perfume mingled with rancid cooking oil. Normally the odor would have repelled him, but tonight everything was so impossibly different, instead his desire was increased by it, the flames fanned by the novelty of her scent.

"Ah, my stallion," she breathed as his ardor increased.

Armand crushed the pliable globes of her breasts demandingly, until she laughed in delight at his touch. Hungrily he sought her mouth, the odor of garlic passing unnoticed on her breath. Her tongue was hot, darting, and he moaned in pleasure.

"*Dieu,* do it now," she cried, seizing him by the hair. Beneath the tattered blanket their bodies thrashed, spilling a patchwork cover unnoticed to the floor. She spread her legs, expertly guiding the projectile, then her mouth on his ear, nuzzling, biting, she whispered: "What is your name, Monsieur Poet?"

"Armand," he whispered as he entered her.

"Why have you got such a name as St. Clare?" the girl asked suspiciously, looking down at the bustling street below, still raining this morning. "Are you an aristocrat?"

"I don't usually tell people this," Armand explained hastily, "but yes, my father was one, a very wealthy man. I am a . . ."

"Ha, a bastard, eh! That's no shame." She grinned as she turned from the window. "That explains your looks and fancy ways. Well, Monsieur Poet, I am a bastard too. My mother, God rest her soul, couldn't resist a man. She was like me, poor fool, pining away her life for an eight-inch broom handle." She cackled at her joke. "She says my father was so handsome, but he left her after she swelled up with me. She never saw him again and spent the rest of her life looking for another just like him." Head to one side like a bird, she gave him a warm, appraising smile. "Ah, now I'm not looking anymore because I've got you. Don't you want to know my name?"

"What is your name?" Armand asked dutifully.

"Fleurette. I have no other. Citizeness Fleurette, ask anyone, they'll know me. Besides, who needs names, I have a body, that's all I need."

He laughed at her frank statement finding her undisguised enjoyment of him both stirring and novel; her open, earthy desire was arousing in its honesty.

"What was your woman's name?"

Armand thought a moment, deciding against the English name of Rosslyn, surprised he even thought of it first. "Marie," he said.

"Eh—the Madonna." Fleurette grimaced. "Was she virtuous too?"

"Yes, I suppose she was."

"Hah, virtue, what is it worth? Did she make you cry out like I do?" she demanded, encircling his neck with her strong chapped arms.

"Never."

"Was she pretty?"

"Yes."

"Prettier than me?"

"No, not prettier."

"*Bien,* and what were her breasts like, were they big like mine?" She grinned, thrusting her plentiful bodice close against his chest.

"Much smaller than you."

"Then I am not jealous of your Madonna. If she did not make you cry out and she had no body, she wasn't a woman, therefore I'm not jealous of her." And without further speech she smothered his mouth with her own, pushing him back demandingly on the bed.

Bernard appeared for their rendezvous dressed in the woolen carmagnole of a revolutionary, his *bonnet rouge* askew and pinned in place with a huge tricolor cockade.

"Greetings, citizen," he said, his voice deep and gruff.

Armand blinked a moment before entering into the spirit of the act, hardly able to believe this pale, jaundiced character decked out so patriotically was the same Bernard Desjardins with whom he had bargained in the back room of the wine shop.

"Thank you for your contributions to the People's Government. We find your documents all in order and are returning them to you."

"Thank you, citizen, I will do all I can to continue to promote our struggle for liberty," Armand replied, making his own voice rough in turn, yet not quite able to master the common Parisian speech.

Avid onlookers patted him on the back at the exchange and turning to Bernard, whom they addressed as Claude, they begged for a speech. By this Armand realized Bernard was adept at this role as he pretended to be a member of the Vigilance Committee from the neighboring faubourg of St. Germain. For the next hour Bernard addressed them in flaming rhetoric, winning thunderous applause. And Armand received a couple of jugs of wine in honor of his friendship with such a loyal member of the People's Revolution.

When he left Jacques' Wine Shop on his journey back

135

to the attic he shared with Fleurette, Armand had his identity card swearing to his patriotism issued by the Committee for Faubourg St. Antoine and a continuous residence certificate attested to by eight staunch and loyal citizens of the New Republic.

"Eh, been stepping around on me already," Fleurette cried when he arrived at her door, temporarily winded after running up the stairs.

"No, it was important business. Ask your friends at Jacques' Wine Shop. I had a rendezvous with someone. Now let me in, it stinks out here."

Begrudgingly Fleurette opened the door and admitted him. She brought him some bread and a small portion of meat she had received in payment for her laundry service that day, then slumped on the bench opposite to watch him eat.

"Who was *she,* this important friend?"

"Not a she, but a man from Faubourg St. Germain. You probably know him; Claude, a pale man with black eyes, gives rousingly patriotic speeches . . ."

"You know *him*?" Fleurette asked in admiration, clearly impressed. "He talks revolution like an angel, but he's no good at making love. I had him one night, pah, what a waste. His fuse is too short," she informed him matter-of-factly as she got up to bring some wine.

"Thank God the revolution is not run by women," Armand laughed, genuinely amused at Fleurette's classification of his cousin.

"Ah, my Poet, in that case you would be a leader amongst men," she laughed, coming to kiss him, her brawny arms locked about his neck. "So you met this Claude, eh! What for?"

"He had my papers which he had omitted to return."

"Oh, that's good. I was afraid you had no papers. I went through your clothing once but couldn't find any."

"What did you do that for? Going to turn me in?"

"No, fool, I wanted to protect you. The Vigilance Committee is very active on this street; already I've heard some rumblings about you. After tonight though, the word will be out. With Claude as your friend no one will say a thing to you."

136

Armand relaxed in the rickety chair, tilting backwards, and he stretched with a sigh of achievement.

"I thought you were with *her*."

"Her?"

"The little bitch who came looking for you today. I gave her short shrift, I can tell you. *Merde,* what does she take me for, she had the nerve to say she was your sister, that the carter told her you were living here." Fleurette cackled in high delight as she went to the bed to turn back the soiled sheet.

"My sister?" Armand croaked, bringing his chair to the floor with a crash. Bernard had made no mention of their English contacts, yet perhaps the crowded wine shop had not been the ideal location for such revelations.

"That's what she said. A pretty thing, I must admit, black curly hair with a face like an actress, flesh to match. If she thinks I'm turning you over without a fight, she's mistaken there." Fleurette gave the pillow an aggrieved thump.

"She came here today?"

"Just before dusk. I had the devil of a time understanding her though, gabbling like a foreigner she was. Must be from the country."

"Yes, she is."

"Ah, then you do admit to knowing her." Fleurette rounded on him, her hand raised to strike, anger turning her face sharp.

"She is my sister. Stop it, for God's sake," he laughed, deflecting her swinging blows. He got out of the chair and dropped her to the bed. "Stop it."

"She is your sister, really? She's not just some trollop out to steal you from me?" Fleurette questioned suspiciously.

"Her name is Jeanette and she's from the country north of here. Oh, Fleurette, there's so much about me you don't know. Can I trust you with a secret? My life is at stake."

Wide eyed, the young laundress sat up, pulling him towards her. "Oh, my poor Monsieur Poet. For what is your life at stake?"

"Members of my family are imprisoned at Conciergerie. My sister and her lover are going to help me free them. Now, you hold our secret in your hands. Will you keep it?"

"Till my dying day," Fleurette whispered, her brown eyes bright with tears. "You can count on me, I swear it."

"My treausre." He kissed her tear-wet cheek. "Where did Jeanette go? What did you tell her?"

"I said I'd never heard of you."

Armand groaned at her words.

"Don't worry, she didn't believe me. I must've looked too satisfied for that to be true, I suppose." Fleurette grinned at him, her tears over. "I told her my man was gone and she said she'd be back later when he was here. I told her it wouldn't do any good, but she insisted she look at you just in case you were the right one. Oh, she knew you, all right, described you too, in a most unsisterly fashion I thought, but then, perhaps it was just because I was so jealous of her pretty face."

"How long ago? You say dusk?"

"Perhaps she watched you come in. Though looking like she does she shouldn't be on these streets at night. Does she have any papers? The Vigilance Committee arrest people on the streets after dark. I was even worried about you tonight. But a girl like that—yes, I can see where she gets her good looks from."

"I'll go down to the street to look for her. Perhaps she's waiting there."

"No, let me go. The patrol knows me. The streets have been closed off by now, and they'll be making their rounds. If they stop me I'll say I'm looking for my cat."

"But you don't have a cat," Armand protested.

Fleurette grinned. "You know that, I know that, but they do not." And with a wave she disappeared through the doorway, clattering downstairs in her wooden clogs on her journey to the odorous street below.

CHAPTER EIGHT

When the door opened Armand reeled back in shock. Not Jeanette, but Rosslyn stood framed in the doorway, urged inside by Fleurette who loudly called, "Here, Kitty," to add credulity to her claims.

"A close one that," Fleurette remarked, slamming the door. "That Robert would've had his hands down her bodice if I hadn't got there in time. Your sister too! Bah! That animal. I gave him a piece of my mind, Vigilance Committee or no. Well, you two, speechless are you? Say something—hello, nice to see you." Fleurette stepped back, head on one side as she surveyed the new arrival.

"Armand, I'm so glad you're safe," Rosslyn whispered. How he had changed! He was leaner, hungrier, and his black hair straggled untidily about his collar, but his eyes still raked her with that familiar appraisal which sent her pulses racing.

"Thank God you're safe too, my sister." Stiffly he drew her to his embrace, steeling his arms and legs against the pleasure, his mind a turmoil of questions about plans gone awry.

As she yielded against the warm, safe strength of him, for no explanable reason, Rosslyn burst into tears. Waiting below in the refuse-littered street, her near escape from that band of ruffians who called themselves the Vigilance Committee, had tried her nerves to the breaking point. And now to be with Armand, at last, only to find she still must share him with this brawny peasant girl, tore her usual control to shreds.

"Come, sweetheart." Cradling her head against his shoulder, Armand motioned for Fleurette to bring wine. "You're safe now. Hush, don't cry. I'm here, Jeanette."

Fleurette paused to watch, the wine bottle suspended in the air, tears of sympathy filling her eyes.

"What if I hadn't rescued her? I hate to think what might be happening now. Dragged into the alley by one of those creatures, filled and pumped, with never a sou to show for it."

"Fleurette," Armand cautioned, shaking his head in displeasure.

"Sorry." Guilty, Fleurette compressed her lips. The wine poured, she brought two mugs, taking her own drink from the bottle.

"Better now?"

Blinking back tears which seemed to keep welling in her eyes, Rosslyn nodded, giving him a tremulous smile. She searched his face and read a warning there. For the time being at least she would have to remain his sister.

"Thanks." Managing a smile of friendship for the other girl, Rosslyn accepted the proffered wine. Out of genuine kindness Fleurette had rescued her in the mistaken belief that she was Armand's sister. The jealousy seething within her at the knowledge of Fleurette's relationship with him was Rosslyn's secret; the crumpled bed very prominent in the small room just added to her pain.

"Have we food?"

Fleurette shrugged. "A crust. I was going to get some in the morning. We usually don't eat this late. I gave you all there was."

"Can you get her something?"

"Amelie may have food to spare. Her man's the executioner. A well-paid job that is these days. I'll see."

When the door closed Armand pulled Rosslyn to him, searching her face, drinking in the sight of her after so long. "Why are you here?"

"Jeanette sprained her ankle. It was either use me or discard the plans. Don't worry about your sister though, she'll be all right. Believe me, I never knew she was that. All the time I thought—oh, Armand, forgive me for what I thought."

"Believing that, you still loved me," he said in surprise, his mouth curving upward in pleasure.

"You didn't know I was such a fool, did you?"

"We have a few minutes alone. Fleurette won't be able to resist telling Amelie about you; they're bosom friends."

Shuddering against the warmth of him, Rosslyn felt that absurd grief again taking possession of her senses, until she pulled away, angry with herself.

"I'm an idiot, but I can't stop crying." She managed, lips trembling to behold him, to see the soft emotion he still felt for her in his eyes.

Armand grabbed her, snapping her head up, the action so swift, her tears were jarred loose. Then his mouth engulfed hers making her shudder with longing for what they once had shared.

"I never thought I'd owe my life to you, *cherie*. How brave you are. How loyal."

Rosslyn gulped at his impassioned speech. Little did he know her reluctance to take part in the plot, the pressure brought to bear against her hesitancy. Yet as long as she lived she would not tell him about her intimacy with Tom Stanley.

"I'm not brave. Down there I was scared to death. You must help me through this; it's the only way I'll be able to manage."

Armand smiled softly at her tearful confession. "I'll help you, Rosslyn, don't worry. Though I'm filled with joy to see you, I wish to God you were still safe at home. This is another world. We risk death once the plan's set in motion."

"I don't mind the risk. Being with you makes it worth while," she whispered, surprising herself at the heartfelt sincerity of her words.

Armand sighed as he released her. "We are not alone. You've forgotten Fleurette."

"You sleep with her?"

"You know I do—listen, please." He caught her hands as she turned away. "The girl means little to me. Her lodging was necessary to our plan. Though I'm not proud of what I've done, the end justifies the means."

Trying to swallow jealousy and failing, Rosslyn numbly stared at the sagging bed. "Where am I to sleep?

"With Fleurette if you wish."

"She'll never allow that. I've only known her half an

hour and already I can see she's mad for you. The floor will do. It's clean."

Armand wanted to argue, to deny her assessment, but in all honesty he could not. She was right. And this was Fleurette's room. "We'll make a clean pallet for you. Do you mind terribly?" he asked, knowing it was a foolish question, sorry he had uttered the words once they were out.

"Mind!" she hissed, fastening glittering dark violet eyes on his. "I mind like hell. I want to slit her throat, grab her hair and tell her what I was to you, what I still want to be. That's how much I mind."

Taken aback by the vehemence of her words, Armand stared at her in surprise, then his face broke into a smile of wonder. "Thank God for that."

Smiling as her anger evaporated, Rosslyn leaned against him, her emotions stirred, but not by anger "You've been in my blood, though I've tried to deny it, since you stared so impudently at me that night of the ball."

"You were a fetching sight. One to make my blood boil," he whispered, sliding his hands over the prominence of her bodice, finding a stiffening response of her nipples beneath his touch.

"Stop, it's more than I can stand," she whispered, her legs going weak.

"Cold, frigid Englishwoman, your body's tormented my sleep this time apart; yet you deny me the pleasure of touching you."

His amused grin tugged at her emotions until she was forced to remember Fleurette as heavy footsteps clumped on the stair. "You have the opportunity to satisfy your lust tonight. I don't." Half in anger she flung from his arms, going to the window as the door handle rattled.

Armand turned his back to the door pretending to arrange papers on the corner chest in an effort to conceal his desire from Fleurette, whose gaze habitually strayed to the revealing tightness of his britches.

"See here, cheese and melons! A pastry too—for your sister, pig," she snapped, as Armand reached for the fruit-filled puff.

Fleurette ushered Rosslyn to the rickety table, spreading out the feast with a flourish on the starched white cloth. Rosslyn ate as if she was starving, nervousness increasing her appetite.

"Will your man be joining you soon?" Fleurette asked, when the food was finished, her eyes straying to the bed where she was eager to retire. Dawn came early these days. And she was not merely anxious for sleep.

"My man?"

"Clarence," Armand supplied quickly.

"Eh, what a grand name. Clarence, is it? What's he? A damned aristocrat too?"

"Like me he's an aristocrat's bastard," Armand intervened smoothly, hoping Rosslyn would understand.

"Oh, Clarence—yes, tomorrow sometime," she whispered, wondering why Armand had told this girl her brother was her lover.

The pallet was soon made with a couple of quilts from downstairs which Fleurette had the forethought to borrow from Amelie. Being in such cramped quarters was difficult for Rosslyn who had become used to endless corridors and vast palatal rooms. The small room was so cluttered with rickety furniture, the bed taking up over half the floor space, there was no room to move. A faded brocade screen in the corner hid the chamber pot and provided privacy for anyone wishing to undress. This luxury was explained by Armand while Fleurette emptied a bowl of dirty wash water out the window.

Her skin creeping with embarrassment, Rosslyn availed herself of the facilities. To her surprise she found her discomfort stemmed more from Fleurette's presence than Armand's; the discovery betraying the new level of intimacy her feelings for him had reached.

From her hard, draughty pallet Rosslyn tried to shut out the murmur of Fleurette's endearments. At the husky whispers pain swelled to her throat in a burning lump; hot tears of anguish trickled from her face to the musty quilts. It was obvious Armand was declining Fleurette's suggestions and though Rosslyn tried to close her ears to them, the girl's disappointed protests came through.

"Eh, Jeanette?"

Rosslyn jumped when a bony finger jabbed her sharply in the shoulder as Fleurette leaned from the bed.

"Yes."

"Your brother's turned all bashful. You don't mind if he . . ."

"Shut up! Leave her alone. I've told you no, so go to sleep."

Cursing, muttering, Fleurette threw herself backwards, creaking and bouncing the bed "Afraid she'll tell your mama?" she taunted.

Armand did not reply.

"Go on, say something to me. No—then I'll tell Jeanette about you—hey, Jeanette, this brother of yours used to be such a fine stallion. Now I think he's turned into a gelding . . ."

Her voice was silenced by a slap as Armand hit her across the mouth, the noise swiftly followed by sniffles and tears. Soon even the sobs from the bed ceased. Now Rosslyn could hear a baby wailing downstairs, the cries of hunger accompanied by a chorus of hacking coughs sounding through the thin partition of the rooms. For a long time she lay awake reviewing the danger ahead. Then, when she would have slept, the noise of the slums penetrated even the barrier of the coverlet until she was forced to put her fingers in her ears to deaden the sounds.

Rosslyn woke to narrow shafts of sunlight on her face. Stretching her cramped limbs for a moment she wondered where she was, then a snore and a grunt from the bed alerted her to the shabby room off the Rue St. Antoine, the raking sun revealing it in all its squalor of peeling plaster and rag-stuffed windowpanes.

A moment later she was staring into Fleurette's brown eyes as, awakening herself, the young laundress was equally surprised to find another female there.

"Hey, for a minute I thought you were a trollop who'd wandered in last night. Want something to eat? There's a bit of melon."

"Thanks, but I'm not hungry."

Rosslyn scrambled to her feet, pushing back her hair

which hung in a tangled mass around her shoulders. The room was stuffy and she longed for a breath of the clean salt-tanged air of home.

Fleurette yawned and stretched on the side of the bed, then glancing at the sleeping man she jerked her finger toward him.

"Eh, what a beauty your brother is. You too. But I don't fancy women like I do men."

Despite herself, Rosslyn grinned at the other girl. She was jealous of Fleurette's association with Armand, yet she could not help liking her. "Have you known him long?"

"Long enough," Fleurette said as she thumped towards the table. "Here, wine to wash out your mouth. It's good stuff. Amelie's husband got it from an aristocrat. No use for it when you've sneezed into the sack."

Rosslyn shuddered at Fleurette's easy jargon for the executions. "Did you know anyone who was— executed?"

With a grimace Fleurette plonked the wine bottle back on the wooden shelf over the window. "A woman I worked for. I'm a laundress, you see. Nice old stick she was. Don't know what they caught her for. Being too clean, probably. I tell you, she wanted everything spotless—Ah, *cher,* you're awake."

Pain stabbed acutely as Rosslyn watched them embrace, the gesture accompanied by Fleurette's husky endearments. The more she realized how much the young laundress appreciated Armand, the more jealous she became, till the too sweet wine heaved sickeningly to her throat. Forcing down the vile-tasting fluid, she managed a smile as he walked to the table.

"And how are you this morning, dearest?" he asked carefully.

"Well. And impatient to be about our business."

"Me too. It's all right, Fleurette knows you're helping me rescue my family from prison. She's trustworthy."

The laundress assumed a broad smile of pride at his words. Then she winked at Rosslyn. "When's your man coming? I want to look at him. Might even want to share him," she joked, nudging Rosslyn in a familiar manner.

145

"This morning, but I'm not sure when."

"Ah, I suppose I'll be out when he comes. Too bad. Still, let him stay to supper. We'll go to Jacques' place and have a feast. I get paid today."

Rosslyn was about to decline the offer when she saw Armand shake his head in warning, so she smilingly agreed to the suggestion.

"If I didn't need the money I'd stay home today. Looks like rain with those clouds building over the river. When your man comes perhaps your bashful little brother will be himself again. We can pair off, thank God."

"We may be out when you get back," Armand informed, not adding that they would be gone permanently from this shabby faubourg. Not to tell Fleurette the truth when she had been so kind pricked his conscience. Yet it was too dangerous to reveal the entirety of his plans, the content of which was not wholly known even to him.

"Mind you, come back in time to eat. Ah, Jeanette, if you weren't his sister I'd not go to work today. Asking for trouble is what I'm doing leaving a man like that by himself. That Amelie! Though I love her like a sister, that sow has her eye on him. Oh, if she so much as touches him . . ."

"You'll be late. Go on, I promise to guard my chastity." Armand grinned as he opened the door. Thrusting her patched blue shawl in her arms he said: "There, in case it rains."

Fleurette smiled beautifully at him, then seizing his face in her strong hands, she planted a thorough kiss on his mouth. "Till I reutrn—*au revoir,* Jeanette."

"*Au revoir.* Thank you for everything."

"It's nothing to accommodate the sister of Monsieur Poet."

Bursting into song on her way downstairs, Fleurette clattered to the cobbled street. Armand waved to her as she passed beneath the window, blowing a kiss in reply to her generous gesture.

"She's insanely in love with you," Rosslyn whispered uncomfortably.

"In love? Nonsense! Girls like Fleurette know nothing of love as you mean it. She desires me. There's no more to it than that."

"Even desire is more than I can stand."

"Ah, sweetheart, don't be jealous."

"I must thank you for your restraint last night."

"To take her with you less than a foot away is too much abandon even for me." He grimaced at her serious expression. "Come, forget her. After today we may never see her again."

"Will we see each other?"

"Before God, I hope so. You should be released before the day's out. I'll wait at Madame Casteel's wine shop, overnight if need be. That's the usual rendezvous. Will Clarence have the plans when he arrives?"

"Yes. He said when it was safe he'd come to the door."

Armand glanced at the shabby street, where doors opened from time to time and shawl-draped heads emerged.

"He's not here yet."

"No. Perhaps it's still too early."

"When the people have gone to work he'll come."

"Yes, I should think so. I'm sure he'll come then."

They stared at each other realizing how ridiculous and stilted they had become. Standing less than two feet apart, yet talking like polite acquaintances, filling the time with pointless conversation when what they really needed was each other.

"Stop it!" Armand snapped, his face tight.

"I can't," she whispered, trembling as he stepped towards her.

"No more! That's an order, Madame Burton."

His words brought a smile to her lips. How long it seemed since she had heard him address her so. "And you, Monsieur St. Clare, what will you do if I disobey?"

His mouth curved upward in a lopsided grin. "I'd hate to make love to a chattering woman; still, it would be a new experience."

Rosslyn fell against him, shuddering at the touch of his mouth against her skin, at the strength of his arms around her.

"For every time you've done it with her I'm going to

punish you," she vowed, seeing the bed and remembering Fleurette.

Drawing away, Armand grinned at her. "How will you do that, Madame?"

"I'll refuse you. For leaving me alone. For taking me. For teaching me what it was like, then discarding me. Oh, you shall pay for it all. I've sworn revenge . . ."

"You little liar." Laughing, he welded her against the hard bruising length of his body and traced his tongue over her trembling lips. "Shut your mouth."

"And then what shall I do?"

Holding her stiffly away from him and imprisoning her in his grasp, Armand did not smile as he whispered: "Open your legs."

The sun was fully up when Clarence tapped on the door. For a long time no one answered, though he heard scuffling behind the door. At last Armand let him in. One glance about the untidy room with its crumpled bed, at Armand's flushed face and his sister's disarrayed clothing, told him what had happened.

"By God! After all that hypocritic twaddle about not wanting to see St. Clare. Criticizing me for my feelings over Jeanette. You've got some—what a hypocrite! You're worse than Adela," he exclaimed, his outraged expression belied by the twinkle in his eyes.

"Oh, shut up, Clarence," Rosslyn exploded, her eyes dark with mingled passion and anger at being disturbed.

Armand clapped Clarence on the shoulder and they began to laugh. "Ah, my friend, how good to see you at last."

"Sorry for the delay, Armand. It couldn't be helped. If it hadn't been for my little sister here, we wouldn't have a chance of doing anything."

"I know. She told me."

"I bet seeing her on your doorstep was a shock. If there'd been a way, I'd have warned you. Lucky you haven't a bad heart." Clarence chuckled as he glanced about the room. He did not ask who paid the rent; he would not embarrass either of them with that.

"When do we go to the prison?" Rosslyn asked, apprehensive now that he was here at last. Now she knew beyond a doubt her role in the plot would be required.

"A couple of hours. First I've got to tell you the plan."

Clarence pulled a chair towards the bed and spread out a rolled map. Rosslyn listened as he discussed the details with Armand, asking her from time to time if she understood. Clarence's French was without accent, something she herself had to be very careful about. His experience at the business of intrigue had obviously served him well. Dressed in ragged workman's trousers, a threadbare carmagnole stretched over his loose frame, he bore no resemblance to the elegantly attired man who was known at Burton Hill.

"Are you sure I'll be released?"

The two men looked up at her question, and from the worried frowns on their faces she knew even they had some doubt.

"If you aren't I'll reward Bernard personally," Armand vowed, his face set with intent.

"Don't worry. We have his word," Clarence assured.

"I've known my cousin longer than you. That is not an ironclad security."

Rosslyn smiled. "Don't look so glum. I'm here now. All we can do is follow through with the arrangements. I'm not afraid." Even she was almost convinced by the lie.

As they studied the street plan, visualizing the site of the Conciergerie prison, thunder rolled in the distance.

"A storm would aid us. I'll pray for it to continue," Clarence said, getting to his feet.

"Let's run through this one more time," Armand decided. "Tell me what you're to do, Rosslyn."

"I leave here, and we go in different directions to the prison. When they let in the visitors I tell them I'm Madame St. Clare's maid . . ."

"Drop the Madame; it's currently a forbidden form of address," Clarence reminded quietly.

"Citizeness St. Clare."

"No, *cherie,* our family name is actually de Gramont—Citizeness Gramont."

"Citizeness Gramont," Rosslyn paused, awaiting further correction. Then noting their approval she continued, "I say I'm bringing loaves. We exchange clothes. She walks outside to Madame Casteel's wine shop just across the bridge. And I wait to be released."

"Bravo. You should be on the stage. A perfect part already learned," Clarence applauded, then his face turned grim. "Remember, litttle sister, we can't go home when the curtain falls."

"I understand that."

"Once you're inside I won't be able to help you, nor will Armand. You won't see him again until the rendezvous. You understand, you can't expect help?"

"I know that."

"The only help you have left is *le Bon Dieu, ma petite*," Armand whispered, taking her hand in his, wishing for one panicky moment that she was all those safe miles away in England.

"You're like old hens clucking your disquieting advice. We'll laugh about it tonight, you'll see."

But later, when she stepped into the dark street where the first cool drops of rain splashed against her face, Rosslyn was not as confident.

CHAPTER NINE

Rosslyn stood in the shelter of a doorway postponing the inevitable moment, listening to the downpour as she watched the debris and filth eddy past down the central gutter.

Hesitating, not daring to look directly at her, Armand rounded the corner and disappeared in the maze of twisting narrow streets.

Taking a deep breath, mentally preparing herself for the irreversible move she was about to make, Rosslyn pulled her shawl about her head and covered the wicker basket of loaves as she resolutely stepped forth.

The smell of wet clothes and wet bodies assailed her in an odorous fog as she waited amongst the noisy, milling throng of afternoon visitors who crowded the staircases and hallways of the Conciergerie. Everyone, it seemed, was either arguing, cursing or sobbing. They had come for vastly different reasons to this dark, gloomy prison without hope. It was called the antechamber of death; looking about with a shudder of fear, Rosslyn found it an apt description.

The very walls of the Conciergerie had a distinctive odor which Rosslyn had never smelled before: a combination born of despair, of unwashed bodies and illness, of foul air, of excrement and death.

At a signal the surging throng moved forward, battling with elbows and fists to reach the front. Rosslyn was crushed in the melee until the wicker basket, hidden beneath her shawl from pilfering hands, cut painfully into her flesh. Kicked and stepped on, her hair torn by coat buttons, she eventually worked her way to the front line where a guard entered names in a book. From some people bribes were taken, the growing assortment of goods heaped behind the table giving the room the appearance of a shop.

"You, citizeness; what have you in the basket?"

Rosslyn revealed the six fresh loaves. The guards took one each to deposit on the floor with the other loot.

The younger one picked his nose as he regarded her speculatively. "Who do you want to see?"

"Citizeness Gramont." Rosslyn spoke loudly, forcing her accent to remain pure as tension stiffened her neck muscles and brought pain to her hands where she clutched the wicker handle as if her life depended on it.

"Gramont." The guard traced down a list with his grubby broken fingernail. "Ah, I know the one. What are you to her?"

"I was her maid."

"Hm. Is it true what they say about her?" he asked, exchanging winks with the other man.

The throng pushed forward then, distracting the guard's attention so that he bellowed at the top of his voice for order, alleviating Rosslyn's need to reply.

"That way." A bystander pointed through a doorway. She fled to the dark stone-walled corridor beyond, down flights of steps to gloomy cellars that were chill even on this summer day as water from the Seine seeped through the masonry and coated the walls with dripping river slime.

Hastening to catch up with a party of visitors led by a guard with a lantern, Rosslyn held her breath against the overpowering stench. One by one people were deposited in cells along the way. Some of the rooms were hideous community cells, so dark, the glowing eyes of their inhabitants gave the impression of wild animals peering through the gloom.

Too late Rosslyn discovered she was alone with the guard, not the man who had spoken to her earlier, but another half-witted creature with gaping mouth and rolling, cross eyes.

"Citizeness Gramont," she repeated with authority, but he only stared at her, a leer spreading over his thick features.

"Gramont," he repeated stupidly.

"Hurry. There's not much time."

To her alarm he stepped towards her instead. Seizing the shawl he snatched it from her shoulders to reveal the basket with the four remaining loaves. Grunting, he picked over the food.

"That all?" he muttered in disappointment.

She nodded, holding the basket before her as a defense against him, for her own danger of bodily assault was all too apparent. The thought of being forced to submit to this half-human creature amid the dripping odor of this hideous prison filled her with disgust.

"What's this?" he demanded, attracted by the gleam of silver at her neck picked up in the glow from his lantern.

Pressed against the chill wall Rosslyn could move no further from his clutching fingers as he reached for her locket. With a swift jerk he broke the clasp, bruising her neck.

"Don't take that," Rosslyn cried in alarm. It was the silver locket Will had given her last Christmas, the secret he had taken such pains to keep.

Fumbling, the guard tried to open the delicate catch with his blunt fingers, keeping the locket out of reach as she grabbed for it.

"What's it worth to you?" he asked, leering close to her face until she gasped in disgust at his foul, garlic-tainted breath, stiffening as he swept an exploring hand over her hips.

So that was it! Chilled at the thought of bargaining with her body, Rosslyn stood silent while he slipped the locket inside his clothes.

"Well, speak up, you can't want it very bad. It's a paltry thing, hardly worth my trouble." His arm went up against the wall as he pressed heavily upon her. "What will it be? A kiss? A feel? Surely it's worth something, citizeness."

Revolted by his nearness, by the ugliness of his unwashed body, she trembled, trying to turn her face away as that garlic-tasting mouth came down wetly on her own, as the slithering tongue probed her mouth until she gagged. His fingers busily explored as she struggled against his weight. When she kicked him on the shins he pinched her nipple in retaliation until she gasped with pain.

"Bitch! You'll not get it now. Come on. I'll finish with you later."

Yanking her by the arm he thrust her before him pressing against her back so that she quickened her steps to elude him. He regarded the action as high sport, renewing the assault until she nearly ran down the narrow uneven passage in an effort to stay away from him.

"Here it is. I'll give you ten minutes. Then we can decide what the bauble's worth to you."

Jangling a huge key ring he muttered in the half-light as he fumbled amongst the long keys for the right one. Close at hand someone sobbed and he bellowed for quiet. At last, the right key found, he inserted it in the lock.

"Here you are, Citizeness Gramont, a pretty little companion to see you. Be careful, don't get too friendly, you've only got ten minutes." Laughing stupidly at his veiled suggestion, he crashed back the metal grilled door, then thrust Rosslyn inside the dark, fetid cell.

In the gloom she could barely distinguish Marie St. Clare's features beneath the towering puff of gray-tinged hair. The other woman stood stiffly apart, not speaking, waiting for the guard to close the door. Finally the key grated in the lock.

"Oh, dear Madame, how wonderful to see you at last. All this time I've been denied a visit," Rosslyn cried, making the words suitably tearful for the guard's benefit.

The man hesitated a moment outside the door, his thick lips curled upward in scorn before he moved away.

"Who in God's name are you?" Marie demanded, swishing towards her.

They stood in the gray, bar-checked beam of light from outside, hostility radiating between them. Rosslyn had been prepared to like his wife, had been prepared to be kind, but the icy regard in the other woman's face precluded friendliness.

"I have come to save your life, Madame."

"Have you indeed. And how do you propose to do that?"

"We'll change clothes; then, when the door's opened you, instead of me, will accompany the guard."

"Don't be a fool. It'll never work," Marie dismissed scornfully, turning on her heel.

"It will work. Bribes have been exchanged. Madame I urge you to waste no more time."

"Who are you?"

"That's not important. The only thing about me you need know is that I'm your friend."

Lightning lit the squalid cell a moment in brilliant relief. "Ah, now I see who you are," Marie spat, her voice bitter.

"You're never met me, Madame. Come, I'll help you to undress."

"Take your hands off me."

Burning with anger and humiliation, Rosslyn kept her arms stiffly at her sides, aware of the minutes ticking rapidly by, of the other woman's lack of cooperation. No one had suggested Marie St. Clare would be anything but eagerly receptive to their plan. This change of direction left her bewildered.

"When you leave the prison you are to cross the bridge to Madame Casteel's wine shop. Do you know where it is?"

"I know. Who's behind this? My loving husband, no doubt."

"The comte has risked his life and a considerable amount of money on this plan. Don't put him in danger through your own obstinacy," Rosslyn snapped, unable to keep her temper.

"Ah, so he is that important to you. I thought as much. You're pretty and he's always had an eye for pretty faces. You're a fool to trust him. There must be a hundred more like you . . ."

Shocked at the words, yet doggedly proceeding with the plan, Rosslyn had already unfastened her gown. Struggling to draw the coarse garment over her head, she gasped, "Whatever you feel about me personally, I beg you to consider your sons. It is for them too. Or do you care nothing for them?"

A sob caught in Marie's throat and she stared with watery gaze at the muffled figure before her. "They mean everything to me. Have you seen them? Are they safe? Ah, God, they tell me nothing."

"Your husband is taking them to safety at this moment."

Rosslyn waited while Marie fumbled with her own gray striped dress, the soiled fabric tearing beneath her trembling fingers. "Why are you doing this? He will most certainly leave you, he always does. My husband is handsome, charming, and totally faithless. He never mentioned you. I'm sure nothing was said about a foreign woman—oh, yes, I know that by your accent—here."

The gowns were exchanged, then the shoes and the cloak. Rosslyn wrapped her head in Marie's gauze scarf in the hope of concealing her own dark hair. Watching her, Marie smiled sadly.

"When I first entered Temple prison my hair was dark like yours; now look at it, gray as someone's grandmother. And my boys. What have they done to them? I hear tell at the Cour des Femmes how they've taken the Dauphin—taught him unspeakable acts, made him say—oh, such things about Her Majesty. I dread to think what my boys . . ."

Cold, bony hands gripped Rosslyn's arm and by the quiver in the other woman's voice she knew Marie wept.

"You must not think about it now. You will soon be reunited, Madame. I promise."

"And what of you? Surely you've not elected to give your life."

"They'll release me later," Rosslyn said confidently. "It's part of the plan. So hurry before that man comes back."

Removing the loaves Rosslyn thrust the empty basket into Marie's hands.

"I'm sorry to have been so unkind to you. It's this prison—and I've always been jealous of his women. Tell me, does my husband love you?" Marie asked.

Uncomfortable at the question, Rosslyn looked away from the faded, anxious face. "Yes, I believe he does."

"At least he says so. What else have we women to go by?" Marie shrugged, then lingeringly she caressed Rosslyn's cheek. "Thank you, whoever you are, for my sons' sake, if not my own."

"I am . . ."

"No, don't tell me. I'd rather not remember your name. Have you children?"

"I had a son. He died," Rosslyn managed to say, finding it still hurt to speak of Will.

"Was he . . ." Marie stopped, unable to continue as her voice cracked. She swallowed and withdrew her hand. "Was your son fathered by my husband?"

"No, Madame."

Footsteps rang along the corridor and in the parting moments of the lurid stormlight, Rosslyn saw Marie smile at her words.

"I'm glad."

Then the jailor opened the door and Rosslyn shrank into the shadows far from the shaft of light, thankful to find a different figure framed in the doorway. "Come, citizeness, time to go." Other feet echoed down the passages, voices and grating locks announcing the general exodus of afternoon visitors while above all booming thunder echoed through the dank stone walls of the Conciergerie. Without speaking Marie raised her hand in farewell before she disappeared, the door clanging behind her with an ominous ring of finality.

It was quite dark now and still Rosslyn waited. She had dozed briefly on the straw mattress after eating some of the bread. Noises seemed to have intensified about her, sounding so close they might have been in the room. Though the walls were thick, the vaultlike rooms magnified sound until the echoes formed a frightening chorus of coughs and moans. Covering her ears to shut out the hideous sound, Rosslyn wondered if Armand had left the prison yet, or whether he had been captured. The thought that he was free to assist her whenever the chain of events led her from this subterranean hellhole, gave Rosslyn a resurgence of strength as she curled on the mattress to wait.

It had been difficult to walk away from Rosslyn, to leave her alone on these dangerous, unfamiliar streets in the pelting rain, but Armand knew it must be done. Hastening through the gloom, head down against the elements, he drew his dark cloak tighter, clutching low over his eyes a battered felt hat, once black, now with a green patina of age.

Entry to the Conciergerie was easy; leaving was the difficult part. Standing in the shadows on the fringe of the crowd Armand waited, hoping there was no one present who recognized him. The wine bottles he clutched beneath his cloak had warmed against his body to become friendly instead of alien as they had at first seemed. People drifted towards the battered desk where the two guards took down particulars, puffed up with importance at their job. For this wet day the crowd of visitors seemed unusually large.

At last his turn came and Armand straightened his shoulders and strode forward. A fat miller, still in his floury apron turned now to soggy paste with the drenching rain, elbowed him out of the way.

"Not so fast. I'm next," he bellowed, glowering at the audacity of this man who dared step ahead of him.

A brief exchange with the guards and money changed hands. Bestowing a parting glare in Armand's direction, the miller rolled through the doorway to the prison proper.

Armand lounged against the wall taking in the bleary-eyed guard and his middle-aged companion, assessing their weakness; not too hard a task, for several empty wine bottles clanked beneath the table.

"And you, citizen, who do you wish to see?"

"The sons of the traitor Charles Gabriel Armand de Gramont, Comte de . . ."

"Enough! This isn't Versailles, citizen," the old one sniggered, wiping his rheumy eyes on a ragged cuff.

"And who might you be, my grand seigneur?"

Leaning nonchalantly on the desk, Armand grinned, displaying the carefully blackened teeth, which in the dark room appeared to be missing. "I'm a free man, citizen, that's who I am. Come to gloat, you might say. I used to be the little bastards' tutor before the glorious revolution."

"Ah, a man of letters," scoffed the first guard. "Here, sign this."

Armand carefully lettered the spotted page René Laurent, who had indeed been his sons' tutor, hoping the men were in ignorance of the man's whereabouts and his true appearance.

"René Laurent," the guard read laboriously. "Well, what are you bringing?"

Like a conjuror producing a rabbit from his hat, Armand whisked forth the gleaming wine bottles, placing them on the desk. "For you, citizen, and another for you. They'll never miss that."

Grunts of pleasure and assent followed as the bottles were examined and exclaimed over.

"A good year that," the young one muttered, unconsciously licking his lips. "Will you join us, citizen."

"How generous of you." Armand accepted the inch of dark wine they offered him, swimming about in the base of a cracked mug. With sighs of pleasure the men upended the bottles and guzzled noisily, eyes half-closed in sheer bliss.

Warily Armand sipped a little of his own wine, wondering how potent was the sleeping draught with which Clarence had laced the offering. Bitterness was a vile addition to the ruby wine, yet the unrefined taste of the guards was a blessing for they suspected nothing.

"Now, am I free to visit the little darlings and gloat over their current predicament?" he asked, leaning forward on the desk and exchanging grins with the men.

"Of course, citizen, go ahead. The rest of you can go home. No more visitors today."

The few remaining men shuffled towards the corridor, knowing pleas were useless once a decision like that had been made.

Staggering to his feet the young guard sat down again abruptly, the key bouncing from his hand. "Ah, a kick like a mule," he chuckled, beaming foolishly in Armand's direction. "On second thoughts you're trustworthy, René Laurent. Here, let yourself in."

Laughing and belching, the two benign guards

grinned at him. Saluting them, inwardly muttering prayers of thanks, Armand took the key and went through the inner door.

The stench of French prisons was a readily remembered horror; he almost did not hold his breath any more as he hurried down the hollow-ringing passage towards his sons' cell.

When he entered the cell, Armand swallowed surprise and pity at their appearance. Emaciated, for all the food he had bought, dirty for all the soap, ragged for all the clothes—

Placing his finger to his lips, he shut the door. At first they did not recognize him and the small boys turned wide, apathetic eyes in his direction before looking back to their game, a form of cat's cradle plaited from straw.

"Louis. Charles. Don't you know me?"

Speechless they looked up, peering in the gloom.

"Papa!" Louis scrambled to his feet, throwing himself like a whirlwind into his father's arms. Six-year-old Charles followed his older brother's actions, but he was more doubtful of this stranger in the tattered, greasy clothes. *His* father had dressed splendidly, had worn his hair powdered and was somewhere miles away with the glamorous courtiers of King Louis's court.

"Papa! Are you really my papa?" Charles whispered, pulling back, somewhat afraid of the stranger. It was two years since he had seen his father, and that was a long time to recall the shadowy image of splendor who rode an immense chestnut and held him aloft, tickling him until he succumbed to squeals of delight.

"I am your papa. Now, can you do as I say? We've little time, so listen carefully."

Squatting on the straw mattress, he held the boys close, shielding them with the strength of his arms, wanting to undo whatever damage this frightening, unnatural existence had wrought.

"Is Mama with you?" Charles asked, interrupting him.

Armand smiled and squeezed his son's bony arm. "She will join us this afternoon."

"Is the revolution over?"

Armand exchanged glances with his older son, who, though he had not been told, seemed to know instinctively what they were about.

"Don't ask Papa so many questions. Shut up and listen," he admonished, giving Charles a push.

"At the desk they know me as Monsieur Laurent . . ."

"Our tutor?"

"Yes. It was the first name which came to mind. Anyway, the men at the desk are probably asleep by now. I've got cloaks for you. When we are outside you are to be my nephews. No one will know you did not come in with me. Can you do that?"

"Of course. Can't we, Charles?"

The younger boy nodded his head solemnly, looking towards his primitive toy. "Can I take this with me?" he asked.

Armand assured him he could. Unwrapping the swathing yards of fabric from around his middle, he handed them the warm garments.

"Now you look more like yourself," Louis remarked seeing Armand's middle decrease by inches.

"Have you water?"

"Over there in the bucket. It stinks. It's from the river."

"Never mind that. Come here."

Armand wet their hair, silencing Charles's loud protests with a stern glance.

"What's that for? It's cold and I don't like it," the boy complained, trying to rub his hair dry.

"Because it's raining outside. Now you'll look as if you've been on the streets."

Louis smiled in admiration at the brilliance of his father's idea, splashing further drops on his cloak and face.

He had been inside the cell less than ten minutes, but Armand was anxious to leave. He opened the door to cautiously survey the corridor. It was deserted.

In single file they hastened towards freedom, amazed at the simplicity of the ruse. Armand hesitated before they entered the guards' room wondering if he would be recognized. He need not have worried for the two men snored contentedly at their desks, oblivious to the milling throng crowding the room where they busily rifled the unguarded offerings behind the desk.

Seizing the boys by the hand, Armand pushed his way to the door, not breathing evenly until the clanging gates of the Conciergerie were closed behind them. The boys stumbled at the required effort, legs stiff with disuse and the daylight, though murky gray, hurt their eyes after months of confinement.

Armand drew them into the shelter of a doorway to wait for Marie.

A few minutes later he saw her coming, recognizable by the proud carriage which accentuated her height, making her head and shoulders taller than most women. Inwardly he wished she had presence of mind enough to stoop to make herself less noticeable. The chilling thought that she walked free on the street because Rosslyn had bought her release by sacrificing her own freedom, flitted through his mind and was immediately discarded. The outcome of the plot was not in his hands. Only by maintaining a clear head could he be assured of the completion of his part in it.

Behind him Charles had begun to whimper. Louis hugged his brother close awaiting further instructions from his father who stationed himself at the shop entrance in order to watch the street. Thunder rolled making the small boy cry out in alarm until his brother held him muffled against his chest so as not to draw attention to themselves.

Watching his wife move rapidly towards them, Armand waited. He did not tell the boys she was in sight and a moment later, when he made a chilling discovery, he was glad. Just as Marie reached the branching of the streets, negotiating the bridge with ease, hastening her footsteps towards the rendezvous, two shadowy figures emerged from an alley to seize her arms. Too surprised to call out, Marie was taken without a struggle.

With heart throbbing so loud he was sure it must be audible to the passersby, Armand stepped deeper in the shadows. They were betrayed! With the discovery came fear for Rosslyn's safety. Had the prison guards discovered Marie's escape she would not have been allowed to leave the courtyard of the Conciergerie, let alone cross

162

the river: Those men who awaited her had known the time and the place. None other than Bernard could have sent them. Trying to plan his next move, imagining unseen agents waiting in the gloom, Armand knew he must get off the street.

"Are you hungry?" he asked his sons, gripping their shoulders.

"Starving for real food," Louis agreed.

"Very well. There's a pie shop next door. Let's see what they have to offer." With sinking heart Armand counted the money in his pocket, rapidly fingering the bills which Clarence had given him for their board. If they made a meal of the pies at the currently inflated price of goods they would have little left over, assignats having fallen to nearly a fifth of their original value. The sudden emergence from the shadows of two somberly cloaked figures who glanced about the street as if looking for someone, made the decision for him.

"Pork pies. Do you fancy those?"

The boys' eyes rounded in delight. With a flurry of tattered cloaks Armand swept them sidling around the bow front of the pie shop from which an enticing aroma wafted into the wet afternoon.

Behind the misted pane Armand watched the two spies traverse the street twice, seeming puzzled by their inability to find their quarry. Just as he expected, the men stationed themselves across the street from Madame Casteel's wine shop to await developments. The entire plan was known to Bernard, so therefore the entire plan as he knew it must be discarded. Frowning, Armand watched his sons devour their food in delight, licking their filth-encrusted fingers, even licking the crumbs from the greasy scarred table where they were seated. The animal behavior of his once refined children caused him little more than a flicker of regret; good manners belonged to the past. He must decide what to do with them now, to find them shelter far from the prying watchfulness of Bernard's spies.

Seeing the food was gone, he paid the bill and put the meager change in his pocket. Taking the boys by the hand, they escaped through the back door of the establishment into a garbage-littered alley.

CHAPTER TEN

When morning came with still no sign of release, despite her feigned bravery, Rosslyn was afraid. What had gone wrong? She was to be released before the afternoon was out; now here it was the following day and still no word.

With her breakfast of a crust of bread and some foul sourness in a battered cup, Rosslyn found three companions thrust unceremoniously inside her cell. When she tried to speak to the guard she was told to shut up.

"You fool, can't you see I'm not Citizeness de Gramont? She overpowered me and escaped in my clothes. Since yesterday afternoon I've been shut in here with no one to attend to me."

The man chuckled. "A good try, citizeness."

"Look at me! You must have seen her. You know I'm not she."

"Yes, I knew her."

"Well then?" Rosslyn tried to keep the sobs out of her voice, though despair was rapidly mounting at his disinterest.

"It's all the same to me. You're here now. If you weren't supposed to be in the cell, you wouldn't be. Gramont, or whatever you choose to call yourself, makes no difference to me. Now shut up and eat your meal. It's all you'll get till nighttime."

Shocked into silence, Rosslyn stared at the door as it swung shut, hearing the terrible finality of the bolts and keys rattling the length of the stone corridor as the man continued his rounds.

"If you don't want your food, I'll have it."

Numbly Rosslyn gave the bread to a middle-aged woman who grabbed her arm. She was a wispy, beady-eyed creature, her scarecrow gown hanging in tatters. Turning her attention to the others Rosslyn saw they were a young woman clutching a child and a girl of about fifteen whose eyes rolled in fright as she huddled by the wall.

"It's a terrible mistake. I'm not supposed to be here," Rosslyn muttered to them, unable to suppress tears which betrayed her despair.

"Can't we all say that?" dismissed the woman with the child. "You're a fool for not eating. You'll be sorry tomorrow."

The women went to the straw mattress which Rosslyn realized she now must share with them. The quarters had been vile enough with only one inhabitant, with five it would be unbearable.

Finding the child grown heavy, the young woman attempted to lay him on the mattress where he was promptly pushed off by the old hag.

Knowing instinctively it was no use appealing to their sensibilities, Rosslyn crouched beside the young mother to assist her with the boy, for the woman's strength was gone.

The middle-aged hag with the wild hair glared hostilely at her, muttering unintelligible insults. She must be the girl's mother for she sat close beside her where she burrowed into the mattress on hands and knees, while her mother, if that is who she was, searched for fleas on their clothing.

"Is he ill?" Rosslyn whispered, not knowing why she whispered as she touched the boy's hot face.

"No, just tired. We were in a cell with ten others. There was nowhere to sleep and they stole our food. At least you were alone. That's much better."

"How long have you been here?"

"Two weeks . . . three. I can't remember."

"My name's Rosslyn. What's yours?"

"Solange," the girl whispered back, peering through the gloom, surprised to find someone who cared enough to ask her name. "He's Luc."

Pain stirring in her breast, Rosslyn drew the small boy against her, reminded acutely of Will when the child gripped her hand in friendship.

"Hello, Luc. Would you like some bread?"

The boy grunted his acceptance, surprising Rosslyn by the voraciousness of his appetite.

"Can I have some?" Solange asked, unconsciously licking her lips as she watched her child devour the delicacy.

"Of course. There's another loaf here. I won't need them. I'm to be released shortly."

"Where've I heard that before," Solange said, seizing the offering, stuffing the heavenly concoction in her mouth. "You must have rich friends to get good stuff like this."

"Yes, I have friends."

The woman on the mattress glared hostilely at them because she had not been offered food nor had she been clever enough to notice the bread in the filthy corner. Had she done so, she would not have awaited an invitation.

"What's the matter with her?" Rosslyn whispered to Solange, eyeing the young girl who had begun a soft crooning to herself, rocking an imaginary baby in her arms while the old one continued the hunt for lice.

Solange shook her head. "We were in the same cell with them before. She had a baby in prison and she killed it. The old one's her grandmother. A couple of whores if you ask me."

"Who're you calling whore?" the old one cried, leaping up to seize Solange by the hair.

They grappled half-heartedly a moment, then parted as if by mutual consent, the old one going back to her task, taking pleasure in crushing the little creatures between her jagged fingernails.

Solange grinned, "Don't look so worried. No one's got enough energy to fight much."

Rosslyn smiled, reaching out in friendship to this stranger who offered her only link to sanity. "Why are you here?"

With a shrug Solange crouched on the floor. "My man was arrested for stealing something from a member of the Committee. He's gone now. We haven't enough money or influence to buy ourselves out of here. They

166

tell me my name will come up soon. They never make you wait long here."

Aghast Rosslyn wondered how knowledgable the girl actually was. They called the Conciergerie the antechamber of death; surely justice was not so swift that her own name would appear on a list before Clarence and Armand were able to free her.

Rosslyn crouched beside Solange, disliking her smell, but needing the warmth of companionship. Besides, she was aware that her own borrowed dress had begun to exude a musty odor. So sure had she been of imminent rescue yesterday, she had either not cared, or not noticed the rankness of this garment. Now its odor wafted to her in all its unpleasantness.

The other girl had great dark hollows under blue eyes which peered shortsightedly from under straggling yellow hair which may once have been pretty, but now was little more than a tangled mane. It was too difficult to learn more about her appearance in this light.

"What was that stuff you were telling the guard? Is it true?"

"Of course it's true," Rosslyn retorted indignantly. "This is all a terrible mistake."

Solange sniffled, wiping her nose on her arm. "It doesn't matter. Even if they know you're not the right one, they don't bother. Last week two women with the same name were executed. The guard said he didn't care which one was wanted by the tribunal, they'd both go sooner or later. Who's going to help you, Rosslyn? Your man?"

"He and my brother."

"Is he handsome?" Solange asked, imprisonment not totally extinguishing her interest in the opposite sex.

"Yes. Was yours?"

Solange rolled her eyes, her mouth turning up in a weak smile. "As good as I could hope to get. I'm just a flower seller. He was a carter. We were managing well until he took that mirror. Not worth it really, because we couldn't eat a mirror. Now, I ask you, why would he take that? So I could see myself, the fool said. Got himself killed just to satisfy my vanity."

Rosslyn said nothing, hearing the catch in the girl's

voice as she explained. "How old is Luc?" she asked at last.

"Three. You have children?"

"No, mine died."

"Well at least you didn't go all crazed like Loopy there," Solange snapped, smiling cruelly as the old woman started to her feet, then fell back. "What did your man do for a living?"

Rosslyn could not help smiling at the question, at the sheer insanity of this situation. Close to hysteria, she smothered foolish laughter which bubbled to the surface. "Nothing," she muttered.

Misinterpreting the meaning behind her statement, Solange patted her arm in sympathy.

"Ha, there are plenty of those about nowadays, shiftless fools. Still, if you had children, he wasn't totally wasted."

For the next hour they fell silent. Rosslyn could hardly bear to watch the crazed girl who alternated between clutching fear and that ceaseless rocking movement.

In the afternoon they were allowed to wash themselves at the courtyard fountain; on certain days clothes were washed also, but for some reason today the exercise period was to be only five minutes. The Cour des Femmes was where Marie St. Clare had obtained her gossip, Rosslyn remembered her mentioning it. This courtyard with its splashing fountain and benches was the social center of prison life. Unthinkable that here, in this filthy hopelessness, women should care to gossip; but gossip they did, their voices rising to a shrill chorus. Yet even here in this seemingly peaceful remnant of sanity the fearful purpose of the Conciergerie probed its icy fingers. A guard came to the gate and rang a bell to announce the arrival of the tumbril for the condemned.

Closing her ears to the tearful parting of the victims from friends and relatives, Rosslyn helped Solange wash Luc in the cold water, wondering if Marie was safely reunited with her children. She prayed there had been nothing prophetic in Marie's question about her intention to sacrifice her own life. Though Rosslyn had decided to help rescue Armand's wife, she had not been prepared to die for her. To have to die for anyone, even for Armand, had been far from her thoughts. Her approach to this situation, this charade, had been too nonchalant. The adventure of it had filled her mind; now she had all the leisure time in the world to repent for her folly.

After a hideous cramped night, the morrow dawned sunny. A pale shaft of sunlight came in the high window, lighting their faces. Rosslyn and Solange stood in the warm beam, rejoicing in the warmth of the sun. Soon they heard the banging passage of authority and hunger drove her to accept whatever food was offered this morning. Rosslyn stood back to allow them to open the door.

To her surprise it was not the shuffling jailor with his rancid offerings, but a man with a rolled parchment in his hand. At the gasp of horror from those behind her, Rosslyn knew without being told this was the dreaded roll call. Someone in this cell had reached the top of the list!

Clasping her hands till her fingers felt close to breaking she waited, not looking about, not wanting to watch their faces when the name was read.

"Citizeness Gramont," the man announced in a sonorous voice.

"That's you," Solange hissed, nudging her forward.

"No, I told you, it's a mistake. I'm Rosslyn Burton. I told the guard what happened yesterday."

The man assessed her a moment without speaking, seeing her frightened eyes forming black circles in the gray light. "So you're the one, eh! He told me you were babbling some such nonsense. So you say you're not Citizeness Gramont."

She shook her head, not trusting her trembling mouth to deny it again.

"Where is she then?"

"I don't know. She took my clothes and escaped."

He bellowed with laughter. "Come on, citizeness, time to go."

"You don't believe me."

"That's right. Even if I did it wouldn't make any difference. A Citizeness Gramont from this cell is on the

169

list. If it isn't those cows, that leaves only you. And you're not half bad, if I may say so. Perhaps we can put you to some good use first."

Stumbling, trying to resist his crushing grip, Rosslyn moved in a daze through the dripping corridor where people were jostled like cattle. Those about her either sobbed or bore their sentence with stoic indifference.

Her trial at the Palais de Justice was farcial. Now she understood the true meaning of the term "antechamber of death." Once you were at the Conciergerie there was little hope of eluding Monsieur Guillotine.

As the nightmare continued, weak from lack of food and fear, Rosslyn huddled miserably on a stone bench with the other hopeless prisoners awaiting the final word.

"Are you Citizeness Gramont?" a man asked at her side.

Forcing her burning, swollen eyes open, Rosslyn saw white britches and clean black boots. Allowing her gaze to travel upward she saw the glint of a watchchain on a brocade waistcoat. Though dull, the man's clothing had the look of quality about it.

No longer did she deny that identity. They had slapped her for telling the truth; they had fumbled her body; they had stopped short of raping her only when their superior came into the room. No, she no longer denied being Marie, it was too painful being Rosslyn Burton. Being Marie Gramont brought her peace.

Nodding, she looked back to the floor, seeing dust and phlegm where the sick had coughed out their lungs while awaiting sentence.

"Come, citizeness, I would have a word with you in private."

Hands raised her from the bench. Used to the normal pattern of treatment, Rosslyn wondered if this man was one of the prison officials who fancied her for himself. They had laughed about delaying her execution a few days to allow them all a sample.

"Where are you taking me?"

He did not reply, only urged her towards a deserted corridor, speeding her faltering steps to a room at the end of the long dark passage.

When the door opened she saw a group of men seated around a table. They did not speak to her, merely looked her over, referring to sheaves of papers before them on the table, mingled haphazardly among glasses and flagons of wine and brandy.

"This is the one?"

"Yes."

"Well, I knew Citizeness Gramont and she never looked like that." The speaker was a young man who stared pointedly at the rent in Rosslyn's tight bodice.

"So you, girl, say you were falsely arrested?"

Gulping, Rosslyn steadied her shaking limbs, leaning on the table edge for support. "Not arrested, Monsieur, detained. I was Citizeness Gramont's maid. She overpowered me and escaped. Though I've tried to tell the guards, no one listened to me."

They smiled at her story in scornful disbelief.

"What shall we do with her?"

The young one laughed rudely. "If you don't know the answer to that question, Partier, you're older than you think."

There followed a round of laughter during which Rosslyn closed her eyes, feeling a wave of weakness wash over her limbs, hating them for their crude attitude. Twisted, crumpled neckcloths and shaggy hair betrayed their class. Yet for all that, they shared that same contemptuous assessment of females as did Jarvis and his titled gambling cronies. How far from Burton Hill she was, yet how near.

"Let me dispose of her."

For the first time the man who had brought her to this room spoke. All eyes swiveled in his direction where he stood beside the door, half-forgotten in their eagerness.

"If you insist. But let me ask, why do you get all the gems, my friend?" the young one demanded hostilely, his hard brown eyes flashing.

"Because, André, I am your superior."

With that he caught Rosslyn's arm and propelled her through the door.

"Do not be afraid, Madame, you are safe now."

In surprise she listened to the smooth soft voice

speaking words which must be part of a dream. Stumbling, Rosslyn steadied herself against the cold plaster.

"Safe," she gasped, thinking she was delirious.

He smiled, his face an uncertain blurr through her misted vision. His mouth moved again, she knew, for she saw the gleam of white teeth, but she did not hear his words for the filthy floorboards slapped her jarringly in the face.

When Rosslyn opened her eyes she was bumping about on a carriage seat, the empty vehicle dark as night with leather curtains secured over the windows. Fear gripped her at her possible destination; yet it could not be the Place de Grave where the towering guillotine awaited, for prisoners were transported there by tumbril. The rattling wheels of those open carts had sounded their death music while she waited in terror for the verdict on her trial, taking the first load of the day to feed that insatiable class leveler.

Banging on the murky pane where she could see the outline of the driver's dark coat was to no avail. The man obviously had orders not to speak to her. All that remained now was to have patience. There was no escape through the carriage doors for they too were tightly secured. Rosslyn guessed she was bound for her rescuer's dwelling, wherever that might be, her duties there a foregone conclusion.

Somewhere in these teeming streets walked Armand, reunited now with his wife and sons, a family once more. It was she who was the outsider. Unknown to Clarence, had this been the intention all along? Nausea gripped her at the thought, until she swiftly quelled it. Jeanette was the intended captive, only by chance had she inherited the role. The trial, even this journey, could be part of the plan. At this comforting idea, her spirits soared. And Rosslyn huddled in a protective ball bracing herself against the bouncing conveyance to await her destiny.

Her reception, when at last the carriage completed its journey, was like a dream come true, complete with hot water, clean clothes and nourishing food. She had not

realized how ravenously hungry she was until the enticing aroma of stew filtered through the air.

When the meal was finished her rescuer made his appearance. Carrying his hat and cloak, he apparently just
reached the rendezvous himself.

Finding her vastly changed from the dirty, pale
wretch he had rescued at the Palais de Justice, the man
smiled his obvious pleasure at her transformation.

"Ah, Madame, my humble apologies for your vile
treatment," he tendered, bowing over her hand.

Still wary of his intentions, yet so relieved to find
herself free at last, Rosslyn could have seized him and
kissed his smooth face in relief. Instead she allowed him
to kiss her hand. While he made his apologies she
quickly assessed his appearance. Possibly thirty, of me-
dium height, his face was pale in startling contrast to his
black eyes and smooth hair jet black against his face.
By his courteous manner and genteel speech she recognized him as a man of breeding, the fact echoed in his
clothes which, while somber, were of impeccable cut.
He was a far cry from the scruffy, desperate group she
had encountered throughout the Palais de Justice who
with their fiery rhetoric condemned the corruption of
the vile aristocracy. He seemed the embodiment of the
very class they vilified. When he gave his name a moment later, she knew the reason.

"I am Bernard Desjardins, Madame. And you?"

Gasping, clinging to his hand in relief, Rosslyn
gulped down her surprise. "Bernard! Oh, God, what
fortune. Yes, I know you. I've waited . . ."

"Your name?"

Surprised he did not know it, Rosslyn suddenly remembered it was Jeanette who was supposedly part of
the plot. "Rosslyn, Lady Burton. Forgive me, I did not
realize you were confused about my identity."

"A thousand pardons, Lady Burton, for your inhu-
man treatment. Had I been in Paris such a thing would
not have taken place. As it was, I was called away on
urgent business. Tell me, how is it possible for a lovely
English lady to become involved in high intrigue?"

"Jeanette was injured and I took her place."

"So you are the Englishman's sister. Ah, now I see.

173

How can I explain? There is no way. I can only beg your forgiveness. Perhaps time will erase the unpleasantness of your recent experience."

"I hope so. Unpleasant is hardly the word."

He smiled as he placed his hat and gloves on the table. The cloak followed to reveal a handsome suit of rust whipcord, frothed with gleaming white linen at his throat. From under lowered lashes he scrutinized the narrow waist and full bodice of this English noblewoman. Her face he had already memorized. Though Armand had not told him there had been a substitution, this woman's probable relationship to his cousin was betrayed by her beauty. Armand never could resist an attractive woman.

"Think no more about it, my dear lady," he dismissed smoothly. "Did you have sufficient to eat? I was unable to accompany you personally, but my staff were instructed to treat you well."

"The food was delicious, Monsieur."

"No, not monsieur. You must call me Bernard. After all, we are not total strangers, you were familiar with me in absentia."

He smiled and Rosslyn smiled back. On the tip of her tongue were a thousand questions which he seemed in no hurry to answer. He must know she burst with worry and curiosity about Armand, about the plans which seemed to have gone awry, unless this seeming rescue from the jaws of death was the natural outcome of their plot.

"Was it your intention to keep me in prison?"

"Until afternoon, no more. Jeanette was not supposed to suffer," he said softly, coming to her side, his dark eyes lit by a smile.

"Those two days seemed an eternity."

"Two days? Oh, my dear, how much you did suffer. Is that all you can remember?"

Aghast, Rosslyn stared at him, at the sympathetic smile he bathed her in, at the air of gentility he exuded. She knew it was his intention to make her feel safe, to assure her of his good intent, yet somehow she felt uneasy instead, not a definable emotion, rather a nagging feeling of doubt deep inside.

"You must be mistaken. I spent only one night." Though she had thought herself convinced, the more he insisted, the less Rosslyn was sure of the accuracy of her own memory. Had she been in Conciergerie longer than she knew? There was no reason for him to lie, no point to it, especially since he had been the one to rescue her from danger.

"Think no more of it, my dear. The passage of time is immaterial. You are safe now."

"But Armand was to meet me that afternoon."

"You seem attached to my cousin, that's apparent from your concern." Bernard turned away and began to pace the room, his slender hands clenched before him as if he wrestled with an immense problem. "Am I correct in saying you are in love with him?"

"Yes. Why else would I have taken such risks?"

"Oh, my dear," his voice was laden with sympathy as he stopped his pacing, studying her in the fading afternoon light.

"What is it? Why do you look at me like that? Is he here?"

Bernard sighed. "I rescued you from prison. No other was involved. In whose carriage did you journey? Was Armand beside you clasping your hand in assurance? Did he worry enough to save you from the tribunal?" The soft voice acquired an edge of anger. "What gave you the idea he would be here?"

Rosslyn swallowed the lump rising in her throat. Desperately she clung to her trust, despite what seemed to be so obviously emerging from their discussion. "When I did not meet him at the rendezvous I thought perhaps he waited for me here," she explained carefully, fighting a wave of shock.

Bernard smiled at her, moving closer, the pungence of his cologne a refreshing change after the assorted smells of the Conciergerie. "How can I say this to you, especially after coming so far, after risking your life—ah, my cousin's a cruel devil. The truth is—he waits nowhere for you."

She stared at him, hardly comprehending his words. From somewhere came snatches of drunken singing and Bernard moved to close the window.

"Forgive me for being blunt. I cannot bear to see you suffer," he continued huskily, reaching for her.

Rosslyn did not want his caresses, but in the numbness of her discovery she was vulnerable to the promise of male strength. Half-sobbing, she relaxed against his arm, glad of the supportive gesture as he drew her close.

"Cry if you must. Best to be over with it now," he whispered.

"But he said he would wait."

"Yes, perhaps he did. A day or two. But you've been close to a week in prison. Madame Casteel's is not a permanent lodging."

"Where is he then? Where are his family?"

Bernard shrugged. "Safely hidden, we must hope."

Gaining her composure, Rosslyn struggled to be free and he released her at once. Uncomfortably aware of the penetrating gaze of those dark eyes, she went to the window. The narrow street was dirty and windblown. Beggars crowded the doorway of the bake shop opposite, its windows dark and empty at this late hour. Constant noise and drab, poverty-ridden buildings seemed to characterize this portion of the city, presenting a medieval relic which had long outlived its usefulness.

"Where will you go now?"

Bernard's voice brought her back to this room and her rescuer, whom she had not yet thanked.

"I have nowhere to go except home to England. Thank you for your concern, Monsieur; without it I shudder to think what would have become of me. Have you no news of my brother? Without him I know nothing of our plans." How serene she sounded, calling desperately on that composure she had often practiced as Lady Burton. No one would have guessed at the pain shredding her emotions because of Armand's desertion, of the near panic which assailed her each time she contemplated the ensuing days in this foreign capital without friends or money.

"Clarence has already returned to London."

The gasp which escaped her, despite the ironbound control, betrayed Rosslyn's great fear. Bernard noted the discovery with pleasure.

"Gone home! Without me?"

"My dear, it was not lack of concern on *his* part." Wanting to offer his embrace in comfort, yet hesitant, knowing she was no mere serving girl, Bernard offered wine instead. "Your brother was unable to delay his return. Your imprisonment, which, had I not been out of the city, would never have occurred, complicated his plans. You must understand his position."

"Of course. I understand, but where does that leave me?"

"Perhaps your husband . . . no, I see what a foolish suggestion that was." Mentally crossing the husband off the list, Bernard continued smoothly. "Until your family contacts you, Madame, may I offer you shelter. My dwelling is in St. Germaine, not lavish, but you are welcome to use it until you can make arrangements of your own."

Touched by his generosity, Rosslyn accepted at once, having no other choice. "You are most kind, Monsieur."

"Ah, but I am honored to have so lovely a lady to grace my salon."

And grace the salon she did.

To her surprise and uneasy pleasure, Rosslyn found a heap of gowns awaiting her when she woke the next morning. Though the gowns had not been made for her, and Rosslyn did not ask him for whom they had been intended, she selected four which gave a reasonable fit. With a maid to dress her hair, a sheer luxury, for since she had left England she had barely managed to brush the tangled mass, Rosslyn found she had not lost the ability to appear elegant, even in borrowed finery.

Bernard Desjardins's blue-shuttered house was situated on a quiet side street. For a revolutionary leader he appeared to live in grand style behind these tall stone walls which hid a small garden and inner court where a fountain tinkled musically through the house. A housekeeper and two maids kept the premises immaculate. The furnishings were in surprisingly good taste. Rosslyn had to remind herself, though he embraced the popular style of the people, Bernard was, after all, born to the aristocracy. His speech and manners were as polished as any gentleman of her acquaintance. And he was Armand's cousin.

Pain stabbed deep at the reminder; tears of dejection came to her eyes. To find Armand gone after enduring the hateful indignities of prison, only kept bearable by the reminder of his love, by the thought that he waited, concerned for her safety, was more than she could bear. Marie St. Clare had been right after all—"a hundred more like you," she had said. At the time the words had stung with venom. But then she had faith in Armand so she had not believed; faith in those sweet vows he whispered, the words of love . . .

"You are divine."

A voice from the doorway broke her chain of thought. Rosslyn turned, her eyes bright and hard with tears. Through the blur a male figure came into focus, an elegant figure in emerald brocade, sparked with amber, in pale kidskin boots, a glittering jeweled stickpin in his cravat.

"Thank you," she managed, forcing her legs to move towards him where he stood, hand extended, in the doorway. The heavy pink satin dress rustled as she walked.

"Divine," he repeated as she came to his side.

"After weeks of rags I find the dresses a glad exchange."

"Perhaps you shall soon have gowns made for you again, Rosslyn."

The husky promise, made with fervent handclasp, recurred during the afternoon to torment her, spoiling her pleasure in the afternoon party. Slowly the realization that things were not quite as they seemed penetrated her mind. Charming Bernard had been the model of politeness, he had made not the slightest improper gesture towards her, yet now, as she dwelled on his manner, doubt assailed her. Was he lingering over the conquest in order to gain her confidence, if conquest he intended?

The grand salon had walls of turquoise brocade lavished with plaster moldings of gilded cherubs. More cherubs played harps and shot bows in the manner of Cupid, dangling precariously from the fan-vaulted ceiling, their naked flesh plumply rosy in the heated candlelight. Swagged brocade draperies fringed in gold hung at the long windows which overlooked the courtyard, matching the gilt-legged court chairs upholstered in the same material. The air of this main salon was one of opulence, the odor of aristocracy at odds with the misborn collection of noisy dissidents Bernard befriended.

Even the manner in which she was treated by the motley assortment of friends who sauntered in and out of the salon throughout the afternoon, sharing gossip over the wine glasses, only heightened her suspicions. It was as if she was the acknowledged mistress of the house, a role which quite naturally, they assumed she fulfilled.

"You, citizeness, are by far the loveliest ornament ever to grace this house," complimented a tall, rakish young man in a sapphire blue suit of rumpled broadcloth, whose trousers of an exaggerated tight cut fitted his bulging muscles like a glove. His craggy face was suffused with a knowing grin which revealed a missing tooth. Large black eyes burned hotly beneath heavy coal-black brows, as dark as the straggling locks which formed a ragged mantle about his shoulders. Clinging to him was the aura of desperate intrigue, of dark plots concocted in small back rooms, of murder in forgotten alleys.

"Camille, enough. You'll frighten Rosslyn. You're enough to frighten anyone," Bernard intervened smoothly, yet behind the soft voice he betrayed his displeasure.

Camille seized her hand, and turning the palm uppermost, he planted a hot kiss there. "Ah, Bernard is an old spinster. If you are lonely, citizeness, ask anyone where to find me. I assure you, I'm quite well known in these parts."

"In brothels and wine shops."

"There too." Camille winked at her, then seizing his black hat in which an enormous tricolor rosette was pinned, he jammed the hat on his head and sauntered to the door.

"Buffoon," Bernard remarked, his eyes grown hard.

"I thought him bold as a pirate," she said in amusement, watching the wide blue shoulders disappear through the doorway.

"A thief, yes. Definitely not the man for you to befriend. Stay away from him."

Taken back by Bernard's swift warning, Rosslyn refrained from comment, knowing her position here was too insecure to raise his ire. His jealous reaction betrayed the answer to her questions however. Bernard had more than a casual interest in her well being, more than compassion behind his offer of lodging. Perhaps this heightened interest also led to lies about Armand, for she did not believe he could have deserted her so callously.

Thinking that perhaps the fierce Camille knew more than Bernard would have liked, hence his warning to stay away from him, Rosslyn waited till Bernard was engrossed with a group of men beside the windows before slipping into the corridor. Peering over the bannister, she saw Camille's blue suit in the shadows by the door. He was talking to someone. A giggle betrayed the identity of the young maid who squealed in delight at his inquiring fingers in the fichu of her bodice.

"Camille, I would have a word with you," Rosslyn called, trying to keep her voice low, yet make herself heard.

The couple sprang apart and the maid sped back to the kitchens. Camille looked upward with a confident grin as Rosslyn hastened downstairs.

"So, you already tire of the old maid," he joked, seizing her hands, not allowing her to pull free.

"Please, I must speak to you in private."

"All right. In here." Camille looked puzzled as he pushed open the door to a chill anteroom beside the entrance. "What is it you want, pretty one? And your name is Rosslyn?"

"Yes. How much do you know about Bernard?"

Camille grinned. "Enough to execute him ten times over. Why do you ask?"

"I thought as much. He told me to stay away from you."

With a shrug, Camille tossed aside his hat. "The

180

warning was twofold. Bernard has never had a woman as pretty as you before—and I have a certain reputation."

"He does not *have* me now," she declared hotly.

"Slow, but he'll get around to it."

"He's the cousin of my lover."

Taken aback, Camille released her hands. Pacing the room, his face turned serious, he said: "So that's why. I wondered. De Gramont is a wanted man."

"We met in England. While I was imprisoned at Conciergerie he was to wait for me, yet Bernard says he's gone. Do you know where?"

Camille viewed her with narrowed eyes. "What is my information worth to you, *cherie*?"

"Worth?"

"I'll expect payment for services rendered."

"I've no money. You can see I'm living on Bernard's charity."

"Before God, that will be a meager existence—ah, *ma petite,* I speak not of money. Being a man of few words I'll come to the point. The question you ask is a simple one. By tomorrow I'll have the answer for you." He came to her then, his large hand rough against her cheek.

"And," she prompted, staring into his bold black eyes.

Camille smiled, fastening his hand in the coiled ringlets to pull back her head before he whispered. "And, *ma petite,* my blood runs hot for you. Yield to me. Then you shall have your answer."

Rosslyn had expected as much, the parrying was merely an action for time. So, if she would learn Armand's fate, she must barter her body to this ruthless young man.

"How can I do that here? Bernard would know," she said, desperate to think of something to obligate him, while not fulfilling the obligation on her own part. But he was too clever for that.

"You give no answer at all. There are other places. Bernard does not hold all Paris in his grasp, much as he likes to think. You play stupid, coy games and I don't enjoy them."

He turned from her. Desperate that he not go without settling the issue, Rosslyn caught his arm. "Tell me where he is. If Bernard has lied to me, you shall have your reward."

Camille stopped, plainly tempted by her offer. With a shrug he turned towards her. "Usually I'm not this foolish, but all right, the offer's reasonable. Meet me here tomorrow and I'll tell you what you want to know."

"There's something else. My brother's part of Bernard's organization."

"Everyone's brother is part of Bernard's organization. Who might yours be?"

"Clarence Warner."

"Yes, I know him."

"Bernard says he's gone back to England. I can't believe he would desert me while I was in prison. If he's still in Paris get word to me."

"For these extras I shall expect extras," he added with a grin. "Come, something at least to seal the bargain."

Rosslyn yielded herself to his arms, pleasantly surprised by the answering feeling he ignited when he covered her mouth with his own. Opening her eyes, she stared into the black pools of light as he assessed her also. His face in shadow seemed evil with its large, hooked nose and heavy brows. Pleasure was reflected warmly in his face as he whispered:

"This may be the best bargain I've contracted all week."

Smiling, Rosslyn moved impatiently in his arms. "Hurry, Bernard will come looking for me. If he even suspected . . ."

"Ah, be careful, he's a man to be reckoned with. Yet of me he is afraid. Since that little Rolandin bitch finished off Marat, I've nearly as much power as he. This August promises to be a hot and bloody one."

To her surprise, while he spoke, Rosslyn discovered his roughened fingers had strayed to her bodice where, against her will, she found shivers prickling her flesh with goosebumps at his knowledgeable touch. Though he was not classically handsome, the forceful masculinity of this man held great sensual attraction for her,

her emotion heightened as he pressed her fleetingly against his muscular thighs.

"Yes, a very good bargain. *Au revoir* until tomorrow."

Leaning breathlessly against a nearby chair, Rosslyn swallowed the racing beat in her throat, surprised at her own betraying emotion. She did not love Camille. She did not even like him very much, yet she found in his arms a moment ago she had desired him.

Moments after Camille had clanged the front door behind him, Rosslyn heard Bernard calling her name. With an answering call, she sprang into action, hastening through the door to the empty hall just as he appeared at the head of the stairs.

"Here I am, Bernard. It was so hot upstairs. I went to the courtyard for a breath of fresh air."

Though he did not question her explanation, Rosslyn wondered uneasily if he believed her, for a frown crossed his face a moment before he assumed his usual benign smile.

The next evening Rosslyn was nervous of the anticipated rendezvous. Bernard had unwittingly invited Camille to dinner during which they were to discuss business. Though she was excluded from the meal, she knew Camille would arrange to see her privately. Convincing herself she must do this to discover the truth about Armand, must settle once and for all if Bernard lied, she still felt guilty at the fluttering anticipation she experienced when she contemplated her surrender. It was not until she heard Camille's footsteps on the stair that Rosslyn realized she had no guarantee he would not also lie if it served him well.

Tonight Camille wore blue and scarlet, replaying the colors of patriotism in his suit. The coat was blue faced with scarlet, the tight pants scarlet, in bold contrast to his white shirt. Sporting the usual cockade his tricorn was worn at a rakish angle even inside the house. In the flickering candlelight his face seemed darker than ever, the satanic cast of his features growing even more pronounced in the changing pattern of light.

"Bernard must go out for an hour, citizeness," he informed from the doorway. And he winked.

"Oh, is it something important?"

"Yes, of vital importance. Being such an influential man he's often called out late at night."

The speech, spoken overly loud, was for the housekeeper's benefit, who could be heard a moment later, quietly clicking her door shut.

Camille winked again as he inched the door closed behind him after an elaborately loud goodnight.

Rosslyn met his gaze, toying nervously with the frills which criss-crossed the front of her peach silk wrapper. It was time to pay, the bargain negotiated blithely enough, yet dreaded and anticipated at the same time.

"I like that dress," he complimented from the doorway, sweeping the length of her trailing gown with an extravagant gesture. "Bernard does not deserve such pleasant diversions. He's unworthy of you, *cherie*. Now, I, on the other hand, am a far better choice; more handsome, more virile, more well endowed, all in all, the perfect . . ."

"Please, be serious. What of your news? That first," she interrupted, smiling at his extravagant self-praise.

Camille grinned as he reluctantly dropped his hat to the chair. "Very well, first things first. Bernard deceived you. Your brother, while not in Paris, is not in London. He must be lying low awaiting word from you. I sent a message so you may expect to be contacted soon."

"And Armand?" she whispered, hating the tremor which crept into her voice when she spoke his name.

"Not dead. Not imprisoned. Not in Paris."

"What!"

"Perhaps he too lies low awaiting word. In my opinion even Bernard does not know where he is. The trap he set for your handsome lover was sprung. A slippery one, de Gramont, always has been. The family—well, that's another story."

Gasping, Rosslyn clutched her robe tighter. "Are they safe?"

"The wife—perhaps your next biggest concern—put

her scrawny neck on the windowsill yesterday while we made small talk and bargains . . ."

Rosslyn's eyes widened in shock at his words, at the throaty chuckle which accompanied them. "Dead! But she was supposed to be set free. Why was I imprisoned if she was already condemned?"

"Bernard had no intention of freeing her. That was a gamble her rescuers took. They lost. As for you, I think you were a mistake which got out of hand. The boys are farmed out on the outskirts of Nemours awaiting money to buy their safe conduct passes from your protector, our charming Bernard."

"Will he have them arrested as well?"

"No. I think he has intentions more towards their father. What do you know about valuables to be bartered?"

Cautiously Rosslyn hesitated, wondering how far to trust this man. "A rumor of family heirlooms, nothing more. Bernard intends to own them."

"Of course. Well, now you know."

"Did Armand wait for me? Do you know how long before he went into hiding?"

Camille shrugged, growing tired of questions about another man. "Forget him. Rich bastards like that are as faithless as fleas. Whereas a good honest citizen like myself . . ."

"It's stupid of me to care, I know it is," she murmured against the hot bulk of hard shoulder and chest. Pictures of Marie flitted through her mind, her words, her warning, reminders of Armand's desertions of the past. He had not asked her to come to Paris. When she arrived on his doorstep what else could he do, even while living with another woman, to whom he had been immediately unfaithful. For him to make love to her had been perfectly natural, what any other man would have done under the circumstance. To feel it implied great love was her own foolish summation. Facts about his later actions told far more than those fevered words of love he whispered so easily.

"What if I had refused to yield to you after you'd given me the information?" she asked, struck by the sudden thought.

Holding her away from him, he laughed deeply, evilly. "Why then, dear Lady Burton—ah, yes, I know who you really are—I'd have taken you by force. As a matter of fact, that may appeal to you more."

"No. I intend to keep my bargain." She lowered her eyes because she did not want to betray what she was afraid he could see there, the sensation she clung to so desperately in an effort to eradicate the smell and the feel of Armand's body, to remove the memory of his touch. This man was an uncomplicated stranger. The force of his virility smote her like a blow, turning her mind to those lustful channels she had never thought she possessed until Armand had awakened her.

"You little devil, you'd probably slash me if I failed to keep my bargain, for all your simpering pretense," he hissed, close against her ear, his hands stealing inside the frilled neckline to cup her ample breasts. At the mutual contact they both shuddered with desire.

Eyes glittering in the candleglow, Rosslyn gave in to the escape he dangled before her, to the oblivion of his maleness.

"Yes, and for your swaggering pretense I'll slash you if you're wrong," she threatened huskily, pulling open the buttons on his coat, then the shirt, exploring the heated expanse of chest, slipping her fingers coolly to his shoulders where she shuddered again at the contact of hard flesh.

"Rest assured, *ma petite,* I make no extravagant claims I can't substantiate."

Smiling into his hard face, she whispered: "That, Camille, will be my decision."

Sweeping her up, he held her inches from the floor in a crushing embrace, burying his face for a moment in the frills at her neckline, his breath hot and damp against her flesh, sending shivers down her back. Then he set her back on her feet.

" 'Tis a fine satin bed," he remarked, glancing towards the frilled counterpane of periwinkle blue edged with lace flounces. "Bernard had it from the palace, or so I've heard tell. Not what I'm used to, but we'll manage. Slippery."

Shivering, she listened to his assessment as he stroked

the smooth covers, his rough fingers snagging minute threads in the luxurious fabric. "Will you talk all night?" she asked, her hand going to his waist, surprised to feel the hard solidity of his frame as if no pound of excess flesh lingered there.

"The bed or the floor?" he asked, half-turning to wink at her as he pulled off his coat. " 'Tis a fine plush carpet. Such a deep blue."

The floor! A flashing memory of the summerhouse amid the pattering rain and Armand's face as he bid her goodbye seized Rosslyn. Watching Camille as he undid his cravat she caught his arms, anxious to blot out the vision, as if to repeat the act with another would hasten the removal.

"The floor," she decided.

With a laugh he gripped her about the waist and swung her high in a half circle. "At once, *ma petite.*"

Then she was against the rug, wondering a moment how she came there so rapidly, finding the breath knocked from her body by his weight as he pressed her hard and painfully into the deep blue plushness. He kissed her. He whispered untranslatable endearments, some of which were not part of her French vocabulary, but because they were part of his passionate lovemaking, instead of cooling her ardor, the vulgarity of the words only fired it. He was almost brutal in his claiming, different from other men she had known, yet so much the same, until she reasoned no longer, gone beyond that point of consciousness.

And then, when it was over, when she returned to the candlelit room with its strange furnishings, when she became aware of the present, shaken though she was, in the emotional aftermath she felt poignant loss. The man she clasped against her, who had become one with her body, was not Armand.

"Eh, are you one of those who cries afterward?" Camille whispered, not moving from her, feeling the splash of tears on his shoulder. Pausing a moment, he chuckled. "Tell me, did I lie, *cherie*?"

"No. And I'm glad of that."

"Come, we've barely ten minutes before your keeper returns. I must be far from here by then or he'll know what happened, already he's fuming at having to wait alone at the Palais de Justice. To catch me in the street would be advertising the deception. Up! Get to bed like a good little slut."

She moved without speaking to him, aware he studied her nakedness as he paused, his hands on his clothing, his hard face suffused by a glowing smile of admiration as his eyes flicked from her satin-smooth hips to the fullness of her breasts.

"*Dieu*, would that I had a little longer with you. Never have I seen a woman who looked like you," he breathed in wonder.

She smiled at him standing immobile as a statue, his shirt, his britches all unfastened while he gaped at her. On some men the state of undress would have proved comical, but there was nothing comical about Camille.

"Hurry, before you're caught," she urged, slipping inside the cool satin covers.

Grinning, he hastily buttoned his shirt, his fingers clumsy in their haste. With an oath he stuffed the material inside his trousers making no effort to conceal his fresh arousal as he struggled to fasten his clothes. "Have you more questions?" he quipped, knowing she was aware of his predicament. "It seems I've a quantity of bargaining left."

At last, hat on his head at the usual rakish angle, he came to the bed to kiss her goodnight.

"Can I come here again?" he asked suddenly, loathe to go.

"With more information?"

"Must it be for that reason alone?"

Rosslyn locked gazes with him, not knowing what to say. She did not really like him. Did not even know his last name and cared not enough to ask—"Perhaps. I'll let you know."

"*Au revoir, cherie.* I was right. This was the best bargain of the week."

Chuckling at his humor he went into the corridor, clattering downstairs, unconcerned about the prying servants.

Rosslyn slid from the covers and lifted the corner of the fringed draperies to watch him move down the street; tall and sinister, his elongated black shadow glanced over walls and cobblestones as he hastened away. Nothing of love tugged at her as she watched him, only the memory of that other fieriness resurged, startling her by the force of the emotion.

"Oh, Armand, how could you leave me when I loved you so," she whispered to the black night, to the jumbled rooftops beneath the tossing clouds. "If only you'd waited. Trying to learn where you are I've done this. And I don't even know his name."

Welling grief filled her eyes as she leaned against the cool window frame and wept.

CHAPTER ELEVEN

A week passed without mention of arrangements for her transportation to England, nor did Bernard seem anxious to even discuss the matter. Beginning to wonder if his intentions were quite as honorable as he would have her believe, Rosslyn was determined to force a commitment from him.

The August day was already hot though it was barely ten in the morning. As was his customary habit, Bernard worked at his desk until noon before journeying to his office in the Palais de Justice. It was during this time Rosslyn chose to confront him in his study, assured at least of his undivided attention.

When she opened the door to the sunny room she saw him writing at his mahogany desk surrounded by stacks of papers. As her purple flowered gown rustled over the parquet floor, Bernard glanced up with a smile of pleasure.

"*Mon cherie,*" he greeted, pushing back his chair.

"Good morning, Bernard. Can you spare me a few moments? I know you're busy, but this matter is so important to me."

"Of course. I'm never too busy to entertain such a lovely lady," he answered gallantly. His black eyes rapidly assessed her appearance, the smile which curved his thin mouth a moment later assuring her of his approval. "May I say how admirably that color becomes you, most flattering to your eyes." With this he stooped over her hand to place a kiss with lips still cool despite the heat.

"You're very kind," she mouthed, quite detached from the polite words, merely repeating what she had learned in the drawing rooms at home.

Leading her to the window, Bernard threw open the pane, breathing deep of the morning air as yet untainted by the odors of the refuse-laden streets, an unpleasantness which multiplied with the rising temperature.

"Have you contacted Clarence?" she asked bluntly. "I thought you intended to do it."

Rosslyn tried to control the temper which flared hotly at his answer. Once more he evaded her questions, but the usual easy dismissal would not suffice today. "You are the one with contacts. I merely await whatever information you produce. As I never leave the house it would be a difficult task."

"But not to send him letters," Bernard reminded, his eyes narrowing. "That was foolish of you, my dear, such missives often fall into the wrong hands."

Color warmed her face at his words. "Oh, you knew about that," she mumbled, feeling somewhat guilty, yet without actual cause: To send a note to Clarence's rendezvous in care of the maid was no crime. "Am I still a prisoner? Am I not to be allowed communication with the outside world?" she demanded.

"On the contrary. The maid received a reprimand for her part in the affair. All such missives should come through my hands first, a fact she well knows. Had you asked me I would have delivered the letter personally."

"If I'm not a prisoner then I may also leave whenever I choose?"

"Assuredly. Except you might find it rather difficult to travel without papers. Naturally, your counterfeit documents were confiscated at the prison."

"Then give me new papers. You do this favor for others, surely I can expect as much. Though you've been very kind, I cannot stay here. As you seem in no hurry to contact Clarence, it's only natural for me to attempt—"

"I've already made arrangements for you. You must learn to be more patient, my dear." He took her hand as he spoke, turning it palm uppermost where he planted a second lingering kiss. "We are soon to journey to my villa in the country. There the plans can be completed."

"When do we leave?"

"Tomorrow. I was keeping it a surprise, but there, you see, you've spoiled it. You'll like the villa. Such a lovely stretch of countryside. Flowers, trees, all the things you tell me you miss about England. Life will be much the same as here; afternoon gatherings twice weekly at which I hope you'll continue to do me the honor of being hostess." He paused awaiting an answer.

"If you wish, but don't rely on me for that function. As soon as possible I intend to return to England. There's nothing for me here."

Slipping his arm about her small waist, Bernard smiled indulgently. "Perhaps, given a little time, I can change that outlook, Rosslyn. All Paris could be at your feet."

Falsely she smiled, allowing him to think her pleased, realizing in his own roundabout way he paid her court. Did he seriously think she would come to regard him with romantic interest? Camille had already affirmed her doubts about Bernard's sincerity over the situation. Very well, she would give him a few more days to prove himself one way or another—but that was all.

On the journey to the villa they passed through a small town nestled at the foot of hills terraced with vineyards. When Rosslyn read Saint Clare on the signpost her hands grew clammy, her stomach lurching to behold it. This green countryside, those vineyards, were Armand's memories. And knowing this, despite his apparent lack of concern for her welfare, drew her closer to him. How easy it would be to meet him here when he reclaimed the jewelry; though the idea was frightening, confronting him was the only way to learn the truth of his feelings for her. Never once did she choose to admit the truth might not be to her liking. How could he cast her aside after the intensity of their love?

Set back from the road behind rolling acres of oak and beech she glimpsed the stone gables of a large house. The walls surrounding the estate were tumble-down, the tall wrought-iron gates swinging crazily in the wind as they clattered past. By its appearance the chateau must be deserted. Marking well the location, she was glad Bernard did not know of her discovery. He dozed in the corner, his head bouncing against the side of the coach where the action served as a soothing rhythm to deepen his sleep.

Her determination to return to Saint Clare, Rosslyn must admit, was a foolish idea. No longer was Armand its comte, nor did scores of retainers wait to do his bidding, nor serve him in the stables or the vast lofty rooms of the ornate mansion. Life as he knew it had ceased. What could the future hold for him in an equal society rubbing shoulders with men like Camille whom she had discovered bore a hearty contempt for Armand's family and others like them? Yet because this house belonged to Armand, because he grew up here and loved this countryside, Rosslyn found herself drawn to the estate.

Looking back when they reached the crest of the hill she could see the outline of the chateau, its roof surmounted by twin conical towers of red tile, making it like a fairy-tale castle. There was a lake, she could see sunlight glinting on a silver ribbon of water before the entrance to the vast gray stone structure.

Presently she dozed to dream of walking beside that lake with Armand. When she woke the warmth of his arm still rested heavy about her waist, the depth of feeling in his smile wrapped her with love . . .

"Wake up. We're here. This is my villa."

Pain churned fiercely within her breast to find Bernard leaning over her instead and disappointment stung with the bitterness of gall to learn it had all been a dream.

During the following week Rosslyn became acquainted with Bernard's country villa, finding that the landscaped gardens overflowing with flowers brought contentment she had thought lost forever. There was an extensive library, not of Bernard's choosing, she was sure, more the tastes of the former owner of this house for the literature leaned towards the romanticists, not a trait she would attribute to Bernard. All of it, confiscated property, Bernard had gleefully told her upon inquiry, not realizing the knowledge diminished rather than elevated him in her opinion.

Though the library and the gardens helped to pass the time, when a week was up with still no word from Clarence and additional hedging by Bernard, Rosslyn was relieved to see a familiar figure crossing the lawn to join her.

Dressed in scarlet serge with white waistcoat and britches, today Camille appeared almost elegant. His thick black hair was brushed back from his face, and though it still hung about his shoulders in dense profusion, the texture seemed softer, looking less like a bramble maze than usual.

"Camille, how nice to see you," she voiced with genuine pleasure, barely containing herself before she began to ask the countless questions which plagued her.

"Do you mean that?" he asked, eyes widening in pleasure.

"Yes. Would I say it if I did not?"

"Perhaps."

Aware they could be seen from Bernard's study, Camille seated himself discreetly at the opposite end of the garden seat. Half-turned towards her, his face thrust in shadow, conveniently obscured from the windows where he was sure Bernard spied, he winked at her.

"Well, over two weeks since I've seen you and, I swear, *cherie,* you're lovelier than ever."

Rosslyn smiled at his extravagance, surprised to see the flicker of sincerity in his dark face. "Do you mean that?"

"Would I say it if I did not?"

"Perhaps." She laughed at him then, at the silly repetition of their words. At the moment he was her only friend, and though she understood his friendship was not given selflessly, it was welcome. "Do you have news for me? Bernard has become as close-mouthed as a confessor these days. Sometimes I think he's made no effort to contact anyone."

Camille moved his hand across the slatted seat contemplating holding her hand, but deciding against it. "Well, you're probably right at that. He's slimy, is Bernard. Slippery as an eel. At this moment he's spying on us."

"Can you see him?"

"Ah, *cherie,* in here I see him." Camille tapped his head. "What say you to finding somewhere less public?"

"We could walk in the gardens," Rosslyn suggested, looking towards the windows of the study, fancying she saw a movement there. "He usually goes into Paris on Mondays."

"He probably knew I was coming so changed his mind. Come. Do you ride?"

"Yes. Though I haven't been on horseback for ages. Don't tell me you've got a mount for me."

Standing up, Camille solicitously tucked his hand beneath her elbow, ushering her sedately over the lawns away from the house. "I intend to mount you myself," he joked, tightening his grip, laughing down at her.

Despite herself Rosslyn had to smile at his statement. "Trust you to twist what I say to a sexual meaning. You're insatiable. Perhaps it's an illness," she ventured, grinning at him. "What did you do away from me for two whole weeks?"

As soon as she had asked, Rosslyn wished she had not. She did not love Camille, nor, except at certain times, did she like him very much, but unreasonably the knowledge he shared his body with others smote her with pain. "No, don't tell me. I don't want to know," she snapped, when he would have spoken.

Camille grinned and said nothing, pleased by the ruffle of anger which moved across her face, pleased to know she had begun to feel possessive towards him. Sometimes with this woman who could change from molten fire to ice in a matter of minutes he was unsure of himself, never knowing another quite like her.

Beneath a spreading oak, two bays placidly munching flowers from Bernard's garden were tethered.

"You brought one just for me?" she gasped, eagerly charging forward before she remembered she wore a muslin afternoon dress. "I can't ride in this."

Smiling at the disappointment on her lovely face, Camille felt his heart pitch foolishly. Surprised, and not displeased by the reaction, he swept her to him. "Eh! ride naked if you wish, *cherie.* Yes, that would please me very much."

Laughing up at him, she let him kiss her. "Be serious.

Can I ride in this?"

"I'll put you in the saddle." With this, giving her no time to change her mind, Camille swept her from her feet, his large hands digging tightly into her waist. Laughing as she swirled about, growing dizzy from the motion, Rosslyn demanded he put her down. He did, slapping hard on the saddle where her dress came above her calves as she sat astride.

Eyes fastened on the white flesh contrasting superbly against the animal's brown hide, Camille whistled his appreciation. "You can ride like that when you're with me. Why hide everything under yards of cloth—aristocrat."

The word was spoken without contempt, meant in humor, yet his reference to her class made her grow uneasy. Camille knew who she was, knew also she had contrived to learn what Bernard considered secret information. In view of his annoyance over her innocent note to her brother, what vengeance would this knowledge bring about? Between them those two men had more than enough information to put her to death. Camille was cruel, hard, merciless; she heard those condemnations from all sides, yet with her he had tried to be kind. Without sentimentality she knew it was because, at the moment, he enjoyed her sexually; once her body began to pall, the hold she had over him would be gone. Shivering at the realization, she urged her mount forward, making him follow with an oath of annoyance. While it lasted she would play her physical attraction to the hilt.

"Come, laggard, where will you take me?" she called, heading the horse along the gravel drive.

"Where do you want to go?"

"How about Saint Clare?"

"If you wish, though it's some distance. Don't you mind the rabble seeing those exquisite calves?"

"Mayhap you'll have to fight them for me," she joked, looking sideways at him, playing the coquette, unprepared for the dark temper which flared in his face.

"I'll spit any bastard who looks askance at you, *cherie,* you have my word on it."

196

"I don't know why we're here. The place is little more than a ruin these days," Camille grumbled as they rode slowly up the gravel drive between those ravaged gates.

A boar's head device surmounted by a coronet supporting the lilies of France was in the center of each gate. It made Rosslyn sad to see the weeds' rank approach to what had once been a splendid residence.

Still grumbling, glancing about with lips curled in contempt, Camille added: "Serves them right, people like them. Too bad the house wasn't burned over their heads."

"Was it purposely destroyed?" Rosslyn asked, confronted suddenly by the formidable building as they rounded a curve of the drive.

"A peasants' march. They probably milked the poor bastards dry all these years working the vineyards, grubbing on hands and knees for crumbs."

"But you don't know that," she reminded.

Camille grinned. "No, but it's safe to assume. Perhaps the de Gramonts were fairer than most, but you can't say owning all this was right. What about the drabs who sleep in alleyways? Or the babies flung on dungheaps because their ignorant sluts of mothers haven't food to feed them? Now those are crimes. Not the destroying of a man who played God to the countryside."

The violent feeling present in Camille's speech made Rosslyn's skin crawl. Thank heaven there were not enough men like him in London, or her family too might be skulking in fear for their lives, the way Armand was forced to do, as she too had done since becoming involved in his struggle.

"Pah! You're not rousing the rabble now. There's only me. And I don't care about all that. I want to see the house." Forcing gaiety to her tone, she urged her mount forward, increasing speed until they galloped straight for the oblong lake before the chateau.

Slipping about uncomfortably in the saddle he pursued her, unused to the frantic pace, for he still rode like a peasant, the skill newly acquired. "Hey, wait for me," he yelled, skidding to a halt before the broad shallow steps leading to the entrance.

Rosslyn was already out of the saddle, scrambling down with difficulty. "Shall we tether the horses?"

"No. Let them roam. Perhaps they can eat some priceless flowers."

Sullen, Camille followed her up the steps. The vast doorway stood open, the oak door a splintered pile of debris heaped in a corner of the black and white marble-tiled entrance hall. Blue sky peered inquisitively through a shattered skylight in the roof, casting a beam of brilliant sunlight alive with clouds of plaster dust stirred by their feet as they climbed over the fallen masonry.

"This is grander than Bernard's villa by far," Rosslyn remarked a trifle smugly, wondering what Camille thought of his compatriot's elegance.

"No wonder he's jealous of de Gramont."

Looking about in wonder at the staircase which circled the hall, Camille slid his hands over the marble bannisters.

"Why did they do this? Couldn't they have left it alone?" Rosslyn whispered half to herself as she saw shards of slivered mirror poking icily from the heaps of smashed furniture.

"That's a stupid question, *cherie*. It proves you know nothing about a mob."

"Well, perhaps you'll enlighten me. I know what an expert you are on the matter," she remarked stonily, ascending the stair.

"Hey, aristocrat. Think you're too good for me today, don't you?"

She did not answer as she climbed the crumbled stairs. Gilt cherubs had been pried from the ornamental friezes. A shattered oil painting, its canvas slashed to ribbons, rested crazily across the bannister.

"Got you," Camille cried triumphantly, grabbing her from behind. "Now, you bitch of an aristocrat, say you're sorry."

"For what?"

"For being so damned haughty. You were almost like the Austrian slut a few minutes ago. I spoke to her

198

once. She swished her skirts away from me as if she was afraid I'd soil her gown. You don't do that at least. In fact, you can be very welcoming at times. How about now?"

His mouth pressed hotly against her neck and Rosslyn felt strangely unmoved as her eyes roamed over the devastation of Armand's magnificent ancestral home. Tattered ribbons of green damask fluttered at a window above, all that remained of the draperies. Huge chunks had been axed from the paneling, even segments of marble had been pried from the geometrical floor below. Insistent, his tongue came wet against her throat.

"Camille, wait till we're outside, please."

Determined not to lose his temper with her today, he shrugged.

"All right. I forgot he was your lover first. Don't feel sorry for him though, he has millions hidden here someplace."

"Did the rabble smash things looking for money?"

"No. They smash things because they enjoy it. In their eyes, poor sods, destroying the symbols of de Gramont's wealth destroys him. Still, what harm did it do? They weren't killing while they did this. There's no room for chateaus in the People's Republic."

"You sound as if you approve," she said in surprise, withdrawing from his embrace to descend the stair.

Camille grinned at her sober expression. "What does it really matter if some thick-headed lout pissed himself silly on a likeness of the Bourbon?" he asked, kicking the damaged portrait as they passed. "People always get hurt during times of change. Thank God it's them and not me."

"So you wouldn't want a home like this?"

"I didn't say that. If I owned this relic it wouldn't be because I'd crushed hope out of people for over six centuries."

"No, it would be because you'd already executed those who had after confiscating their belongings for yourself."

"Eh, you catch on fast. *Certainement!* For them to own it is wrong; for me, because my people have had it coming to them since the Dark Ages, such a mansion would be a fitting reward. Now come, you make me say too much. Will you see the rest of the place or go back? It's much the same upstairs."

Clouds crossed over the sun, darkening the room oppressively until Rosslyn decided she had seen enough of Château Saint Clare.

"Let's go outside. I'm cold," she said, clutching her bare arms tight about her body in an effort to remove the chill which gripped her at the loneliness of the ruin.

Smiling, pleased by her decision, Camille clasped her against him. At his insistence she wore his fine red coat to dispel the temperature drop, though once the brooding house was left behind she had no need of the coat. Outside the air was warm and almost immediately Rosslyn found her humor returning.

Camille stretched full length on the grass verge beside the ornamental lake, trailing his hands in the water. In the bright sunshine his thin shirt revealed dark growths of hair around his shoulder blades where the sweat-damp fabric molded like a second skin.

"Sorry if I was a pig to you. I'd forgotten how attached you were to him," he apologized, not looking at her when he spoke.

"The house depressed me. It's all right," she said, resolutely turning her back on the square-built stone house with its castlelike turrets, its sightless eyes where pigeons fluttered like white ghosts through the paneless windows.

"Perhaps, like Bernard, I'm jealous of de Gramont. He had so much. All my life, up to now, I've had nothing. Men get values twisted sometimes."

"So greed is the basis of Bernard's involvement?" Rosslyn voiced in surprise, squatting beside him on the grass.

"You didn't know that? He hates his cousin like poison. If you weren't such a dish," he said as he pulled her down against him, his hands trembling to caress her neck, "I'd think he wanted you out of spite."

Rosslyn smiled at him, pleased to see that burning intensity in his face. Theirs was a strange relationship, one of bartered needs; yet his admiration gave her a sense of power. The insistence of his hands, stealing lower, fired that emotion that knew no love. Rosslyn breathlessly asked her question, knowing that if she did not cement her request before he took her, he would never agree to it afterwards. "Will you bring me here to talk with him?"

Camille's hands stiffened on her body, the smile of pleasure frozen about his mouth. "Why do you ask me that?"

"Because you're the only one who has the means."

"But not the desire."

"Ah, you have desire, more than any man should have. You have your share and that of ten others beside."

"Bitch! You twist my words."

In relief she watched his frown dissolve at her husky words. "Can you not grant me this one thing?"

Caressing her face he finally agreed. "I'll bring you here to talk with him, but not alone. How do I know you won't couple in the bushes, so hot for the sight of him you seem. To be party to that would rip my peace of mind to shreds."

He appeared to jest, but Rosslyn saw the telltale expression in his eyes; they appeared black and hard as coal. It was easy to see how he had earned his reputation, as he revealed a side of his nature she had rarely glimpsed before.

"If I promise to behave like a convent virgin, will you let me speak to him? Five minutes is all I ask. That will be long enough to tell me what I want to know."

"What's that? If he still grows hard for you?" Camille said contemptuously. "Stupid aristocrat, the man's not born who doesn't do that," he growled, gripping her arms till his fingers left bruises.

"Not that," she whispered against his face as he pressed the breath from her, his black hair smothering, tickling her nose. "I must learn if he deserted me. What he feels for me. If only to settle my own conscience."

"Shut up! Must we always discuss that arrogant bastard when we're together?" he snarled, growing impatient.

"I promise not to mention him again today," Rosslyn whispered, stilled under the pressure of his heavy body,

"That's better. Sometimes I want to break you, so violent do you make me feel," he confided, smiling into her eyes. "But then, *cherie,* I'm usually content to split you asunder."

Forcing the tormenting picture of Armand from her mind, his smile, the tenderness in his eyes which plagued her constantly, Rosslyn concentrated on the man in her arms, the man who rapidly became one with her body.

The party that evening smacked of the despised court, with liveried musicians playing chamber music on a dias at the end of the grand salon. Bernard was dressed in black satin, diamonds in his cravat and on his fingers. The rings were new additions; the obvious way in which he stretched out his hand at the slightest provocation, half-admiring the fire-flashing gems as he spoke, told Rosslyn that. A prickle of disgust crept through her at the thought of the fate of the jewelry's owners who either languished in a filthy, rat-infested cell or had already been dumped in the communal grave of the friendless guillotined.

Camille, his hair brushed, his boots shined, strode importantly about the room. Whenever Rosslyn looked up he was watching her. His obvious attentions were disquieting, for though Bernard might be trusting, he was not a complete fool.

"Why do you stare at me so?" she hissed in agitation as Camille brushed against her.

"Stop. Talk to me, *cherie,*" he said aloud, the laughter in his words taken for flirtatious banter by the other guests.

Annoyed by his recklessness, Rosslyn went to the buffet table where sliced meats were artistically arranged amongst olives and golden cheeses. Thrusting a crystal glass of champagne in her hands he smiled at her above the gold-edged rim of his glass.

"I thought I'd have to ogle you all night, bitch. Why wouldn't you talk to me?"

"You've been so obviously cow-eyed, it's a wonder Bernard hasn't guessed what goes on behind his back," she snapped.

"What a temper! They told me Englishwomen were placid."

"Camille!"

"Listen, your wonder man should make his move before the week's out. The two boys have been readied for travel."

Rosslyn gasped at his startling news, at the thought of actually seeing Armand within days. Though it was something she had long awaited, now that a confrontation was imminent, her mouth grew dry with fright. "Are you sure?"

"Reasonably so. You still want to talk to him? He may not tell you what you want to hear," he suggested gravely, the bantering smile fading from his face.

"That would please you, wouldn't it?" she demanded, spots of color clinging to her high cheekbones, temper brightening her eyes.

"No. It would not please me to see you hurt." With this he turned on his heel and strode away.

Rosslyn stared after him, surprised by the concern in his face. A general reshuffling of guests was taking place, the confusion hiding him momentarily from sight as the musicians played music for dancing. Those who did not take places in the dance moved to the fringe of the room, leaving the center clear. There were a dozen other women present, mostly courtesans, their occupation betrayed by their loud laughter and coarse, painted faces. Viewing them with haughty disdain, Rosslyn had done no more to make them welcome than was expected of her as hostess, knowing instinctively that Bernard accepted these women only because they were companions of his acquaintances. To her surprise Camille now led a giggling hussy to the center of the room; a blowsy woman with fiery dyed red hair, her white bodice stretched almost transparent over large breasts resembling melons which bounced and jiggled in accompaniment to her parody of a minuet. Impatient with the staid music, Camille ordered the musicians to play the carmagnole, his suggestion greeted with a cheer of enthusiasm. Soon the room was throbbing with their raucous voices chanting the words of their antimonarch ist song, as they clumped about with more enthusiasm than finesse.

"Peasant pigs," Bernard hissed in her ear, his lip curled in contempt as he viewed the assembly.

"They are your friends," Rosslyn reminded.

"They are my colleagues, my dear Rosslyn, never friends. A man in my position has no friends. He has enemies, and potential enemies, but never friends."

"Why do you invite them here if you don't like them?"

He smiled, taking her hand, still admiring the winking diamond on his finger. "It suits me to humor them. Though they are gutter rabble there's much power in their hands. Don't forget, I was not born a man of the streets," Bernard added, uncertainty flickering through his face as he watched the noisy throng. "Look at Camille, a glorified stonemason with more muscles than sense. The drab he chaperones becomes him. No doubt they've both got Caen dust beneath their broken fingernails. I saw you talking to him earlier. What does he want?"

The question, slipped in so casually, almost took Rosslyn off guard. They were right about Bernard's character. Slippery, Camille had called him.

"Because he is what he is, a member of the aristocracy is interesting to him," she dismissed with equal nonchalance.

"Interesting? In what way are you interesting?" Bernard demanded, his grasp tightening. "If the dog seeks to bed you, I'll . . ."

"Oh nothing of that nature," Rosslyn dismissed the suggestion in haste. "He wanted to talk. Perhaps he finds my attention flattering."

"I forbid you to give him any attention," Bernard commanded, his voice tight with emotion. "A man like that isn't good enough to lick your shoes. Dog of the gutter that he is. And he ruts in a like manner. That scarlet-haired bitch has a litter of assorted pups, no doubt he had the dubious honor of fathering several."

The venom in his voice took her by surprise. Nostrils flared in anger, chin held high, at this moment Bernard betrayed his background, reminding her for a fleeting moment of Armand. In hauteur the family resemblance had betrayed itself.

"His sleeping habits are of no concern to me," she said, her indifference belied by a nagging, twisting pain which settled deep in her stomach.

"That's good. Let me know if he offends you. If they end this barnyard frolic before they all succumb to drink, will you dance with me?"

She smiled and nodded in reply to his question, keeping her eyes on Camille and the red-haired woman. To be thus betrayed by him was a blow. "I'll be delighted to dance with you, Bernard," she said.

At long last the perpetual carmagnole came to an end. Signaling for the musicians to play to his liking, Bernard took her to the middle of the floor where they began a stately dance. The guests laughed and clapped for them, but they did not join the dance, their contempt for the ways of the aristocracy betrayed on many of their faces. Uneasily Rosslyn saw what Bernard did not: Just as he did not count them as his friends, likewise they did not accept him as theirs. This dance was too much a reminder of the gulf which stretched between them.

When they came off the floor amid applause and laughter, Rosslyn caught Camille's glance, seeing jealousy flaring there before he successfully masked it. Suddenly the blowsy woman on his arm did not matter anymore as his eyes followed her to the refreshment table, piercing her sky blue taffeta dress as if he would strip it from her, discounting the masking frills of lace with a hungry, burning gaze which came to rest on the fullness of her bodice. With a sigh of relief, Rosslyn turned away, knowing she had not lost her hold over him. Whatever that woman with her flaming hair had once meant to him, she was not the one he watched with hunger tonight. Until his passion strayed elsewhere, Rosslyn knew she was still secure in counting on Camille's aid.

After the dancing was over and the food was consumed as if by a starving mob, the company began to talk, making speeches of revolutionary policy and pointless incitement until Rosslyn retired to the corner to nurse her throbbing head, thankful for the moment to be left alone.

These past weeks of listening to Bernard's friends had given her a clearer picture of the revolution. She discovered it was not a simple uprising of the oppressed poor as she had at first thought. Even the marches on prisons, those riots where simple washerwomen spurred their compatriots to violence were exposed to her as sham: Men in women's clothes had rallied the mob; fiery dissidents poured evil notions into receptive ears, backed by pamphlets turned out as fast as the presses would roll. Nor were the victims of Monsieur Guillotine all the decadent fugitives from Louis's opulent court; they included artisans and shopkeepers, beggars and prostitutes. Taking advantage of public outrage against a lavish court expenditure while food prices soared to prohibitive heights, until many of the poor starved in the streets, men like Bernard and Camille fueled the fires of hatred to further their own ambition. It had become a vast struggle for political power using any means available, as leaders changed places in a frantic race to the top. Since the murder of Marat by the Rolandin supporter, Charlotte Corday, Robespierre's supporters mounted in power, setting the stage for this new acceleration with many political reprisals still to come.

It was almost as if that murder had been arranged, so fortunate a crime was it for people like Bernard. When they spoke of the ugly Marat with his sore-encrusted body, a legacy of lurking through Paris sewers, they jested. When they spoke of the baskets of heads collected in the aftermath of the guillotine's busy days, they jested also. Like madmen they found no horror in the proceedings, knowing only a driving urge to incite, to lash the power of the populace, to commit further madness. And above all to reign supreme, drunk with their own power.

CHAPTER TWELVE

The garden was heavily fragrant in the afternoon sun. Rosslyn took her book to the white wrought-iron bench in the rose arbor, but found she was too unsettled to read. In an hour Camille would be here. She had waited for the disclosure of Armand's whereabouts in great anticipation, wanting to be assured circumstance had kept him from her, anything but the reason suggested by Bernard. Today Camille had promised he would have definite news.

Though she tried to convince herself the disquieting emotion swirling through her body was generated only at the thought of Armand, Rosslyn knew she deluded herself. Naturally Camille would expect the customary favors for his information; had he not she would have been disappointed. Though she would never seek him out, relying solely on him for the pursuit, Rosslyn had begun to eagerly anticipate his arrival, using him as consolation for the ache in her body, to appease in part that voracious thirst generated by Armand. Men had always used women for bodily satisfaction; now she discovered women could also use men. At one time to have suggested that she, Lady Burton, would stoop to physical contact with a man of Camille's background would have seemed preposterous. Yet when he held her in his arms, when the hot ardor of his desire fused with her own, it was hard to remember he was a man of the streets. Afterwards she sometimes felt ashamed, but the emotion was not forbidding enough to make her forego those encounters. She even pretended he loved her a little, for it was the only thing which eased her misgivings. Honest in this one thing, however, Camille never complicated matters with sentiment. He treated their relationship as no more than a pleasant diversion.

When at last he strode over the lawns, he reminded her of a scarecrow with his black hair flying loose about his shoulders, his crumpled shirt and britches looking as if he had slept in them. Breath choked in Rosslyn's throat to acknowledge it was time once more to pay.

"Ah, you've waited faithfully for me. Such affection. I'm flattered," he joked, stooping beneath the arbor entrance.

Blinking against the light Rosslyn looked up at him thinking how much like a gypsy he looked today. She had seen them beside the Kentish hedgerows squatting around their campfires; wild dark hair, coal black eyes, bronzed faces where white teeth flashed in grins of approval at her appearance, all contributing to an air of mystery. Yet those young men with their lithe bodies were deceiving creatures, prepared to steal what they could not wheedle—such a man was Camille.

"Hey, are you sunstruck, *cherie*?"

Rosslyn smiled at him. "I was thinking all you need are gold rings in your ears to look like a gypsy."

"Do you fancy gypsies? Maybe I can learn some Romany words of love," he suggested, going to his knee before her when she did not rise. "Tell me, what do they say to their sluts?"

"How would I know?"

"Ah, you disappoint me. I thought perhaps you'd sampled one, you wanton creature."

He grinned wickedly at her, imprisoning her hands in his large fist, tightening the pressure until she gasped.

"Have you news?"

Camille's wide mouth turned down. "Ha! that's my romantic bitch. Always remembering business. What about the other business, eh? That's far more to my liking."

"A business relationship was your idea," she reminded.

"So it was."

"If you tell me your news we can get down to the other." Her own boldness surprised her, yet something

208

in Camille immediately touched the inner self which she often hid from strangers.

He grinned at her suggestion, standing, drawing her with him. "*Eh bien,* a good idea."

When he would have kissed her, Rosslyn turned her face away, finding the decision hard to make, knowing she must insist on information first, for once Camille had her body there would be nothing with which to bargain.

"First tell me your news."

"Our runaway aristocrat is within ten kilometers of here." At her gasp, he squeezed her hands tightly. "Sh! would you interrupt me? He brings heirlooms to buy his safety."

"From Saint Clare?"

"Must be."

"But you said we should meet him there," Rosslyn cried, feeling cheated.

"So I was wrong. He does not write a letter to inform me every time he moves. You must accept your luck. This time it was bad."

"That's all?"

Camille grinned, tracing his thumb over the exposed flesh above the neckline of her gown, lifting her heavy hair so he could explore unimpeded. "He will see Bernard today. And, *cherie,* they will certainly not invite you to their afternoon social."

Rosslyn considered his news, her heart plunging at the discovery. Armand must know she was here, such news traveled rapidly, even in the underground sources he used. Why hadn't he contrived to send a message? Surely he did not think she stayed with Bernard out of choice, he must realize, stranded as she was on her release from the Conciergerie, there was little else she could do.

"Now, the first part of our business is concluded we can move to the second," Camille suggested huskily.

Staring into his black eyes, Rosslyn compared them for the first time to those others she so well remembered, to the expression which had the ability to make her shudder with delight. There was no comparison. In

Camille's face she beheld desire and amusement, but there was nothing of love.

"Well," he prompted, moving his attentions from her back to her shoulders, to the lace-edged neckline and beyond.

"I'm ready." Almost viciously she seized his face, forcing her lips to his, wanting to hurt him as part payment for his failure to be the man she loved.

Far from giving pain, her assault gave him heightened pleasure, so that he laughed and grabbed her with his strong hands, turning her about, pressing against her back as he devoured her neck, allowing his hands the delight of plundering her rose-sprigged bodice.

For a moment she stiffened, holding herself aloof, too aware of Armand's memory to enjoy Camille's lovemaking. Then her own nature took over, thrilled at the hard length of maleness pressed hot against her back, at the hands pursuing their conquest. She closed her eyes, shutting out the bright daylight, his picture, giving herself up solely to desire.

In the shelter of a fronded willow an observer watched the figures in the arbor, finding them like some hideous painting come to life, opulently framed by cabbage roses. Flower-sprigged blue-striped gown wrapped intimately about the man's long legs. Sickened, he turned away as her white flesh became imprisoned in eager brown hands. Armand vomited his disillusion in the cool grass.

He watched no longer. A moment later when he passed the arbor the figures were no longer framed in its entrance: he could guess the reason. Head down, he strode purposely towards the white stone villa, anger turning his face white and hard, pain churning sickeningly in his stomach. She had deceived him and not only with Bernard; that he could perhaps understand, if not forgive. But to take that low-born rabble rouser as lover heated his rage to boiling point.

Indoors it was dark, the vast-ceilinged rooms pleasantly cooled by deep windows left open to the breeze. Once he too had owned a luxurious home like this, far better than this, he noted with tightened mouth. Bernard's stolen mansion must have been owned by a lesser aristocrat, for there were only two stories, the number of rooms appearing minimal.

"Monsieur." A white-haired servant, who, despite the shabby clothing of the visitor, had served the nobility long enough to recognize a member of it when he saw one, bowed to him.

"Citizen Desjardins is expecting me."

"Ah, yes. This way please."

Making no comment about his audacity in stepping through the open windows, at not waiting to be announced before entering, the servant took him to a room overlooking a placid lake where two swans glided majestically over the green water.

"My dear Armand. At last."

Bernard rose from his desk, coming to greet him with arms extended, offering friendship which Armand sensed was false.

"Good afternoon, citizen."

The servant quietly closed the door leaving them alone.

"Do you have them?" Bernard demanded, coming close, his dark eyes glowing with greed to contemplate the jewelry.

"Where are the safe conduct passes first?"

"You don't think I keep them here, my dear Armand?"

"Why not? Isn't that your desk?"

"Ah, but I have several offices."

"So you expect me to part with my only assurance of cooperation with nothing in return for it?"

Bernard shrugged, trying to curb his impatience. "You have my word."

"I had your word about the escape from Conciergerie. Marie is dead. Oh, yes, though you sought to keep it secret, I know. Public executions are hard to keep quiet, my *dear* Bernard."

Pausing in the assurance he had been formulating, Bernard scowled at him. "Who told you? I'll have his head."

"It's of no importance. The same source also revealed the whereabouts of a certain lady used as decoy for Marie."

"Oh, well, yes, Rosslyn's here with me. I intended to tell you."

"I'm sure you did."

"Come now, do I detect anger? Resentment? The lady is quite old enough to choose, Armand. She chose me."

Staring at Bernard's smiling complacency, Armand suddenly realized he did not know about the couple in the arbor. And for a moment the knowledge gave him pleasure.

"How fortunate she found herself destitute, otherwise her choice may not have been unduly influenced."

Hands clenched to suppress his annoyance, Bernard smiled.

"Jealous? Well, over so beautiful a lady who can blame you? If you feel she's kept here against her will, why don't you seek her out? She's reading in the gardens."

"Is she?"

"Every afternoon while I attend to business. Most obliging, don't you think?"

How much he would love to remove that smug smile with the truth. Content for the moment in dwelling privately on the situation, Armand said: "Enough of women. Let us get down to business, to my passage aboard ship to be exact. Seeing as your obliging lady love allows you time to work, surely by now you've managed a trifling signature or two."

Eyes narrowed, Bernard watched his cousin affect that air of arrogance he had inherited from his father, disliking it, nay, hating it, for he was excluded by it. Son of the wastrel brother, mothered by a provincial matron of little consequence, during his entire life Bernard had strived for power. He did not even use their name, he loathed it so, preferring instead the name of his stepfather, the clerk his mother married when François de Gramont obligingly succumbed to a stroke. Scorned by Armand and his like, the promotions offered by the People's Revolution presented everything he desired.

"Do not patronize me," he warned, dropping all pretense. "You can't afford it. Now give me the valuables first."

Armand hesitated, casting about for a solution. Bernard was determined to have the jewelry before he gave him the passage, and he could see no way around it. To say he had not got them, when spies must have already reported his progress, would avail him nothing. Not to present them to his cousin would be to not obtain the tickets nor the passes; it may even be to place his head on the proverbial windowsill, for Bernard seemed ill humored, despite his obvious advantage.

"Very well, putting myself entirely in your hands, relying on your integrity and the bond of blood between us—here they are."

Removing a pouch from around his waist, Armand spilled the stones on Bernard's desk, the rubies bouncing like huge drops of blood across the white papers. Emeralds like pullet eggs came next, followed by a pearl-encrusted pendant.

"Is this it?"

"All I brought with me. The rubies were taken from their setting before they were hidden. I don't know where the gold is now. The loyal man who was entrusted with its safety is probably a thousand miles away."

Mouth curving in a smile of delight, Bernard held the largest emerald to the light, fascinated by its myriad flashing design.

"Exquisite!"

"The passage. I have little time, Cousin."

"Ah, yes, at once. Far be it from me to keep so eager a traveler where he does not wish to be."

Crossing to his desk Bernard unlocked a small upper compartment. He placed some papers in an envelope.

"Don't put your seal on that just yet," Armand interrupted as Bernard withdrew wax and candle. Grimly he slit open the envelope taking several minutes to thoroughly read the contents before he was assured of their authenticity. "They seem all right. Here."

Bernard snatched the packet with bad grace, fuming to have his word questioned. "Such trust," he muttered as he pressed his ring into the hot wax.

"Farewell. I hope, for my own safety, we do not meet again," Armand dismissed, stepping towards the door. "Don't bother, I know my way out. By the way, Cousin, how are the roses this year?"

"Roses? As always. Why?"

"I thought a stroll by the arbor might prove enlightening."

"What do you mean? You're talking nonsense," Bernard dismissed him impatiently, his eyes straying to the gems glittering on his desk.

"Some foreign varieties are rank with deceit, my dear Bernard. But you shall discover this for yourself before long. *Au revoir.*"

Running over the smooth lawns, racing away from the flowery nook where Rosslyn delighted in another lover, Armand found his legs moving as if they belonged to another while he remained detached from the movement. Over and over again he pictured her with *him*. The man was well known to him, to all of Paris: Camille of the fire-breathing speeches, son of a stonemason from Saint Michael. But Rosslyn's knowledge of him was the only part which hurt.

Faithless! This one woman who had seemed different from the others, the love she offered him valued above all else. Now that love was cast so easily aside. Camille was virile, his lack of finesse, that animal brutality of the people no doubt appealed to some perverted part of her character. There was violence in her, he had long known that. Perhaps that taint met a like response in the muscular animal of the streets whose voice had the ring of truth, but whose heart was as black as Bernard's.

His horse was tethered by the gatehouse and Armand climbed to the saddle, his anger painfully tensing his muscles. Well, she was welcome to them both if that was her wish. Perhaps Camille's brutality, and Bernard's ineffectual performance held the opposite requirements needed to spice her hot-blooded demands. It was fortunate he had seen them together today. The excuses he had made to himself when he heard the rumors had seemed valid until confronted by the sight of her nestled in another's arms, by the knowledge that other man was buried deep within the heat of her body. He would go aboard ship with his sons never to return to the country of his birth, making instead a new life in the Americas.

Determination tightened his jaw as he fought the emotional remnant of his attachment to her. No longer was he drawn back by that intangible foolishness called love, the desire to protect her. Rosslyn Burton seemed well able to look after herself. And he turned his horse's head towards Paris, the anger throbbing in his blood painfully mingling with the rhythmic hoofbeats.

September! Regardless of the determination of the revolutionaries to rename the months according to their own calendar, it would always be September. Looking across the rain-drenched grass Rosslyn was poignantly reminded of home. Burton Hall, where her husband undoubtedly waited in puzzled anger for her return, was not the place her heart craved. It was the windswept headland, the woods and pastures which beckoned with nostalgic pain. The balmy haze of the month lay like a mantle over the wooded farmland, where trees changed slowly to russet and gold. Crisp nights, the smell of woodsmoke, all these things were so real she felt she had only to put out her hand to grasp, to possess at last . . .

"Why so sad?" Bernard asked coming to her side, resting his soft hands on her shoulders.

"I want to go home."

Almost as if he had spoken it she sensed the resentment, the withdrawal at her words.

"This is your home now."

"But I don't want it to be. My visit was to be of a few days' duration until Clarence could be contacted. The time's lapsed from days to months. If you're unable to contact my brother, then at least lend me some cash, or get me a ticket aboard a packet for Dover."

"Are you not happy here?" he asked in surprise, noting the flush spreading across her cheekbones in a banner. "Haven't I given you all you could ask? Gowns, jewels. Is this life so terrible?"

"You don't understand, do you?"

"Is it because I've made few demands on you, too

215

few, perhaps?" The words, soft spoken, were accompanied by a caress as Bernard misunderstood her reason for sadness. "There's nothing I wouldn't do for you, Rosslyn," he vowed. "All this time I've longed to make love to you, yet because you didn't invite it, I've stayed aloof. Can this be the reason you are unhappy?"

When he would have kissed her she twisted away. "You've been kind to me and I appreciate that. While I was glad to be your hostess, I don't wish to be your mistress."

He blanched, his mouth withering to a thin, tight line.

"Why else do you think I've showered you with gifts?"

"Mistakenly, I thought out of kindness and compassion."

"You've cheated me."

"I never promised my body to you, we never even discussed the matter. Week after week I've waited for news from home or from Armand . . ."

"I've already told you he deserted you. Gone long since."

"Ah, that is what you told me, but I know it to be a lie. He's in Paris."

Spinning on his heel Bernard strode towards his desk. Noisily shuffling papers he stopped to demand: "Who told you that?"

"It's unimportant how I know. I want you to tell me if it's true."

"Why? Do you fancy yourself in love with him still? Is that why you're so anxious to leave?"

"Whether he be dead or not, I would still want to go home," she vowed, tears stinging her eyes with the futility of their discussion.

"Strange you should make such a prediction, this time next week he most certainly will be dead."

Rosslyn gripped the chair arm at his statement. "So you do know where he is! All this time you've lied to me just to keep me with you."

Bernard smiled to see the shock on her face, to watch her composure disintegrating before the power of his knowledge. Intoxicated by the feeling it gave him, he cast all caution aside. "To want you, is that a crime? To admire your beauty? Armand doesn't deserve you. He's unworthy of you. He attempted to escape and was arrested. It's out of my hands."

"You liar!" She was on her feet and she raced towards him pounding his chest in anger.

Exhilarated by her fury, Bernard seized her wrists, imprisoning her in a grasp surprisingly strong for one so slight. Then he pulled her close to kiss her mouth. "Would that I could arouse such ire in you more often. Your behavior excites me, Madame."

"You had an agreement with him. Only at your word could he be arrested," she accused, eyes flashing as she struggled to be free. Abruptly he released her so that she fell to the floor.

"True, I have absolute authority over those matters," he agreed. "Sufficient to say my cousin displeased me, so for that he must pay. You fool, still grieving for him when he cared so little for you. You should be glad of the chance for vengeance."

"Though he never wants to see me again, he need not die for it," she whispered, sitting where she had fallen. She wondered if she begged Bernard, if she promised herself in return for the favor of setting Armand free, he would grant it.

"What, aren't you going to weep at my feet? Aren't you going to implore me to spare your lover?" Bernard asked sarcastically, staring down at her.

Anger blazed at his statement, convincing Rosslyn she would not be humiliated by asking him for Armand's release, the scene he obviously anticipated with pleasure. One look at the smugness and the dead black eyes, told her Armand would be destroyed whatever her sacrifice in his behalf. There must be a way to save him, but at the moment she did not know it.

"That would please you, wouldn't it? To see me grovel so you could have the satisfaction of refusing. I've no intention of begging. Tell me, what happened to the heirlooms which were to buy his freedom? To the passage aboard ship for the Americas?"

"Ah, the passage is quite safe in my desk, retrieved intact when he was arrested. As for the jewelry, at this moment it is in a vault below the Assembly. If you promise to mend your manners, perhaps I'll have the rubies set in a necklace for you. How about a pendant to dangle provocatively at the cleft of your so lovely breasts?"

Reaching out, he gripped the front of her bodice to yank her to her feet, tearing the material in his anger.

"You are odious. If you think after this I'll consent to . . ."

"There's nothing to consent to, my dear Madame, you have no other choice. If I wish I can have you arrested, tried and guillotined before sunset tomorrow. Do you want to earn that ignoble fate solely through pride? I think not. You will find my personal demands are moderate, far more controlled than my hot-blooded cousin's, whose women form a large, if not too select, assembly. Now, go to your room and freshen your appearance. We are to entertain at dinner tonight. It's already after six."

Drawing herself to full height Rosslyn stalked from the room. Her mind in a turmoil, she puzzled over a plan of action until she heard the rumble of carriage wheels announcing the arrival of the first guests. Automatically she reached for a gown, hastily struggling into a maroon silk, the neckline trimmed with garlands of silk camellias. As she dressed she pictured Bernard's smug assurance over his triumph, any chance of liking him extinguished by today's revelation. Though at times she thought she hated Armand for deserting her, she did not want him to die. As Bernard so proudly reminded her, he had absolute power in the matter. Without the necessary papers it was not possible to move freely about the country. Denied Clarence's support, she did not have those documents to assure her safety. Now the hope of obtaining them from Bernard, of ever seeing England again, had dimmed to obscurity. As she pulled on long white gloves, checking her appearance in the gilt-framed mirror above the dressing table, an idea, chilling her with its consequences, came winging through her mind. Camille desired her also. She had never asked him for favors she had not paid for. If Bernard were dead, Camille would benefit from the vacant position. Would he willingly commit a crime for her? There was little doubt the chosen victim would meet with his approval, for he spared no love for Bernard.

When she cornered Camille beside the fountain in the spacious garden later that evening, he laughed at her suggestion.

"Cherie, what is this, too much brandy? Are you insane? Me, murder Bernard! Why? We are partners, not enemies."

"He's *my* enemy," she spat, blood pounding to her throat in fear of finding she had betrayed her intention to unsympathetic ears.

"Why spoil matters? He's not gifted with undue perception. We've eluded him these past weeks. Don't spoil things."

She turned from him when he would have embraced her, walking rapidly towards the garden, far away from the detested white villa overflowing with music and light, from those people who were Bernard's friends, therefore her enemies.

"Don't cry, Rosslyn—ah, you know I'd do anything for you, but not that," Camille soothed, pursuing her, catching her in the shadow of the cypress hedge where he pulled her to his body.

Rosslyn shivered in his arms, sobbing, cold, desolate, taking the comfort he offered, but angry with him for denying what she asked. For the second time today a man had vowed he would do anything for her, but it was never the thing she craved most. The only actions they contemplated were for their own satisfaction.

"I'm not crying now. It's over," she said flatly, drawing away from him before their bodies demanded further. "Let us go back."

Camille shrugged. "Very well, you strange woman. Though I had thought out here in the moonlight would have been our perfect rendezvous. Lovers are turned magical by moonlight—did you not tell me that once?"

Moonlight. Yes, that night so long ago, lifetimes away when Armand had wanted to make love to her in the garden. When he had revealed his desire, it had been one of the most magical nights of her life. To violate those memories with Camille was unthinkable. Her mouth twisted bitterly, Rosslyn nodded, drawing her wrap tight about her shoulders to drive off the chill of the September evening. "Insanity on my part, don't you think?"

"But I find your insanity most interesting," he whispered, catching her about the waist and swinging her towards him. "Come. I want you. What's wrong with moonlight?"

Tonight the fire of his desire tempted her only mildly, she was too preoccupied with the problem of Bernard. "Please, we're usually honest with each other. Tonight I'm not in the mood."

Surprised at her answer he pulled a face. "When, pray tell, will you be in the mood?"

It was Rosslyn's turn to pull a face. "Who knows. Listen to me, Camille. Seeing that you'll not bring about the end I seek, if I do it, will you help me escape?"

Taken aback at her words, yet still treating the entire conversation as a joke, he grinned. "Eh, you are insane. Of course I'll help you. No man with any sense would discard a piece like you. Something tells me you'll be in the mood if I promise this assistance."

"Perhaps—but not now, there are too many people and their presence spoils it for me. But you do promise?"

"*Allons donc?* You're serious aren't you? Poor little girl, what has our terrible ogre done to you?" Camille whispered, holding her close to him, not allowing her to go when she would have moved to the terrace.

"Don't ask too many questions. Have I your word?"

At her insistence he kissed the top of her head. "My word. If it's tonight I'll be at the inn in the village. Be careful, *cherie*."

"I will. Thank you, Camille, I don't know what I'd do without you."

Swiftly she kissed his face then fled through the open windows to the glittering salon, leaving him touching his cheek in surprise for her fleeting attentions, staring at the moon, worry niggling his stomach at her suggestion. He did not care if Bernard Desjardins was strung from the nearest lamppost. He had even contemplated such an action himself until he discovered Bernard was more

220

valuable to him alive than dead while he enjoyed the dual personality of Claude the revolutionary and a member of the Assembly.

For Rosslyn he would do anything, even that. Fear she would involve herself in a plot from which he could not easily extricate her caused his uneasiness. He liked to think he was invincible in times of confidence, but in times of honesty, he knew he lied. There were too many enemies to rest secure. Camille turned to watch her, but Rosslyn had already disappeared, lost in the moving throng of the brightly lit salon. Brooding, he leaned against the orangery wall, a heavy scowl drawing his brows together. His reaction to her tonight surprised him. Honesty was a rare bedfellow in his daily life; now he forced himself to assess his true feelings for the woman. Could he be in love with her? His mouth twisted in a cynical smile and he came from his leaning place as if shot from a catapult. Insanity was not just reserved for women on moonlit nights. With an oath he gestured obscenely to the silver ball shimmering above.

"And that to you," he muttered, slouching towards the stable, disgusted with his treacherous emotions.

When the guests had gone home Rosslyn hurried to her room to freshen her appearance before she embarked on her important mission. The crime she contemplated failed to move her; too much had happened lately for her to feel remorse at the taking of Bernard's life. Growing hatred for his treachery swirled through her like strong wine as she rearranged her hair, pinning a full-blown rose to the side of her looped-up ringlets. He must suspect nothing; therefore, she would appear her most lovely. Bernard would be easily convinced by his own conceit that she had changed her mind about becoming his mistress.

"Come in," he answered gruffly to her timid knock on his bedroom door.

Rosslyn entered the second-floor bedroom with trepidation, having never ventured there before. Thankfully his infrequent kisses and embraces had not demanded further, and she had not been tempted to join him of her own accord.

"Are you busy?" she asked, giving him her most charming smile.

"For you, no." His answering smile betrayed his sheer delight in her being there, the glint of imminent conquest turning his dark eyes hot. "So you have changed your mind."

"Yes. I'm no fool."

He came to her with outstretched arms to begin the experience he had dwelled on so long in private. She was his at last. Not Armand's anymore. In this competition at least he had proved the master. "You look very lovely. In fact, tonight you had a reckless gaiety about you which I found very enhancing. Dare I hope the emotion was spawned by your wise decision?"

Rosslyn lowered her dark lashes, hiding her violet eyes from him, firing his desire by the coquettish gesture, until he gripped her arm with such intensity she gasped. "You're right, my decision caused my changed mood. Now, please, dearest, you're hurting me. Would you have me bruised?"

Laughing softly he released his grip. "Only with kisses of love," he murmured, pressing his mouth into the warm hollow of her neck, breathing deep of the violet perfume with which her skin seemed drenched, a scent which plunged him deeper into madness.

Rosslyn looked about the room noting the drawn rose-colored curtains, the preparations for retirement. Outside the wind had risen obligingly so the noisy rustling sound of branches would muffle the deed. Belatedly she glanced about for a weapon, not thinking beforehand that there might not be a convenient missile. Besides a marble cherub with weighted base the only possibility was a silver letter opener lying on the coverlet beside a scattered pile of envelopes.

"How exquisite you are. All my life I've dreamed of someone like you to care for me," he murmured against her neck.

"It's to my fortune you find me so appealing," she said with a little laugh, gently nudging him towards the bed. Realizing her intent, he smiled, his eager expression filled with joy and relief.

"Ah, so lovely and so eager. What more can I ask."

His fingers fumbled with the hookings of her bodice and she slid to the coverlet with a giggle, playing her part expertly while wondering if she had the strength to plunge that mock sword deep enough for a mortal wound. She lay full length, smiling up at him, inwardly despising him for the desire flickering over his face, for the fumbling haste of his trembling hands.

The dress came down from her shoulders, slid to the beginning of swelling flesh. With a throaty laugh, she took him by the ears to press his burning face against her body, hiding his eyes so he could not see. Moaning love-nonsense, not really knowing what she said, Rosslyn strained towards the knife. Another moment and it was cold in her grasp, seeming so small and delicate beside its potential victim. With her free hand she stroked Bernard's neck, patted his hair, soothing him into a security of passion, teasing, pressing his head closer while she poised the dagger above its mark between his narrow shoulder blades encased in brown velvet.

When he would have moved she urged him to more love kisses, knowing her breasts must be an ugly pattern of purple; so inspired was he by her enthusiasm, he did not need to be held in place. Using both hands she gripped the knife, gritting her teeth, arms tensed, willing all her strength to this final act, for there would be no second chance. And the blade descended.

Gasping in pain and shock, Bernard struggled up, the letter opener protruding from his back, his eyes black holes in a parchment-pale face.

"You bitch!" he gasped, transfixed with horror.

In panic now, knowing the knife had not driven deep enough for a mortal wound, Rosslyn twisted her leg about his as he staggered backward from the bed. Brought off balance, he thudded to the carpet, driving the blade home to the hilt.

Crouching over him, Rosslyn stared back at his wide eyes, hating him, yet feeling mounting fear at the knowledge she had taken a man's life.

"It was for him I did it," she whispered. He asked her to help him, to pull out the weapon, to bring assistance; without pity she ignored his hoarse pleas as she fumbled around his neck for the silver key which un-locked his desk.

Too startled still to call for outside help Bernard stared up at her, then realizing what she sought, he chuckled, the sound gurgling through his lungs. "Fool . . . you'll never leave the house . . . no papers."

Surprised by her strength she yanked the chain free, reminded momentarily of the jailor who had robbed her of Will's gift during that nightmare introduction to the Conciergerie.

"For all you've done to him, and to me, and to all those countless others who were fool enough to trust you, you deserve to die."

At her vehement statement his eyes flickered wide as he grasped the extent of his wound.

"Die!" The incredulous gasp was accompanied by a struggling effort to prop himself upright, but his elbow slipped sideways and he thumped back, crying out at the renewed tearing of the weapon.

Waiting only until she knew he was dead, Rosslyn threw a wallhanging over the body, trying not to look at the white face, at the spreading crimson mantle congealing on the floorboards. The cover made a mound on the far side of the bed; perhaps it would go unnoticed by anyone glancing inside the room. She drew the damask bedhangings before placing Bernard's shoes at the foot of the bed. It nauseated her to touch his feet; though still warm, the touch of his flesh repelled her. The knowledge that she was the bringer of his death caused her heart to pound loud as a drum.

The staircase was dark. Feeling her way towards his study, afraid to light a candle at so late an hour and arouse the servants, Rosslyn fumbled for the door handle. The study was cold and smelled of woodsmoke from the fire Bernard had burned here this afternoon. With the door safely closed, Rosslyn lit a candle at a faltering flame still sputtering about the edge of the charred logs.

With trembling hands she unlocked each drawer in turn, searching for anything which could be the boat tickets. Her search was fruitless. Conscious of the rapid passage of time, of the need to flee the house before the murder was discovered, she grew frantic in her search, upending drawers as she rummaged through the contents. All her search produced was a crumpled envelope with Bernard's own seal; it was hidden, so it was obviously of importance. Ripping open the paper she shivered with relief to find identity papers made out in the name of Armand St. Clare and his sons, Louis and Charles. There were two papers with the name of the ship, *La Belle Amie,* assuring passage for three on its next voyage. The date written there made her gasp with surprise, September twentieth. Surely that date had passed? Bernard told her she had been in the Conciergerie over a week. Rounding on the rolled gold calendar on his desk, she read today's date, September sixteenth. So he had lied about that too. The reason behind his lies had become apparent today; to make her think Armand had deserted her, that he had not waited those days of her confinement was Bernard's intention, so that in her pain she would turn to him. For a while it had almost worked. Now she knew Armand had not forsaken her, love flooded back, warmly comforting in the face of danger.

Thrusting the papers inside the bodice of her gown, where the stiff paper clawed her flesh, Rosslyn opened the deep windows to the balcony. It was too much of a risk to go back through the house, far better to drop the few feet to the terrace.

As she raced over the lawns to cover, knowing she made a perfect target against the silver moonlight, Rosslyn heard a man's startled cry from upstairs. Someone had discovered the body.

Gasping, feeling as if her lungs would burst, she leaped behind the bank of orange blossom separating the lawns from the rose garden. Resting to catch her breath, she watched the house in alarm as a network of lights moved from room to room. They sought the assassin. How long before they found she was gone?

Chilled at the thought, knowing that her only hope lay in immediate escape, Rosslyn began a stumbling flight to the stable. There was a horse there beside the carriage animals; she had heard it last week, but whether the nag was rideable remained to be seen.

It was difficult to find the equipment in the weak illumination of the moon's light. From his stall the horse watched with interest. Hefting the saddle over the high-ridged backbone, she shuddered at the discovery of his advanced age, wondering if the animal could bear her weight. God, he was old!

At last she scrambled into the saddle, wadding her maroon ball gown in a roll around her knees. At first the horse refused to budge. Urging him, alternately cajoling and cursing, Rosslyn got the stubborn animal moving towards the stable door. A hum of increased sound filtered over the gardens from the house which had fast become a blaze of lights. They still searched, she could see dark figures etched against the lighted windows, holding lights aloft, seeking Bernard's assassin.

Turning the horse towards the narrow lane which ran behind the estate, she cursed anew to find the gate padlocked. Moving the length of the rock wall, she found a tumbledown spot where she urged the horse forward, praying to God he would jump. Surprisingly, the old horse rallied with enthusiasm, scrambling over the low barrier, kicking stones loose as they crossed. Patting him, giving him reams of extravagant praise, Rosslyn urged the nag to maximum speed, which was little faster than a walk. The village was less than a mile, yet it was the first logical place they would look for her after the house search revealed her disappearance. She must get to Camille before it was too late.

CHAPTER THIRTEEN

Rattling into the innyard on that ancient bag of bones, Rosslyn found the shutters closed. It was so small an inn, she imagined there was only one sizeable guest room which must be the room with a broken balcony overlooking the weed-choked fish pond. She gambled that this was where Camille slept.

Choosing a small rock, she pitched it against the shutter, cringing as the missile slid the length of the low eave with clattering passage. There was no response. She repeated the action. Was it her imagination or could she already hear carriage wheels on the road?

A moment later she was rewarded by a rattling noise at the window as the shutter reeled drunkenly outward on its broken hinge.

"Camille, is that you?" she hissed.

"I'm Camille. What the devil do you want?" the man demanded, poking out his shaggy dark head in the moonlight. "Christ—you!"

"Let me in. They'll be coming this way soon."

"That horse! God, it should have been soup long ago." He laughed, and she realized he was not wholly sober.

"Let me in, damn you. You promised."

The smile vanished from his face as he tensed, forcing his muddled wits in order. "Promised?"

"Yes, this evening. In the garden."

"You've done—it?"

"Yes."

With an oath he leaned forward, his strong hands reaching over the wooden bannister. Standing in the saddle, Rosslyn gripped the welcome lifeline, allowing him to pull her upward while beneath her the old nag shifted so that she bumped her hips against the stone-work. Finally scrambling upward, ripping nails as she clutched the coping to brace herself, his arms went like a vice choking out her breath as he crushed her chest wall. Rosslyn then stood beside him on the ramshackle balcony.

"Now I've got to dispose of that stew meat," Camille muttered. "Get inside. In the bed."

Dropping to the ground, he seized the horse's bridle and ran with him towards a thicket of trees. Panting from his exertion, he patted the bony rump as he looped the reins over a forked branch. "There. Go to sleep, you bag of bones."

Obediently the horse collapsed on the ivy-covered ground and Camille raced back to the inn, the rumbling sound of carriage wheels growing louder.

He had just scrambled under the bedcovers when pounding fists loud enough to wake the inn's occupants sounded on the door below, dangerously shaking the precarious structure which appeared to hang by a few worm-eaten struts.

"Tell me what happened!" Camille hissed in the darkness, taking her against him for she trembled with cold and shock.

"I killed him."

"*Sacrebleu*—how?"

"With his letter opener, only it didn't kill him at first—not strong enough—then I tripped him so he fell backwards—and he bled all over the place."

"Are you sure he's dead?"

"Yes. I made sure his heart wasn't beating before I left."

"Why? *Bon Dieu*—why?" He groaned, cradling her against him beneath the musty covers, wondering how he could save her.

"He lied to me about everything. Oh, Camille, he wanted me to sleep with him—he threatened me. And I needed Armand's papers, his passage. Bernard had him arrested."

"Yes, I know."

"You knew and you didn't tell me," she gasped.

Camille was silent, then with a sigh he muttered. "Why should I? You're mine now."

Rosslyn began to sob softly, wearily, the emotional upheaval of her day taking its toll. Gently he held her while he raked his mind for a way out. Footsteps sounded in the corridor, then a thump shuddered the door.

"Citizen! A thousand pardons." The landlord was unsure of his treatment after waking such a powerful man. Yet those at the door spoke of murder and treachery.

Extricating himself from her arms, Camille padded to the door. "Yes, what is it?"

"Have you heard any disturbance tonight?"

"Not until now. Why?"

The landlord smiled sheepishly. "I told them you would know nothing, but they insisted I ask. They even wanted to search the rooms, citizen. Asked me when you arrived too."

"They?"

"Men from Citizen Desjardins's villa down the road. Perhaps you know it."

"Yes. I'm acquainted with the good citizen. Has there been trouble?"

Lowering his voice, the innkeeper leaned close. "Murdered, in his own bed, poor man. Now, citizen, what say you to that?"

"It's unbelievable! Such a loyal man! I'm shocked. Who's his assassin?"

"Who knows? There are thousands who could fit that bill, if you'll pardon me for saying so, citizen," the landlord added hastily, afraid in case he had said too much.

Camille winked, immediately assuring his confidence. "Agreed. There are many who bear grudges. No, I've heard nothing. While I don't normally interfere with justice, bringing them here tonight is out of the question." Camille stood aside so the landlord could see the mounded female form in the bed.

"Oh, a thousand pardons, citizen—I had no idea." The landlord winked as he backed away. "I'll see to it then."

"Thank you, citizen."

Camille closed the door and came back to bed, listening for the man's footsteps to die away before he spoke.

"While I talked to him I've thought of an idea. Come, get out of bed, *cherie*. We can't stay here. If they know who they seek, you're a dead woman."

In less than an hour they were on the road for Paris, Rosslyn muffled in Camille's black cloak which fitted like a tent. As they swayed from side to side, hitting ruts which flung them unceremoniously in each other's arms, Camille's mind darted through all the possibilities until he had formulated a working plan.

"Don't worry, you'll be safe. I've an acquaintance in St. Antoine parish, Dr. Belhomme. He runs an asylum."

"For the insane?" Rosslyn gasped.

Camille chuckled at her horror. "Aye, 'tis supposedly for the insane, but 'tis more of a prison these days. A very expensive prison. Only for those with wealthy friends, if you get my meaning."

"He takes in emigrés?"

"Political prisoners with money who are too ill to stand trial. 'Tis a recent thing, this traffic, and for us, most fortunate. You've no need to fear it, *cherie*. Would I put you in danger?" he whispered, taking her icy hands in his, chafing warmth to the numb fingers. "Trust me."

She smiled in the darkness as she heard the tender sincerity in his gruff voice. "Yes, I trust you, Camille, with my life."

Her words touched him, moving him close to grief. Alarmed at the unexpected reaction he noisily cleared his throat. "Last night in the garden I thought about this—Rosslyn, don't bargain with me any more."

"All right."

"Promise?"

"Now it's my turn, is it? All right, I promise. Why do you ask that?"

"Because I love you."

The deep, matter-of-fact statement rumbled through the coach, taking rhythm from the crunching wheels speeding her to Paris. "In love?" she gasped.

230

"Don't sound surprised," he snarled, "I'm capable of emotion, you know, little aristocrat bitch."

"Camille, please don't be hurt; or angry. It's just that I thought you didn't believe in love . . ."

"Bah! And so I don't," he growled, withdrawing to his corner of the carriage.

Touched, yet bewildered by his declaration, Rosslyn tentatively slipped her hand in his. "So how can you love me, then?"

His throaty chuckle rumbled in the darkness. "Don't ask me, *cherie,* I've no answer. Come, sit beside me."

Lulled by the warm safety of his presence Rosslyn dozed, not waking till the carriage halted with a lurch. Pale dawn light filtered through the half-closed blinds. The noise of clattering produce carts and the shouts of their drivers filled the air as they jostled for places in the stream of traffic awaiting admittance through the city gate.

"Are we there?"

Camille nodded, putting her from him. "Stay over there. 'Twill be better for appearances."

With churning stomach Rosslyn obeyed, wondering what would become of her now, or how endurable would be Dr. Belhomme's asylum. She could trust Camille not to knowingly leave her in squalid or dangerous surroundings, yet she was penniless, so the quality of her treatment was not assured. Even at the Conciergerie for those with enough money luxuries could be bought, such things as clean mattresses, food and wine. Not far from the Conciergerie gates, chicken and champagne could be purchased for inmates if one had enough money to bribe the jailors . . .

"Citizeness," Camille rapped, turning her attentions toward a red-nosed guard who peered at her through the grimy window. The shade had been opened to allow an unobstructed view. Wild-haired, grimy-faced, enveloped in the voluminous black cloak, Rosslyn realized she must look the part of a desperate fugitive.

"Papers," the guard demanded, finally looking at the male occupant of the carriage, swallowing as he quickly identified him, then trying to erase the slip with an ingratiating smile. "Citizen, what a pleasure to meet you in person. All Paris knows . . ."

"I thank you, but can we speed up entry? This prisoner is due for Belhomme's asylum before nine this morning."

The guard nodded, leaning on the window which had been obligingly opened to allow him the scrutiny. "Dangerous?"

"She may have murdered someone. It's very sad, such an attractive woman too. Mute you know."

"Ah, is that so."

The guard turned reddened eyes toward her, leering, scrutinizing the folds of the dark cloak in an effort to determine the size of her breasts. Camille viewed her gravely. He had given her the perfect reason to remain silent. Eyes downcast, Rosslyn stared at the floorboards, resisting a hysterical urge to laugh.

"I have her papers here, citizen. You'll have to give me a moment. I've injured my hand and I'm slow." Camille made the gesture of reaching inside his coat with his left hand, but the guard waved him aside.

"Ah, no need to bother with that, under the circumstances. I hear they don't waste the pretty ones at places like that, regular brothels so I've heard. She'll make a good entry, though with that wrapping I can't see much."

Camille made no move to uncover the merchandise. Waiting a moment, then realizing it was in vain, the guard straightened up and waved them on.

"Good day, citizen. You're a good, patriotic man. I'll see that your superior hears about it," Camille assured.

Thrilled at the commendation, the guard shuffled from the coach, chest puffed out with pride, raising his voice to order the scattering townspeople away from the carriage, demonstrating his leadership for Camille's benefit.

"Posturing fool," Camille sneered as they moved forward, leaving the guard marshalling the vegetable sellers about like infantry.

"We're lucky he is a fool: I've no papers."

"Don't you think I know that? Since the Suspect Law

232

that's immediate cause for arrest. They won't ask for papers at Belhomme's, thank God."

The narrow dark streets were nearly deserted at this early hour and Rosslyn stared dismally through the window at the crumbling, rat-infested hovels where beggars crouched like so many bundles of rags in convenient doorways. How far away seemed the peaceful tranquility of home.

Opposite, slumped in the corner, Camille smiled reassuringly at her. His expression changed suddenly to anger when the carriage was forced to stop a second time before being admitted to the sector where Dr. Belhomme resided.

"What is it?" he demanded, letting down the window with a thump.

"Ah, it's you, citizen," the guard smiled in recognition, his hand on the door. "Routine, nothing more. There's been a murder, nearly as terrible as that of Citizen Marat. I suppose it's another Rolandin sympathizer—you haven't heard? Citizen Desjardins was murdered in his bed. Terrible it was. A woman most likely. His latest piece. We've a warrant for immediate seizure," he added, waving a paper at the window.

"Is that so. Well, it's no concern of mine. I'm taking this prisoner to the asylum. And be careful, though she appears quiet, she's very dangerous," Camille warned as the man leaned inside the coach. With surprising speed, the narrow head was withdrawn and Rosslyn was viewed speculatively from a safe distance.

"Mad is she?"

"As a hatter. She may have killed several men."

In awe the guard reviewed the pretty face half-obscured by a cloak pulled close about her chin. "Go on—never would have thought that. She's a pretty one too. Anyway, citizen, if you see anything suspicious you'll know what to do."

"Of course. And thank you for your information. I'll report to the Palais de Justice and see what I can learn."

Waved on once more, the carriage rolled over the cobblestones towards the appointed place.

"Too bad they've identified you already, that'll make

it harder to get you away," Camille muttered, rubbing his eyes, deep in thought.

"What of Armand? How will I get these papers to him?"

"Forget him. You've your own skin to think about now," Camille snapped, then regretting his ill humor, he took her hand. "Give them to me, or keep them till you can make your own arrangements. Whatever you want to do. I suppose you're afraid I won't give them to the right party, so you'd better keep them. You can receive visitors so Clarence will come to you at the asylum. If I have my way you'll be aboard ship in less than a week. At those prices I can't afford much longer. Six thousand livres is the old bastard's going price, for that your papers get conveniently lost in Fouquier Tinville's files. If I can get you admitted before he really knows what you've done, we'll be all right. Once he finds out, the price will probably double."

"Six thousand livres! Where will you get so much money?" Rosslyn gasped in surprise at the astounding fee.

"From some fat aristocrat, *cherie*. They've got it hidden away. Let them buy me something I want—yet, you know, maybe I don't want that. I've just realized . . . once you set sail I'll never see you again."

They stared at each other. Rosslyn was surprised to see the unaccustomed pallor of Camille's strong face, the dull blackness of his eyes. "Perhaps someday we'll meet again," she soothed.

At that moment the carriage lurched to a stop, flinging her in his lap where he crushed her in a farewell embrace till she thought her bones would snap.

"Here we are, you stupid aristocrat bitch, 70 Rue de Charonne," he muttered into her hair. "If you hadn't taken matters into your own hands we could have— *Merde!* Women!"

In exasperation he flung her from him and swung open the carriage door, aggravation plain in every movement. Miserably, Rosslyn followed him, gathering the trailing cloak in both hands so she would not stumble, not wanting to go inside, not wanting to leave behind the last hope of protection she possessed.

The asylum of Dr. Belhomme was more like a country villa than either a mental institution or a prison. Pleasantly surprised by the surroundings, Rosslyn found that the villa sported a large tree-dotted park where one could stroll. There were gardens and a courtyard with benches arranged about a fountain, even an orchard fragrant with apples. Blinking, fully expecting the pleasant surroundings to dissolve before her eyes, Rosslyn was filled with gratitude for Camille's decision to bring her here.

The inmates were served palatable meals, selections from the bill of fare decided by the amount paid to Dr. Belhomme. It was obvious that these mental patients were members of a very elite set, the few actual cases of insanity shunted upstairs to the distant attics so as not to offend the more distinguished clientele. To her surprise Rosslyn found the evenings were filled with music and card games enjoyed in the company of guests whose carriages lined the streets outside the asylum.

For three days Rosslyn enjoyed this unreal existence watching the incoming visitors for signs of Camille. Instead of Camille, on Wednesday evening, another tall figure in a plain brown suit stepped inside the main salon, head and shoulders above the other chattering guests.

"Clarence!" Rosslyn almost swooned with delight to see her brother sauntering through the salon as if this social evening at Dr. Belhomme's establishment was a normal Wednesday routine for him.

"Dearest sister, I trust you are feeling much recovered today," he said, loud enough for the bystanders to hear. Taking his hand she led him outside to the secluded gardens where few dallied once the evening social hour had begun.

"Oh, God, Clarence, I'd given up hope of ever seeing you again," Rosslyn gasped, fighting tears as she trembled in his arms.

Clarence held her close, surprised by the unexpected display of affection. Though he knew his sister loved him, her emotions were usually under tight control; this was a far different person from the slightly frivolous girl

235

who had accompanied him aboard the ship for France two months ago.

"Steady. Come on. It's really me. For God's sake, where have you been hiding?" he demanded when at last, smiling through her tears, she released him.

Rosslyn led him to a bench on the open grass with no adjacent shrubbery to conceal eavesdroppers.

"Hiding! I might ask you the same question. All this time I've been waiting for you to contact *me*."

Clarence grinned. "Sorry, but until recently I'd no idea where you were. After that Conciergerie disaster everything went haywire. Our communications were nil. Armand's in prison, you know that, don't you?"

"Yes, I discovered it yesterday. Can you talk to him?"

"No. He's allowed no visitors."

Reaching inside her gown, Rosslyn extracted the folded envelope with Bernard's seal. "Here, these are his papers and passage for the Americas."

"Where the devil did you get those?" Clarence demanded, taking the packet, putting it safely inside his jacket as he spoke.

"That's a long story. Maybe you know part of it already."

"This fellow, Camille, what is he to you?" Clarence asked suspiciously as he studied her face.

"A friend."

"I'd heard that you and he were lovers."

"Does one sleep with one's enemies?" Rosslyn challenged, holding his gaze.

"Then it's true! How you've changed," he said, shaking his head in bewilderment. "I hardly know you."

"I hardly know myself. Now, we're not allowed much time, so before you go something must be settled. Enough days have been wasted as it is. There's a warrant out for my arrest . . ."

"The charge?"

"Murder."

"My God!"

Rosslyn smiled at his shocked face without humor. "Camille brought me here. He saved my life. I'll always owe him that. He says he'll arrange passage for me to England, but before I leave, we—you—someone, must free Armand. The ship sails on the twentieth. You've the guarantee of his safety in your pocket. Outside Paris the provincials won't care enough to question who Armand St. Clare and his sons are. They'll just see the official seal. Now that Bernard's dead there's no one else who'll pursue a vendetta. We should be able to free him if we can get money for bribes. Bernard has hidden the jewelry in the vaults—"

"Forget it, love. Armand's already been tried."

"What!"

Taking her hands, wanting to ease a little of the shock, but unable to do so, Clarence said, "He's to be executed on Thursday. There's no way to arrange matters in so short a time."

Pain burst within her heart in a stifling, choking wave. Rosslyn gritted her teeth to keep back the cry of anguish which rose to her throat. She had even committed murder to save him and it was all in vain.

"No—say it's not true," she cried in a small, strangled voice, turning away so that he wouldn't see her betraying emotion. "Then there's no hope?"

"While he lives there's always hope," Clarence decided, standing up, beginning to pace the length of the path while deep in thought. Coming back to her he knelt, slipping his arm about her shaking shoulders. "Don't cry, love. I've just thought of something. It may not work, but we can try it. What about that girl he stayed with? What was her name?"

"Fleurette." Speaking the name twisted the emotion painfully deep in Rosslyn's heart. Trust Clarence to say "stayed with"; that was such a nice way of putting it.

"That's right. Do you suppose she'd help us? Lord knows, everyone in her district would help if she asked them, I'm sure of that. That type of woman's always . . ."

"Clarence, maybe I'm being unduly stupid but I don't see the connection," Rosslyn said, making her speech careful and deliberate.

"Well, I'm not sure I do either at the moment. We

could rescue him from the tumbril. It's the only way. His cell guards are a rarity—honest. I already tried to bribe them."

"How can we take him from the tumbril? And why will Fleurette be of help?"

Clarence smiled. "Don't worry about that, love. Let me do the worrying. If this Camille can be trusted to help you, then I'll turn all my attentions to Armand. What I don't understand is why a revolutionary's helping *you,* especially someone like him. Lord, he virtually sets the crowd alight every time he speaks."

Smiling, forcing back fear and worry, Rosslyn pushed his arm. "Well, you certainly underestimate my charms, brother dear. Tell me, are you still being honorable with Jeanette?"

Clarence did not reply to her question, though his fair cheeks were suddenly suffused with stinging blood. Rosslyn had her answer.

"Now look here, that was unfair," he protested, grinning shamefacedly at the triumphant look she flashed.

"Don't waste what you have, it doesn't last forever," she whispered, gripping his hand, fighting absurd tears of self-pity.

With the swift assurance of his utmost efforts to free Armand, Clarence took his leave. Rosslyn watched his broad figure until he disappeared from view in the misty lamplit street.

CHAPTER FOURTEEN

Fleurette answered the demanding summons at her door, anxious lest the other occupants retaliate for the disturbance by reporting her to the neighborhood committee. One had to be that careful these days.

"What is it? You'll wake the dead," she grumbled, slipping back the bolt, pulling her ragged dressing robe tighter as she saw the dark shape of a man outside.

"Fleurette? It's me, Clarence. Let me in."

The hissed urgency of his words tempted her. Hesitating, Fleurette wondered if his life was in danger, so desperate did he seem in his ragged clothing. His eyes flashed in the gloom. Blue they were, such pretty eyes, she had not noticed before. A dawning smile lit her face and she decided to open the door. She was lonely these nights.

"*Eh bien!* But be quiet about it."

Safely inside the room Clarence breathed a sigh of relief.

"Thank you. You may have saved my life. I was being followed."

"Are you still trying to save prisoners, you fool?" She chuckled, reaching to the shelf above the window for a wine bottle. "Here, this'll oil your throat. Then you can tell me what's happened to everyone. Two months I've waited but not a word. I tell you, I'll string that bastard friend of yours up by his—what is it? You're white as a ghost."

Clarence dashed his hand over his eyes, falling into a nearby chair. Swigging the wine, he wiped his mouth on his sleeve. "Ah, it's more your choice of words after such an exacting pursuit."

"I don't follow. Too fancy talking from you and your

239

friend Monsieur Poet. What happened to him anyway? And your woman, Jeanette?"

Managing a weak smile Clarence sighed. "They'll both sneeze into the sack tomorrow unless I can help them. I've tried everything, been everywhere, no one can help."

Eyes grown round with shock, Fleurette plopped on the edge of the bed. "*Bon Dieu*—what a pity! Such a man!" Tears filling her brown eyes tumbled in swiftly moving streams over her cheeks, sallow these days, the rosiness gone.

"Will you help me?" Clarence pleaded, taking her hand, covering the reddened flesh with his own square palm. "You're my last hope."

"But me?" Fleurette gasped, sniffling, dashing tears away with her arm. "What can I do? I know no one of importance. The closest I got to the men in power was Claude."

"Oh, do you know him?" Clarence asked in awe.

"Not any longer. Our relationship ended before it began. Anyway, he only wanted me in bed. He'd probably not speak to me on the street."

Clarence smiled and she smiled back, glad of the comfort of his hand, of his presence, finding the more she looked at him the more attractive he became.

"How did your woman get caught?"

"Our plans went wrong. That's why you never heard from us. Armand was worried about your welfare, but there was nothing he could do. Any word to the outside has to be payed for and we are paupers."

"I know all about that," she agreed, sympathizing immediately with his plight. "It's a wonder we're alive these days, the price of food. Speaking of food, are you hungry? I've bread."

Clarence accepted her offering, relaxing in the chair as she visibly warmed to him. There was hope after all.

"Is your woman to die?"

"Yes," he whispered, hanging his head.

Fleurette clucked in sympathy. "Don't be sad. Ah, I know how you feel. Like me knowing poor Monsieur Poet is to die. Too bad I can't help. Many's the night I've wakened praying to heaven he'd come to the door,

240

but I knew he wouldn't." She sighed as she crossed to the cupboard to get out a loaf.

Clarence ate and thought. He smiled at Fleurette understandingly. He intercepted her appraising glance flicking the length of his body, the sure way to her cooperation. His conscience did not even flicker with remorse at his intention. Though he had never known a woman like this one, he had often heard stories about her type. He had once believed Armand's good looks alone had wooed her, now he understood it was more the voice of her blood which hastened the persuasion.

"To part with you must have caused Armand many regrets," Clarence said at last, holding her gaze, smiling at her round peasant face with its deep brown eyes.

"Don't flatter me. There are a hundred more he could've had. Amelie upstairs would have given her last sou for a night with him. I was just lucky," Fleurette dismissed.

She did not know the real reason Armand had chosen her. Though he must lie to her to gain his ends, Clarence was not cruel enough to reveal the truth of St. Clare's attachment. Let her think she was lucky. It would serve his purpose. Anger with St. Clare would finish any chance of cooperation.

"Don't belittle yourself. Men talk. Armand told me you were a woman in a thousand."

Fleurette found her heart missing a beat at his husky voice, at the startling knowledge of Monsieur Poet's flattery. Emotion twisted hotly within her as Clarence took her hand in his, transferring the throbbing warmth of his blood to her own chill fingers and stirring that other so-easily-aroused feeling until she gasped at the flaring surge.

"What must I do to help you?" she whispered, drawing closer to him, fascinated by the blue eyes which shone like glass in the flicker of the lone wax stub sputtering in a chipped saucer.

"At one Armand will be taken by tumbril to the place of execution. If you could arrange with some of your friends to pull a farm cart across the street, upturn it, anything to block the way, the tumbril would have to detour. There's an alley nearby where I'll wait. It's just wide enough to take the cart, but I need your friends too. Without them I can do nothing."

Stupidly Fleurette stared at him, trying to fix his plan in her mind. "A farm cart to block the street. What do you do then?"

"I'll pretend I'm going to slit his throat to save the guillotine work. Instead I'll pull him to safety. When the tumbril goes about its journey it will be one victim less."

"What about your woman?"

Clarence caught himself, forgetting for the moment he had told her Jeanette was also imprisoned. "She'll be dealt with later. They are in different prisons."

"Oh, so you want me to help you with Monsieur Poet first?"

"Yes. Can you—will you do that for me?"

Fleurette smiled softly at him when he pleaded, his face softened by the candleglow, his blue eyes drawing her. That stirring emotion inspired by the man's touch had gripped her intoxicatingly, as if she'd taken far more than a mouthful of red wine. Tentatively she stretched out her free hand to stroke his brown hair.

"Are you lonely?"

Clarence nodded.

"Me too. It's been so long—your woman—do you fancy you're in love with her?"

Clarence shrugged, tightening his grasp, opening the way for her as he said: "It's so long since I've seen her, I'm not sure any more."

Pulling her hands free, Fleurette stroked his face, shuddering at the smooth heat of his flesh. "I don't think Jeanette would mind, especially if I'm going to help save her brother's life. We're both lonely. It's not wrong when you're lonely," she whispered, her voice quivering with emotion.

Making her decision for her, Clarence swept his arm about her shoulders drawing her close, both repelled and aroused by the smell of her. The voluptuous bodice pressed demandingly against his chest, burning through his thin shirt.

"We won't tell her," he suggested, kissing her cheek,

moving in moist passage to her full mouth where he shuddered at the heated response she gave.

"No. There are some secrets worth keeping, after all," she whispered, laughing in excitement, running her hands through his hair. "You are too fine a man to be lonely, Clarence."

She blew out the candle. Dawn was slipping over the tiled roofs and murkiness illuminated the small room. He saw her smile as she pulled down the neck of her patched nightgown, pleased when his gaze followed her movement.

"Tell me about your plan later, *cher*. At the moment I have some plans of my own," she said as he began to speak. Laughing, she slid her hand over his thighs, clucking in pleasant surprise at what she found. "Hey, we should be very good together, you and me."

Overcast skies threatened rain as Rosslyn looked through the broad windows of Dr. Belhomme's salon awaiting news of Clarence's plans. Camille had not been to see her once, nor had he sent word. Though she realized it was dangerous for one of his importance to communicate, she had hoped he would find a way. Perhaps he was still angry with her over Bernard's death.

Within the secluded environs of this establishment only snippets of news filtered. Like Marat's murderer everyone assumed Bernard's assassin was politically motivated, taking a foreign identity as a clever ploy to disguise the real intent. Flaming Bernard with passion, this traitor had killed him in his own bed. There were reputed to be other revolutionary leaders with whom she shared her favors; now they too were spending sleepless nights awaiting the sting of the assassin's knife.

The nature of these rumors made her smile. She knew whom she had to thank for the stories. Camille had spread the gossip through his many contacts in order to cloud her identity. Several fellow patients had asked if she knew it was rumored that she was the mysterious murderess. Laughing at the idea, Rosslyn assured them if that were the case, she would already be in a cell at the Conciergerie, an idea they laughingly corroborated.

To her surprise one of the hospital staff came to inform her she had a visitor. Ordered to get her cloak for traveling, Rosslyn found her heart stifling with fear. Had something gone wrong?

When she approached the cloaked male figure who waited beside the front door she wondered if it was Clarence, but a glimpse of wiry black hair pulled back beneath a large hat betrayed his identity.

"Camille," she whispered, in mingled surprise and relief.

He did not speak, but led her outside to a waiting carriage. Once inside, he ordered the coachman to drive slowly about the district while they talked.

"*Cherie,* have you been treated well?" he asked huskily, his hands trembling as he held hers.

"As well as can be expected. Thank you for taking me there, you saved my life. Also for those stories about Bernard's assassin. We heard them from such reliable sources too."

He smiled fondly at her. "They were easy things to say. Rosslyn, you're probably wondering why I came for you today."

Her face clouded at his sober change of expression. "I'd thought you came to put me aboard ship," she whispered, trying to read more in his dark face, suddenly afraid of the reason for being taken from Dr. Belhomme's.

"You're half right. Come, sit beside me. Ah, *cherie,* how I've missed our old bargains. Would you like to strike up another?"

"Bargain?" she questioned, leaning against him, yet not allowing herself to relax.

"Aye, I'm such a fool for bargains. In my pocket are your papers. There's a ticket aboard the next packet, yet I don't want you to go. Rosslyn, will you stay with me? Here?"

"How can I?"

"There are ways. We could not be together, but we could still see each other. Such an alternative is all I can manage."

"You mean in hiding?"

He nodded, searching her face for acceptance. "You

see, I do love you. Strange though that may sound coming from me—oh, I know I'm not what you're used to, I've not de Gramont's finesse. Isn't that what they call it? I've got only myself to offer, my arms for comfort, and that part of me you've found satisfying in the past . . ."

"Camille, stop! You know I must go back. At any moment I could be arrested. As long as I stay in Paris, despite your wonderful stories, I can be identified. Besides, my heart's set on England. Please, if you love me as you say, grant me this. Let me go."

His heavy brows drawn together in a scowl, Camille listened to her tearful plea, hating it, yet knowing it was only what he had expected. "So you don't want me?"

"It's not that. Please, try to understand."

Trembling against him, she began to sob.

"Hush, *cherie,* I know what you want. And it isn't me. First, before you decide, there's something I must tell you: De Gramont's execution is this afternoon."

Rosslyn stiffened in his arms at the dread news. Clarence had failed in his efforts to free him. Ideas flashed through her mind, wild thoughts of bartering herself in exchange for Armand's life the way she had sought to do with Bernard. Camille would not delight in watching her grovel for favor as Bernard would have done. He wanted only one thing; her body.

"Before you beg me to save him, let me tell you I cannot," he said, his voice heavy, rough, ploughing on as she gasped, "nor do I want to. Why should I release the one man you'd go with above all others, who need only snap his fingers for you to come running."

"You're wrong. I think he does not love me . . ."

"*Merde*—don't tell me that. Whether he loves you makes no difference. You love him, that's all it takes."

Through tears she stared up at his hard face, set in deep aging lines, haggard in the gloomy coach.

"So whatever decision I make will not save Armand?"

Glancing at her, then away again, Camille agreed it would not. For a few moments they were silent, deafened by the clang of hooves and wheels rattling over cobblestones.

"Then I must go home to my family."

Camille sighed at her words. "Yes, I knew all along you'd say that. I could have you imprisoned, could even have you executed. I know who you are, what you did, above all people, I know . . ." he paused, noting the shock which froze the expression on her face. Softly he smiled at her, stroking her cheek, slipping his hand gently over the prominence of her breast beneath the shrouding cloak. "I know it all, yet I intend to betray my cause for you, little aristocrat bitch."

Rosslyn's breath escaped in a long, shuddering sigh of relief at his softly spoken words. "Dear Camille, I was tempted by your offer. At last I see your regard for me. But you know I can't stay, much as I might want to . . ."

"Shut up." He clapped his hand over her mouth, his eyes glinting with moisture. "Here's my betrayal."

Camille reached inside his coat pocket and withdrew a paper wound into a tight spiral. However, when she would have accepted it from him, he shook his head.

"Am I to bargain for it then?" she asked, smiling at him.

To her surprise Camille shook his head. "No. It is a parting gift from me," he growled, trying to hide the emotion in his voice. "Much as I'd like to bargain one last time, we've only ten minutes to get to the rendezvous. I've often serviced sluts in carriages, but with you I'd be useless as someone's grandfather. There—see how you've ruined me," he muttered. Seizing handfuls of her hair, dragging her face to his, Camille kissed her so fiercely her lips were bruised. Then he thrust her aside, forcing her to keep to her side of the carriage. "Stay there with your hot little mouth. And here, put this between your tits to keep it safe. I'll envy that paper for the rest of my life."

He grinned as he watched the stiff paper disappear to safety between the mounds of white flesh until, shuddering, he looked elsewhere as they rode parallel to the river.

"Do you mean today I'll be aboard ship?" she gasped, her eyes shining with delight.

At the sheer beauty of her smile, he gulped, looking

away, cursing himself for a prize fool to send her to England when all he wanted to do was keep her with him in Paris, hidden, imprisoned, it did not matter as long as he could come to her sometimes.

"Yes, God know me for an ass, but I've arranged your passage for today. A man with a cart will meet you at the rendezvous, from there you'll go to the coast. Act mute. You're his idiot wife. Maybe you can slaver, roll your eyes, whatever comes to mind."

"Oh, Camille, thank you. Wherever I go, I'll not forget you," she vowed sincerely, clasping his hand. But he disentangled her grasp.

"No. Don't tempt me to arrest you, *cherie,* you don't know how close I am to doing that."

Appalled she stared at him, confused by his statement.

"Arrest me!"

Camille smiled but said nothing. Glancing through the window to assure himself this was the place, he tapped on the glass for the driver to stop.

"Here you are. Now, get out of my sight before I change my mind."

Rosslyn kissed his cheek, finding the jaw tense as steel beneath her mouth. "Goodbye, Camille."

"God protect you, little aristocrat bitch," he hissed, brushing her cheek with his mouth, hard with controlled passion. "The pastry shop at the corner of the alley is where you're to meet him. When the clock strikes the hour he should be there. He'll order mutton pastry, paying with a bag of change. Blue knitted cap, striped hose."

Half-pushed from the carriage, Rosslyn stumbled against the wooden door before her. Almost at once the rattling conveyance started up, the horses' hooves slipping on the mire of filth-slimed cobblestones. She waved, but Camille did not look back. Knowing why he did not answer her wave, yet resenting his desertion, she grasped her cloak, lifting the flowing garment above the steaming piles of horse dung mounded beside her.

Inside the pastry shop she was greeted by a fat woman in a dirty cap, who winked when she saw her, knowing this was the one, because she had just watched the carriage pull away. Who could mistake the identity of that well-known citizen?

"Eh, Lally, thrown out were you? You worthless little slut, who'd be surprised at that. Here, have some food. Hercule will be here presently."

Taken aback by the immediate acceptance, yet knowing this woman must be part of the plan, Rosslyn allowed herself to be led to the corner table where she had a view of the street.

A few minutes later, puffing and blowing, her fat arms shaking huge rolls of fat, the shopkeeper banged a broken pie before her. "There, I dropped that one. Go on, it's still good. Hercule didn't pay me a sou for your food yet."

Picking at the yellow crust, Rosslyn finally succumbed to the wafting aroma of meat. Surprisingly the pastry was good, the filling more potatoes than meat, but tasty nevertheless. A few moments later a black-bearded carter thumped inside the shop, clad in work clothes and a blue knitted cap and striped hose. Yelling for the proprietress, he glanced about finding only one customer beside Rosslyn, an old man in a patched smock. The sound of a booming church clock echoed through the building as it struck the hour. One o'clock. Her heart thumping, Rosslyn realized in less than an hour the man she loved would be dead. Perhaps Camille was right, regardless of whether Armand loved her, she knew she still loved him. She was a fool, but it was a feeling she could no longer deny. After today the depth of her emotion would matter to no one but herself, its pain something to be endured the rest of her life.

"Hey, Lally, here's your man," the pie woman yelled.

"Bah, that dirty slut. Who wants to notice her," the carter growled, glancing towards her and nodding. "Give me a mutton pastry. One of your best. And I've got money to pay for it this time."

Grinning to display rotted teeth, he smashed a leather bag of coins on the wooden counter.

Rumbling wheels sounded outside and the old man

248

who had been dozing jumped from his chair with surprising agility. "The tumbril," he cried, bolting for the door.

The shopkeeper and the carter glanced with jaded eye towards the street. And the carter spit on the floor.

"Poor old bastard, it's all the fun he gets."

The fat woman laughed and whispered something to the carter, then they both looked in Rosslyn's direction and guffawed. Whatever the woman's suggestion, the carter shook his head. Feeling her face flush with blood, Rosslyn instinctively knew what the woman said and she could have torn her frowsy hair from its moth-eaten roots to think Camille paid her good money for her part in the escape yet she was already putting vile ideas in the lout's head. No doubt he had thought up that idea himself long ago, discounting it only because of the power of his employer.

A commotion sounded outside and curiously the two went to the door to see what had happened.

"Christ, has the tumbril cast a wheel?" the woman cackled, forcing her quivering bulk through the narrow doorway.

"Naw, some stupid bastard's cart's upended. Mine's back the other way. Look at them, the sniveling wretches. Down with aristocrats! Run 'em to the lamppost! Don't bother with the guillotine," he yelled, doubling his fist, spittle frothing his lips.

Not wanting to see, yet somehow compelled to look at those unfortunates during the last moments of life, Rosslyn followed them to the door. Her steps speeded alarmingly as she realized there was a chance this tumbril could be the very conveyance which took Armand to his death.

Like a hideous nightmare she looked towards the half-dozen prisoners, knowing even before she saw, he would be there. A bolt of shock radiated through her body, stiffening her spine, quivering her legs with fright. There he was, black hair pulled back sharply with a narrow ribbon, face lean and pale. A clean white shirt was plastered across his wide shoulders with sweat in the stormy afternoon heat. At first he did not see her,

249

looking with practiced detachment above the heads of the screaming rabble who had begun to pitch clods of filth at the tumbril's hapless occupants. Set mouth and tense jaw betrayed the emotion locked within him, as yet not betrayed to the mob, who chortled with delight when a worm-eaten, dung-fouled cabbage leaf slapped across the narrow face of a woman in gray silk. Disdainfully the woman removed the filth, keeping her composure, though Rosslyn saw tears of humiliation fill her eyes.

Standing so close she could almost touch him, Rosslyn was afraid to draw attention to herself in this rowdy mob by speaking to him. Concentrating, she willed him to look in her direction. As if by the sheer force of her will the deed was accomplished. A moment later she looked up to encounter startled gray eyes which made her spine prickle with remembered excitement. He had betrayed himself with a gasp before he regained composure, staring blankly at her, his mouth tightened to a narrow line of anger.

Pain as wounding as a blow seared her heart, for his eyes were cold. Was it because he feared for her safety or his own? Or was it more because he cared nothing for her?

Blinded by tears, she found herself thrust backwards by a ruffian in ragged clothing, whose long legs protruded naked from the fringed bottoms of a workman's canvas trousers.

"Let's string the bastard from a lamppost. Or I could save Monsieur Guillotine the job," the man yelled, his coarse voice echoing the sentiments of the carter.

A murmur of assent rose from the crowd as the tumbril was maneuvered about and rerouted towards a narrow alleyway between the shops.

Blinking back her tears, Rosslyn saw, to her horror, they referred to Armand who was the only man in the tumbril. The ragged workman leaped aboard the vehicle, clinging there, yelling to the crowd, spurred on by their shouts of encouragement. Reaching to his waist a knife blade flashed suddenly in the murky light. Another roar of approval met the action. Clenching her fists, Rosslyn saw what he intended to do: Once inside the dark alleyway he would slit Armand's throat, then throw his body to the mob.

"Come! To the other end! We'll divide him between us," screamed a wild-haired amazon, her mouth dark as a tunnel while she screamed her suggestion to the others.

Appalled, Rosslyn surged forward with the crowd as the tumbril neared the narrow entrance. For a moment she was close enough to look into the desperado's face where he stood shielding Armand from view behind his broad frame. Shock, relief, numbness seized her in a paralyzing wave as the man looked back at her, registering nothing beyond a flicker of recognition in his blue eyes. The desperate revolutionary was Clarence.

The tumbril rattled out of sight. With a yell of triumph it was pursued by a couple of men, but the rest of the crowd raced through an adjoining passage to beat the vehicle to the other side, eager to dabble their hands in the blood of their hated victim.

"Hurry up, you slut. Dip your hands in his blood, maybe your whelp'll be born with lace frills," a girl cackled beside her, pushing her aside in the milling crowd.

Unable to see above their heads, Rosslyn heard a roar of anger from the mob as the tumbril emerged amid a watery burst of sunshine which turned the dismal street yellow. Armand was gone. Gasping with relief, she hugged herself tight, ignoring the painful coldness of his gaze, ignoring everything but the fact that he was safe. Somewhere in that narrow alley had been an escape route.

"So! Now you are happy?"

At the familiar voice she turned around, shocked to encounter Camille's dark face beside her, his hair tumbling wildly about his face, his black eyes alight with the power of the crowd.

Rosslyn realized he knew what had happened to Armand. If he chose he could direct the mob to those doors along the alleyway which in a matter of minutes would be torn from their hinges. The mob would enter the buildings, dragging both Clarence and Armand to the nearest lamppost. Her mouth quivering with fear she held his gaze, wondering if he intended betrayal. Pointing in the opposite direction, he inclined his head meaning she should go.

"*Allons! Allons!*" he cried, leaping aboard the tumbril.

At the sight of him the crowd's attention was immediately diverted. Holding out their arms, grimy faces wreathed with adoring smiles, they cheered as he waved to them like a conquering hero. With audacity he caught the young noblewoman in gray silk about the waist, roughly pulling her to him, laughing when she kicked at his ankles. Then he pinned her arms behind her back and kissed her while he ran his free hand intimately over her bodice, complaining to the crowd about its meager content. All the while the mob roared approval as they ran alongside the tumbril, determined to follow it to the completion of its journey at the Place de Grave.

Stopping to watch no more Rosslyn raced in the direction Camille had pointed, finding it took a circuitous route to the pie shop. There waited the carter, his face breaking into a smile of relief at her appearance.

"Lally, you stupid bitch, following the crowd. Come on, we've got to be home before dark." Seizing her arm he swung her against him, gripping her shoulder, propelling her forward as he waved farewell to the proprietress of the pie shop.

The farm cart was loaded with refuse, with sacks of grain, with decaying cabbages he had not sold, yet it was to be her carriage to freedom. A few moments later they trundled over the now deserted cobbled street towards the Paris gates. The roar of the mob could be heard in the distance. They were singing the Marseillaise now and the male voice raised above all the others belonged to Camille.

Tears of gratitude stung Armand's eyes as he thanked his rescuer profusely, hardly able to believe the miracle he had wrought. Yet while his mouth moved in praise, his heart grew leaden by degrees beneath the crumpled cambric shirt. She had come to watch him taken to execution. And she had not come alone. Through the worm-eaten door he had heard the mob shouting their hero's name.

CHAPTER FIFTEEN

The light morning haze lifted over the Channel and Rosslyn saw the white cliffs shining in the sunshine. Emotion choked her at the longed-for sight. Always a moving scene to the returning exile, those green-topped cliffs represented life itself, imparting a sense of security at last. How she longed to set foot on English soil.

During the nightmare flight from Paris in the odorous farm cart, scuttled through byways, stopped at numerous checkpoints, it seemed as if she would never reach the harbor where her ship awaited the tide. All the time, threading its way unhappily through her thoughts, was the memory of that cold stare of indifference Armand had given her. He, who all this had been for. Tensing her jaw, she forced back tears of self-pity which threatened to squeeze between her lids. In all probability she would never see him again. The passage aboard *La Belle Amie* had been for today. At this moment he was sailing to the opposite end of the world, the reason for his betrayal of her heart's devotion remaining a secret.

Resolutely she turned her face into the stinging salt spray whipped to a froth by brisk winds, determined to put the horror of those months in Paris behind her. Whatever had caused the rift between them was no longer important. The nature of their love had been aptly described by Armand that day on the cliffs as "a flower in season." Her mouth set in a bitter line to acknowledge how quickly that passionate flower had withered and died.

By the time she reached Burton Hill it was late afternoon, the sky darkened by threatening storm clouds. Instead of going directly to the Hall, Rosslyn ordered the coachman to drive to The Hollies. Despite the hideous shame of Jarvis's wager with Tom Stanley, she knew Adela would still welcome her.

To Rosslyn's dismay when they rattled up the gravel drive neatly framed by an avenue of towering hollies, the house had a curiously deserted appearance, the windows unlit despite the afternoon gloom. Ordering the coachman to wait, her heart sinking with an uncharacteristic premonition of disaster, Rosslyn banged on the elaborate lion's head knocker.

The door was opened by a young maid who did not reconize her in her present shabby state.

"I wish to speak to your mistress," Rosslyn announced, realizing what a strange picture she must seem in her tatered maroon silk ball gown. It was the one she had worn that last night with Bernard and every night since. Much the worse for wear, the silk camellias which once framed the neckline had all but disappeared, while the skirt was rent in a dozen places. When the woman looked her up and down with distaste Rosslyn arrogantly informed her, "Though my appearance belies the fact, I am Lady Burton. Your mistress will receive me."

Clearly surprised, the girl repeated: "The mistress?"

"Yes, Mrs. Warner. Are you a half-wit?"

The maid continued to stare, then her plump face crumpled like a dried apple as she burst into tears. "The mistress passed away," she managed between sobs. "We're still not recovered from it. The house is in mourning—all but the master."

White-faced, Rosslyn received the shocking news. "Adela dead!"

"Yes, mum. Not gone a month yet and already—oh, I can't bring myself to say it. That French baggage! Disgraceful, that's what it is."

"Is your master home? I'd like to speak with him," Rosslyn asked, not knowing if Clarence remained in France.

Large splotches of rain began to patter on her head as the maid snapped: "No he bain't, and good luck to him!" she added, anger sparking her eyes.

"Your master is my brother. Now, will you tell me

255

where he is?" Rosslyn said. "I should like to come indoors to wait for him. Can't you see it's raining, girl?"

"Sorry, mum, but I can't admit anyone. Those are me orders."

"From whom?"

"Well," the maid replied with a toss of her carroty head, "I can't say as 'ow that's any of your business." With this the door was slammed in her face.

Speechless, Rosslyn gaped in disbelief at the solid mahogany panel where the polished lion's head snarled ferociously at her. To have a door slammed in her face was absolutely unheard of. But then, looking like this, perhaps it was not the first such incident she must endure before she was restored to her normal appearance. It was a blow to find Adela dead, impossible to accept after the laughter and gaiety she had so often shared with them at The Hollies.

"You sure you got enough money to pay for this?" the coachman demanded, leaning from the box as she approached the coach.

Hastening to get out of the rain Rosslyn answered curtly. "My word's good. Now take me back the way we came. I'll go home instead."

"Home!" The coachman chuckled as he clicked to the horses, shrinking down inside his caped greatcoat to avoid the rain. "S'pose that's the kitchens or the dairy, my girl. Go on, you with your fine airs. We'd better get let in there, or I'm having me money and getting out of here. You'll have to shift as best you can."

Refraining from comment, Rosslyn banged the coach door. Huddled in the corner, bleakly surveying the passing countryside as they sped along the rutted road to Burton Hall, Rosslyn found her pleasure at being in England slowly evaporating. In all her thoughts of coming home not once had it been to that cold mansion where Jarvis waited. How could she explain her absence? How could she face everyone, for by now there must be no one in a twenty-mile radius who did not know the intimate details of her experience as high stakes in Jarvis's birthday wager.

Forcing herself to sit upright, defiantly raising her head, Rosslyn determined to brave this through. She had endured the rigors of Parisian life during the Revolution, she could not waver now at the thought of the sneers of their neighbors.

Her joyful intention of spending a few days with Adela while sounding her out on the current social opinion of that wager, exchanging clothes and reams of sympathy, had evaporated. Never strong, Adela had most likely succumbed to another aborted pregnancy. Rosslyn knew she should be weeping for her friend's death, should feel something, yet her senses were stunned. Today she seemed incapable of reacting to the news. Clarence must not have kept his secret over Jeanette as well as he had thought; by her anger it seemed the maid was well acquainted with the affair, a shock which may have hastened Adela's demise.

Scowling at the splattering rain, Rosslyn wondered what curse Armand and his family possessed to damage those whose paths crossed theirs. Before he arrived in England she had managed reasonably well in her ignorance, pampered and well dressed. At the time those things had seemed enough.

"Where to now, me girl?"

Directing the red-faced driver, Rosslyn tried to rearrange her tumbled hair, but it seemed an impossible task. Then the thought that perhaps Jarvis would find her more appealing if she arrived looking like one of his village sluts, stayed her hand. Yes, if he wanted to think that, it would serve her well. She had learned in Paris that one must use others to one's own advantage whenever possible.

Struck by the feeling of slovenliness and decay about the deserted mansion, Rosslyn moved through the chill corridors, marching ahead of the servant who alternately muttered and wept at her unkempt appearance. Ignoring the old man's blubbering, Rosslyn decided a spirited offense was her best approach. Jarvis deserved to know how angrily humiliated she was over his behavior, how much she despised his weakness which had placed her in such a situation in the first place.

"Gad! Am I seeing things?"

Stopping short in the doorway of his study, Rosslyn

was as shocked by Jarvis's appearance as he was by hers.

"You may go, Mostyn," she said coolly, dismissing the shuffling man, who also seemed to have fallen victim to the contagious decay.

Jarvis tottered to his feet, obviously drunk by his unsteady gait. His soiled, rumpled clothing betrayed that he was too often in a like state, amazing in one who had once taken such pride in his appearance. But then, at one time, she too had been a fashion plate.

"This is the state I'm forced to endure, thanks to you," she cried, her eyes flashing.

"Eh, thanks to me?" he repeated stupidly, bumping into the desk as he tried to come to her.

"You're drunk."

"Of course—get drunk every day. Shouldn't surprise you, Ross, shouldn't surprise you at all."

Stiffening her spine, she held her head high, watching him come towards her, stumbling like an old man. He had lost weight, for his clothing hung on his large frame like a scarecrow's. His once thick hair had thinned, his heavy ruddy face sunk to greenish sallowness.

"Have you been ill?" she asked, a wave of compassion for him taking hold, despite her former resolve to harden her heart. His angry reply soon dashed any sympathy she might have had.

"Ill? You might say that—ill with worry over your shenanigans. Little slut, where've you been? Suppose Tom Stanley's had you holed up somewhere for his amusement. Told me what a piece of goods you were, the bastard. I hate him, that's what." Panting, fuming, his pale face suffused with blood, he grabbed her arm. "You'll answer for this, Madam. I'll have you flogged, making a laughingstock of me."

"The laughingstock was entirely your own doing," she hissed, turning cold with hate for him now. Standing there accusing her, making no apology for his own part in the situation. "You should be ashamed to visit our friends. Ashamed to hold your head up in public after what you forced me to endure," she spat, retreating a couple of steps when he grabbed her skirts.

The fabric gave beneath his grasp, so that he stared foolishly at the piece of maroon silk in his hand.

"What's this fancy get-up? A party, eh?" he muttered, studying her at close quarters through poorly focused eyes, wondering at her grime.

"You fool! Are you so besotted you can't see how I've suffered?" Mind darting quickly for an explanation of her disheveled appearance, Rosslyn blurted: "I was robbed. All my clothes were taken."

"Should've stayed here where you belong," Jarvis snarled, pulling at the bellpull which came away in a cloud of dust.

Amazed by the incident, Rosslyn asked: "Why is everything so filthy? Where are the servants? Only Mostyn came to welcome me."

"Gone, all of them, the disloyal bunch. Slip 'em a few sovereigns and they're off."

"Jarvis, either you're drunker than I think, or I'm losing my mind. Who slipped them a few sovereigns?"

"Stanley!" The word hissed out in sheer loathing took her by surprise. Swaying to a nearby chair, Jarvis eyed her with bloodshot gaze. "Taken them, the lot. Horses. Carriages, all his."

"What? How is that possible?"

"Unlucky run, that's all," Jarvis muttered, glancing about fiercely at his once lovely home. "Don't worry, I'll get everything back. Now you're home things'll be better. You're my inspiration. We'll show 'em, me dear, we'll show 'em."

Appalled by his words, Rosslyn looked about her critically, seeing the grime thick on every piece of furniture in the room. The house had a damp chill which came from lack of heat; the dirty hearth overflowing with ashes seemed to have been neglected for weeks.

"How many servants do you have left?"

"You met him."

"Mostyn! That old man is all that's left! What of the women?"

"Those silly hens were afraid of their own shadow," was all he said.

Increased drinking on his part, violent temper, an advancing state of disrepair: it must have been a simple task to persuade the maids to take positions elsewhere. There was nothing here to hold them.

"You'll have to stop drinking and gambling."

"What!" Stupefied, he stared at her, his eyes growing watery with the effort.

"How else can you hope to gain back what you've lost?"

"By gambling, you stupid bitch. All I need are some lucky throws. Do you think I like it like this? Do you think I like owing my last pound to that scoundrel knowing he's laughing at me behind my back? Got me where he wants me at last, he thinks, kindly letting me stay on here. The insolent bastard! Letting me stay! My own home!"

Rosslyn turned on her heel, leaving him muttering to himself in an alcoholic daze. Rousing his wits, Jarvis stumbled after her.

"Stay where you are. I order it!"

"You're in no fit state to order anything."

"How dare you? Insolent bitch. Learned that from him, I suppose. Brought me crashing down, reduced me to the level of pauper, so he boasts. Well, what'll he say now you're here? I'd like to hear that. Said you'd never come back to me."

"He was right."

"What!"

"I only came to get my things."

"Things?"

"You don't think I intend to spend the rest of my life in these rags, do you?" she challenged.

Jarvis leaned against the wall, and he began to laugh. "Go upstairs. Take a look. See if you fancy what's left," he suggested finding great humor in her proposal.

A wave of shock swept over Rosslyn as realization dawned. Not only Jarvis's possessions, but her own as well had been taken to settle debts. As Tom Stanley had a legion of women acquaintances, the sumptuous dresses would come in useful.

"What am I supposed to wear?" she gasped.

"I don't give a damn what you wear. Nothing would suit me." He chuckled as he lurched towards her. "Now, sweetest, how about a welcome-home kiss. Just the two of us here."

Rosslyn slithered from his grasp. "Don't ever touch me again. I'll take what's left when I leave."

"Leave! You can't leave."

"Do you expect me to stay with you, when you hardly draw a sober breath? Without servants or clothes? If there was even a hope of remedying the situation, if I honestly thought you'd try . . . "

"I promise, Ross, if you stay I'll try," he mumbled pathetically, reaching for her arms before she whisked away.

Purposefully mounting the staircase, Rosslyn ignored his pleas as she heard him stumble on the stairs. Turning when she reached the second-floor landing she saw him crouched there, his head in his hands. At first, when she thought he wept, pity smote her until she recognized the muffled sounds for laughter. The sound hardened her heart. Any smattering of feeling for him which might have remained after the Tom Stanley incident, frail though it might have been, was destroyed then.

It was dark now so she fumbled about the upper rooms looking for a candle. Finally she found one glowing in the master bedroom. Carrying the sputtering light she went to her room, shocked to find the bed with its lovely blue hangings gone. The closet doors stood open to reveal the yawning emptiness where her finery had been; her jewels, even the chest which held them, had all disappeared.

Setting the candle on the floor she reached inside the vast empty space, searching for some garment left hanging there. Three things remained: an old cloak she had kept for sentimental purposes, being a birthday present from her father, a brown worsted dress and a taffeta mourning dress with fringed shawl to match. These pitiful remains must have been too drab to be presented in payment for sexual favors.

Clutching the garments, she took the candle to search the room. In the blanket chest by the window she found the battered valise where she stored donations for charity. The bag yielded a pair of woolen stockings, pink satin slippers and two sets of cambric underwear. To these she added the contents of her dressing table drawers, finding them to be the plainest or oldest of her possessions. A woman must have chosen the items, no man would have taken enough time to be discriminating: a man would have grabbed the lot, then discarded at leisure what he did not want. The thought that one of Stanley's disreputable women had greedily scoured through her possessions stung worse than anything else.

When she went to the kitchens to heat water for washing, Rosslyn saw no sign of Jarvis. This dark, deserted house seemed only a ghostly shell of its former self. Piled about the room seemed to be two months' dishes loaded with scraps of refuse, leaving a feast for a family of rats who boldly scuttled past her feet. Shuddering, Rosslyn sent a soup ladle after them, dispersing the rodents, though she was acutely conscious of their bright eyes watching from the murky recesses of the kitchen.

After a hasty wash, she donned the black mourning dress, then folded the other dress and cloak and stuffed them in the bulging valise. Why not a mourning gown, she thought with a trace of hysteria, catching sight of her dark reflection in a copper boiler. She was mourning. Oh, how many things she mourned today, she felt bowed down with the weight of them. Loss of her way of life, her possessions, her husband; Adela too had disappeared forever. And there was Armand. It was the loss of him which caused the most pain.

Lugging the heavy valise, Rosslyn went to the dark stables only to find them bare. Not one horse remained to ease her departure from Burton Hall. She had only five pounds left from the packet of currency Camille had given the carter for her. Whether the man had first extracted a sizeable bonus for himself, she had no way of knowing.

Leaning against the woodwork in the black starless night, Rosslyn allowed herself to think of Camille in a fond manner. At least he loved her. In this world such devotion was rare indeed.

Hefting the baggage she set out across the stableyard heading towards the road, turning her worn shoes on the gravel, wrenching her ankles. Once she looked back to see the vast house in darkness save for two pinpoints of light; Mostyn in his cubbyhole, Jarvis in his study. The former probably polishing his boots, the latter polishing off the inevitable bottles of port. The humor of her assessment made her smile, the first such expression she had managed since she arrived at Burton Hill.

Turning out onto the flinty road, Rosslyn glanced towards the small family cemetery wondering if she should go to Will's grave, then resolutely deciding against it. What was past was past, no point in reliving it with painful clarity. She must turn her back on everything here, even Will. When she first set eyes on Jarvis she had known it would come to this. At least she had somewhere left to go. The white-washed cottage overlooking the cliffs at Dover seemed infinitely desirable at this moment.

CHAPTER SIXTEEN

Rosslyn looked about the small, chintz-decorated room with pleasure, finding it a haven of security. In this white-washed three-roomed cottage she had resumed the threads of her life. Tonight was the anniversary of a month's residence at Sea View.

The arduous journey from Burton Hall on foot and farm cart when she was fortunate enough to beg a ride, had been only the beginning of her ordeal. The five pounds were soon spent. And if not for a kind neighbor a few hundred yards along the cliff path who had taken her under her wing, Rosslyn did not know how she would have survived these last weeks. An old sailor's widow, Mrs. Kenney had a heart of gold. Thanks to her, the transition had been less painful.

It was difficult for Rosslyn to rekindle her vague ideas of cooking, what little skill she possessed having vegetated since her marriage to Jarvis, and to be honest, put into little use even before that. Her father may have been near bankruptcy, but he had always maintained a front which included servants, carriages, good food and clothes. There had been little need for her to practice domestic skills beyond a raspberry ice for a special summer garden party, or delicate butterfly sponge cakes of which she had always been so proud.

Smiling with pleasure, she sniffed the aroma of stew with a feeling of accomplishment to know the dinner bubbling in the iron cauldron over the hearth was of her own making. These crisp November afternoons increased her appetite, but the thought of winter just around the corner took away some of her pleasure. Mrs. Kenney had tactfully suggested she take in sewing to provide an income, something she had decided to try.

At least she sewed a passable seam, her work much exclaimed over by her neighbor, who made her own livelihood in that fashion. A poor seamstress living in a seaside cottage, not in the least the way she had pictured herself once life in England was resumed.

One dull November afternoon a visitor arrived. At the sight of Stella's plump face surrounded by bobbing moss green plumes sprouting from the brim of a velvet hat, Rosslyn's limbs were turned to ice. This was the first time she had received a visit from any friend or relation. Though she had not announced her new place of residence, they had obviously guessed she had gone to the only sanctuary she knew on the Dover headland.

"My dear! How wonderful to see you," Stella cried, turning back to dismiss her coachman. "Be back in an hour, Webster. An hour, mind."

An hour; at least the visit was not to be of long duration, Rosslyn thought thankfully. "Hello, Stella. This is a surprise. How did you know where to find me?"

Stella bustled inside the small room, taking in the worn upholstery and the black stew pot hanging over the hearth in one critical glance. "My dear, what a quaint little place this is. Kitchen, scullery, bedroom upstairs I suppose, yes, very quaint."

Rosslyn's mouth tightened at the phrase. Wanting to defend her home she snapped, "Well, at least it's mine."

"Oh, yes, quite." Stella managed a glossy smile, her eyes flicking incessantly about the room as if counting the vases and the candlesticks. "Now then, tell me all about what you're doing with yourself. Is this a retreat from reality?"

"This is reality to me. Would you like some tea?"

"Not, not at the moment. I've just eaten a huge luncheon at Squire Pendergrast's—oh, but you wouldn't know them, would you?"

Rosslyn shook her head. Well, at least Stella admitted she had not put herself out for this visit. The Squire must live in the vicinity. "How disappointing. I thought you'd driven down specially to see me," she cooed with sugar sweetness, pleased to put Stella in the uncomfortable spot for once.

Not quite knowing what to say, Stella smiled painfully. "But I did. The Squire's invitation was a second thought. After all, we are sisters."

Rosslyn smiled and waited. Perched on the lumpy edge of the small couch, for the first time in this house she felt uncomfortable. She became acutely aware of its shabbiness which she knew Stella must be absorbing in great detail to recount to their friends.

"Soon it'll be winter. Rosslyn, dear, you must come home." Stella leaned forward, taking her hand in her own kid-gloved palm. "I always come straight to the point, you know me. That's why I'm here."

And of course, you only have an hour, Rosslyn added mentally, the addition making her smile. "Did Jarvis send you?"

"Well . . . not exactly," Stella hedged, looking away. "The family thought I should come."

"Why?"

"Oh, Rosslyn, you don't know how far Jarvis has sunk! Oh, it's terrible. We sometimes fear for his life. Now, if only you would come home . . . "

"Nonsense. Jarvis will drink whether I'm there or not. And he'll gamble. Sometimes I wonder if he can't help himself. This isn't something which happened overnight."

Stella smiled and began to untie her bonnet strings.

"No. You're right, he's always had such a weakness for port. Runs in the family, you know. Dear Papa was a terrible one for drink, it finished him, you know. And his gout, well, that was something you just had to see to believe."

"Then how will I be of help?"

"Because your return will give him the incentive to reform," Stella announced triumphantly, vigorously shaking her blonde curls to fluff them after the pressure of her bonnet. "We know you can do it. Things just aren't the same on Burton Hill these days. Everyone keeps away. Now, if you'll come back, I'll arrange a few teas. We can have our old card parties to let everyone know things are back to normal. They'll soon come around once they know . . . "

"Stella, you're wasting your time. When you can honestly tell me he has stopped drinking and gambling; when you tell me the house is a house instead of a pig sty, I might consider it. Certainly not until then."

Stella's smile dissolved and she pursed her lips in annoyance. "Well, I think the least you could do is give it a try."

"That's because you were never forced to endure the indignity of being bartered. The humiliation of knowing that the details of that encounter were circulating the neighborhood drawing rooms, whispered and laughed about behind ivory fans. Much of that gossip begun by you, I've no doubt."

Stella gasped, appalled at the statement. "Well, to think I came all the way out here to beg you to come home, then have you treat me like this! How dare you say that to me!"

"I say it because I, of all people, know you. When I needed help you never offered it. You wouldn't be here now if you weren't afraid of the gossip, or if you hadn't been to the Squire's dinner party. Don't try to delude me. At least allow me the dignity of the truth."

Drawing herself to full height, Stella faced Rosslyn in the cramped area before the hearth, glaring at her, the only sound beyond her harsh breathing the bubbling stew. "Very well. You want the truth. True, I came to ask you to come home for appearance's sake. The family name's being dragged through the mud, you living here like some bought woman . . . "

"No man supports me, Stella, least of all your drunken brother. My husband's never offered me a penny for food. So, you see, I find it hard to be convinced of his concern at this late date."

"Money! Oh, Rosslyn, if that's all that's holding you back, here." Stella opened her reticule and handed a fat wad of money to her.

Rosslyn's arm trembled with longing to take the offering; pictures of fuel, food and much needed supplies flitted through her mind. Yet if she took it she was beholden to Stella. In this new world of bargaining she had been introduced to in Paris, Rosslyn knew that with money went a host of unvoiced promises.

"No. Heavens knows, I could use it, but I won't accept your charity, Stella. I know there's a web of requirements attached. Put it back." Pushing the fat, gold-ringed hand aside, Rosslyn mustered all her dignity as she said: "If you wish to visit me because you are truly concerned about my welfare, then you are welcome. If it's a repetition of this afternoon, then don't put yourself out."

Stella angrily grabbed her bonnet, puffing out her round cheeks in anger. "I never thought you'd have such little regard as this for dear Jarvis's health. If he drinks himself to death, then it'll be on your conscience, because I've done my best. I always knew you and your brother wcrc not of our class. When Papa arranged your marriage to Jarvis I suspected as much. Old blood-line, he said, sound business. Nonsense! Anyone who's forced to engage in trade is not of the nobility. We wouldn't deign to work with our hands or to dabble in filthy foreign currency . . ."

"No, you'd sooner drink yourselves to death amid cobwebs and rats than turn an honest day's work," Rosslyn interrupted quietly, surprising herself by the truth of the words.

"Well, if that's all the satisfaction I'm going to get, I'm off. I'll leave you to it, my dear. Perhaps that little French strumpet will visit you. And that worthless brother of yours. He's scandalized the entire district with his shameful carryings-on with that maid. And poor Adela lying ill in her bed all the time. Brought to bed of a stillborn babe at that. And no one knowing where he was, gallivanting heaven knows where with that woman. I tell you, the Warner name's not worth tuppence amongst our friends after that."

Rosslyn knew where Clarence had been, not a trip of pleasure, but of desperate bravery. Only she could not reveal his whereabouts even to clear his reputation. Facing up to Stella's glare, Rosslyn quietly pointed out, "Perhaps Clarence stepped over the line by making his infatuation public, but I doubt if anything he did could be any more shameful than when your brother auctioned me to the highest bidder. Don't you think some of his present predicament has been brought about by the reaction of our friends? I saw none eager to succor him, to talk him around or help him with money or friendship."

Stella flushed at the truth, not trusting herself with words. Outside on the road came the sound of hooves as the carriage returned.

"As I'm not welcome, I'll take my leave."

"Stella, I just don't have any pity left for him. If he wants me back he'll have to do a lot of changing. You may tell him that; we'll see how much he wants me home by his reaction."

Her sister-in-law left without another word. Rosslyn watched the green plumes nodding angrily as Stella thumped down the path without casting a backward glance. The carriage spun a moment on the rocky track before lurching forward. When they were no more than a blur on the horizon, Rosslyn moved from the window, finding her hands still shook with emotion.

Mechanically she stirred the stew, reviewing Stella's words, shuddering to think what pitiful state Jarvis must have reached to prompt this visit. Stella was not one to ask favors, and though she had not done it in a gracious manner, it had been asked nevertheless.

During the following year Rosslyn received no further contact from the family. With the exception of visits from Clarence and Jeanette, she might have been dead; all the friends she had once thought she had on Burton Hill ceased to acknowledge her existence. Sometimes she wondered if she had been foolishly stubborn in her refusal to accept a bribe to return home. When food became scarce or the loneliness almost unbearable, she thought with increased fondness of the parkland through which she had ridden with pleasure, of that headland where she raced her mare. Poor Alice, who rode her now? Hopefully they had a gentle touch for the young black mare had a sensitive mouth.

For all this, when she recalled Jarvis in all his unpleasant degradation came with the bargain, she remained strengthened in her resolve.

Huddled in her old Nithsdale riding hood of scarlet serge, Rosslyn hastened down the cobbled street, shivering as the wind swept icily from the quay. Golden light radiated in blurring circles over the pavement as the cold brought tears to her eyes, stinging her cheeks, chapping her lips with its raking blast. Unconsciously she ran her tongue over her parched lips, catching the eye of a lounging sailor as she did so. Assuming the gesture was an invitation, he smiled, interested in making her acquaintance; she crossed to the other side of the street, not anxious to make his.

The poulterer's had a scrawny bird which she purchased with misgivings. To waste money on a roasting fowl for one person seemed a terrible extravagance, yet Christmas tradition was deeply ingrained. And the bird cost far less than a round of beef, or the inviting haunch of pork decorated with oranges and parsley in the forefront of the window. She could make several days' meals from it before using the bones for soup.

After the poulterer's, Rosslyn went next to the bakery where she stood a few moments breathing in the heavenly aroma of fresh-baked bread, warm from the oven. When she complained about the price of a loaf, the baker twisted his ruddy face to a grudging smile.

"What can you expect, Missus, with a war on? Tell those bloody Froggies about it, will you."

Still not at ease when dealing with tradespeople, Rosslyn let his grumbling pass, hastening to be gone. In the larder was a cabbage to go with the fowl and bread, and there was a bowl of mincemeat given to her by Mrs. Kenney, who felt sorry for a high-born lady reduced to genteel poverty. Squandering her last shilling on a dollop of lard for the pastry and a bottle of cheap claret, Rosslyn put the purchases in her basket, covering them with a teacloth as protection against the grainy moisture which blew intermittently in the wind.

"Going to snow before tomorrow, mark my words, Missus," the grocer's wife commented, smiling at her. "Here, take a bit of butter, love, seeing as it's Christmas."

"But I haven't enough to . . ."

"A gift from me."

Tears stung her eyes at the woman's unexpected kindness. Thanking her profusely, Rosslyn went into the cold, warmed by her restored faith in humanity. The sailor waited at the curb for her, winking invitingly when she caught his eye. She was so lonely, so emotionally bereft, that for one insane moment, Rosslyn toyed with the idea of returning his interest, for he seemed as lonely as she. He was young and strong, with regular features. His curly hair was blond . . .

Resolutely she started in the opposite direction, ignoring his plea for her to talk to him. Stiffening beneath her fur-lined hood, Rosslyn held her head high, making her way towards home. As she passed a recessed gateway a couple pressed further back in the shadows, standing close locked in broad daylight, bodies pressed tight against the cold.

Jealousy, pain, she did not know which, stabbed her, bringing forth easy tears of emotion. What a fool she was of late, morose, crying at the slightest provocation. Yet the surge of exquisite feeling kindled by the sight of those lovers was not easily doused. And she leaned against the stone wall on the corner to regain her composure. Armand! It was he who invaded her thoughts, who tormented her nights. How warm his arms had been, how sweet his kisses. She would settle for the innocence of a kiss today, for the assurance she was loved. Often the searing, throbbing need aroused within her at the memory tormented her like a sickness. Their love was over. Did he ever spare a thought for her far away in the Americas with his sons? How many women there must have been during this year apart, perhaps one who had become special to him, since he was free to marry.

An undiscovered need to torture herself, for self-inflicted punishment must produce those thoughts. He was gone. There was no point in reliving their affair. So painful was the memory, to even watch lovers brought tears to her eyes. She hurt for all she had lost, for all she craved and could never have again. There were other men, but only one Armand. Though Camille satisfied her briefly, her use of him did not make her proud. The fact that he had greatly enjoyed his servitude did not enter her mind as consolation. She had used his maleness, his heat, as a substitute for what she had lost.

Gathering her wits she moved forward, toiling up the sloping lane towards her cottage. High hedges cut the sea wind, but did not take the icy blast from the air, and it was a relief to know a fire welcomed her once she reached home. Sometimes when she toyed with the idea of swallowing her pride and returning to Jarvis, when she weakened, that small living room with its blazing hearth and the mementos of her happy childhood, drew her back.

Shaking the moisture from her hood, Rosslyn looked about the room, gaining some comfort from the familiar surroundings. Not enough, however. Christmas would be cheerless again this year. Rosslyn knew why today she even failed to find pleasure in this small world she had carved for herself. It was because of Armand's letter.

Though she knew its contents by heart, she took the battered missive from behind the clock on the mantel. A month ago she had received this letter written the preceding spring, taking whatever circuitous route was available to reach her.

"My dearest Rosslyn," he began. Fiercely she crumpled the page, taking pleasure from the action. Therein he spoke of love, of only just learning of her whereabouts, but it was all false. Since spring he would have pushed her completely from his mind. It was almost a year. How many lovely women must grace those ballrooms of the exiled aristocracy, emigrés known to him in the past, native-born belles, dark-eyed quadroons, enough females to last him for years. In view of that, what a fool she was to hold out hope of lingering in his thoughts. Oh, Marie had known him well, and she had not.

A tap on the back door brought her to the present and Rosslyn went to answer the knock, knowing instinctively who it was.

Mrs. Kenney, her closest neighbor, had brought a cake full of fruit and spirits. Overcome with gratitude and having little with which to repay the kindness, Ros-

272

slyn offered the widow a small glass vase decorated with violets which had belonged to her mother.

"Here, this is my Christmas gift to you—no, take it, I know how you enjoy flowers." It was her turn to feel warmth from giving as Mrs. Kenney's eyes lit up with pleasure.

"Oh, you shouldn't. Why, that must be worth a fortune, cut glass with them pretties." The middle-aged woman gasped, holding the glass towards the light where it sparkled like diamonds. "Oh, my lady."

"In spring you can fill it with primroses from the wood."

"Aye, or violets, now them would be nice. By the bye, love, you 'ad a visitor today."

"A visitor!" Rosslyn gripped her hands together, turning the knuckles white, absurdly thinking about Armand. Her shock dissipated a moment later when the identity of her visitor was revealed.

"A grand lady, but if you ask me, she's common as dirt underneath. I can always tell." The gray head wagged knowingly and Mrs. Kenney carefully wrapped the vase in her apron. "Pranced up to me door big as you please asking when you'd be back. 'My good woman,' says she, 'pray tell me when my Lady Burton intends to return?' 'Now that I don't know, Missus,' says I, putting her nose out of joint I might add, for even I knew she was gentry. 'I'll have you know I am Lady Redding,' says she, all hoity-toity. 'Lady Redding or not, me answer's still the same,' says I. Well, with that she marched away, black as thunder. Do you know her then?"

"Oh, yes, my sister-in-law, come to wish me cheer for the season or, more accurately, to ferret out a tasty piece of gossip."

"Maybe she brung some news from that brother of hers," Mrs. Kenney suggested, her mouth tightening as it always did when she was forced to acknowledge Rosslyn's husband. In her opinion any man who would let a lovely girl like this alone and impoverished needed a good thrashing.

"Perhaps. But I doubt if she'll bring me news he's

reformed, or that he has his possessions again debt free."

"Drinkers find that hard going, love. My Jack was a drinker. Rum. Seamen's always got that weakness. Sweet as a lamb when 'e was sober; but drunk, cor, like an 'eathen savage. That like your old man?"

Rosslyn smiled and nodded agreement. "Somewhat. They must be all the same, Mrs. Kenney."

"Well, don't you worry, love, it'll all come out in the wash, I always says. Thanks for the vase. I'll treasure it like bloomin' gold, I will."

Smiling as she waved at the departing figure, Rosslyn felt unease lying leaden in her stomach at the knowledge of Stella's visit. What could she be here for? Surely not to give the tidings she almost dreaded to hear, that Jarvis was in full possession of his faculties. She had halfway promised to come home if Stella could ever bring that message, yet now, despite the loneliness, she could not bear the thought of succumbing to his heartless embrace. And he would expect that. Not for one moment did she delude herself into thinking her return would not signal the resuming of her marital responsibility. How often had she longed for some compassion from him in the past. Now she dreaded his embrace, for she knew she could no longer respond to any touch of his. The very thought made her flesh crawl. Since that time there had been other men able to fire her blood, and though only one had she taken with love, the experiences had been mutually rewarding. Picturing the men she had known intimately, Rosslyn sighed, trying to evade the disquieting squirm of guilt the memories evoked. Detached by time and place she had to admit she had obtained some pleasurable response from them all, even Tom Stanley, yet to recall that interlude chilled her with unpleasant memories. Though none made her sing with joy as Armand was capable of doing, the gnawing ache in her body had been temporarily dispelled.

Now Camille was dead. The admission gave her a twinge of pain for he had said he loved her. She learned his fate one day when Mrs. Kenney had brought some vegetables wrapped in tattered newspaper. A glorious newspaper which she pored over beside the fire, thirsty for news of the world's events. There, tucked away in a corner between the account of a hanging and His Majesty's latest illness, was the report of the Parisian mob turning on their former hero, denouncing Camille as a traitor and placing him in the Conciergerie. Two days later he was guillotined. Poor Camille, who had believed as deeply as any of them in the cause, yet like all the others, larceny was too deeply ingrained in his soul! He had followed an illustrious roll call, the most important victim being Marie Antoinette herself.

Now it all seemed so far away, those embraces they had shared, his gruff voice breathing vulgar endearments. Paris, the terror, all remote as if another had endured that violent summer of passion and bloodshed. France was still their enemy. Patrols manned the coast watching for invasion. Yet the one thing which stayed longest in her memory was the sweet hope she had squandered in that land: the hope of being with the man she loved.

With a sigh she picked up her current sewing job, a delicate lawn nightgown for a young girl's trousseau. And while she stitched she fought the splashing tears which dampened the fabric, blurring her eyes, until she stabbed the needle viciously into her unprotected finger. Mutely she watched the welling crimson drops, reminded of the blood-fouled cobbles about the guillotine, the channels they had later dug to carry the blood. Perhaps Camille had died because of her. Who knew what secrets had been uncovered by jealous friends about Bernard or the details of her own escape. The thought that Camille may have been condemned by his own misdeeds did not enter her mind. She could not allow herself that much comfort.

And comfort was what she craved most of all. To be loved, to be held warm, safely nestled against another human being. And to hear those whispered words of love which she had not heard for so long. It seemed another lifetime away.

The wind eddied coldly around the ill-fitting window, stirring the black fringe on Rosslyn's shawl. How bleak and forlorn was the garden where dried seedpods tossed in the winter storm. White feather-soft flakes drifted to the windowsill, the headland slowly paling under a covering blanket.

Abruptly she turned from the reminder of her loneliness, swishing the curtains closed. The orange sprigged fabric added a little cheer to the small room, the color taking its brightness from the struggling fire in the hearth. Poked to sluggish flame, even the grate glowed.

Crouched before the hearth, her hands held to the warmth, Rosslyn stiffened as she heard the crunch of hooves on the frozen-rutted track outside. Could it be a messenger from Jarvis? Had he relented in his stubborn refusal to send comfort as long as they remained apart? Or was it Stella? If so she was leaving it late. The Christmas guests would already be thronging Redding Place, each newcomer a splendid source of information. The image tugged a moment until a hollow crashing on the door announced the traveler's arrival. As the sound of the knocker echoed away, Rosslyn moved to the door, not eager to learn the identity of her visitor.

In the icy gloom a man's dark frame blocked the doorway, snow-dotted, wind-raked, his cloak clasped tight about his body. Rosslyn's gaze traveled upward to his face, hidden beneath the shadowing brim of a black, snow-covered hat.

"*Joyeux Noël,* Madame Burton," he said.

At the husky, longed-for voice, Rosslyn found her legs beginning to tremble. Gripping the folds of her gown in clenched fists she gasped, "Armand!"

"The same. May I come in? It's snowing again."

Like a sleepwalker she pushed the door wide to admit him, watching as he went to the hearth, shaking snow from his hat in a sizzling cloud. Still in the doorway, she kept her distance, hardly able to believe he stood there in person, thinking it was more likely an embodiment of her dreams conjured up in the loneliness of dusk.

That face, darker than ever from the fierce southern sun, his eyes, pale as a winter sky, watching, assessing his probable welcome—or rejection.

"Are you alone?"

Coming to life she mumbled her assent.

"Didn't you get my letters?"

"One," she croaked, her throat dry and painful.

"But I sent a dozen. So that's why I never heard from you. I thought—well, you know what I thought."

He pulled off his sodden cloak and draped it around the ladderback chair at the table. Warming his hands at the fire he held her gaze, drawing her, beseeching with his eyes until, against her will, her feet moved forward.

Eyes flashing in sudden anger, he demanded huskily, "After more than a year, is this the welcome I dreamed about?"

"Oh, so you dreamed too, did you?"

"You know I did."

"To make ends meet I've had to take in sewing. See, how fine a seam I sew, the flowers are delicate too . . ." Clutching the half-finished nightgown she was stitching for the local minister's daughter, she thrust it towards him, her eyes hot with pain. "Do you know how long it is since you cared enough to inquire about my welfare?"

"To the day—but it was not for lack of concern."

"What then?"

"Lack of opportunity. Apparently letters are poor messengers."

As if a barrier existed between them they stood in the small room, the fireglow flickering eerily from face to face, lighting the gleam in her eyes, the flash of white teeth against lips so red their ripeness was a pain twisting in his heart. She was thinner, but the beauty was not diminished, only grown more ethereal, as an unattainable painting he coveted till the beauty became pain.

"You left me to die in the Conciergerie!" she spat at last, unleashing the resentment she had harbored all this time, forgetting Camille's vague assurances of Bernard's duplicity in the matter, remembering only her own pain at the desertion.

"Never! Before God, that you should think that."

"Why did you not wait for me?"

"Bernard double-crossed us, surely you knew. I had to get away, put the boys in hiding before they too were recaptured. How was I to know that part of the plan would not be carried out as arranged. Marie lost her life! Do you think I would have entered into something with so great a risk had I known the plan was a deception? I had to hope, to believe—Don't you think it's caused me sleepless nights?"

Swallowing some of her anger, Rosslyn ground her hands together, discarding the embroidery on the chair.

"If it wasn't for Bernard I'd be dead now," she reminded him icily.

"If it wasn't for Bernard you wouldn't have stayed there in the first place," he countered, his mouth twisting to a bitter line. "Well, thank God he is dead, murdered by one of his compatriots, traitors all . . ."

"I killed him."

The words, calm and icy in the quiet room, hung like lead. Armand stared at her, his eyes dilated with surprise, his hands clenched on the chair back. "You! Oh, *cherie* . . . you."

"Yes. I did it for you, to get your passage to safety. There are many things I've done for you, of which you're not aware, that being the most spectacular."

"Why didn't you tell me?"

"How could I? Should I scream the message through the streets of Paris when they are looking everywhere for his assassin? Without a certain friend I would have been taken."

Armand tightened his jaw, knowing she spoke of the revolutionary, Camille. He recalled the day he had watched them in Bernard's garden, close-locked in that fragrant lovers' rose bower where she allowed liberties he had thought reserved only for him, memories which, at the time, had made him vomit in the grass, which even now sent his stomach churning in distress.

"Oh, yes. Him I marked well. You never knew it, but I watched you with him, his hands in your bodice, his mouth devouring yours. Had you groped him in return I wouldn't have been surprised, so hot for it were you . . ."

Paling at the venom in his voice, Rosslyn gasped to know she had been discovered. "I did not love him," she whispered.

"For that small favor I'm grateful," he snapped with sarcasm. "You don't know how much at ease that sets me."

"What of your women? How can you sit in judgment on my behavior when you tumble every wench you meet, when your mistresses are legion."

"I suppose my charming cousin Bernard presented that gem of information."

"No, Armand. It was your wife."

Taken aback by her statement, he bent to pick up his cloak. "This meeting was a mistake. Never go back, they say, how right that advice is. Seeing that I disturb you with my presence I shall take it elsewhere. Ever mindful of my welfare and knowing my despicable carnal appetites, perhaps you'll direct me to a local inn where the wenches are comely and obliging. Travel for a Frenchman at this time is a somewhat dangerous thing."

"So you are going," she whispered, nearly swooning with shock and pain, wondering why everything had gone wrong when she had dreamed for over a year of this very meeting.

"Don't tell me you mind. After the condemnation you've heaped on my head, Madame Burton, I should think the decision would please you heartily."

Numbly she watched him grab his hat, stooping to find his gauntlets which had slid to the floor. Though his clothing was not as well tailored as it once had been, his figure was still the same, those broad shoulders and slim hips, the muscular thighs—Oh, she remembered too plainly what it was like to love him, what ferment his touch created within her soul. He was here at last and she was driving him away.

"Will you go back to the Americas?"

"I had thought not, but this afternoon you've changed my mind. After settling my boys with relatives, I sacrificed the chances of a new life to return to you in the mistaken belief you still cared. Foolishness is not an exclusive failing of youth."

Eyes huge watery pools Rosslyn watched him cross the room in anger, her feet chained, it seemed, to the Turkey red carpet, unable to reach for him, or even to speak.

The door handle creaked as he fumbled to open it and she came to her senses.

"Stay—Oh, God, Armand, you don't know how much I've waited for this."

Frozen, his hand on the knob, he looked at her, pain and withdrawal reflected in his face. "What?" he said.

"Stay. I don't care what's past. I don't care about the others. You are here now and I want you so."

Stiffly he moved, unsure, contemplating her words until she flew to his arms. For an agonizing moment his hands stayed at his sides. Rosslyn sensed his rejection, terrified she had lost him, until warmth came crushing about her as his arms went around her back.

"God, yes, I'll stay. After coming six thousand miles it's the least I can do," he whispered into her hair.

Seizing his face in her hands, she fused her mouth on his, swaying against him with the heated pain of it, exploding with all the long-remembered fire she had cherished for this moment alone.

"There's never been anyone I love like you," she whispered when their lips parted. "No one has even come close. You are everything to me."

"I know, but I never tire of hearing it," he whispered, his wide mouth curving in a smile as he imprisoned her face between his hands. "Tell me again."

"I love your mouth, your hands, your body; when we make love I think I'll go insane so possessed do I become . . ."

He smiled in pleasure at the revelation, feeling the same way, treasuring the memory of it. "Yes, all that too. Come to the hearth where it's warm."

They sat together on the couch, basking in the warm safety of each other's touch, in the pleasure of embraces. Outside the snow came down silently, whitening the horse's tracks, casting gray-white light through the cramped mullion windows which reflected the leaping orange glow of the fire.

Rousing himself, Armand finally remembered his horse. "Good God, I've left the nag tethered to a tree stump. Have you a barn to house him?"

"There's a garden shed. Perhaps he can shelter in that."

Kissing her in parting, Armand seized his hat and cloak and hastened outside to attend the animal.

In his absence Rosslyn laid the table for a meal. When she purchased the luxury Christmas bird she must have known he would be here to share it. When she baked the mince pie warming on the hearth, she must have known he would come. Subconsciously she had expected someone, why else would she have squandered her hard-earned money on Christmas cheer for one. Out of the snowy gloom he came, bringing warm assuasion for all those lonely months.

When Armand came indoors he sniffed the air with pleasure.

"Food. What is it?"

"My Christmas duckling. See, I knew you were coming."

Rosslyn set out a plate of candied relishes, lavishly using her mother's crystal on the table, putting the butter in a silver server, not telling him what a sham she presented, or how many days' food money it had taken to present this feast. To tell him would be to spoil the day.

When they had eaten and the table was cleared, they sat before the blazing hearth to toast the festive season in cheap wine. Armand had brought nothing with him for he came directly from the coast where he had landed scant hours before a storm whipped the Channel to dangerous swells where no boat would venture. All his money had gone on a mount and a meal at a tavern where he asked direction. Next week he would make the rounds of the London firms in the hope of securing a job where his genteel upbringing and fluency in two languages was an asset.

Though she did not consciously do so, Rosslyn found she was postponing the time when they would come together in the feather bed beneath the heaped blankets, half-afraid of the inevitable ending to their day. Had she thought she could have spent this many hours with him, yet held herself aloof after so long a separation, she would not have believed it, yet aloof she had stayed. Armand had not pressed her to yield to him, content with the knowledge of her love, content with caresses and kisses—but not for long.

"Are you tired?" she ventured at last in a small voice.

The smile which curved his sensual mouth set her pulses racing. "I thought you'd never ask."

"Armand, I don't know why, but I'm afraid. God knows, all this time I've shuddered to recall your touch, gone hot to picture you—and now, when at last—I'm skittish as a virgin."

Lazily he stroked her cheek, his fingers soft, gentle as they moved to her hair. "Then I'll treat you as one."

She caught his hands, pressing them to her mouth, covering them with kisses. But still she stiffened when he cupped her breast, the warmth of his hand sending prickling heat along her spine which tingled ice cold after its passage.

"Won't you discover how much I still want you," he whispered, his breath hot against her ear, the veiled invitation bringing both panic and delight.

And when she saw, the confirmation turning her fingers clumsy with haste, she would have gone upstairs; instead, he held her fast. Slowly he removed her brown wool bodice, then the chemise, releasing what he sought with such longing, he shuddered as if fevered when their bodies touched. In the warm golden glow of the hearth they shamelessly made love. Snow sizzled on the logs, mournful wind cries surrounded the cottage, but she didn't hear them. All the heat of her passion came forth to drown the sounds and she was no longer afraid.

CHAPTER SEVENTEEN

"You're a bigger fool than I thought you were," Stella snapped, dropping all pretense of friendship.

Stiffening, Rosslyn tried to keep her temper. This warm, early spring day had been so beautiful before Stella's visit. It had been so long since her sister-in-law's Christmas call when she had fortunately been away from home, she had quite given up the idea of seeing her again. Then today, like the unwelcome return of winter after spring flowers bloom, Stella had come riding along the chalk path, her face set like a thundercloud.

"Because I won't do as you wish does not make me a fool," Rosslyn said evenly. Since Armand's return she had gained confidence in herself, something she had thought lost forever. Now she felt able to battle with Stella on her own terms.

"Oh, yes it does. What could you possibly see in this type of life in a hovel? No parties, no friends, though I must admit, it seems cheerier than I recall on my previous visit. Some new furniture too. Is there a rich old man lurking in the district?" she cooed, turning artful, her smile challenging.

"I'll ignore that insult."

"You can do whatever you want. But mark my words, if you don't come home, you'll be very sorry."

"Why? What can you possibly do to hurt me now?"

And because she knew she could do very little, Stella gritted her teeth in fury. "Oh, you'd be surprised. So incensed is Jarvis over your stubborn resistance, he threatens to publicly name Veasey as his heir!" There, it was out. Biting her lip, Stella found her heart palpitating at the thought.

"That should thrill you. Though I doubt if there's much of the estate to leave beyond the title which goes to Veasey in any case," Rosslyn said, pouring herself a cup of tea as she forced herself to be composed.

"Stupid woman! Do you know what that'll do? My Prudence will never make a good marriage. I had my heart set on Bishop Gardener's son. He's such a catch."

"Stella, I fail to see what difference Jarvis's heir can make to Prue's marriage. Besides, she's only a child."

"She's not. She's fourteen. Quite old enough to make marriage plans." Loathe to tell Rosslyn what she had kept secret for so long, Stella knew she would be forced to explain fully if she expected any consideration out of her sister-in-law in the matter. "Rosslyn, naming Veasey as his heir is more natural than you think. Oh, won't you come home. I told you, Jarvis only drinks socially now. He doesn't gamble . . ."

"Probably because he has nothing of value to wager these days," Rosslyn added with conviction. Nothing would induce her to return now, not if they stripped her and flogged her through the town for being a harlot would she go back to her husband. But she could never tell Stella the reason.

"Oh, damn you, sitting there with your smug smile. Sometimes I think I hate you," Stella cried, thrashing her gloved hands together. "All right. You're going to hear the truth, though God knows I've gone to enough pains to hide it all these years."

"It's about time you told me why you really want me to come home," Rosslyn agreed, maintaining her composure as she wondered uneasily what the actual reason was.

"Veasey is Jarvis's bastard—no need to gasp, sweetest, anyone else would have guessed years ago, as alike as they are."

"Why did you take him as your own?" Rosslyn asked, inwardly cursing herself for a fool. Despite the startling physical resemblance she had given little more than passing attention to that possibility, so secure did Veasey seem in Stella's household. This was why he had been schooled by Jarvis in the finer arts of drinking and seduction; a bird in the hand in case the worst happened to Will. And God help her, it had happened before there was another child to take his place.

"In itself it's no real deterrent to respectability in our society: half the men we know have little bastards scattered about the country. It's part of being a gentleman," Stella added, managing a smile. "However Jarvis isn't content to leave it there, he intends to reveal the circumstances surrounding the boy's birth, which could prove embarrassing. I can't think why, unless it's to punish me. He can be quite vindictive at times, especially since I stopped loaning him money."

"That's really none of my concern. Surely you don't think I'd return just to prevent gossip. Don't you think enough has been said about our family by now? A little more can do no harm."

"The boy's mother was Charlotte Gardener, Bishop Gardener's daughter by his first wife. She came to spend the summer with me. Jarvis was young, but not too young. Charlotte fell madly in love with him. When she discovered she was pregnant she was devastated. You see, her family would have cast her adrift for her sinfulness had they known—stupidly strait-laced. They still are. Anyway, I offered to take her to live with me as my companion when I moved to Redding Hall. I was already married, just staying with Papa while the hall was being redecorated."

"Did Jarvis care for the girl?"

"Oh no, she ran after him. He told her to get rid of the baby, but she wouldn't. I was really very angry with him, suggesting a thing like that to a girl of her background. Anyway, I pretended I was the pregnant one. When Veasey was born we smuggled him to my room. It was so exciting, but then, I was young and silly, it seemed a great adventure. Charlotte's brain was turned by the birth. She followed Jarvis about like a sick calf. So angry did he become, he struck her several times. Well, to cut a long story short, she drowned herself in the lake. Threatened him with it. But he said, 'Go ahead,' never thinking, mind you, she'd do it. Now, if he reveals she really committed suicide instead of falling out of a boat as we pretended all these years, what will that do to us? Oh I hate to think of the long drawn-out questions, perhaps charges for concealing the deed. Think of it, Rosslyn, all you have to do is come home for a little while. I'll pay you to do it if you like. Do this tiny, tiny favor, for all the friendship we've shared," Stella wheedled.

"I can't."

"What do you think Prudence will think of her Aunt Rosslyn when she knows you've ruined her chances like this? She's very much in love with Charles Gardener—in a nice, girlish way, of course."

"No, Stella."

"Oh, damn you, still as selfish as ever."

"If the Gardener family has overcome the shame of Jarvis's behavior toward me, the complete ruin he has brought upon himself, then I'm sure they'll take this news in their stride. After all, it's their family skeleton, not yours. The boy's been raised like your own. They can't fault you for that."

With one more trick left to play, Stella burst into tears at Rosslyn's words. "You don't care what happens, do you? Here I am, virtually begging you to come back, just until the marriage at least . . . "

"They've no idea about Jarvis's drinking, have they? They haven't even heard about the famous wager."

Sniffling, twisting her mouth, reluctant to admit anything, Stella finally shook her head. "No. They live up north, you see."

"You were hoping to make my marriage appear normal, regardless of the cruelty I've been forced to endure. Just as long as I put on a front with heaven knows what—even my bedroom furnishings were sold." Rosslyn's voice shrilled as she faced Stella, anxious to be rid of her and all the disturbing memories she evoked.

"Very well, have it your way," Stella snapped, retreating a couple of steps. "But I warn you, if you don't come home you'll be very sorry. Jarvis doesn't like to be crossed . . . and neither do I."

Glaring hostilely, Stella snatched her hat and gloves from the table. Beside herself with rage, she had belatedly discovered Rosslyn could be just as domineering as she.

"Your threats don't mean a thing here. I'm so remote from Burton Hall, Jarvis's wishes don't affect me. Besides, if he's so concerned about me he should have considered my feelings when he bet Tom Stanley . . ."

"Oh, Lord, don't launch into that again! Anyone would think it was the worst thing ever to happen to anyone," Stella snarled, clumping towards the door.

A sharp rap at the back door took Rosslyn's attention. Leaving Stella alone a moment, she hurried through the cool, stone-flagged kitchen to answer the knock.

Twisting her gloves into an angry spiral, Stella glanced about the room as she waited, desperate to think of something to change Rosslyn's decision. No doubt Prudence would recover from the loss of her suitor if the ugly truth came out, but the Redding family finances wouldn't. Poor, sweet child, she had no idea how close to bankruptcy they too had slid. As the Gardeners were immensely rich, marrying Prue to Charles Gardener was the prefect solution. How, oh, how could she convince Rosslyn to do the right thing? Appealing to her family loyalty had not worked.

A bundle of letters propped behind the clock on the mantel caught her attention, and thinking perhaps they were overdue bills she might offer to settle for a price, she snatched them for a hasty look. Her blue eyes bulged in fury at what she read on the opening page. A glance at the addressee's name confirmed her suspicion—how had that scheming Rosslyn managed to snare Armand St. Clare when she herself had tried desperately hard to interest him without success? What injustice, especially when Rosslyn never had appreciated a man's attentions as they should be appreciated. Only a woman with blood instead of ice water in her veins deserved someone like Armand St. Clare. Face dark with fury, Stella stuffed a couple of condemning pages in her pocket, determined to make use of them somehow. Rosslyn would never get away with this. To refuse a favor was bad enough, but this was the final straw. No wonder she didn't want to come home, the wretch. This isolated cottage was their trysting place secure from prying eyes. Or so they thought. She'd soon change that.

287

Without waiting for her hostess's return, satisfied Rosslyn was safely engaged in conversation at the scullery door, Stella gathered her belongings and flounced outdoors. Her mind was a seething turmoil as she planned how to use her knowledge to ruin Rosslyn and that damnable Frenchman for his deceit.

One cool April evening, when the gardens sparkled crystal fresh after a shower, Stella decided to confront her brother with the letter. Though she had spent several days wondering how best to hurt Rosslyn with her information, no brilliant idea had come to mind. Determined to have at least the satisfaction of vengeance on her sister-in-law, Stella decided to reveal the scandalous secret to Jarvis. His pride would suffer a death blow when he learned his supposedly frigid wife was enjoying a passionate affair with their former tutor. That would serve him right for causing such an uproar by his spiteful proposal.

Surprised by his sister's unexpected visit, Jarvis turned jaundiced eyes on her plump figure, bustling with determination through the study door, reminding him of a plump wren in her chocolate serge habit.

"Well, demme, if this isn't an honor. Come to check if I'm sober, Stella?"

Stella smiled and patted his arm. "Nonsense, dear. You know I trust you. If you say you're not drinking, then I believe you."

Jarvis snorted at her sugary manner. "What do you want then? Seems as if you're another one who's made herself scarce since my fortunes took a plunge for the worse."

"You hurt me to the quick when you say things like that," Stella pouted. "Fancy, your own sister who loves you dearly."

Letting that pass, Jarvis bundled his account book back in the desk and stood up, wincing as a colic-like pain stabbed his midsection. "This damned liver of mine, need to replace it with a new one, eh." He chuckled, attempting humor, but Stella's attention was elsewhere.

"How badly do you want Rosslyn home?"

"The wretch can stay where she is for all I care," he growled, his face tightening at the question. "You're the one always worrying about her. S'pose if she were here we could play house to suit your fancy Gardener clan. Then once Prue has her hands on their money, I suppose we can all go to hell."

"Now you don't mean that. Say you don't," Stella soothed, taking his arm as she led him towards the windows overlooking the garden. "Sit down there, sweet. Everything looks so fresh after the rain. I've something to tell you. Now I don't want you to get angry—"

"That bad? Need me sitting, eh!"

"If Rosslyn came home to nurse you, to oversee your household, don't you think you'd feel better?"

Jarvis curled his thick lips. "Can't say I've missed our quarrels. It's made life a hell of a lot quieter."

"But she is your wife."

"Yes."

"And her place is here at your side, especially now you're not in the best of health."

"Yes. Damned woman's shirking her duty all right."

"If she was here you'd be able to keep servants. After all, even you must admit this place is beyond Mostyn, and I can't spare my girls more than twice a week. It's spring, so you're going to need the gardeners. Rosslyn could organize everything for you, just like she used to do."

Eyes turning distant, Jarvis wistfully recalled how smoothly life had run in the old days. Free to do as he pleased, enough money for pleasure as well as necessities, and Rosslyn by his side had made him the envy of every man they met. Life had been good then, only at the time he had not realized how transient his blessings were.

"She's coming back to me then," he rumbled, gripping his stomach which pitched alarmingly at the thought. Things would be like they used to be! The situation would gradually right itself if she came home where she belonged. Since Rosslyn left him everything had come crashing about his ears. "Well, I don't mind, if she behaves herself," he condescended, drumming his fingers on the chair arm. "In time I can bring myself to forgive her for her desertion." His voice had deepened to the old tone at the prospect of life returning to the happy state it once had been. A beaming smile replaced his usual wan demeanor as he stretched his legs, basking in his dream of the future.

Annoyance tightened Stella's mouth as she watched him stretching there like a placid tomcat. Never once, in all this time, had her brother blamed himself for his own misfortune. Even now, when she had worked so hard to bring about what seemed an impossibility, he condescended to admit his wife to their home. She wanted to rage at him, wanted to call him the fool he was, but she steeled herself to remain calm.

"Not exactly, Jarvis. Not yet anyway."

"What! Does she have the gall to make conditions?"

"I've something here which I think will change our dear Rosslyn's mind. A little blackmail may be in order."

Jarvis glowered at his sister. Levering himself from the deep leather chair, he marched towards the port decanter on his desk. "Not begging her to come home, if that's what you mean. She can stay in that hovel, can rot in loneliness for all I care if she expects me to beg. I asked. You asked. That's as much as she can expect. I'll not give her a penny, do you hear, not a penny."

Stella watched him pour a half glass of port, waiting till he came back to the windows before continuing. "I truly agree with you, her behavior's been shameless, but this latest episode tops it all. There's another man."

"What!" Eyes bulging in shock, Jarvis clutched his glass, then gulped the contents in one go. "That iceberg has a man!"

"Not just *a* man but that insolent ex-tutor of yours."

"St. Clare!" Jarvis managed, his voice cracking in shock. "You saw him there?"

"No, but I know what's going on. I have a letter sent to Rosslyn. The shocking things that man writes, he should be imprisoned for even thinking them, let alone putting it on paper," Stella added, feigning shock, but secretly hating the fact the lovers were close enough to be able to say such things. No man had ever rhapsodized over her body, the omission turning her livid with jealousy.

Taking the closely written pages to the window, Jarvis began to read, his color going from white to purple as his rage mounted. Growling his distress, he flung the letter to the carpet where he ground his heel on the paper. "Filth! To my wife no less. By God, I'll have him hanged for this!"

Alarmed at the anger blazing in her brother's face, Stella tried to pacify him, seizing his arm only to be shaken free like a terrier shakes a rat. Beside himself with rage, Jarvis had gained in strength.

"Please, remember how ill you've been. It was not my intention to . . ."

"Leave me alone. I know damned well what was your intention, why else would you show it to me? Get out! You've had your fun. I'm reacting the way you wanted. I'm hurt to the quick. Is this the final indignity I'm to endure, having to read how much of a harlot my wife's become from the pen of that bastard?"

"No, Jarvis, never that. I want to use the letter against her by threatening to make public what that audacious foreigner wrote. Threatening to expose her shoddy secret should change her mind. It wasn't to hurt you. Not for vengeance. You must believe me."

Glaring at the tearful, blubbering woman, Jarvis flung free of her ineffectual grasp, finding himself charged with a new strength of purpose. "Well, whatever your intention, my sister, you can have an immediate reaction: I'm going to run him through."

"No!" Stella came to life, racing across the room to stop him as he charged through the door. "Have you forgotten what a swordsman St. Clare is? Didn't he give fencing lessons to your Will?"

Pausing at the foot of the stairs, Jarvis chuckled, a mirthless sound which made Stella's skin crawl.

"Aye, fencing lessons to my son—it's the lessons he gave my wife for which he's going to pay."

Sweet spring air washed the headland. In the coarse sea grass, flowers showed pale pink heads, clumps of blue harebells making a drift like water beside the gorse. This year the sea seemed to be deeper blue, the sky too. Smiling at her imagery, Rosslyn knew it was only because she was in love. Not only that, this time she felt secure in the knowledge that the object of her affections loved her deeply in return. Even Mrs. Kenney had noticed her changed mood. And though she never mentioned seeing her male visitor Rosslyn knew the widow must have watched him pass her window on the way to Sea View.

Sighing with pleasure she turned her back on the sea, hastening towards the cottage where a joint of meat roasted in the oven, the fragrant aroma challenging the fresh sea air for mastery. Armand would be here any minute. He said today he would have important news for her and she prayed it would be what she most wanted to hear. She wanted to go away with him. Clarence had given Armand a place in the family business which seemed to have taken an upsurge for the better these days. Perhaps there was enough money to move to a house of their own where neither Stella nor Jarvis would ever find her. Jeanette was now the new Mrs. Warner and more happy a couple she had never seen. Since her bother sold The Hollies, she had only seen Jeanette twice, those visits occupied with descriptions of the home they had purchased near Petersham with a garden backing onto the Thames. How lovely if Armand too could settle there. Yet to arrange such happiness for herself seemed too much of an impossible daydream.

When she walked through the white-painted garden gate a shadow loomed from behind the rose hedge.

"Armand!" Crying, laughing in her pleasure, Rosslyn was swept into his arms where she pressed close against the warm safety of his body. Whenever he held her time moved so fast, sometimes she desperately tried to recall everything about him to last through their next parting. It never worked. Though she knew him well, each time she saw him again there was always something about his appearance she had omitted from the dream image.

"Did you think I was a footpad or one of those randy sailors who give you the eye in town?"

"Neither. Oh, you're early. I was taking a walk before dark. Come, the meal's almost ready. Roast beef, roast potatoes and carrots, down-to-earth English food, but I'm proud to say I prepared it all myself. You'd be surprised to know what I can do these days," she added, walking up to the door with him, her arm about his slim waist.

"Oh, I am surprised, every weekend when I turn faint with delight," he joked huskily, squeezing her shoulder. "How much time can I steal from the fabulous roast beef dinner?"

Her heart quickened to know the unvoiced meaning behind his words. Rosslyn seized his face in her hands and kissed him thoroughly, fighting the wash of weakness he always caused, drinking in his smell, a mingled scent of leather, sea-tanged lips, and that hot delight which only his skin produced.

"How much time do you need, Monsieur?"

"Five minutes will be ample," he whispered, smiling into her eyes, dark now with passion.

Pleasantly sated, they lit the fire as fog rolled in with darkness. Blissfully content in Armand's arms, Rosslyn wondered about the promised news of such importance.

"You've never told me your news. Are we going to elope to darkest Africa?"

Armand rested his face against her hair, his smile dissolving as he inwardly phrased a sentence knowing both of them would rather not hear voiced. "I have to go home."

"What?" Fear shot ice cold through Rosslyn's body, stiffening her limbs with pain.

"Just for a little while, *cherie*. I promise I'll come back. Sources assure me I may move without danger now. The Revolution's all but burned itself out. It's only a matter of time before sanity is restored. Trust me. Would I leave you if there was any earthly way around it?"

Pain spurred those old doubts which sped swiftly through her mind. Would he really come back? Had this been but an idyllic interlude?

Forcing tears from her voice she asked him bluntly, "Why must you go back?"

"All my lands will eventually be restored, yet it's important to time things right. I've an offer for sale of my vineyards, more money than I'd thought anyone willing to pay for those hillside acres. That's one reason for my return at the moment, the other—well, I'm still the official owner of valuables deposited in a vault in Paris. My source tells me as there's near chaos in Paris at the moment, it would be a simple thing to reclaim my property."

"My God, more intrigue! Your sons are safe. Your wife's dead. Yet you still can't stop. When will it end? Aren't you done with tempting death? Wasn't that aborted ride to the guillotine real enough? I don't understand you anymore. When we have so much here, when we're together . . . "

"Cherie, don't cry," he soothed, looking above her curly black hair to the sputtering hearth. Of all the things he cherished most in this world after her love, the quiet solitude of their seaside cottage was the most valuable. Yet he must return to Paris. A force, without sense, pulled him home, made him gamble one last time.

"What if your source is wrong? What if it isn't safe? They could be trying to trap you."

"Yes, I suppose they could, but this man has no axe to grind. He's not even a Frenchman."

"My God, not Clarence?" she cried, anger mounting swiftly at the thought that her own brother should seek to destroy her happiness.

"Shh, not Clarence."

"Who then?"

"I can't tell you, Rosslyn, not yet. He's someone who's known to you. Once the danger is over perhaps he'll come forward of his own accord, at the moment secrecy is imperative."

"So you don't intend to tell me."

"No."

"What am I to do while you're gone? Take in sewing again?"

Armand sighed. He released her and went to the windows to stare out to sea where a light blurred through the fog as a ship rode at anchor awaiting the tide. "I didn't expect you to understand, only I always hope you will. This time I'm going home to reclaim that which has belonged to my family for centuries, which was wrested from me by a rabble spurred on by insanity. When I'm able you shall come there with me. At the moment I have so little to offer you. The salary your brother pays is hardly a fortune."

"I don't care about fortunes. Haven't you learned that much about me by now? Once money and clothes were vitally important to me. Surely, after living here all this time, you don't still think I crave a mansion and all that goes with it?"

"I don't know what you crave, Rosslyn, but I know what I must do. Risking this quarrel with you, I was determined to tell you in person. Clarence thought I should write a letter to be delivered after I set sail . . ."

"Oh, yes, Clarence would," she exploded, unreasonably angry with her brother, with her lover, with the whole world, resentful of having her bliss shattered by such an unexpected event. Never had she thought Armand would consider returning to France until the Revolution was over. That the fury of that insanity was running out was not security enough to protect him from an angry mob.

"Do you want me to leave now? Or shall we spend our last weekend in happiness?" he asked, turning to face her, his face grown serious.

Battling inwardly, Rosslyn's nature made her want to scream at him, to accuse him of not loving her, of risking his life out of disregard, the way she would have done with Jarvis. But Armand was not Jarvis. And she could not risk losing him.

"No, don't go. I'll need something pleasant to sustain me while we're apart," she whispered.

He smiled at her words. "It won't be for long. You have my word."

Rosslyn buried her face against his shoulder, drinking in the familiar scent of him, the mixture of skin and soap, of pomade and leather. The intoxicating aroma she had grown to love, to respond to in full passion.

Soon he would go away. Their entire relationship seemed to consist of partings and reunions. But more partings. They were sadder and longer remembered. So sure he seemed of his own safety, yet how could one be sure as long as the guillotine operated in the Place de Grave, its insatiable appetite satisfied by the condemned from the Conciergerie.

The fire died down to a rosy glow, the embers giving off gentle heat. Silence, broken by the ticking clock, by Armand's breathing as he lay beside her, filled Rosslyn with pain. This last night she must grasp to have forever. And the hours fled at breakneck speed. All too soon it would be dawn and time for parting.

Thundering on the front door startled her so that she jerked upright, nearly falling from the couch. Armand was immediately awake.

"Who can that be at this hour?"

"I don't know," Rosslyn whispered, beginning to tremble. How real were the rumors of French agents combing England for emigrés? Had someone discovered Armand's identity and turned him in? "Get a light," she said, as the door thundered again.

To her horror as the bolt was drawn back and the candleflame held aloft to identify the traveler, Rosslyn saw a familiar face, haggard, older, but still recognizable.

"Oh, God—Jarvis!"

Thrusting the door open he marched inside, admitting a stream of vapor from the fog, damp and chill.

"Where's the bastard?" he growled, his voice thickened by the three ports he had downed before the final stage of his journey to give him courage. Though the rotgut stuff was working its poison on his liver, he felt better for it. The wine gave him a great jolt of courage. To face a swordsman on his own ground required courage: that much courage could probably not be found in a whole keg of port.

"Do you mean me?" Armand stepped from the shadows.

"You bastard! Thought I wouldn't find out, didn't you? Suppose it was going on all the time under me own nose, damn you. Treacherous damned foreigner! Give

296

you a position, pay you damned well when you haven't a penny to your name and this is all the thanks I get. If Stella hadn't shown me it in black and white I wouldn't have believed it."

Glowering, his old belligerence returned, Jarvis leaned a moment against the wall to catch his breath after the exertion of his bellowed speech.

"Stella told you? How could she know?" Rosslyn gasped, fighting the panic which fluttered through her stomach at the imminent confrontation.

"Too careless with your filthy letters, my dear, that's how."

"She stole a letter from me. Is that how you found out?"

"That's right. You should thank her for the crime, Ross. I intend to take you back with me. I'll not stand for you living a life of sinful degradation with that foreigner."

Glowering at Armand, who had so far held his tongue, Jarvis lurched forward, fumbling beneath his heavy serge coat to produce a sword which had banged and clanged when he came indoors, but which in the dark Rosslyn had thought the sound of his spurs.

"Look, Burton, you're in no fit state to fight a duel. You know I'm a better swordsman. There would be no contest."

Panting at the cool speech of his enemy, Jarvis found his breath strangling in his throat. "Coward! Fight like a man. Always had me doubts, always wondered if you Froggies were quite as manly as you pretended, all that hand kissing, those stupid compliments . . ."

"I have no sword. As you've probably noticed, it is not quite the fashion it once was to carry sidearms," Armand pointed out, standing his ground, wondering if he could take the bigger man if it came to a scuffle with fists.

"Well, by God, that's no excuse. Use that damned saber up there on the wall. I'd hate to murder you without you lifting a hand to your defense."

Jarvis snatched the sword hanging over the hearth, a relic of Rosslyn's uncle's army days, and he thrust it into Armand's hands.

"Rosslyn's old enough to decide what she wants from life. To settle her destiny with swords is pointless . . ."

"Shut up, you damned Froggy, and fight," Jarvis bellowed, beside himself with rage, not caring to debate the question any longer.

Without waiting for Armand to position himself, Jarvis lunged with his sword, tipping over a table, splattering a vase of daffodils to the carpet. Realizing his opponent was deadly earnest, Armand took his stance, parrying the blow with his arm. Repeatedly he defended himself, not choosing to run Burton through, though he would have delighted in the action. It would not only rid the world of a pompous fool, it would serve to avenge Rosslyn's treatment and make her a widow at the same time.

"Bastard! Fight me! Stop all this damned playacting," Jarvis yelled, closing in as he lunged towards Armand's chest. With a clatter his weapon flew towards the scullery as Armand disarmed him, coming to rest with a jarring fall on the tiles.

"Have you had enough?"

Blustering, clutching at his chest, Jarvis stared in disbelief at his sword.

"For God's sake go home while you're safe," Rosslyn cried, her throat painful with emotion. She gave Jarvis a push and he staggered towards the hearth. Like a flash he seized the huge brass poker and whirled it over his head, leaping towards Armand, surprisingly agile.

They wrestled on the carpet, Armand borne down by the attack. Jarvis raised the heavy brass poker to hit his opponent, momentarily off guard. Seizing his opportunity, Armand pushed him backward, toppling his balance. With a cry of surprise Jarvis fell hard, the poker flying across the hearthstone.

Crying in relief, Rosslyn raced to Armand's side where he assured her he was unharmed. After a few moments, during which she alternately wept and clung to him, they turned their attention to Jarvis who lay unconscious on the hearthstone, ashes dusting his brown hair.

"Fool. Why couldn't he take the opportunity when he

had it?" Armand muttered, crouching beside Jarvis to lever his bulk from the cinders.

"He hit his head on the hearthstone. See, there's a lump," Rosslyn said, holding the light close to the egg-sized swelling on his temple. "He's so still! Are you sure he's all right?"

"Probably. Here, move those things. I'll put him on the couch."

Dragging, struggling, Armand got Jarvis to the couch, where they propped his head on pillows. Fear began to throb through Rosslyn's body as she stared at her husband's inert form with its gray-tinged face. So still. Not even an eyelid flickered.

"Is he dead?"

"No, knocked cold. That's all."

But when Armand straightened up, after checking the pulse in Jarvis's thick neck, Rosslyn saw the mounting tension in his set face, the creeping pallor. "Oh, my God! He is dead!"

Armand nodded, his warm arm a welcome support as she grew numb and cold with shock. Together they stared at the bulky figure, arms and legs drooping to the floor.

"It was an accident. Had I wanted to kill him I had the opportunity a dozen times. When he was disarmed it would have been a matter of moments to run him through . . ."

"Shh!" Rosslyn placed cool fingers on his mouth, silencing the defense. "There's no need. I know you never intended this. Heaven knows, if you had, I wouldn't have stopped you. But will others believe your innocence?"

Appalled, Armand stared at her, his eyes dilated to black in the candleglow. Flames moved a pattern over the walls casting giant shadows on the ceiling as they stood silent, shocked to inertia by the events of the evening. Though alone in this remote cottage on the fog-shrouded headland, it seemed as if the whole world must already be aware of the crime.

"Christ—it's as if he hatched some diabolical plan to prevent me going home. He couldn't have chosen a worse time had he planned it," Armand croaked, dashing his hand over his eyes, swallowing, unable to think of a solution. "Who must we contact?"

"Contact," Rosslyn repeated, her mind already racing to solve his predicament.

"About the death. The coroner. Someone."

"Why contact anyone?"

"What?" As he saw the flicker of a smile play about her mouth he cried: "No. If we bury him ourselves we haven't a chance of clearing the crime. What do you think everyone will suppose then? Besides, someone's bound to make inquiries about him."

At his dismissal of her plan she scowled. "Don't be an idiot, don't you think they'll condemn you anyway. My lover, the drunken husband—it's a classic situation. No, much as you want to be honest about this, sweetheart, honesty will be fatal."

Taken aback by her calmness, by her unexpected ability to cope in such a situation, he smiled in admiration for her courage. "*Cherie,* where do you learn these things? My little Rosslyn calmly planning to hide a body."

Armand surprised her by his soft laughter uttered more from nervous tension than humor. She smiled reassuringly at him before taking a deep breath, feeling in control as never before in her life.

"The Conciergerie was a painful apprenticeship," she dismissed. Going to the window she lifted the curtain to assure herself the fog still held. The hazy light from the water still pierced the white billows, reminding her they were not totally alone on the headland. "Do you think the other cottagers heard the horse?"

"Sound's distorted in the fog. I suppose so. Why?"

"Too bad. We can't pretend he never came then."

"Look, *cherie,* I know you want to help me, but I can't see how we can get around the truth. He rode along the path. He came to the cottage. He died here. It's that simple."

"You want to set sail tomorrow, don't you?"

"You know I do."

"Very well, if you march to the magistrates and confess the crime, what chance do you think you've got of ever seeing France again? Jarvis is an Englishman, you are French. We are at war. Don't you think Stella's spread the gossip far and wide about us by now? When Jarvis is found dead they'll come to one natural conclusion; you murdered him."

"Put like that you don't give me much chance," he said, his mouth tightening. "What then, my diabolical little schemer, do you have in mind?"

"It's something I read in a history book, though why it stuck in my mind I don't know. As a girl I never thought to be putting it to use myself." Rosslyn let the curtain drop back in place, trying to avoid looking at the man on the couch, finding it hard to believe he had once been the object of her girlish affections, harder still to believe he was dead. Now he seemed smaller, less forceful, almost an object of her pity.

"All right, I won't scoff. Tell me." Moving to the fire, Armand stoked the faltering blaze, adding a couple of spars of driftwood. The room had grown icy cold, or perhaps it was his own blood which ran chill at the thought of trial and death at the hands of an alien nation. Death was a fate he had faced many times before. Somehow he felt this would be one time too many. He had used up his very last chance that day he was led to execution.

"We can put him in the saddle and send the horse over the headland. In the fog the animal will be terrified. It's a wonder he found his way up here as it was."

"Do you expect him to go over the cliffs?"

"No, I don't want the horse killed. We'll fasten Jarvis's foot in the stirrup. When he falls from the saddle the horse will drag him. By the time his body's found no one will know how he got the lump on his head. What do you think?"

Armand pursed his mouth considering the plan. Not familiar with English history he asked, "What unfortunate met with this fate?"

"A king, a prince, I don't really remember. But it worked then. And they didn't have fog on their side."

"What if you are questioned? Things could run afoul."

"How could I get a man Jarvis's size into the saddle? By the time he's found you'll be on your way to France."

"Very well. It's as good a plan as any," he agreed.

She smiled at him, her eyes glittering in the firelight and Armand chilled to find how much she had changed. That time in Paris learning the duplicity of Bernard's schemes and consorting with the revolutionaries had produced the change. Even her intimacy with Camille had played its part in hardening her character. He winced to picture them together. How painfully disillusioned he had been then; now it was of little portent, so long ago did it seem. With a prickle of shock he remembered the circumstances of Bernard's death. Lord, why should he be surprised by this comparatively easy scheme when she had successfully negotiated the murder of a revolutionary leader, following it up with her own escape from the capital city while pursued by an army of agents.

"Come. We wouldn't want to be surprised by daylight," she urged, reaching for her red cloak. "Can you lift him?"

"Don't worry. Open the door for me."

Pulling, pushing, they managed to get Jarvis outside. Fog billowed like smoke as Rosslyn shivered at the cottage door. Light in the sky forced her to swift action; though the fog may hold till late morning, people would soon be stirring. How ironical if the animal careened into someone's yard bearing his grisly burden before the plan had time to be completed.

The dark shadow of the horse could be seen tethered to the garden gate. Rosslyn went to soothe the animal while Armand dragged Jarvis down the path. It was a struggle to put the heavy figure into the saddle as the horse whinnied, uneasy at the smell of death. Throwing back his head, changing feet, the stallion became an unwilling accomplice compounding their difficulties. At last Jarvis slumped against the horse's neck, reminding Rosslyn of his appearance when he came home drunk, clinging to the horse's mane, relying on the animal to take him home. Twisting the stirrup, Armand tangled Jarvis's spurs in the leather, pulling sharply to test its strength, hoping it would support a heavy man long enough to carry him a safe distance from the cottage.

"Are we ready?"

He nodded. "Let me go with him. As heavy as he is, we wouldn't want him deposited on your path."

"It doesn't matter where he falls as long as the horse drags him far enough away. Just enough to make it look authentic," she pointed out, tension mounting as she noticed the lightening sky towards the Dover road, the mist already thinning to isolated pockets.

"Have you thought the animal may stay where he is when his rider falls?"

Gasping, Rosslyn clapped her hands to her cheeks, now suffused with heat. "He can't! How did they manage their scheme?"

"Probably prodded him in the rump. Don't worry, *cherie*, I'll take care of the necessary details. Get back in the house."

A few minutes later, Rosslyn heard him open the front door, the deed accomplished.

Running to Armand she clutched him tightly, losing herself in his arms. She wished she could turn back the clock to last week, last month. To have him leave her was punishment enough, now to have this terrible disaster which she had arranged to face alone hanging over her head, seemed too much to bear.

"*Au revoir, cherie.* Only a little while," he whispered, kissing her mouth, welding all the heat of his nature to her chill lips in that kiss of farewell.

Wanting to cling, to plead, Rosslyn released him. She tried to implant the memory of his smile within her heart; she wanted to remember the sweet promise of his eyes when he looked at her.

"Write if you're able," she said, fighting tears.

He nodded. "Send word through Clarence. Pray God the events of this terrible night are over safely."

Silently she handed him his hat and gloves, watching as he slung his dark cloak about his shoulders, picturing the warm strength of his body pressed to hers, the smell, the pulsing need he aroused. She would have to live on memories for a long time.

They kissed again, then resigned to leaving, Armand pushed the door open, striding purposefully down the path to the shed where he housed his horse. Mounted, he raised his hand in farewell, pausing on the road, the thinning fog weaving spirals of white about his dark-clothed figure adding an air of mystery. Like an apparition he slowly dissolved in the fog, the muffled hoofbeats drowned by the rush of suppressed grief which deafened her senses.

CHAPTER EIGHTEEN

The hours that followed Armand's departure seemed like days. Around mid-morning when the last trace of fog had disappeared, Rosslyn could stand the suspense no longer. Taking her wicker basket, she set out along the cliff path to town.

Unable to inquire if a rider had been found, she learned nothing of value from the shopkeepers' gossip. There was no sign of a horse or of a rescue party when she walked home in the bright sunshine. The green headland seemed bare of life. Uneasiness gripped her at the thought of what might have happened to the horse and rider. At this moment the animal could be enjoying a bag of oats while doctors examined his rider, taken carefully from the saddle, all signs of murder clearly apparent.

She was being a fool and she knew it. There were a dozen explanations why Jarvis had not been found. Guilt caused the alarm, accumulated guilt for numerous crimes, yet probably the most damning crime of all was her lack of remorse for the deeds.

Just before nightfall riders halted outside her garden gate and she knew Jarvis had been found.

"Lady Burton?" the first man asked in surprise, doffing his black hat, hardly expecting to find Her Ladyship in this white-washed cottage.

"I am she."

"We've bad news, Your Ladyship," the other, older man said, taking charge of the situation. "Don't want to alarm you none, but we might've found your husband down at the foot of the cliffs. Terrible accident it was, mum. Broke 'is neck. I understand you wasn't living together at the time."

305

White-faced, Rosslyn nodded, clutching the door jamb for support, willing strength to endure the next hours as she prayed for the duplicity not to accidentally reveal the truth.

In the fading yellow sunset the men led her down the winding cliff path to the site of the accident, less than a hundred yards from the cottage. To think Jarvis had been down there all this time, so close, yet she had not known it. The thought made her shiver.

"Only a quick look, mum, don't need no more'n that. We usually sends for someone else, but you being so close like. And Mrs. Kenney says she's sure it's your 'usband. Mick, 'ere, well he follows coats of arms and such, 'e says that's the Burton arms all right. Well, mum, after that, only thing I could do was fetch you."

Rosslyn nodded, walking white-faced over the wet sand to the small tableau crouched about the horse carcass. Poor animal. It had not been her intention to kill him too. He must have stumbled over the cliff in the fog, frightened out of his wits by the inert rider dangling from the stirrup.

"That's him. I recognize the horse," she murmured, turning away, not wanting to see the battered blue-black face which was half-twisted in the sand. Tears, more for the horse than the man, formed, trickling slowly down her cheeks. Observing her sorrow, the investigating group grunted their condolences, then thrust the tearful widow into the waiting arms of Mrs. Kenney who led her sobbing to the warmth of her cottage while the body was carried on a stretcher up the chalky path.

The inquest which followed was merely a formality. With His Lordship's reputation for drink; the foggy night; a treacherous, unfamiliar path; an accident like this was a foregone conclusion.

It was a glorious June day when Rosslyn rode up the drive to Burton Hall, finding none of her distaste for the house lessened by Jarvis's death. Memories of their life complete with its bitterness lingered in the masonry, in the furniture, only the overgrown garden seemed innocent of pain.

Wearing a black dress, her face obscured by a heavy

mourning veil, she entered the chill rooms. Like a ghost of her former self Rosslyn ascended the wide stairs to the room made available to her for her brief stay while the will was read and the estate settled.

The house seemed better kept than it had been on her previous visit, though the servants who greeted her were strangers. The rest of the family, Stella and her children, were here also, though they made no effort to greet her on arrival. Veasey would inherit the title after all, without embarrassment, or revelation of his true parentage. That at least should pacify Stella.

To Rosslyn's surprise, when she was summoned to the study for the reading of Jarvis's will, she found only Tom Stanley and his lawyer, James Millington, awaiting her.

"I understood the will was to be read this afternoon. That is why I'm here, is it not?" she asked stiffly, forcing the speech even though her heart raced with unease to find these two there like conspirators. She was immediately reminded of that other legal document to which the unscrupulous Lawyer Millington had put his seal.

"Rosslyn, still charming as ever. And quite as beautiful," Tom Stanley complimented, coming towards her and bowing over her hand. "Do sit down. Everything is in order."

"Are we waiting for Stella?"

"No need for that, Lady Burton," James Millington chuckled, shuffling papers at Jarvis's huge desk where he seemed miniscule behind the oak vastness.

"Even mourning becomes you," Tom Stanley said with a warm encompassing smile. He took a chair opposite hers, moving his booted legs within inches of her black satin slippers. "What we have to tell you may come as a shock."

Millington cleared his throat. Holding the sheaf of papers aloft, he pushed back the red leather chair. "This will, while quite in order, fails to present a true picture of your situation—your financial situation, that is, Lady Burton."

Rosslyn managed a tight smile at his words. "My assumption is that it's disastrous."

"Quite, quite," Millington chuckled, glancing towards

Stanley for affirmation before continuing. "As a matter of fact, the property known as Burton Hall and its surrounding grounds is heavily mortgaged."

"What!" Rosslyn's eyes widened with shock. She had assumed though Stanley had taken most movable items of value, the house itself still belonged to her.

"I'm the lucky mortgage holder," Stanley explained, moving closer, setting his tan polished boots on either side of her feet, imprisoning with his grip. Then leaning forward, so that the spicy odor of his cologne wafted headily in her face, he explained. "Jarvis lived here under my beneficence alone. He was an absolute pauper. So, my dear, as you can see, there's absolutely nothing left of the estate for you. The title, which is worthless as a means of support, goes to Veasey Redding, the closest male relative."

Eyes fastened on his in shock, Rosslyn struggled to her feet, suddenly light-headed. "I don't believe it!"

Smiling, his glance still bearing that same assessment of her bedding qualities as he swept the length of her body, Stanley tossed her a sheaf of papers. Hitting her skirts, they fluttered to the carpet. He picked them up, holding out the evidence with a smug smile of satisfaction.

"Quite legal. Filed, accepted by any lawyer in the land. But you may have them checked yourself for your assurance."

Stonily Rosslyn took the papers, her eyes blurring over the legal sentences weighted with verbiage, seemingly too real for comfort. Finally abandoning the task, she met his gaze, trying to maintain composure so he would not know the shock this document had been. "What am I to live on? Was there no provision for me?"

Stanley signaled Millington to leave. Bowing quickly, the white-whiskered lawyer glided from the room to leave them alone.

"How long it is since I saw you!"

The tone of his voice had become warmly intimate, so much so, Rosslyn half-expected him to embrace her; instead Stanley walked to the windows, throwing them wide to admit the warm fragrance of the June day.

"I don't have pleasant memories of our last meeting," she rapped.

The sunlight turned his light hair to gold as he stood by the open window, reflecting fire flashes from the buttons on his violet cutaway coat as he turned towards her. From the lawns came the sound of children playing. Stella's children. No wonder they had not been waiting in the study like vultures ready to pounce with beak and talon, demanding their share of the inheritance. There was no inheritance to divide.

"How can I ask your forgiveness for my drunken folly that night," he said with a remorseful smile. "You, of all people, surely must know how drink can change a person."

She nodded, but gave him no more satisfaction than that. "Is there an allowance for me?" she repeated, wishing to cut short his idyllic reminiscences. As he gave her that bold assessment once more, she flushed, feeling naked beneath his raking, hot-eyed gaze.

"No."

"Then we have nothing further to say to each other. The house, the land, everything in it is legally yours. I wonder why I was called at all." That was her voice sounding unnaturally tight. Rosslyn made the statement as if another spoke the words through her. The one thought pounding in her brain was she must return to Dover, to the only place in the world she could call her own.

"Not so hasty, Rosslyn, you aren't dealing with a stranger. That you can speak so formally to me after what we've been to each other . . ."

"What we've been! My God, we were cat and mouse, what other construction could you place on that relationship?" She was on her feet, her voice shrill with anger.

He quickly closed the window, anxious to keep their exchange private. "You know it was more than that. We both know it."

Rosslyn saw he was coming to embrace her. Stunned, she stood waiting for his touch, wanting to escape this room with its bitter memories yet unable to move.

Sweeping her in his arms, Tom Stanley kissed her

mouth, crushing her against his body with renewed vigor. "Ah, yes," he breathed, looking into her eyes flashing dark in anger, "exactly as I remember. Come, we can arrange a settlement of mutual benefit to both of us."

Rosslyn slapped his face. Unlike the last time she had resisted him there was no reprisal, he only pulled her tighter, laughing at her anger.

"Let me go! There's no settlement I wish to make with you."

"Don't you want me still? Pressed this close, renewing the memory of what it was like," he whispered, well aware of the increased arousal she ignited in his body, knowing also she was aware of it. "Don't lie. Be honest for once. Tell me how much you enjoyed it with me."

Rosslyn thrust ineffectually against his chest, wanting to forget that shameful coupling, hating the hot insistent pressure of his thighs which only awakened her memory of it. Twisting in his arms to avoid his hot wet mouth, she gasped:

"All right, you want honesty, you shall have it. Though at the time I may have used you to satisfy some hunger, there's absolutely nothing there now. My appetite was generously appeased; if any remains it's for a different food."

Not expecting to be met at his own game, Stanley stared down at her shocked to find she spoke the truth. His smile tightened to a grimace sending lines crisscrossing his thick lips.

"So, you are saying whatever I do, or do not do, you will never let me take you again?"

"Right." Challenging him, she looked him straight in the eyes, no longer afraid, nor shrinking from the confrontation.

"You know I could rape you now. No one would know, or even care."

"Right again. You're far stronger than I am."

Surprised to see no fear, Tom Stanley slackened the pressure of his embrace. "How you've changed."

"A lot of people tell me that. And I suppose they are right. Now, Mr. Stanley, as we've nothing further to discuss, with your leave, I'll return home."

"No! Must you call me Mr.—isn't Tom more appropriate?"

"Mr. Stanley, Tom, it's all the same. It doesn't change my mind."

"But Rosslyn, darling, I still want you. Don't you understand I'm willing to reinstate you at this house, to give you an allowance, if you'll resume our two-week bargain."

"The time we spent together was more like two days," she corrected.

"That was your fault." He smiled, already gaining control as he overcame his surprise at her refusal to bend to his will. "The situation is simply this; I want you, you want what I can give. Why can't we strike a bargain."

Bargain! The words brought her to weak laughter. How alike men were, always eager to bargain with her, their collateral of varied composition, hers always the same.

"Why do you laugh at me? By God! I'll not have you laughing," he growled, snapping her against him, his face gone grim.

"If you only knew how many bargains I've been forced to strike during the years you would not ask. I'm sorry. It's not at you I laugh."

Calming somewhat at her explanation, Tom Stanley rested his hot cheek against her hair, breathing in the clean, salt fresh odor of it. "Rosslyn, it's not in my nature to beg. Is that what you want of me?"

"Though I admit your offer might seem appealing under different circumstances, I want nothing from you. Least of all your lovemaking. Too much happened to me in France. I'm not that same girl—yes, girl. I hadn't the intelligence of a woman. An interlude abroad completed my education."

Anger flared in his face yet he said nothing. With a push he released her, striding to the desk to pour himself a glass of wine. He offered her the filled glass but Rosslyn declined, glancing longingly at the sun-sparkled lawns beckoning freedom from this situation which was not of her choosing. All the hatred she had once nurtured for Tom Stanley seemed to have flown. It was a surprise to find she was honestly trying to let him down gently, to protect that very delicate male ego, so fragile when sexual failures were involved. And he had failed in his seduction of her this afternoon.

"You're waiting for *him,* aren't you? That's the reason."

"Him?" Rosslyn repeated the word stupidly, her heart seeming to poise a moment before beginning a frantic plunge.

"St. Clare."

"What do you know of Armand?"

"Everything there is to be known. I could almost tell you the times he came to your bed, both here and in France. I know about the little escapade you enjoyed while slumming with the scum of Paris in the person of one brave revolutionary by the name of Camille. There's absolutely nothing I don't know about you, my little darling, even your crimes."

Stunned by his knowledge, Rosslyn perched on the edge of her seat, her throat going dry to learn she was discovered. "How," she croaked, barely managing speech.

"Because, my dear Rosslyn, my money directs the operation."

"You!"

Tom Stanley smiled at her shock, pleased to see the pale cheeks, the fluttering pulse visible in her so white throat. "Yes, sweetheart, it's my money which freed your handsome lover and dozens of his compatriots. Surprised by that, aren't you? Oh, I know how you've despised me for coming from nothing, you and the whole aristocratic plague who live on this hill. Well, now I hold the cards, and they must come to me because I own the biggest part of this snobbish settlement thanks to Jarvis and his incurable bad habits. I intend to own you as well. Putting it simply, there you have it."

Stunned by his words, Rosslyn clasped her hands tight, the knuckles white. To find her most intimate actions betrayed filled her with dread. She had always supposed those guilty secrets to be shared by an elite few.

"You've no need to worry. I know that much about a hundred others too. I've no intention of making the facts public."

Her sigh of relief was so audible he smiled when he heard it.

"Does your continued silence depend on my bodily cooperation?" she asked suspiciously as he walked towards her.

"Not entirely. Have you changed your mind about the future?"

"No. I'll never change my mind."

Anger colored his face and he seized her arms, drawing her from the chair.

"Very well, you bitch, if you could lie about with men like Camille and still refuse me, when I offer you everything, you can damned well settle the mountain of debt your husband left behind at his untimely demise."

"You know I've no means to settle debts."

"Exactly, sweetest. The prisons are full of paupers in the same condition."

"Debtor's prison! My God, you can't be serious," she gasped, numbed at the thought.

"Oh, can't I. You just try me." With a vicious thrust he pushed her from him. Snatching the sheaf of papers from the desk, he pointed to a list of figures all purportedly owed on different occasions by Jarvis. None of his bad debts had been settled for the past two years.

"How could I have any hope of paying this? You must know, seeing as you are so well informed about my movements, that I'm forced to take in sewing to support myself," Rosslyn cried, white-faced with anger and despair.

"Oh, I know, don't you think I've taken that into consideration? Why do you think I've come to this? Because, you damnable woman, I'm determined to have you at any cost."

"If I'm in debtor's prison I doubt I'll be too appealing," she remarked caustically.

"Knowing you, you'll give in long before that. Now you have my permission to go. You also have my permission to stay away for sixty days; but at the end of

313

that time, you'll have either the money or you'll be arrested for debt. You know the other alternative. After Burton Hall you're my next goal. That comforting thought should cheer your days. Till August then, Rosslyn, my sweet."

CHAPTER NINETEEN

The heavy fragrance of white stocks filled the air as Rosslyn mechanically plucked dead rose heads from the pink bush overflowing the stone-pillared wall. To contemplate giving up this house, which would also be confiscated to settle debts, to give up her freedom for a squalid foot of prison floor, was an unthinkable horror. Today, in the sparkling August sunshine, Tom Stanley and his threats seemed unreal. Yet she knew in a few days he would ride down that cliff path demanding payment.

Going inside the cool house, Rosslyn wrestled uneasily with her decision. To call it conscience would be to lie, for since Camille, since the confrontation of Parisian mob violence, since the crime she herself committed without flinching, the idea of a conscience was laughable. Though she did not relish the idea, more repulsive than ever since Armand's reappearance, succumbing to Tom Stanley was preferable to the Fleet or Newgate. People would know from the beginning what she was to him. But that did not matter anymore. Nothing seemed to matter these days. Still no word from Armand and though she prayed fiercely for his safety, Rosslyn could draw but one conclusion; he was either dead or a prisoner. In mid-July Robespierre had been executed, his death halting the reign of terror and paving the way for the return of hundreds of aristocrats. After the first excitement of the fall of the regime and still no news from Clarence nor letter from the packet boat, her hopes dwindled to nothing. Time pressed too rapidly for her to remain faithful indefinitely to a memory. Sixty days of freedom were over; now the debt must be paid. For money she would use the only asset she possessed: her body. And if her fears were founded, that would not stay desirable for long. Her sudden bouts of sickness, recurring dizzy spells all pointed to one end. She was sure she carried Armand's child.

A carriage arrived at noon the following day and Rosslyn's heart plunged when she identified the broad-shouldered traveler in his expensive clothes.

"Well, Rosslyn, expecting me?" Tom Stanley asked, alighting from the carriage. He was perfectly turned out in a beige broadcloth coat and britches, his tall brown riding boots polished like a mirror.

"You're like misfortune, always expected," she commented icily, holding wide the blue painted door for him to enter the dark cottage.

Looking about with interest, he commented: "Small and comfortable. You appear so at home here. If you wish, I'll let you keep it as a weekend retreat."

"That's very generous of you."

He smiled, flicking the chair arm with his gauntlets. "Still the same old Rosslyn, a mouthful of venom with every bite. Don't you ever give up?"

"I might ask you the same thing."

"Ah, but I have vast sums of money at stake and something just as valuable as money."

At his warm smile, she dropped her gaze, not wishing to read what was so plainly spoken in those green eyes, unable to witness the open triumph of his smile.

"As you well knew, before you came, I've not been able to raise the money."

Tom Stanley nodded with satisfaction. "I hardly expected it. After all, sewing is not a highly profitable profession."

"Why did you make the bargain then? Do you mean if I'd managed to produce the money our debts would be settled? That I'd be free of all obligation to you, or had you another condition up your sleeve?"

"I hardly gave that possibility a thought. Yes, I suppose had you begged your brother to supply you with funds, I'd have had to give in. Ah, but I know you've not spoken to a soul."

Angered by his self-assurance, Rosslyn snapped, "What makes you so sure? Perhaps I have the cash."

"But you forget, you already told me you have not." He grinned at her, chucking her under the chin, his grip becoming bruising when she would have pulled away.

"Perhaps I lied," she whispered, enduring the pain, refusing to flinch and give him the pleasure of knowing he hurt her.

"Perhaps. Yet, had you told that courageous brother of yours he'd have been at my throat weeks ago. I happen to know he has not the money to bail you out, even if he knew your predicament. No, Rosslyn sweet, our agreement is known only to three people, the illustrious James Millington being the only outsider. It is a little settlement between friends—very good friends."

Pulling her against him, he seared her mouth with his kiss. She struggled a moment, then decided against the effort. Staring up at his gleaming eyes, mocking as he laughed at her, Rosslyn resigned herself to the inevitable.

"I should have chosen prison. That would give me such sweet revenge."

His face darkened at her hissed words. "You still have that choice."

"You know me better than to think I'd choose that. One dose of prison life was enough for me."

Through the window she watched the leafy tree branches tossing in the breeze, having a perfect view over his shoulder as he nuzzled her neck. Bleakly she wondered what Armand would think when, or if, he returned to find her gone, the cottage locked up and deserted. And then, when he found out what she had done to avoid imprisonment, would he be understanding? A bitter smile twisted her mouth at the answer. Never! Rage would incense him until he was fit to kill her, the way he told her he had felt when he knew about Camille.

"You seem detached. Have I lost my touch?"

The drawling voice brought her back, so that she gave a guilty start of surprise. "You must understand there are bound to be misgivings when a woman enters into an arrangement like this."

"By now I'd have thought all misgivings were dead and buried. Don't tell me you are still afire for the Frenchman?"

Rosslyn smiled and did not answer, knowing it would infuriate him, pleased when it had the required effect.

"You stupid little bitch, what do you think he can offer? How successful will he be springing you from an English jail? You're not dealing with a handful of wine-besotted Froggies."

How like Jarvis he sounded, so much so that a chill moved through her body. "If you have that opinion of the French, why did you spend money freeing them?"

He shrugged. "Excitement. Investment possibilities. Some of those people can serve me well once order is reestablished. You forget they came from the richest families in the land."

"Most of the very rich went to Cologne with d'Artois."

"True, but they still left holdings, relatives behind. For the price of their safety they were willing to sign their possessions away. I can't wait to travel to my new acquisitions. You shall come with me. It will be our unofficial honeymoon."

Gasping at the thought of touring that ravaged place at his side, Rosslyn slid from his arms. "What of Château Saint Clare?"

"What of it? If you mean do I own that, no."

"Armand has many acres of vineyards, and a buyer. That wasn't you, by chance?"

He laughed at her thinly veiled inquiry. "Look, sweetheart, why don't you come right out and ask me about him. No, it isn't me. The owner is a fat, rich German, who never intends to set foot on French soil. As for your handsome lover, he's greedily rounding up his possessions which have scattered over the continent to refurbish that shell of a mansion he owns. Are you satisfied?"

The news turned Rosslyn white with shock. He wasn't dead, or imprisoned, merely otherwise engaged.

At her bleak expression Stanley smiled, reaching out to pat her arm.

"Come now. You can't expect a man to be faithful forever. Money and rank can be powerful mistresses, especially to one who's enjoyed them all his life. Forget him. I'll guarantee after a few nights with me, you'll never give him another thought."

Clenching her hands, Rosslyn fought the sickening wave of grief which rose like gall in her throat. "Will you expect me to come with you today?" she managed.

"That was my idea. Of course, if there are things you must settle, I can put up in Dover for a few days. Whatever you wish. I intend to please you in the matter. See what a fool I've become since I rose to this rank. Patience is a virtue the rich can well afford."

"Yes, by tomorrow or the next day I should be finished," she said, seizing the added reprieve, hoping some miracle would come forth during those remaining hours to save her.

"I'll be back tonight."

Her eyes widened in shocked surprise. "No!"

"Why not? What difference will a couple of days make?" he demanded in anger, clenching his fist as if wanting to strike her, but thinking better of it.

"But I thought not until we reached Burton Hall . . ."

"What do I care where it is? I want you, woman, and I'm going to have you. Tonight, here, will do as good as anywhere," he growled. Then reaching inside his coat he brought forth a paper. "Here, shy one, this is the accounting of your debts. It will serve to quicken your blood for me when you read it."

Silently she took the paper, not bothering to open it.

"While not quite as eloquent as Jarvis's agreement, it nevertheless is legal. 'My black-maned riding filly,' " he chuckled, "a damned good description of you." He caught a handful of her hair, pulling her to him for a kiss. "You don't know how hungry I am for this ride."

Then, still chuckling, he strode purposefully to the door without looking back.

Like a statue Rosslyn stood before the empty hearth, the crackling paper clutched in her hand as she heard the carriage wheels trundling along the path. It was all over. The last vestige of her hope had been quenched by his revelation about Armand. She should have expected as much when he failed to write. Too busy to spare much thought for her, he would have the shock of his life when he finally strolled back to find her gone. Faithless, Marie had called him. At the time Rosslyn would have defended him to the last, but now, she too had growing doubts. Pictures of the shattered house at Saint Clare flitted through her mind, even the memory of that exquisite dream when she had walked at Armand's side beside the lake. Gone was the hope she had cherished of realizing that dream. Even the child, a fragment of life connecting them forever, would never know his father's name. Assuredly Tom Stanley would claim that distinction. There was nothing left but to go forward. The path behind her was too painful to relive.

It was dusk when she heard the hoofbeats on the track. The long summer twilight was dwindling to a close, the sun a molten disk far on the horizon, turning the sea a shifting pattern of silver and black. For the last time she gazed at the scene through the bedroom window, drinking in the memory of it. Gulls wheeled a half circle through the orange light, crying mournfully as they sought their nests. In a few moments she would relinquish her freedom. No longer would she belong to herself, instead she would be bound in servitude to Tom Stanley for the rest of her days.

With a sigh she turned from the window. She had chosen a flower-sprigged gown for the great occasion, made from a length of material Mrs. Kenney had purchased, then discarded. Rosslyn had put her new-found skill to use by making a gown for herself. It was the prettiest she owned. No extra money for lace at the neck, she had stitched small ruffles from the dimity instead, applying a rose pink bow at the center of the bodice.

Catching sight of herself in the dingy mirror beside the bed, Rosslyn turned about, critically eyeing her appearance. The gown looked like a servant girl's Sunday best, yet, what, after all, was she at the moment? Those dozens of satin and silk gowns, the velvet day dresses, fur-trimmed, spangled, jewel-edged, all belonged to someone else. If Tom Stanley had kept them for her, she would at least be able to appear her old self on the outside. If he had divided the loot among his whores, then she would demand other clothes. He would be pushed to the limit, just the way she had done with Jarvis. This man would take more careful strategy. He would soon discover, though he had her body, he would never have her heart. And for every begrudged embrace she would find a way to make him pay.

Head down, contemplating the revenge which brought a cynical smile to her mouth, Rosslyn walked into the gloomy hallway. To her shock she collided with a hard black shape. A man had just rounded the corner from the stairs, stepping lightly, clearly intending to surprise her. Arms imprisoned her tightly, so that she struggled, desperately trying to identify her assailant. Then, as hot lips pressed against her neck, she shuddered at the remembered touch.

"Armand! Oh, God, God, you!"

Holding her slightly apart from his body, he stared at her, surprised by her words, by the anguish on her face. "What is it? Did you think me dead, *cherie*?"

Still she did not speak, only stared at him, at the dark hair expertly barbered this time, at the clothing fitting so well she knew it too was of the highest order. Weakness, pain, both robbed her of speech.

"I'm sorry to frighten you so. I thought you'd heard the horse, that you waited upstairs for me as you sometimes used to do," he explained, reaching for her again, surprised by the unyielding form in his arms. "What is it? Are you angry with me?"

"Angry is the most inadequate word you could use," she whispered, her voice weak with distress. "Why couldn't you have come last week? Yesterday? Why did it have to be today, especially now?"

He smiled stiffly, not understanding. "Because, my dear Madame, only today was I able to finish my business. Had I known how unwelcome I was to be, I'd have delayed the journey even longer. When, pray tell, will be a convenient time for me to visit?"

"Stop it, damn you, stop! You've no idea. Oh, God, you don't know." Bursting into a fit of tears, she fell against him, nearly knocking him off balance as he wavered on the top step. Supporting her body, his heart raced in alarm at the sheer misery of her huddled form.

"Tell me. Come, let's go to the bedroom."

Purposely he led her back the way she had come. Then sitting beside her, he cradled her weeping form against his shoulder, wondering what could possibly have gone wrong.

"It's too late now. There's nothing I can do. Oh, Armand, why must our love always be like this? Too late. Everytime we've been together there's always something to interfere, to spoil it, to thrust us apart. Is it because we weren't meant to love?"

"Cherie, I don't understand. How can it ever be too late for us? I came to you as soon as I could. Heaven knows, the mountain of tasks I've managed since I landed has surprised even me. I expected happiness, not this."

Bleakly she stared at him, seeing all the things about him which tugged at her heart. His handsome face, the cleft in his chin, the way his dark brows made a line over those gray eyes which chilled her to the bone with anticipation whenever she stared at the expression of love they held for her. All that would soon be gone. His arms, his passion, lost forever to her. So near to happiness had she been, so close, to have it all destroyed.

"You must go," she urged, remembering the hour and who she expected. Straining for the sound of hooves, she only heard the waves breaking on the shore.

"Go! Why?"

"Someone's coming."

"Another man—God, are you that faithless? I'm gone for three months and already you have another?" Thrusting her to the bed, he leaped up, his face set in anger.

"It's not like that. He comes to me for that purpose, I can't deny, but it isn't by choice."

Glaring at her tear-stained face, Armand drew himself stiffly apart from her, refusing to succumb yet again to the pathetic sight of her grief. "Who is he?"

"Someone you know well. Until you'd left for France I never knew the truth about him—it's Tom Stanley."

Speechless, he stared at her, unable to grasp what she had said.

"Stop looking at me like that!" she cried, beating her fists into the covers.

"That you prefer that coarse stallion over me, should not come as a surprise when I consider your feelings for the stonemason. He and Camille are perhaps very much alike."

Appalled, she stared at his arrogance, standing before her judging something he knew so little about.

"Damn you, you're not God Almighty. How can you know the way I feel? For you I did so many things. At least I'll admit this last is entirely for me."

A cynical smile lifted his wide mouth and he turned contemptuously on his heel. "Of course. I had no doubt of that."

"Listen to me! Damn you, don't go like this. At least hear why," she screamed, leaping to her feet to clutch his sleeve. Tension stiffened the muscles beneath her grasp and he shook her off.

"I'm listening. Though I doubt if I have the stomach for what you intend to reveal."

Glaring at him, anger making her hostile, Rosslyn stood her ground. "It is not the delights of his bed which lure me, though I know you expected me to say that. He holds the mortgage to our property at Burton Hill. Jarvis owed him a mountain of debt. As I'm unable to pay he threatened me with debtor's prison unless I agree to the alternative. I don't have to tell you what that is."

Armand stared at her, his jaw set hard, his eyes pinpoints of steel gray in his stern face where the tan had faded to a jaundiced cast. "You are selling yourself to him? Is that what you're telling me?"

"Yes, that's it. It's not the first time I've had to bargain with what God gave me. And, Monsieur le Comte,

323

the first time was strictly for you. Revile me, spurn me, but never forget what I bought for you with my body, at which you now look with such loathing. Say it, go on, call me the name that's on your mind. It won't be the first time I've been called that. Now I'm not even sure it's still a lie."

In the fading light they faced each other, tense, the air so emotion-charged it seemed as if it could be cut with a knife. A screaming seabird circled close to the windows making them both start in alarm, breaking the icy silence.

"I'll not call you whore. I've never thought of you by that name," he whispered, his face working to control his emotion. "How much money do you need to buy off Stanley?"

"More than I'll ever have in three lifetimes. There's a neat accounting of the debts downstairs if you wish to study them, Monsieur le Comte."

"Don't call me that."

"It's your correct title, is it not? I well remember one day you told me . . . "

He seized her in his arms, welding his mouth to hers, the fierceness of his embrace making her shudder with mingled fear and delight. "Enough!" he growled, bending her back. "Do you think I'd ever let another have you now? Show me the debts. And my name is Armand."

Excitement fluttered her heart as she looked into his stern face where she read the sheer mastery of his will. If she struggled, he would probably strike her; if she resisted him, he would probably rape her. Never before had she seen him so angered, so thoroughly in control.

"We must hurry. He'll be here soon," she gasped as he released her abruptly, making her stumble against the bed.

Downstairs she lit a candle so he might study the document, anxiously watching his face as he read. Was it her imagination or did she already hear hoofbeats on the road? Probably only the pounding surf, but she could not be sure.

"You have a day left to raise the money. The sixty days aren't over until tomorrow."

Blankly she stared at him. "What difference will one day make to me?"

"Have you asked Clarence for help?"

"I've asked no one. This final shame I've borne alone," she announced with dignity.

"You fool! It's not something to boast about. Sheer stupidity is never something to be proud of."

Her head snapped up in anger at his words, when she saw he smiled as he beckoned to her, the paper fluttering back to the table.

"What?"

"Come here. Now, give me the greeting I expected after so long an absence."

Moving as if in her sleep, Rosslyn found herself in his arms, her blood thundering through her limbs at the warm pleasure of his caresses, at the pressure of his mouth and legs against hers.

"When he comes you are to tell him you have the money."

"How can I say that? He'll soon know I don't," she argued, shivering deliciously as he traced the top of her dress with his tongue.

"You will say it because it's true. I intend to pay your debt."

Eyes wide in shock, Rosslyn stared at him. "You?"

"That's right. I have money now. In my pocket is a letter of credit from a leading English bank. My holdings in France turned out to be more profitable than I suspected."

"You sold your home?"

He shook his head, kissing the top of her brow before he put her from him. "The chateau, for what it's worth, still stands. The grounds too are mine. I've even located some of my possessions as it's my intention to rebuild the place for my sons."

This time she was not mistaken, there were definite hoofbeats on the path. "Oh, God, he's here!"

"Do what you must. I'll wait in there."

Armand darted towards the scullery. Belatedly Rosslyn wondered where he had tethered his horse. Then there was no further time for thought as Tom Stanley's large, broad-shouldered frame filled the narrow doorway. Stooping he entered the cottage, his eyes sweeping over her in pleasure, noting the full, frilled bodice, the narrow-sashed waist which promised him long-remembered delight.

"All ready and eagerly waiting are you?" Coming to her he swept her off her feet, reminding her in a sickening wave of Camille who often used the same greeting. Perhaps it was a habit of large men to demonstrate their strength.

"Yes, I'm eagerly waiting because I have news for you."

"News?" Warily he glanced about as if some instinct told him they were being watched.

"You told me if I raised the amount of money for the mortgage, for Jarvis's debts, you'd be forced to accept it, did you not?"

"Yes, yes I did." Smiling in amusement, he caught her arms, drawing her close. He bent his head and kissed her chest, letting his tongue stray toward the outward thrust where the top of her breasts were visible beneath the frilled neckline and slipping his large hands over the prominence covered by wild flowers and fragile white cloth which he longed to rip aside.

"Surely the sale of our furniture, the agreement Jarvis drew up when he offered me as collateral has more than settled his gambling debts," she continued, hoping Armand could not see Tom Stanley's hands on her breasts, ashamed at the thought of his witnessing the spectacle.

Stanley raised his head, temporarily losing his amorous intentions. "He still gambled after you left."

"Yes, but my jewels alone must have paid off much of that. I'm no fool."

His face set in a scowl, he released her. "This is a pointless debate. Since yesterday, when you were admittedly without funds, you surely have not magically acquired a fortune. What happened, a visit from your fairy godmother?" he asked with sarcasm, flinging his

326

cloak over a chair. "All right, saying you owe only the mortgage on the house for argument's sake, I still see no further need to discuss the matter. We both know you can't pay."

"And I have until noon tomorrow to make the debt good. It says so here in the agreement."

He sighed in exasperation. "Yes. Is this another ploy to keep your body to yourself for another night? I'll not put up with it, woman. I intend to take you with force or without. It's up to you. But don't make me wait too long . . . "

"I have the money."

"What!" Thunderstruck, he stared at her, his green eyes glittering in the candlelight. "I can't have heard properly. You said you have the money?"

"Yes, or more correctly, it's in a London bank. There's a letter of credit here."

Dark with anger, his face set in a scowl as he accepted the parchment. Carrying the letter to the candleflame he noted the official bank letterhead. "Christ in heaven, that goddamned Frenchman has bailed you out?" he yelled, spinning on his heel to face her. Suddenly a different expression came to his face and thrusting her aside with one arm, he held the letter above the candleflame. "I could burn this, then no one would be any the wiser. It's your word and his against mine. Who'd take that, a penniless widow and a foreign refugee. Yes, that's exactly what I'll do."

Tom Stanley's back was to the kitchen door as he goaded Rosslyn to try to prevent him, thoroughly enjoying the situation as he teased her by holding the parchment high, barely allowing the heat to curl a corner of the page. Suddenly the door burst open and a flying figure shot from the darkened room, bearing Stanley to the floor, taken completely by surprise. With a thump the large man fell and Armand seized the valuable letter which he thrust at Rosslyn for safekeeping.

Catching his breath, Stanley sneered at the other man. "So, your knight-in-shining-armor arrives. How very fortunate. I wonder how much protection you'd give her if you knew the truth?"

327

Uneasily Rosslyn felt her heart lurch as she wondered what lie Tom Stanley was going to tell. Then, fear choked her as she remembered the truth would be sufficient: She had never told Armand about the details of Jarvis's wager, letting him think Stanley's assault was never completed.

Armand allowed the other man to get up, eyeing him warily for signs of attack. "I probably know more about Rosslyn than you," he said, lighting another candle so they could see each other better.

"Is that so? By that I know she hasn't told you everything. Shall I tell him, my dearest, or will you?"

Her voice quivered over the words until Rosslyn found herself unable to utter them. Armand looked askance from one to the other, awaiting the revelation, his fists clenched on the table.

"Well, Sir Knight, your lady fair was included in the birthday bargain. Quite good value for my money, wouldn't you say?" Smiling that smug expression of satisfaction for what he had just revealed, Stanley stretched his long legs lazily before him, making himself comfortable against the couch. "Now, are you sure you still want to sacrifice your hard-won fortune to settle her debts? Wouldn't you say she deserves what she gets and welcome to it? I assure you, she'll be most lovingly cared for. If I do nothing else right, I at least know how to please a woman, even one as hard to understand as Rosslyn."

She leaned against the wall, nauseated with shock at his statement. Armand did not leap to her defense, almost as if he weighed the decision: She against the cash from the sale of his vineyard. He said he had received more than he thought possible for the land, yet he still needed immense funds to refurbish the chateau, the home he intended to preserve for his sons.

The clock ticked unusually loud in the quiet room. Beyond the open window came the shrill warbling of a night bird to break the silence.

"You are familiar with that bank?" Armand asked, his voice gruff as he held out the letter.

"Bank—yes, it's mine, as a matter of fact."

"Then it will not inconvenience you to make the withdrawal of sufficient funds to cover the mortgage . . ."

"Now look here, there's more money than that owed," Stanley cried, leaping to his feet.

"Don't try to get more than you're entitled to out of revenge for losing Rosslyn. I heard you tell her that was all that was owed. Or have you forgotten?"

"That was only because I didn't expect her to pay. If you've got the money you can damned well pay for that too."

"Don't tempt me to withdraw my offer. However desirable Rosslyn may appear, I doubt you'd enjoy her much in jail. As I'm only prepared to pay for the mortgage, you'll have to accept that."

Tom Stanley chuckled. "Well, you both seem to have overlooked one important alternative. I can accept neither, and I've still got Rosslyn."

"No, it's you who've overlooked something. Before I'd let you do that I'd kill you."

To Rosslyn's surprise when Armand brought up his hand she saw a curved-bladed knife glittering there, inches from Stanley's waistcoat with its diamond-centered flower buttons. Calmly Armand popped one of the buttons free.

"Strike out all the entries but the mortgage on the property."

Glowering, yet declining to argue with the knife, Tom Stanley crossed through the columns of figures with the pen Rosslyn gave him.

"Sign it. Initial each change. I wouldn't want you saying you never wrote it," Armand cautioned, smiling at his victim, pleased to see perspiration beading his forehead. Tom Stanley, after all, was a coward.

"You'll never get away with this," Stanley growled, wiping his upper lip where dampness formed a film. "I'll have my lawyer draw up other papers, I'll . . . "

"If you want to live you'll do nothing. Now write, paid in full. I'll sign over the correct amount to you. When you take this letter to the bank tomorrow you'll get your money."

"What use is that cavern of a house to you, St. Clare? You're not even an Englishman. You've got your roots in France." There was a pleading sadness to Stanley's face as he asked the question, as if all the fight had suddenly gone out of him.

Surprised by his question, Armand shrugged. "The house is for Rosslyn. I don't intend to live there."

"Will she? Alone?"

Remembering the lifelong ambition he held of owning the house, Rosslyn offered, "I'll sell it back to you for the mortgage price. If that's what you want?"

"You'd do that? After all that's gone between us?"

"Yes. The place gives me chills. Is that satisfactory to you?" Turning to Armand she was surprised to see him grin.

"Lord in heaven, after all this, you're going to turn the place over to him. I don't believe it."

"What good is Burton Hall to me? I wouldn't dream of living there alone without money for servants . . . "

"Very well." Wearily Armand seized a piece of paper from the bureau which he thrust toward Stanley. "God knows why she's doing this; whoever knows the way a woman's mind works? Write a receipt for the price of the property, then we'll both sign the agreement to sell. At least doing things solely on paper speeds the transaction. And I don't think we'll need this anymore." He put the knife away.

Stanley sighed with relief at the knowledge that the coveted house was still his. He deeply regretted losing Rosslyn, but there was only one Burton Hall. There were a hundred women he could be content with just as long as he was master there. If those were the Frenchman's terms, he must abide by them.

The papers exchanged, Stanley stood up to leave.

"Am I allowed to return to the inn? Not a prisoner or anything?" he asked, a tentative smile curving his mouth.

"You're free to leave. And Stanley, don't try to deceive us. We have many mutual acquaintances, not all of them happy with your business dealings."

330

Stanley's eyebrow twitched at the reminder. Taking his cloak, he draped it over his arm. "I'll remember. What is it they say, honor amongst thieves? You are welcome to visit me whenever you wish, Rosslyn. But do come alone."

With that he walked through the door, quickening his pace when he reached the path as if unable to believe his good fortune in being allowed to go free without pursuit.

"I should have slit his throat," Armand muttered, watching the dark figure clamber into the saddle, wheel his horse around and head for Dover.

Weakly Rosslyn began to laugh, a moment later, the laughter verging on hysterics, she sank to the couch, her face in her hands. Armand sat beside her, cradling her against his chest where she began to sob.

"Hush, *cherie,* it's over. Sometimes it's necessary to become melodramatic."

Smiling at him through her tears, Rosslyn whispered: "What can I say to thank you? Risking the money you needed to rebuild the chateau."

"Ah, don't worry about that. I still had a few tricks up my sleeve. As long as you were safe, that's all that mattered. Now, as it turns out, we have our money back. How was I to know Tom Stanley would prove to be such a paper tiger? We are free at last."

"Freedom. That's what this strange feeling is. For years I've been bound to someone. Now at last I'm my own free agent. I might be poor, but then, freedom never comes cheap, does it?" She rested her head against his, watching the shadows dance across the wall as the draft stirred the candleflame.

"Mine did not. But you are wrong, you're not free. I still have a claim on you."

She smiled up at him and taking his face in her hands she kissed his mouth, the touch gentle, caressing. "No, it is I who have a claim on you. Before I did not want to mention this, especially since I didn't know if you'd ever come back, then I wasn't really sure . . . "

"Come on, don't keep me in suspense. What's this

secret? Am I to spend our passage money on yet another debt?" he whispered, pulling her tumbled black hair from her face, smoothing the curls from her brow with gentle hands.

"Passage money! You intend to take me back to France with you!" she gasped.

"*Certainement.* You're so fond of reminding me what you've endured on my behalf, it's only fair I take you to share my munificence, even though it's a roofless, windowless ruin."

Lying in his arms, gazing up at the firm tanned jawline Rosslyn sighed a deep satisfying sigh, snuggling herself deep in his embrace, thrilled to be able to tell him the secret she had hugged to herself for weeks.

"Well then, Monsieur le Comte, you are about to obtain a bargain on your passage."

"How is that?" Lazily he unfastened the hooks on her gown, his hands warmly thrilling against her bare skin, so that she shuddered with delight, hardly able to stand the suspense as the warmth slid with tantalizing slowness to her breasts, tauter in her early maternity.

"You will get three passengers to France for the price of two . . . I'm pregnant," she whispered.

He smiled, slow, lazy, his eyes warmly appraising.

"You couldn't have given me a greater gift," he whispered holding her close, cherishing her in his unexpected happiness.

"My poor little son will be third in line, perhaps he never will be able to be called Monsieur le Comte," she complained softly as he wrapped his arms about her, covering her face with kisses.

"Then we will have a lovely daughter instead. Who, if she looks like her mama, will easily marry a prince." He laughed. His gaze lingered on the beauty of her body and his humor died; his expression changing to grim determination.

Reaching up, he snuffed out the candleflame. Eagerly they sought each other, pushing all that had been between them to the past, determined to live for the years ahead. They were free to love each other at

332

last. The sound of the sea and the trilling birdsong filled the dark room; soon the rhythm of the waves mingled with the sound of their labored breathing as the two became one.